THE PENGUIN BOOK OF

Contemporary
New Zealand Short Stories

Susan Davis was born in 1960 and has an MA in English from
Auckland University. She lives in Auckland where she works as a
senior editor at the publisher Longman Paul. She contributes to and
co-edits *Antic*, a journal of literary and art criticism.

Russell Haley was born in England in 1934. In 1961 he and Jean
emigrated to Australia with their son Ian, moving to New Zealand
in 1966. He has an MA in English from Auckland University and
has held the ICI Writing Bursary, the Auckland University Literary
Fellowship and the 1987 Katherine Mansfield Memorial Fellowship.
Russell Haley has published two books of poems, three collections
of short stories, and a novel, *The Settlement*. His most recent work
is a biography of the artist Patrick Hanly.

THE PENGUIN BOOK OF
Contemporary
New Zealand Short Stories

Edited by
Susan Davis and Russell Haley

PENGUIN BOOKS

PENGUIN BOOKS

Penguin Books (NZ) Ltd, 182–190 Wairau Road, Auckland 10, New Zealand
Penguin Books Ltd, 27 Wrights Lane, London W8 5TZ, England
Viking Penguin Inc., 40 West 23rd Street, New York, New York 10010, USA
Penguin Books Australia Ltd, 487 Maroondah Highway, Ringwood, Australia 3134
Penguin Books Canada Ltd, 2801 John Street, Markham, Ontario, Canada L3R 1B4

Penguin Books Ltd, Registered Offices: Harmondsworth, Middlesex, England

First published in 1989
1 3 5 7 9 10 8 6 4 2

Designed by Richard King
Typeset by Typocrafters Ltd, Auckland
Printed in Hong Kong

CONTENTS

CONTENTS

INTRODUCTION

We began this project two years ago with the simplest of guidelines. We would consider short stories which had been produced within the last ten years by any living New Zealand writer. From this period we would try to choose work which hadn't been previously anthologised. Because our rules were self-imposed, we allowed ourselves the freedom to break them if it became necessary.

To the best of our knowledge, only one story falls just outside the last decade, and most of these short stories were either published quite recently or they are making their appearance here for the first time. We are reasonably certain that we have not included any previously anthologised works, and this fact alone would make the volume unusual. Anthologies in New Zealand tend to feed off each other, but we've put together, we believe, the most varied and comprehensive selection of New Zealand short stories to appear in recent years.

We regret that several established New Zealand writers are not represented in this anthology. Noel Hilliard, for example, wished us well but he had no recent work which we might use. O. E. Middleton had some unpublished short stories but wanted to retain them for his own future collection. We wished to include a story by C. K. Stead but terms could not be agreed upon.

While we hoped to include stories from our major established writers, we were also committed to looking for what we came to call 'edge' work. Such a notion, with its cluster of usages such as 'keenness', 'tension', 'sharpness', and 'danger' applies, as we would expect, to the fictions of our best-known writers. In the process of selecting our stories we had anticipated that we'd encounter 'edge' fiction predominantly in the newer voices. Innovation, we found, isn't necessarily the prerogative of the latest generation of writers; but neither can all the mature and assured work be gathered under an Establishment banner. 'Edge' fictions can be found throughout this anthology. Our first priority, however, was always to collect the most interesting recent stories from New Zealand authors. It is, of course, finally up to the reader to decide what individual risks these writers have taken.

As editors we had to settle the sometimes vexed question of who *is* a New Zealand writer. Authors were included if they were born here; if they reside in Aotearoa; or if they maintain literary connections with the country. With the exception of Compton, Sutherland, Johnson, Kemp and Ihimaera, all the writers in this anthology currently live in New Zealand.

Within our guidelines we chose stories which appealed to us — an enjoyment enhanced by the diversity of forty-four individual voices. It seems reasonable to suppose that the breadth and variety of current short stories in this country is related to the accelerating rate of cultural change in New Zealand. Certainly many of the works in this volume explore the social, political, and literary upheavals of the past decade.

If we have new ways of perceiving and describing what is happening around us then perhaps we also need fresh critical approaches to our writing. We have deliberately included texts which disrupt readers' expectations as to how prose stories function. A number of works, for example, foreground language itself, where utterance is both the means and object of fiction.

In looking at the collection as a whole we found that existing descriptions of New Zealand short fiction were not always appropriate. There have been suggestions that the powerful influences of Sargeson and Mansfield have created a kind of bi-polar literary force-field in which the whole of present-day short fiction is still magnetically articulated. Our reading experiences over the past two years would not support this argument.

Another truism about our fiction — that a primary theme concerns the search for a New Zealand identity — is no longer foregrounded in the work of contemporary writers. Indeed, a large number of stories are set overseas, where narrators, at ease with their New Zealand identity, make very little of their being 'Kiwi'.

Much of this work needs no introduction, but we should perhaps comment on our interpretation of the word 'contemporary'. While we have tried to select work from the last ten years, our employment of the word has as much to do with the notion of the 'new' as with chronological parameters.

We are not talking, however, about trying to establish an *avant garde*, since the 'new', here, is defined by many differing voices and fictional strategies. Some works may appear visually unfamiliar, some are stylistically explorative. And our interpretation of the word 'short' has been flexible.

On a personal note, we would like to thank Geoff Walker of Penguin, who suggested that we work together. After establishing our guidelines we made our preliminary selections independently. We found that our intuitive responses to the stories were surprisingly close. This was one of the unexpected pleasures of working on the collection.

Susan Davis
Russell Haley

FIONA FARRELL POOLE

Footnote

Kirmington. Page 63 in the *Motoring Atlas of Great Britain*. There is no store in Kirmington. No public telephone. Nowhere to buy a magazine or a drink. The church stands stolid in couch grass overlooking a raggle-taggle bunch of inter-war cottages, an early Victorian rectory and a light-electrical firm. The air is filled with the agitated humming of Euro-executives jetting in and out of the Hull International Airport down the road. Only the verges are beautiful, pink yellow-white, thick with Queen Anne's lace. She walked round the church twice before she found them. There were eight Quickfalls. Their stones were stacked one against the other in a corner by the rectory. Joseph, Elizabeth, Francis. Another Elizabeth. Brothers, sisters, cousins, aunts. But not Jane. Jane had gone away.

It's so little to leave behind. A scrawl, 'Jane Kendall' (born Quickfall), a photo. A faded fleshy woman in a dark dress. How could anyone live so long and make such a tiny mark on the earth? It's the scratching of a nomad. The imprint of a transient. Skilled trackers are needed to tell where such travellers have stood. Where they have eaten. Where they have lain down.

. . . all morning she'd been watching him from the creek where she knelt, scrubbing. Keeping up appearances, keeping down the bugs. They'd abandon ship temporarily, but give them a week and they'd be back. Peppering her linen, crawling and biting and hopping and breeding. She stood up amongst the ferns to straighten her back, feeling her knees cold against the heavy wetness of her woollen skirt. Looks up through leaves and branches to see him bending in full sunlight, cutting wood. He is a short man. Square. With thick red-brown hair. He lifts his arms. Brings them down and a piece of mahoe springs in two, clean as new cheese. He bends, gathers one and chop chop chop it lies in neat straws to kindle the fire. Sweat runs down the crevice along his spine. Sunlight on his arms and shoulders. She kneels on the stone and draws the white linen towards her against the current . . .

11

How could anyone have endured it?

Here
lies interred the body of
THOMAS QUICKFALL
who died 24 January 1810
Aged 71 years

and underneath, the limestone peels leaving sudden patches:

black some by blazon'd heralds shine
And backwards trace their ancient line;
blank heaps of blank and others raise
blank monuments of blanking praise;
Let others boast their pompous state
of merit void, ignobly great:
One truth, o'er these remains below
Inscribed, more honour will bestow,
Than lineage, wealth or grandeur can.
Here lies interr'd an HONEST MAN.

She traces the words with her finger, kneeling on damp earth threaded
with purple worms, snail slime and the white veins of bruised grass.
The Quickfalls, square and grey, stand ready for the last trump under
the hawthorn.

Tickling. Like a moth caught in cupped hands.

*. . . she lay under the table looking up at rough wooden planks and
thought, 'So this is it. This is adultery. The seventh commandment.' But
no angel drew back the blanket over the door and stood with flaming
torch directing her out into consuming darkness. There was no thunder.
No lightning. The table stood solid over her head. She reached an arm
up and ran her finger along the grooves left by her husband's adze. And
with her other hand she traced the deep cleft down this other back (he was
asleep), still damp and warm. Outside kereru kereru, pigeons drunk on
soft red puriri berries, the creek and sea sighing, moaning, in and out,
in and out. 'So this is adultery,' she thought and waited for dogs to howl
and Jezebel to be torn to pieces . . .*

They had been driving for two hours. Rain poured against the car, sealing them into a small grey world. Vivaldi on the radio, buzzing advancing and retreating. Jeff liked long drives, liked pointing the car north and driving through. 'It'll be a long day,' he'd say apologetically, knowing she hated this rush, wanted to potter up side roads, inspect cathedrals, or stop for picnics. He always promised a slower pace next time. But when next time came round, there they'd be, driving at 70 over hundreds of miles of motorway. She'd sit and read the Guide as they passed the road signs: 'Rievaulx,' she'd say. 'A monastic ruin in a secluded valley.' Or, 'Lincoln: cathedral city, noted for its Roman gateway . . . the oldest house in England . . .' But he'd have a meeting to get back to, or an appointment which couldn't be re-scheduled. They'd leave with just the time necessary to make the journey direct and arrive, tired. Tired of each other and sitting in the same place, tired of motorway meals because there was never time to look for somewhere better. (And it was cheaper too, she thought. Another characteristic she was coming to hate: his stinginess. As he got older he earned more and spent less. Wore the same clothes year in, year out, bought books he never read from bargain bins. Saving for what?) But enough. They were caught in the car together, two more hours to go. It wouldn't do to start worrying at grievances as one prods at a throbbing tooth. Vivaldi pranced nearer dum *de* dumdum, dum *de* dumdum and the rain swept down.

. . . she had a baby to him of course. Lay on a bed and brought forth her 'spurious brood'. The sheets were covered with blood. The baby lay on a piece of cloth, legs waving frantically like an insect's. 'Hold me, hold me.'

Who helped her? Did one of her countrywomen buttoned against contamination venture into that house heavy with the smell of blood and sin, to boil linen? Tightlipped by the fire bathing her beautiful boy? Did they give her brandy to restore her strength? Was her husband somewhere near, or off bobbing about half-seas over babbling guilt and guns on some trader? Impossible to know. No letters, no diary. Just a scribble on sand . . .

Kirmington was her idea, of course. They'd left London at one (Jeff had an appointment at LSE and no, it couldn't possibly be made for any other time). 'We'll just make it,' he said as he accelerated onto the motorway, pleased at the urgency of it all. But there were roadworks near Stevenage, and on the A15 past Peterborough. They crept in single file behind lorries, Jeff cursing monotonously and repetitively. She saw the sign-post by accident when they were nearing Hull. There was another diversion. A truck jack-knifed on the motorway, a collision, a petrol tanker perhaps? She could see a dense column of smoke rising to the west as they snaked off through the countryside following the scarlet arrows along smaller roads. The car moved slowly in heavy traffic, Wrawby, Barnetby-le-Wold, past fields, pubs, houses with peas on crossed sticks. Jeff muttered. They'd be late he'd arranged to meet Gordon at five they were all going to have a drink together and now look at it they'd be hours late Jesus Christ get a move on did you see that? just cut in . . . Then there was Kirmington 9 miles. She'd insisted. 'We're late anyway,' she reasoned. 'You can ring and tell Gordon not to expect us. Ring from Kirmington.' Besides, it would be useful background for her book. Jeff gave in. So they came to the village, the raggle-taggle cottages and the church and its heap of Quickfall dead in the late afternoon, and the rain cleared and the clouds rolled back and she walked round the church with its plain tower and its plain windows, her jeans wet to the knees in the long grass. And found the Quickfalls stacked for heaven like the Sunday bread. Jeff couldn't even find a telephone. A desert place. Surely Paternoster Valley couldn't have been worse than this?

Tickle. Tickle. Twitching under her navel.

. . . *rum is the answer. At night, in the dark, clinking of cup on bottle as the children slept, wrapped in rows in blankets. She sits on the bed drinking slowly. Fire in the grate, banked up for the morning, blanket round her shoulders. Fumble, pour, drink. Fumble, pour, drink. At least she always uses a cup, hasn't yet descended to drinking straight from the bottle. One of the children cries out, flings an arm out of his blanket warding off some other smaller devil. Husband away for months, the community prying. God looking into her very heart, and if not God then one of God's delegates, alert to the slightest falter, eyes bright behind their prayer books at morning service. And no words. No letters. No diary. Who can she talk to who can guess at Kirmington and despair and the exact nature of temptation? She's the woman with no head in the joke; the silent woman. Fumble, pour, drink . . .*

Back on the motorway and her turn to drive . . . Rain again, and the wipers move back and forth. Jeff seems to doze but when she brakes suddenly his foot jams against the floor, driving with her. They don't talk. Strange that. Once they drove to Auckland from Dunedin in his old VW and talked all the way. That first time. They camped near Kaikoura. His wife had packed him a picnic dinner. They ate Shirley's chicken, drank Shirley's coffee, then tumbled into the tent and she made love to Shirley's husband while a sudden gale nipped at their bare bodies and threatened to lift them and the tent clear away. By the time they reached Auckland Jeff had said, 'I'll leave her,' and he did. As he did anything he'd decided on. It was what drew her to him at first, his decisiveness. She would spend hours, gnawing her pen, looking out the window at the harbour, trying to decide which essay to write for his economic history course. 'Which dress will I choose?' she'd ask him, buy one, and instantly regret it. Not Jeff. He wanted her. He didn't want Shirley. So it was clear. He left his home, left his children who were teenagers anyway and old enough to cope (almost as old as herself she remembered, as she changed gear and they climbed towards the Humber Bridge). To begin with she loved his sureness. The way he drove from A to B. The way he stood in the mornings, still wet from the shower simply putting on his clothes; no dither, no agonising over this shirt with these trousers. He was strong, loved her with vigour and pleasure. He cooked when it was his turn without consulting a recipe book, adding spices, herbs, a glass of wine, tasting. Always certain.

. . . *'And they called Rebekah and said unto her, Wilt thou go with this man? And she said I will go.' But how was it really for Rebekah among the Canaanites? And Ruth? 'Whither thou goest I will go and where thou lodgest I will lodge.' Ruth the Moabitess? What was she thinking of, there amongst the alien corn?*

They'd discussed babies of course, back then on the way home from the Auckland conference. 'No,' he'd said. He didn't think he'd want any more. He'd had four, was too old. And she wanted a job, didn't she? Babies and jobs didn't mix easily. Shirley could tell her that. (Poor half-a-BA-Shirley. Poor-part-time-librarian-Shirley . . .) 'OK,' she'd said, that young girl driving down the Desert Road through tussock and skylarks, one hand warm between Jeff's thighs, her hair whipping in the cool wind off Tongariro. She loved him. He loved her. She'd given a good paper. She was a Young Professional Woman, on her way, intent on a Career, and that was that. Soon after they began living together, Jeff went out one Saturday morning and had a vasectomy.

. . . when confronted with her sin she'd confessed of course. Anyone who could count to nine could tell anyway. Husband gone eleven months, belly swelling under her black dress. (The delicious tickling of hands and feet in her belly . . .) She was pregnant to the hired man, an ex-convict. Two of the women come to her house one morning, stand in the doorway: 'You are a shame to us all how can we preach the Christian faith when one of our number openly flouts all the values we profess? a fornicatress an adulteress.' They spit chapter and verse at her. She holds onto the table for support. And when she has had enough she picks up a wooden beater and they step back. Two dark shadows. Two angels flying from her sunlit door. 'We shall pray for you' their final threat . . .

Across the Humber, river oily and the wet road. Tomorrow she'd visit York, gather more pieces for the puzzle, her book on missionary wives in the South Pacific. She'd unpack her neat white file cards, add a fact here, a name there. Kirmington. Those gravestones might be useful. They were stone. They were certain. They gave dates and places. No eminent greybeard would be able to lift himself from his rock at some conference and woof, as one had woofed already, 'Yes, but is it history?' Jeff takes out the conference folder and fumbles for his glasses. 'He's old,' she thinks suddenly, watching him from the corner of one eye as they wait at the toll booth. 'His hands have grown old.' Stiff-fingered, he fights with the glovebox catch. She puts out her hand and rests it on his thigh. He pats her, spreads the conference map and peers at names and numbers. It's getting dark. Soon too dark to see.

She loved him she supposed. Simple, 'Jane loves Tom', something carved on a tree with an arrow through. She lived with him for years, had his children, watched one of them die. 'I will go,' she'd said. And meant it. 'Till death us do part,' she'd said. And meant it. But there are difficulties. You find yourself alone, pitching about on a place they said was a fish, where charts and rules run slap against despair. In a harsh new light where old certainties fade. Or you find yourself wanting a baby so much you can't bear it any longer. You have a Mature and Loving Relationship. Your work is going well. You even have a Reputation. You receive grants to do research abroad. Students leave notes in your box at the end of the year, 'A stimulating year. Thank you.' And you're thirty-seven and one day your period, always so reliable, never any bother, doesn't come on time. It's early. You're at the beach for the weekend to get some writing done away from the telephone, and you're not prepared. Two days of making do with torn dusters (no shops for miles), and it stops again. Nothing to worry about, though. Your body, it seems, is preparing for The Change. This is it. So what do you do? If you are Anna you raise the matter with Jeff (one must be honest with one's partner) and he says (because she cries), 'If you want it so much, I'll see about having the vasectomy reversed.' And finds it might be possible. But the night before he is to go to the hospital he wakes you. Lies there in the early morning half-light, sea breathing, one bird calling. 'No. I can't go through with it.' He won't explain. But when she turns over to look at him, he is shaking. And since this is an adult relationship (no one has any rights over another's body) she can't press. She walks alone on the beach and cries of course. But it is his body the doctors must cut and snip and rearrange. So there you are. Then, if you are Anna, you go to a party three weeks before you go to Britain on study leave. Jeff is away tramping with his younger son. You talk to a German *lektor* out for the year. You offer him a lift home. He is an efficient and pleasant lover, and thanks you for the coffee in the morning. ('The only good coffee I have had since I am in New Zealand.') And you throw up in the Ladies Room at LA airport. You eat nothing but Indian food for the first three months in London.

The car is approaching Hull. Jane sits in her whare playing with her baby. The boys are swimming in the creek, their brown naked bodies whiplash from the tree and splash. 'He who would valiant be,' hums Anna to keep their courage up and switches on the headlights. The tickling starts again, a moth in her belly and unmistakeable. In Hull they'll talk, they'll sort it out in their rational adult fashion. But in the meantime, she asks Jeff for a peppermint.

JOHN CRANNA

History For Berliners

The first time I saw Jan and Klaus they were standing naked together in a dormitory in Lipari. Jan faced the window, his arms stretched out to the sill, while Klaus rubbed scented oil into his back. They spoke to each other in rapid German, their conversation punctuated from time to time by Jan's high laughter, and seemed oblivious to the conventions of discretion and reserve that tend to be observed by strangers in hostel dormitories. It only occurred to me much later that this little scene was for the benefit of the other Germans in the dormitory, geology students who had come to the islands in order to climb the volcanoes and who never appeared in anything less than their sturdy mountaineering underwear.

The previous day I had taken the ferry from Sicily with these students, straightforward, friendly men with beards and professional-looking rucksacks. There had been a slow swell on the sea and the day had been very clear, so clear that we could make out a smudge of black smoke on the horizon in the direction of the discontented Etna. At the time the papers were reporting a scheme to redirect the lava flow of the volcano through a series of controlled explosions. The students were discussing the plan, in English for my benefit, and when they had agreed that it was an ingenious notion, one of the Germans turned to me and said, 'But of course we are in Sicily. First the old men of Palermo must be certain they can make money from this plan.' It seemed appropriate, somehow, that here in their ancient homeland the influence of the Mafia extended even to the regulation of volcanic activity.

In the lee now of the island's ashy shore, we moved across a mirror sea. Behind me the Germans were gathering up their rucksacks and securing their geologists' hammers to thick leather belts. The climax of their expedition, they had told me, was to be an ascent of an active volcano on the outermost island of the group. They had brought with them an impressive amount of gear, and later, when I made my way up to the hostel through the narrow streets of the old port, the students preceded me like a train of Sherpas. I found myself feeling absurdly underequipped, as though by coming to the islands in order merely to lounge about and lie on the beach I was betraying the more serious geological obligations of the visitor to these parts.

In the morning the students rose early and either tramped into the interior of the island or caught ferries to the other islands in the group. After they had gone, I made my way down to the old port and sat with a cappuccino and a three-day-old English newspaper in a cafe. In order to avoid reading the newspaper, I watched an old man on the breakwater performing a mysterious operation with wine casks. Water was drained from the cask, fresh sea-water funnelled in, and a series of pebbles dropped through its bung hole. Each cask was then turned a little on its axis and wedged still against its neighbour. I had been watching this operation for half an hour, trying to decide whether it was a scientific operation or an ancient superstitious practice, when a ferry drew in to the breakwater and unloaded its cargo of passengers. All of them, it appeared, were islanders returning from the mainland and they quickly dispersed along the waterfront, until the breakwater was empty again except for the old man and his wine casks.

At this point the two Germans from the dormitory emerged from a side street and ran down to the breakwater. When they saw the ferry, moored and empty, they stopped, looked up and down the waterfront, and hurried over to the old man filling his casks. It was plain from the old man's passivity and by the increasingly urgent gestures of the Germans that he was failing to provide them with the information they needed. Then one of the pair, the more serious-looking of the two, came across to the cafe to where I sat.

'Excuse me,' he said. 'We are looking for our friend. Her hair is cut like this,' he made a flat gesture across the crown of his head, 'And her eyes are not working.'

'You mean she's blind?'

'Sometimes she is blind, ja.' I thought of the steep drop from the breakwater into the harbour, but thought better of suggesting they look in the water. He continued. 'You were here when the ferry arrived?'

'I'm sure she wasn't on the ferry. I would have noticed her.' He called in relief to his friend, who was still trying to communicate with the old man. I noticed that his friend didn't break off the encounter straight away, as though reluctant to abandon the interrogation before the old man had shown some willingness to help. When he came across to the cafe I was struck immediately by how absurdly good-looking he was. Dishevelled blond hair, fine high cheek-bones and the shadow of a pencil moustache — the whole effect of ambiguous Prussian beauty was underlined by a mole on his right cheek in precisely the place where an eighteen-century lady would have worn her beauty spot.

The three of us discussed ferry times for a while, and agreed that their friend was likely to arrive on the afternoon sailing. Then Jan, the blond-haired one, said, 'Your accent . . . you're not English?'

'I'm a New Zealander.'

'So. Sir Edgar Hillary. Why then aren't you with our Bavarian friends on the side of one of the volcanoes?'

'Sometimes New Zealanders get tired of climbing mountains.' Jan laughed the high, tense laugh I had heard the night before in the dormitory; not so much, I felt, at my reply, but because of the opportunity to continue the mocking tone of the conversation.

'Perhaps you will not be too prejudiced against us,' he said. 'We are from East Berlin.' I looked at his friend, who gazed back at me as seriously as before.

'You've been very enterprising in getting to Sicily,' I said.

'So. You're suspicious because everyone knows we Communists are kept locked up behind our borders. However, the father of Klaus,' he laid his hand on his friend's shoulder as though introducing an asset of immeasurable worth, 'is an official of the Politburo of East Germany.' I looked again at his friend, at his brown, serious eyes and for an instant I saw the offspring of a dutiful high-ranking Communist. The story was implausible enough to be true. Only a month before, when hitch-hiking near Turin, I had been picked up by two young Hungarians, a laconic pair who had driven their battered Skoda across the Apennines in the grip of a ferocious death wish. One was a teacher, the other a journalist. They told me that they were both members of the Hungarian Communist Party and presented me their Party cards when I showed scepticism.

'And now,' said Jan, getting up from the cafe table, 'We will leave you to recover your strength, so that you may once again follow your national calling.'

'Thanks.'

'The island is not so big. The privacy of the Anglo-Saxon cannot always be guaranteed,' he added cryptically. 'Ciao!' I watched them make their way along the quay, Jan's hand on Klaus's shoulder, until they disappeared among the ochre hulls of upturned fishing boats.

In the evening I ate alone in a restaurant hung about with glass floats and fishing nets. Fastened to the walls were the remains of unnamable sea creatures, the bones gleaming in the candle-light from the tables. I had failed to charm the waiter with my crude Italian, the food was unexciting and as consolation I was nearing the bottom of a litre of red wine. I thought back over my Italian grand tour, the three months that were drawing to an end, and the images of a hundred towns unreeled themselves in my imagination, the memories of some already blurring a little . . . was it Vicenza or Cremona where I had seen a hearse run out of control in a crowded street? And the pensione where a tiny monkey had answered the door to guests — was that Siena or Perugia? I recalled a long train journey to Naples, of being immobilised in the aisle of a shabby carriage with peasants taking produce to the city, wicker baskets and bundles of vegetables, white hens rocking with the movement of the train, their heads in fitted black hoods like condemned men . . . had I ever felt more free than on that train journey?

Behind me, near the door of the restaurant, I heard a commotion, voices arguing in German and then the unmistakable high laughter, a little drunken this time. I turned to see Jan threading his way among the tables. With him was Klaus, and behind them a slim woman with Slavonic features and closely cropped hair.

'Excuse us again,' said Jan. 'Please meet our friend Krista who after all did not drown in the harbour this morning.' The woman smiled a taut smile. She looked angry. Jan went on, 'Now we have the chance to celebrate this lack of a tragedy. We must buy you a drink.' Klaus, who was already drunk, but who still managed to look very serious, called the waiter over and ordered another bottle of wine.

'Una bottiglia grande,' he said with a large gesture. 'Una bottiglia rosso, alto, rotondo e profondo.'

Jan eyed him speculatively. 'When Klaus is drunk he likes to become the great Latin poet,' he said. Then, turning to me, 'We were having a small disagreement between friends. We need the views of someone who is unbiased.' Krista said something succinct in German that could have been obscene. Jan raised his hands in mock defence and grinned.

'Let me explain to you what has happened,' he said. Some time earlier the three of them have met a couple of Italians in a bar. The Italians, who appear to be very wealthy, are en route from Genoa to the Adriatic and their yacht is at present moored in the harbour. After an hour in the bar together the Italians excuse themselves, but invite their new friends to visit them later at the yacht, explaining that there is no shortage of room on the vessel and that they are welcome to stay overnight if they wish. It is apparent that one of the men has taken a fancy to Jan, and there is a suggestion that a little cocaine may become available.

'You see now the terrible temptations that are placed before the loyal Party member when he is abroad?' said Jan.

Krista broke in. 'So, another little joke. Let me guess that Jan has told you we are from East Berlin, perhaps also that Klaus is the son of the Party Secretary. But he has told these Italians that he and Klaus are the heirs to a West German newspaper empire and has invited them to visit him in the family villa on Lake Geneva. Unfortunately none of these things are true.'

Jan did not seem at all embarrassed by this disclosure. He spoke sadly to his wine glass.

'Krista can always bring the free spirit back to the earth when it thinks to fly too far away.' Then he looked up. 'It is good to try on other skins, don't you think?' I said that I didn't think it was too harmful. I was annoyed at myself for having believed Jan in the first place.

'We still have the problem of whether to visit these wealthy Italians and help them use up their expensive drugs,' said Jan. Krista said flatly that she was not going and Jan ordered another bottle of wine. While he was arguing over the price with the waiter, Krista told me that all three of them were students in West Berlin and that they had been coming to Lipari every summer for four years. By the time we finished the wine, Jan and Klaus had decided that they would take up the yachtsmen's invitation.

When they had gone, Krista and I faced each other a little awkwardly across the table. I asked her why Klaus seemed to get more gloomy the more he drank.

'Klaus is like that. Also he's trying to have a relationship with a girl here in Lipari. This would make anyone depressive. Even in these times the fathers of Sicily keep their daughters locked up like wild dogs.' She got up from the table. 'We must go. Soon the hostel will be closing for the night.'

The hostel lay in a Venetian fortress overlooking the bay. It was approached through a tangle of narrow streets that ran down to the harbour. At night, the streets all looked similar, and this fact, combined with the effects of the wine, made us unsure of our direction. Krista told me about her eyesight, which at present was reasonably good. She suffered from a condition which badly affected her vision during a severe attack, but whose name she did not know in English. She was explaining what brought on the attacks when I realised we were lost, and by the time we had retraced our steps and followed the correct route, the heavy doors of the hostel were closed. The institution was run by a sandy-haired Italian whose moods fluctuated according to invisible laws: when I first arrived he was exceptionally friendly; however, earlier that day he had been curt and scowling, and now as we banged on the great studded doors I was apprehensive of what we might provoke in him. In the event there was no response from inside, the hostel remained dark and silent.

Part of the grounds of the fortress were marked off as an archaeological site, and as the night was warm and still, it occurred to me that this might be the safest place to sleep.

'How do you feel about spending the night among the bones of medieval Sicilians?'

Krista shrugged. 'Dead Sicilians I don't mind so much. It's when they are alive that I have problems with them.'

I looked into the inky digging, obscurely offended on behalf of a people I had not yet got to know and among whose ancestors I was about to bed down.

'Why bother to come here at all then?'

Krista was silent, and then she said, 'The difficulties for women — Klaus's friend for example — and for myself when I was travelling, perhaps they make me too cynical.'

We made our way cautiously through a series of linked pits, until we found what appeared to be a sheltered part of the digging. We lay on our backs looking up at the opaque Mediterranean night while Krista spoke of her journey through mainland Sicily. She said that she had spent several weeks in the mountainous interior, where she had stayed in 'thirsty villages containing only doves and old men'. She described the countryside of the interior, its bluffs and barren valleys, its scattering of lemon and lime trees, fixed in their places in the harsh soil by an unrelenting sun.

It had begun to get cold, so we pressed together for warmth, and some time that night, with the accumulated history of Lipari laid bare but invisible in the darkness around us, Krista and I became lovers, although my memory of how this happened, or which of us initiated events, is not at all clear. I woke in the morning to a fine rain falling on my face. Krista lay huddled against the wall of the pit. Between us were dislodged wooden markers, and I was wondering how far we had set back local archaeological research in our blind stumblings of the night before, when Krista sat up abruptly and looked around her.

'Scheisse. I'm soaking with water. Why are we sleeping in this stupid place?' She was looking at me with genuine anger. I wondered whether she had drunk more than I realised, and was beginning to remind her of our attempt to get into the hostel, when she got up, rubbed her eyes furiously with her fists and walked off through the site in the direction of the hostel. By the time I arrived in the lobby she had disappeared. the sandy-haired Italian watched me without curiosity as I signed the register in a hand so damp that the violet ink ran all over the page.

I lie on a blinding pumice beach. Nothing moves and I let the light seep through to the shuttered eyeball. With my fingers I penetrate the skin of pumice until I touch the damp layer below, the first rain that has fallen on Lipari in four months, the rain that despite its warmth and lightness has apparently so upset Krista. Now, after the morning clouds have cleared, the day is very hot, and ten metres away the Tyrrhenian Sea meets the pumice in a train of benevolent slaps. I am expecting the Berliners, who have told me that because of its seclusion this beach is their favourite on the island.

Jan's laugh announces their arrival from some distance off. He is with Krista and they wave at me across the dazzling pumice. Jan looks unusually pleased with himself and Krista too seems to have cheered up since the morning.

'Good, good,' said Jan, squatting beside me and inspecting me approvingly. 'You are getting some colour on your sad pale body.' With the deft movements of practised sunbathers, Jan and Krista took off their clothes, folded them carefully and stretched out naked beside me. Jan settled into the pumice and let out a contented sigh.

'It is only the sun that can purify the body after the sins of the night,' he said.

After an appropriate pause, I asked, 'How were the Italians?'

'The Italians were very interesting. If all the people of Genoa are like these Italians then Genoa must be a very decadent place. Perhaps next year I will go to visit this city and its wonderful people.'

'First, however, you must entertain them at your villa on Lake Geneva,' said Krista.

Jan laughed his brilliant laugh. 'You're right, honey. First I must do that.' He took out a tube of lotion and began to rub the almond-scented liquid into his skin.

'For Klaus, the night was not so good,' he said. 'Klaus is drinking to forget the girl who is shut away from him in the evenings. After a little more wine, Klaus became very excited and made his big speech about the barbarian fathers of Italy, using much foul language. Fortunately when Klaus is excited his Italian is not so good, and I think our hosts did not fully understand this speech. However, they understand when he lies down on the floor of their expensive yacht and vomits his stomach into their carpet.'

'And after all this, they still believed you were the sons of a wealthy publishing family?' I asked.

'But of course,' said Jan seriously. 'This is absolutely correct behaviour for the sons of wealthy newspaper families.'

Krista pulled a face. 'It's also absolutely normal behaviour for Klaus,' she said. She got up and picked her way gingerly across the hot pumice to the sea. She stood in the shallows with the water lapping around her ankles.

Jan called to her. 'Honey, your string is hanging down.' Krista half turned towards us, looked down and then tucked her tampon string up between her legs. Jan went on, 'And if you go into the water leaking out blood you will attract all the sharks of Africa to this beach.'

Krista picked up a piece of pumice from the shoreline and threw it at him, the way boys are taught to throw, with a flick of the whole arm. Although the projectile had been aimed casually, it only narrowly missed Jan's head. Then Krista waded into the water and swam out into the bay with flat, even strokes. I told Jan that I thought he deserved to have been hit. He gave me a mocking smile.

'But you are such a gentleman.' He propped himself up on one elbow. 'You see, Krista and I have known each other for a very long time, since we were twelve years old in fact. At that time we made some sexual experiments with each other. However, these experiments were not so successful . . .' He trailed off, and for a moment I thought he was expecting me to offer my commiserations. 'Since this time we have been very close,' he continued. 'But we no longer allow sex to make any complications in our relationship.'

I lay on my back, absorbing the heat from the pumice, trying to imagine the desultory coupling of twelve-year-olds in that distant grey city, trying to picture Jan and Krista growing up in a place that existed for me only as a collection of newsreel images, and I felt an irrational wave of depression at the unimaginable difference of our childhoods.

Jan was saying, '. . . when Krista's eyesight began to cause problems, some very sensitive doctors told her that she could be starting to go blind. This is a particularly stupid thing to tell an angry person of six-teen years old. On this occasion, Krista also did something very stupid . . .' He trailed off again, as though concerned that he was being indiscreet, then said abruptly, 'Berlin in the winter is a city with great dangers for the soul.'

Krista was swimming back from the headland towards the beach. Several times, involuntarily, I caught myself searching the bay for moving shadows beneath the surface.

'This is our fourth year of coming to Lipari,' Jan said. 'We have some kind of affaire with this island, Klaus, Krista and myself. Perhaps it is the strange affaire of Germany and Italy, which has been going on for a long time now. In the winter of Berlin I dream of lying on this beach and watching Krista swimming in the green water, and of arguing with Klaus about his crazy lusting for the girl who is locked away.'

'Klaus has been after the same girl all this time?'

Jan nodded. 'Each year it is the same. Sometimes I think that Klaus was born to be the sadist to himself.' He looked down at his own perfectly tanned body and frowned, as though baffled by the sheer perversity of Klaus's obsession. 'I tell him to lust instead for the Italian boys, who are not locked away at all.'

Krista had come up from the water and was standing beside us, drying her shock of blonde hair and listening to our conversation. Her laugh was muffled by the towel.

'And when you and this wealthy yachtsman from Genoa are lusting for each other, what is his friend the other yachtsman doing?' she said.

Jan smiled. 'He's getting a little jealous, perhaps. However, he is much older, and some of his hairs are falling out, so he must be careful not to drive his friend away into the arms of some beautiful young man.'

'Like yourself, perhaps,' said Krista.

'Honey, you are very kind.'

In the evening the three of us went to the bar where Jan had first met the Italians. A little while later they walked in, dressed in immaculate white and with cashmere sweaters knotted casually about their necks.

The younger of the two, Fabio, a languid youth with long eyelashes and an easy laugh, quickly joined Jan in a joking conversation concerning Klaus's misadventures on the yacht. Jan explained with transparent condescension that Klaus was out on another of his doomed missions at that very moment. Krista and I, who had avoided saying anything significant to each other all day, sipped vermouths and listened to the conversation. The Italians seemed charmingly straightforward and I wondered whether the decadence that Jan had spoken of was another of his compulsive inventions.

Eneri, a well-preserved man with the manner of a successful academic (he appeared to be Fabio's senior by at least fifteen years), even gave the impression of being progressive in his politics. As the evening wore on he spent some time explaining the tenacity of the Mafia in Sicily in terms of the protection given it by the right-wing political establishment. Jan, who was still playing up to his role as scion of the West German ruling classes, and who in any case was in competition with Eneri for the affections of his young friend, disagreed with his analysis, at first quite politely and then, when Eneri persisted, with a passion that became almost comical. It was undeniable, Jan declared, that the only serious threat to the Mafia had been during the Mussolini years, when Il Duce's man in Palermo had been unafraid to treat the families with proper savagery, to the point of throwing the wives and children of prominent Mafiosi into jail.

Eneri said mildly that the years of fascism had been a special case and that he had been speaking of the political establishment since the war.

Jan gripped his glass and sat up straight in his chair. 'So you think that fascism was a special case in the history of your country. This is also what Germans would like to believe . . .' Krista laid a hand on his arm. She spoke to the Italians as though excusing the behaviour of a brilliant child.

'Jan is an enthusiastic student of these matters, and it's dangerous to start on such discussions with him. Unless of course you're keen to hear about the whole of your history since the time of Garibaldi.'

Eneri said that he would be very interested to hear such an account of Italy's history, but perhaps, yes, it would be better to leave it for another occasion. Jan was not going to be deterred so easily. His pupils seemed unnaturally dilated and he spoke very fast.

'Perhaps you believe it's better that we push these things into a dark corner of the mind. Of course the Germans and Italians are afraid to look too hard at this part of their history. We like to think that the fascists were just very clever men who fooled the people with their brilliant propaganda.'

I said, 'Surely that's partly tr . . .'

Jan cut in. 'It is a lie. Fascism grew up within the culture of the nation. Our parents and grandparents have spent forty years trying to pretend this is not so. They prefer to believe that they were fooled by the evil genius of Goebbels and Hitler. Until they accept that they were guilty, the soul of Germany will stay with its poison.'

Fabio, who had given the appearance of being bored by the conversation, carefully inspected his fingernails and said that this might be true of Germany, but he did not think it was true of Italy. I was surprised by Jan's outburst, and it had clearly not endeared him to the Italians, who not long afterwards made their excuses and wandered off.

We sat at the bar in silence for some time. And then Jan said, 'This may be the last we see of the wealthy yachtsmen from Genoa.'

I ordered Jan another drink and Krista said, 'Think of the difficulties if you had fallen in love with Fabio.'

'Perhaps I have already fallen in love with Fabio,' said Jan with unconvincing defiance.

Krista linked her arm in mine. 'And perhaps I have fallen in love too.'

Jan looked from one to the other of us, visibly shocked. 'Is this true?'

'Of course it's not true. We have only known each other for a day or so.'

Jan smiled a wan smile, but he had already begun to look more cheerful. 'Honey, you should not play jokes at such moments.'

Krista and I spent a lot of time together in the next few days, although our previous intimacy was not discussed. We went for long walks on the deserted coastal roads, we passed the pumice quarries on the northern end of the island, their monolithic hoppers, mobile gantries and vaulted conveyer chains functioning without any sign of human intervention. A pall of white pumice dust hung over this end of the island, as though the land was throwing up a veil in order to decently obscure the violence being done to its geological heart. Often we walked in silence, intruders in a scene of studied monochrome, the sky empty of birds and the sea leaden and subdued.

In this part of the island, autumn in northern Europe did not seem so far away, and Krista talked of her return to Berlin, of the claustrophobia that overcame the city in winter, and of the deterioration of her eyesight that followed the cold.

'The problem with Berlin,' she said, 'Is that there is no escape from the past. When Jan says the Germans refuse to look at their history, he's correct, but in Berlin itself we have the opposite problem. Everywhere we go we run into the past — in the form of a snake of concrete that runs through our city. So Berlin also has its sickness. Too much of this past is as bad as too little.'

We had come to a headland at the end of the island and the path we had been following ended suddenly before a long drop to the sea. I said to Krista that in Polynesia such places were considered to be stepping-off points for spirits on their way to the underworld. We looked over the sea to the spectral shapes of the outlying islands and I considered the idea that this anonymous piece of ocean was eventually continuous with the vivid Pacific.

Krista said, 'You're very lucky to come from a country which is too young to have the problems of Germany.'

'We have our own nightmares from the past,' I said. 'A country as far from anywhere as mine finds it easier to keep these nightmares secret.'

'I think these are quite small nightmares, in comparison,' Krista was standing near the edge of the bluff watching a boat at the base of the rocks. Far below, two men were lifting lobster pots from the sea. She moved a little closer to the edge, perhaps to obtain a better view of the fishermen.

'I like your story of departing spirits,' she said. 'As a spirit I would feel privileged to leave from this point.'

She was at the very edge of the cliff now, and she raised a finger to her lips as though listening for the sighs of departing wraiths. But it was very quiet up there on the bluff, and the only thing that broke the silence was the disembodied slap of oars from the base of the rocks.

Krista stepped back from the edge, threw her arms around my neck and cried.

'Today the spirits are staying at home!'

Making love in the white dust of an abandoned valley, Krista talked of the spirits she had listened to the last time we had been together, spirits that hummed in the chambers of the digging below the fortress. She told me she had stayed awake half that night while the history of the place had risen up around us in the dark. Now, moving together in the white dust, she talked of Arabs and Venetians, invaders who had come to the islands across the millenia, who had settled and died here, and whose bodies now fertilised the earth beneath us. Fucking and talking like this, she said, was a medicine, but when I whispered 'For what sickness?' she wouldn't answer me. Wraiths ourselves, with the pumice dust sticking to our skins, we followed the valley to a beach and washed it away in the dull sea.

Later, in a crowded cafe in the main town, Krista covered her eyes with a hand and spoke softly to herself in German. When I asked her what was wrong, she answered irritably, still in German, and wouldn't explain further. Jan and Klaus were consoling themselves with drink that evening, Klaus for the usual reasons, and Jan in preparation for the departure of his yachtsmen, who had been seen preparing their vessel for sailing. We sat on the terrace of a bar that overlooked the main harbour, while Jan and Klaus sang sentimental German folk-songs and we drank from the neck of a bottle of grappa.

'By next summer,' said Klaus, his voice thick with the drink, 'I think this barbarian father will have forced his daughter to marry a Sicilian boy.'

Jan put an arm round his shoulders. 'This is very serious. We must look for another girl immediately. Without this lusting it is impossible to imagine a proper summer on Lipari.' Klaus shook his head and muttered that this girl was impossible to replace — he would go mad before he could forget her . . .

Jan passed me the grappa. 'You see now the optimism of the true native of Berlin.' I asked Klaus whether he had considered running away with the girl. He peered at me, bleary-eyed.

'That is out of the question,' he said with bleak finality.

Jan said, 'The barbarian father might arrange for the Mafia to search out the fleeing couple.' He seemed to savour the sheer infamy of the idea. Since the argument with the yachtsmen, speculation on the influence of the Mafia had been a regular feature of conversation. We spent some time discussing elaborate plans for releasing the girl from captivity and ruses for throwing the Mafia off the trail.

At last Klaus broke in. 'This is quite stupid. She would never agree to such crazy ideas.'

Krista shrugged. 'Then perhaps you're wasting your time with this girl.'

'However, we can't just abandon her to the savage father,' said Jan.

'If she won't consider escape,' said Krista, 'perhaps she's not so keen on this romance as you believe.'

Jan eyed her reproachfully. 'Honey, that is most unkind.'

Krista shrugged again. 'Perhaps it's time for Klaus to wake up from his dream.' Suddenly she sounded very angry. 'Perhaps it's time for all of us to wake up. Fantasies about the character of the Latins. Dreams of the beautiful Italians who can save us from ourselves. Is this how we are going to spend the rest of our lives?'

Jan bit his lip. 'So. Everything is clear. Italy is no longer good for us. The playing ground has been closed off. Next summer we will all make love to New Zealanders.' In an attempt to retrieve the situation, I tried a feeble joke.

'I'm afraid we only make love above certain altitudes.' But Jan and Krista were no longer listening.

'Why do we come here year after year?' said Krista. 'So we can gaze at the Italians and pretend to have exotic romances? Unfortunately these romances are always dead before they are born.'

Jan sat rigid in his chair. 'And of course you will be able to tell us why this is the case.'

Krista slammed her glass down on the table, her face suddenly ugly with despair.

'Are you so stupid that you can't see it for yourself?' Her movement had upset the bottle of grappa, and now it spun across the table and shattered on the tiles at our feet. We sat there immobilised, while the creamy dusk descended over the sea and settled among the cane tables and chairs of the bar. And then Krista was on her feet and away down the path from the terrace, while the rest of us sat and watched the dregs of the grappa disappear between the black and white tiles.

I looked for Krista at the hostel and at the bars in town. Then I checked the port area and the arms of the piers enclosing the harbour. I took the road along the coast, pausing to check the beach where we had gone to sunbathe. At dusk this part of the island was even more desolate and at intervals along the road, like the desiccated victims of a drought, stood the spindly shapes of prickly pears. Now I was half walking, half running. I passed the valley where we had made love in the white dust of pumice, past the remains of a boat beached far beyond the shoreline by an invisible hand, until eventually I approached the headland at the end of the island.

I could imagine now the sighs of wraiths, the whispers converging in a susurration that thickened the dusk. Krista's Arabs and Venetians, the foreigners who had voyaged to these islands down the ages, and whose histories of colonisation and death had returned to obsess her. . . . I heard them as they rose on the air and flooded out towards that high point overlooking the sea. I was caught up among them now myself, impelled towards the headland on a tide of whispers that had taken on the strength of a steady breeze. I ran up the path that led from the road to the bluff and cast around in the half darkness. There was no sign of Krista. I called into the dusk, but my voice was snatched away by the eddies that moved swiftly over the headland. At the edge of the bluff I looked down to where the ocean sucked and drew on the rocks, but the light was fading now and the jumble of granite withdrew into the gloom. I stood there on the top of the bluff while a dark wind carrying the memories of Krista's labyrinthine fears blew past me on its way out to the horizon.

When the sea had turned black, I walked down the path to the road. The air was still, the whispers had faded with the light, and I walked in a cocoon of silence along the road towards the lights of the town. The effects of the grappa had worn off, and I felt dull and stripped of emotion. I passed the moonscape of the pumice quarries, their stark architecture pitched up against the night sky. Whatever happened, I knew that my time in Italy was over, and that I would leave the islands as soon as possible.

Krista was sitting on a sand-dune near the road, and I would have missed her in the gloom if she hadn't called out as I went by. Her voice seemed unnaturally loud. She said that she had been on her way to the headland when her eyesight and the failing light had prevented her going on. She had watched me pass from the dunes above the beach. I had looked very grim, she said, and smiled. I stood there for a while in silence, thinking of the headland at dusk, and of the metallic sea that stretched away to the coast of Africa. Then she held out a hand, and I pulled her to her feet. 'Why don't you come and stay in Berlin for a while?' she said.

We walked arm in arm towards the lights of the town, while images from an old newsreel turned in my mind, women cleaning bricks among blackened churches, the Reichstag against a white sky . . . barbed wire, airlifts and the sluggish river Spree.

PATRICIA GRACE

The Pictures

After all she and Ana wore shoes to the pictures now, and hers had the toes and heels out, and she'd been promised stockings for the winter. 'I might get me some earrings,' she said to Ana, as though earrings grew on trees.

They'd spent most of the afternoon getting themselves ready for the pictures, heating the irons on the stove and going over the skirts and blouses — pressing and steaming, reheating and pressing. Then they'd taken the basins outside and washed their hair, and now they sat on the stile waiting for it to dry. 'And I might get me a haircut,' Ana said. Charlotte drew in her breath, 'Ana, we wouldn't be allowed.'

'Yes, well. I might get me a haircut anyway — and I'm putting mine up for tonight.'

'So am I.'

'Let's go and try it now. See if it suits us. You do mine and I'll do yours.'

In front of the bedroom mirror with clips and elastic. Charlotte pulling the wire brush through her hair. Pounding the brush on to her scalp, dragging it down through the layers of thick tangles. Scraping up now, and out, up and out. Until the room is filled with flying streamers of Charlotte's hair.

Ana spread the circle of elastic on her fingers and worked carefully, putting the ends of Charlotte's hair into the band. She let the band close, then tied a ribbon tightly over the band and pulled the bundle of hair up and under at the back of Charlotte's neck. She spread the fold so that it rested thickly about Charlotte's shoulders. A clip above each ear to hold the hair in place. Finished.

Charlotte looked into the mirror smoothing and patting. Not bad. Not too bad. As long as the elastic would stay, as long as the clips would hold. Ana was hovering, 'It suits you. It does. It suits you.' 'Ye-es. Not bad. Not too bad.' Charlotte could see Macky and Denny Boy peeping round the open door at her but she couldn't be bothered with them, not with her hair done up, and it suiting her. She arched her eyebrows and stroked her hair, 'Get those kids, Ana,' she sighed. 'Get those nosey brats out.'

'Get out,' said Ana, making a face and slamming the door. 'We don't want any kids hanging round — Yes, it suits you, Charlotte.'

'It's okay. Course when I get dressed up. With the skirt . . . and shoes . . . I'll do yours now. Then we'll go over to Linda's and do hers and tonight we'll wear some old boots on to the road to keep our shoes clean.'

'Are those kids still hanging around?'

Ana opened the door. 'They've gone,' she said.

The boys had wanted it to be a cowboy one but it was going to be a sloppy one after all, with kissing and people singing — La la la . . .

'La la la,' Macky sang with one hand on his heart and the other extended to his love Denny Boy. 'La la la, will you marry me?'

'No,' Denny Boy sang. 'No I won't, my darling.'

'Thank you. La la la . . .'

'Anyway,' said Denny Boy, flopping down on to his stomach, 'we mightn't be going yet.'

'We'll go. We'll get there.'

'Aunty Connie won't give us any money. I just walked over her scrubbed floor — by accident. Just by accident.'

'What did she do?'

'Picked up her mop. So I took off. She's in a bad mood. For nothing.'

'We better not ask her for any.'

'No . . .'

'What about Uncle Harry?'

'He's too mingy.'

'We could hoe his garden for him, and chop his morning wood.'

'Boy we'd be working all day.'

'And he mightn't give us anything. He might be broke.'

'And we might work all day for nothing.'

'Let's go and see Aunty Myra then.'

'Okay, she might.'

'But she mightn't.'

'But she might.'

And there was Aunty scratching her borders with the rake and all her ducks scrummaging into the loose soil at her feet. Wonder what sort of mood she's in.

'Tena koe, Denny Boy.' Talking Maori ay? Must be in a good mood — not like that Aunty Connie.

'Hello, Aunty.'

'Tena koe, e hoa. Kei te pehea korua?'

'Kei te pai, Aunty.' Talk Maori back to her.

'Yeh. Kei te pai, Aunty.' That'll keep her in a good mood.

'Ka pai.'

'We came over to see you.'

'To see how you're getting on with your flowers.'

'And your ducks.'

'Kai pai ano. Kei whea o korua hoa?'

'Down the beach.' Hope that's right.

'Yes down the beach. And Charlotte and Ana are do-dahing themselves up for the pictures.'

'The pictures tonight.'

'Ah.'

'It's a good one.'

'Yes real good.'

'Kei te haere korua?'

'Not him. Not me, but all those others are going. Everyone else.'

'But him and me, we can't go.'

'Na te aha?'

'Because . . . because . . . Aunty Connie's in a bad mood. For nothing.'

'Yes just for nothing.'

'Kare aku moni, e tama ma.'

And that's easy enough to understand, she's bloody well broke. Shit what a waste of a good mood . . .

'Well . . .'

'Well . . . we have to go, Aunty. I hope your flowers are all right.

'And your ducks.'

'Haere ra e hoa ma.'

Uncle Harry was hoeing up the dirt round his kumara plants. They could see him from the willows at the back of his place.

'All that and he might be broke, like Aunty Myra.'

'Wait a bit longer. When he gets to the last two rows we'll go and help.'

'If he's broke we'll have to try to get Aunty Connie in a good mood.'

'That's too hard.'

'Mmm. Worse than hoeing up Uncle's kumara.'

'All this trouble and it's only a sloppy love one.'

'Yes. La la la . . .'

'Shut up, he'll hear.'

'Anyway he's nearly finished. Let's go and help.'

'Hello, Uncle. We came to help you hoe up your kumara.'

'Hello, boys. Good on you. Get another hoe from the shed and one of you can have this one. I'll sit down and have a smoke. You two can be the workers and I'll be the boss.'

He sat down and began shredding tobacco along his paper as the boys started to mound the dirt up under the vines.

'That's the way, boys. Heap them up. When we dig them there'll be plenty for you to take home.' Well it wasn't a bag of kumara they wanted.

'Plenty of potatoes too.' Or spuds.

'Those others are playing down the beach, Uncle.'

'Yes they're lazy.'

'Just playing. But Macky and I, we like to come and help you with your garden.'

'Instead of playing.'

'That's good boys. Keep it up. Careful of those vines.'

'After this we'll chop your morning wood for you.'

'That's the way. Good on you, mates.'

'. . . Uncle?'

'Ay?'

'You know what Charlotte and them are doing?'

'No.'

'Looking at their ugly selves in the mirror.'

'And ironing their clothes.'

'Ironing their clothes ay?'

'They think they're bea-utiful like ladies in the pictures.'

'And their hair is all done up funny like rags.'

'And they got banjo feet and gumboot lips, but they think they look bea-utiful, la la la . . .'

'Hey, Uncle.'

'Ay?'

'You know why Charlotte and them are ironing their clothes and washing their hair?'

'No.'

'They're going to the pictures.'

'Ah the pictures. What's on tonight?'

'Well it's a good one . . . a cowboy one.'

'Yes, a good cowboy one, Uncle . . . All those lazy kids are going.'

'All of them, ay?'

'Yes, all.'

'Well, boys, you've done a good job there.'

What was the matter with Uncle Harry? Wasn't he listening? They'd hoed up two rows of kumara and now they were lopping the dry brush heads off the manuka and tying it into a bundle to start his stove in the morning. They'd told Uncle that all those lazy kids were going to the pictures but he wasn't listening.

'Good, good. Put your hoes away in the shed now, and stick our axe in the block.' Was he deaf or something?

'Got any more jobs, Uncle?'

'No that's all, boys.' Deaf all right. No ears. All that hoeing, all that chopping. And old Uncle No Ears going up his steps and in his door . . .

'See you later, Uncle.' Deaf Ears.

'OK, boys. Hey don't you want these?'

Up on to the verandah, pecking the coins from Uncle's big dried paua of a hand. Running, shouting. Shouting . . .

'Thank you, Uncle.'

'Thank you.'

'La la la.'

'La la la.'

Lizzie was coughing again. Mereana ran with her down the track past the garden, Lizzie's eyes bulging like two turnips, her chook hand clawed over her mouth. Running into the dunny and banging the door. Then the coughing. Mereana kept watch outside because they wouldn't let Lizzie go to the pictures tonight if they knew she had her cough.

And from where Mereana waited, she could hear the cough gurgling and rumbling up Lizzie's throat then barking out of her mouth as though Lizzie was a dog. Then after a while the gurgling and rumbling and barking stopped and she could hear Lizzie spitting down the dunny hole.

Coming out now with the bottom half of her face all white and stretched and her pop eyes watery and pink. 'Come down the beach,' Lizzie gasped at her. 'So they won't hear.'

Down through the lupins with the black pods busting, which was nothing really, only a sound. Lying on the beach stones and licking them for salt. Lizzie gurgling and squeaking, and Lizzie was nothing but an old crumpled bit of paper there beside her. What if Lizzie died right now?

'Lizzie, Lizzie! There'll be a lot of kissing I bet.'

'Mmm. Plenty . . . of kissing.'

'And she'll have lovely dresses, Lizzie.'

'Yes. . .'

'The men will fight over her. Ay?'

'Mmm.'

'But the best one will marry her.'

'Mmm. At . . . the end.'

'And they'll have a long long kiss.'

'At the end.'

Bending over the sea now. Her neck stretched and lumpy like a sock full of stones. Spitting on the water. 'Don't cough, Lizzie,' Mereana called. 'Don't. They'll hear you. They'll make you stay home.'

Oh but it wasn't that. Not the staying home. The cough was too big. Bigger than the sea — bigger than the sky. Now standing up, pulling a big breath in, 'Yes . . . I bet she has . . . lovely dresses.' And another long breath. In. 'There'll be a long long kiss . . . at the end . . . I bet.'

At the gate where the road began, Charlotte, Ana and Linda took off their old shoes and hid them in the lupins, then carefully slid their feet into the good shoes and smoothed the skirts, patted the hair. Ahead of them the others were running along the sea wall yelling. Leaping down on to the sand, running back up the wall, but they were only kids. They didn't want kids hanging round. Mereana and Lizzie dawdling along behind them and that Lizzie barking her head off. 'We'll sit up the back,' Charlotte said, 'so we won't have *kids* hanging round.'

Not that the others wanted to anyway. Charlotte, Ana and Linda stank and had canoes for shoes and rags for hair. What's more, Charlotte and them, they had hairs under their arms and they were growing tits as well, just like cows. Along the top of the sea wall, flying now, and landing in sand. Cold. Sand goes dead at night time, up the wall again. Bits of shell everywhere, winking, on the road getting blacker every minute.

And waiting. At the store waiting. Lollies and a drink, then up the verandah poles, swinging and sliding — except for stinky Charlotte and them. Not Lizzie and Mereana either, Lizzie coughing like an old goat and baby Mereana nearly crying. Then . . .

'Here it comes.'

'Here it comes.'

Two eyes rounding the corner, bowling downhill. Jack had his foot down tonight.

Slowing down. Stopping.

'At last.'

'Yes. At last.'

Money in the tin. Smart the way Jack flicks you the ticket.

But Charlotte, Ana and Linda were waiting till last. What was the hurry? Damn kids. Always in a hurry. Always pushing. Always in the way. Well . . . well . . . Might as well get in.

'Might as well get in you two.'

'Might as well.'

'Go on then.'

'No you.'

'You first.'

'Go on.'

Up the steps. Gum rolling, eyes down. Wondering who's staring. All those big eyes in the bus must stare — or were they? Have a look, look away. They knew it, people *were* staring.

'All looking pretty tonight, aincha?' Jack yelled.

Bloody Jack. And now that Ana. That Ana had started giggling. Charlotte and Linda were wild with her. No wonder everyone was staring. No wonder . . . And look at Linda. Now Linda was going to. Sneaking along the bus with her hand up over her mouth, snorting behind her hand. Gee they made Charlotte wild those two — and Jack. Everyone staring.

Now Linda was looking at her with cow's eyes, rolling her fat eyes at her and cackling like a chook. Then oh! Oh shame. She, Charlotte, could feel all the little dribbles of laughter gathering in her throat — climbing, pushing . . . Pushing. She threw herself on to the seat between Ana and Linda as the sounds fizzed and exploded behind her hand.

The boys who had sat behind the girls at the pictures got off the home bus at the store and followed the girls along the beach road. They were tossing bits of shell into the girls' hair and shoving each other. The girls were giggling and telling each other secrets. Those kids were going to get a good hiding too, running up and down the sea wall. Shouting, 'Give them a kiss.'

'Kiss.'

'Kiss, kiss.'

'Kiss, kiss, kiss.'

Making sure to keep out of Charlotte's way because she wasn't really a beautiful lady you know. You had to watch Charlotte for the left hook and the leg trip, yes.

Ack, those big boys were dumb following Charlotte and them. Whistling between their teeth and chucking things.

'Give them a kiss.'

'A kiss.'

'La la la.'

But no. No kiss. The boys had stopped now that they had come to the end of the road, and they were calling out to the girls.

But Charlotte, Ana and Linda weren't answering. They had remembered something and were walking ahead, not talking, not turning, not looking down . . .

Their hair suited them.

Their skirts suited them.

They had shoes to wear to the pictures.

They might be getting earrings.

And stockings.

And haircuts.

And they'd just remembered.

And now Macky and Denny Boy had remembered too. 'Hey, you girls. What about your old boots you hid in the lupins?'

'Your old pakaru boots.'

Then away for their lives over the dark paddocks, through the thistles and plops. Lucky they had a head start. Up over the stile and jump the creek. Lucky they could see in the dark, those smartheads would never get them now — across the yard and in. Canoes for shoes. Rags for hair. Not till tomorrow. They'd kill them tomorrow.

But that's tomorrow.

Yes.

HUGH LAUDER

Finland Station

Each Wednesday afternoon he tells me the same story, always with the same opening — that's one way of describing the passage to the Finland station. He goes on to say that as a failed student of Freud's he set up business in Zurich as a hypnotist. He describes himself as a small-time scavenger who cleans up after the titanic psychic battles are over. Ladies with phobias about spiders, children who hate the sunlight, and then he mentions the name Vladimir Ilych.

As the train pulls out of Berlin on its way to the Finland station Lenin is rolling a cigar between his lips, contemplating the pleasure of lighting up. After so many years he can afford to wait a little longer . . . but then returns the match to its box. For Lenin is trying to kick the habit. In Zurich his voice was fading and there was a fear of throat cancer. That's where our friend the hypnotist stepped in. Freud's pupil claims he is the originator of the parrot treatment. Imagine, he said to Lenin, every time you draw on a cigar that it tastes like a parrot's arse.

I leant back in my chair, stretched, and eyed the man through the grille. I knew his next lines perfectly and as he talked on I was tempted, once again, to break the rules. This wasn't the kind of story for which one received welfare, it didn't conform to the regulations but I began to write out the cheque anyway. I thought he'd stop talking then and besides I had other things on my mind. I'd wanted this story to be about the woman I'd met yesterday.

Contemplating that cigar as the train pulled out of the Berlin bahnhof, *that*, Freud's pupil says, was the decisive moment in history. It was the moment he realised it was now or never.

Thinking of the woman I'd met yesterday, I said, I'm not so sure there are decisive acts. But my friend was not to be put off his story — when Lenin arrived at the Finland station he was in a foul mood. That picture of him outside the station, his arm outstretched, the taste of parrot shit on his lips — that's the kind of man who starts a revolution.

I was having doubts, giving him a welfare cheque for a story like this could get me into trouble.

Of course I'd checked, he'd never been to Zurich and he'd never known Freud. He'd never left the working-class suburb he'd been born into. I looked into his ham face. Outside there was a spring southerly blowing all the way from the Antarctic. It was dead on five and my friend watched as I signed his cheque. You know, he says, Freud never wrote a single song and he turns his back on me, wheezing.

On the way home I thought of that woman I'd met yesterday, imagined she was waiting for me, a smile like fresh cut flowers as I closed the door, and having climbed the ladder kicked it away, so to speak.

SHONAGH KOEA

Oh Bunny

They nosed in the gates after lunch, taking advantage of a lull in the traffic. The car came soundlessly down the drive like a shark taking a small bay with a shoal of herrings, the bold red and silver paint at odds with the wily approach. There was a car hire motif on the driver's door and Louisa thought it would have been in the cheaper range, an older superseded model, and that would be like them.

They had stalled in the gateway, jerking wildly to a halt beside the pink florabunda rose as if the big foot stroked the accelerator too lightly and that would be like them too, she thought. They liked to get something for nothing, an advantage for scant investment. She heard the motor splutter again and then, as the car glided forward over the safety humps, it was turned off and the free-wheeling vehicle slid through the trees without a sound, like a mean insinuation. Its bright colour alarmed all the birds and they flew away from the bird-bath, shrieking.

Inside the house, at bay on the top landing, Louisa stood with the old cat, Bunny, in her arms. The landing, with its encompassing view of the garden, had forgotten the flimsy innocence of a quarter of a century of peaceful yesterdays and today provided the sudden shocking sight of that prowling approach. The shape of those two remembered heads was as familiar as her own reflection, instantly recognisable, though so many years had passed that the memory seemed more real than the sight.

'I hate you,' she had said to them, small green cardboard suitcase in one hand and the busfare to a distant town in the other. 'I loathe you all. I hope I never see any of you again.'

'Just remember,' her father had shouted out the window with that lewd sideways jeer, 'you're just dirt, you're scum.'

'If I am, then you're worse, all of you.' A bleak northerly enveloped her on the way to the bus stop and she stopped only once to look back, saw his fleshy face with the compliant garland of the other two at the pane.

'Going away to work, are you? Just finished school, have you?'

asked the bus driver and the merry sound of the clipper on her ticket provided him with any answer that was required.

'Oh Bunny,' said Louisa now, and the old cat lay back with a sigh and licked her arm with a warm red tongue, sensed the old horror. 'What do they want, Bun-Bun? It's all such a long time ago.'

A pigeon, almost tamed by a season of scattered crumbs, rose from his perch at the top of the big magnolia and flew straight up in the air, preparing for some of his usual insolent aerobatics.

'Oh Bunny, they've frightened everything,' whispered Louisa and together they stood on the landing, watched the pigeon flip over several times like the pages of a book in the sky.

She had been happy a moment before, a rare and ephemeral pleasure, hard won, based on a thousand unexpected knocks at the door that turned out to be as innocent as the days on which they occurred. A thousand times she had listened carefully, dried her hands on a tea towel, and said to the children, 'Please, don't answer the door. Please, go into the other room and shut the door. I'll answer the door,' and she had marched stalwartly forward like a small soldier. It had always been a neighbour or a friend or the butcher with the order and the horror of today's sight became a forgotten alarm, the peacefulness of this thought breeding a faint happiness like the memory of fine music.

'Time for our siesta,' she had said to old Bunny, and Bunny waited to be picked up like a fond child.

'You talk too much to that damned cat.' That was what Philip always said. 'You talk more to that damned cat than you do to anybody.'

'But I love Bunny, Philip. Bunny wouldn't ever hurt me. I have nothing to fear from Bunny.'

'I hate them all,' she told Bunny now. 'I hate them all,' and Bunny, recipient of all unpalatable truths, lay back again with a sigh and showed a derisive pink tongue, the warning of the clicking gates forgotten.

The gates were stiff and needed oil, provided a small and comforting alarm with their protests.

'Don't you understand,' she said to Philip once as he tramped up the drive, oilcan in hand, 'I don't want the gates to be easy to open. I don't want to make it easy for anyone to come in. I want to be left alone.'

'And don't you understand,' he said, 'that it's all so long ago that they'll have forgotten? You must be objective, my dear. Think it through. Of what interest would you be? Now? I don't see,' he said, 'what the problem is.'

'You don't know how relentless they are. You don't know how they track people down and use them and bully them. If they knew what I have now they'd want it all.'

'Mrs Paranoia,' said Philip then, and one of the children told him how she went lily-pale when the doorbell rang.

'You were screaming again in the night.' Philip often said that. 'Do you remember me waking you up at three nought nine?' He had a digital clock.

'I was dreaming. I dreamt I went out to the letterbox and there was a letter in it.'

'You and your dreams. What else would there be in the letterbox?' Philip laughed.

It was the handwriting that made her scream, her mother's malevolent and impenitent handwriting, that crushed crabbed script that scratched its way across the paper like old alchemy for poison. The letter, sliding in that nightmare's letterbox, was a silent triumph. I have found you at last, Louisa. No matter how fast you run or how far, I'll run you to earth, Louisa. I will invade all your sanctuaries and soil them, I will show you photographs of your father on his latest beach holiday so you can see again his hairy hands, photographs of ourselves avidly watching other sights.

Bunny stirred uneasily as the doorbell rang five times, a great clamour of noise through the house. Most people rang only once or gave the bell a polite half-turn.

There had been no sound of the car stopping, no slight squeak of brakes, no sound of an opening door. They had relied, she thought, on complete surprise. Faint footsteps could be heard now on the front verandah, a muffled and furtive sound. They unsettled a young thrush which hopped wildly over the front lawn and lost itself in the privet hedge.

'I'd have that out.' Now there was the sound of a car door slamming behind the second person.

'What?' Her sister always overworked the word. 'What, what,' she used to say, 'Watt invented the steam engine.'

'I'd have that hedge out. I'd rip that old privet out. I wouldn't give those dahlias house-room. I'd get rid of that bird-bath and those birds, stinking things.'

Louisa leaned forward, looked through the gap in the curtains. They were standing on the front steps.

'Oh Bunny.' The whisper seemed to lose itself. 'Mummy won't answer the door, Bun-Bun. Isn't it lucky everybody's out.' The old cat shut her eyes and began to snore faintly as Louisa leaned closer to the curtains again.

'I saw something move up there. I saw something up inside that window.' A victorious cry.

'What? Where? I didn't see a thing.'

'Up there, by that balcony thing. I'd pull that off, useless silly claptrap. I'd spray that creeper. I'd get that old rose down. You wouldn't catch me having that.'

Louisa glided slowly back to the safety of the big bookcase at the head of the stairs. No sudden movement must alert them again. Fright had driven her too close to the window for a moment like a little doomed animal.

'It looks as silent as the grave to me.' Her sister's voice was so positive. 'It's bedrooms up there. You wouldn't be up there during the day, anyhow. You'd be down in the lounge laying about watching telly. You'd be showing off to your friends and eating cream cakes. You'd be sitting pretty,' she said, 'in a show like this.'

'That little madam had her head screwed on the right way.' The maternal whine had never changed. 'Louisa was always one to fall on her feet.'

Louisa drifted down the stairs, listening at each step. The voices were quite clear. They had begun to think that the house was untenanted, that the gathering spite was safe to utter and her own small smile bloomed out at her from the mirror in the entrance hall, crooked and dazed like that of a man poleaxed as he falls.

'How old would she be?' The sister's voice.

'Louisa,' said her mother grimly, 'wouldn't be any spring chicken.' They were round the back now, knocking on another door.

'More white flowers. White flowers make me sick. I'd have all that white muck out. I'd have something worth looking at.'

Those burgeoning white daisies gave an abundant shelter to baby birds after flying lessons but today the trusses of flowers sank down to the lawn as if exhausted.

'Mum, you and your big ideas.' Could that monumental figure really be her sister Sylvia? Louisa climbed up a few steps and obtained a better view through the stairwell window.

'I see a cat, a big ginger cat.' How clearly the voices carried through the stone walls. The house, on her behalf, would present an austere and aloof facade. The cat would be Sergeant from next door, a big tom with a face like a boot.

'She was always mad on cats. This'll be her place all right. Here puss, puss, puss. It won't come. Take that then, you great ugly brute of a thing.' A pine-cone from the basket beside the back door flew through the air and Sergeant galloped away, following the thrush's path through the hedge.

'Look what you've done, Mum. You've ruined her artistic arrangement now.' There were muffled sounds of tumbling, falling. Perhaps all the cones had fallen out of the basket.

'See if I care. Blow her and her short shirt. She can pick up her own basket and stuff.' So the basket itself had fallen down into the garden. 'Don't talk to me about her and her artistic arrangements. You could thrash the little devil to within an inch of her life and you'd never get rid of her big ideas.'

Louisa sat carefully down on the bottom stair so Bunny was not disturbed, but the old cat opened one big green eye.

'I think we're safe, Bunny. I think they think Mummy's out. We're safe, darling.' Bunny breathed heavily.

'Talk about stubborn. Talk about a fuss. You could belt that child into the middle of next week and it was still fuss fuss fuss, fiddle fiddle fiddle.'

'I can see a sort of shed down there, Mum.' That would be Philip's begonia house. 'I'm just going to run down and try the door. I'll run her to earth if it kills me. She's going to hear a few home truths from me, I can tell you.'

'That's right, you tell her where she gets off. All these years and never even a card at Christmas. Louisa,' said her mother, 'was always selfish to the bone.'

'Come out. I know you're in there.' Sylvia seemed to be beating on the door of Philip's garden house. 'I saw you. Don't think you can get away from me.' Silence fell on the garden, impenetrable.

'I'd get all those old roses out.' Her mother was wandering round the rose bed. 'I'd get those new luminous ones with the bright colours. I'd get those stinking old oaks ripped out, them and their acorns. I'd have them all looking in from the street to see what I'd got.'

The scent of flowers came faintly through the windows like a distant cry for help and Louisa moved carefully towards the back of the house where the windows had an unparalleled view of the visitors.

'Is it locked from the inside or the outside?' Her mother had joined Sylvia on the lower lawn. A gap in the blinds provided a sudden glimpse of an old hand clawing at wild white curls, a hand once generously endowed with heavy stinging flesh.

'Use your loaf, stupid. How do I know if it's locked on the inside or the outside?'

They were coming towards the house again.

'I'd think I was Christmas in there. All that back part could be mine. You could have a granny flat there. I'd rip out those old steps. They'd have to think of my bad leg.' The hand clawed the wild curls again.

'You could sit around all day in there, Mum, all dressed up like a fourpenny hambone.'

Louisa clutched the sleeping Bunny.

'I feel sick, Bun-Bun. Oh Bunny.'

Sylvia seemed to be turning away, looking towards the begonia house again.

'I've just had a brainwave, Mum. I'm going back down to get that ladder. I'm going to see if Lady Muck's hiding.'

'Mind my stockings. Mind my knees. Don't you snag my best socks with that thing.' The hand had left the curls now and guarded the knees while Sylvia struggled up the slope with Philip's pruning ladder. It was high enough to reach the top of the big apple tree, high enough to reach the kitchen windows.

'It's the kitchen. I can see right into her kitchen.' Another triumphant cry and that sudden shadow on the floor must mean a face was pressed to the glass.

Shadows, thought Louisa, I must watch my shadow, and stepped backwards carefully, always backwards to the safety of the stairs.

'Can you see anything? Is she hiding?' The older figure had remained at the foot of the ladder.

'I can't see a soul.' The shadow had grown larger. Sylvia had possibly cupped her hands round her face to shut out the light. 'It's all just so. It's all as the hen laid it. You ought to see all the stuff.'

'Any sign of cream cakes?' The old lady cackled. 'Nothing but the best for her, I suppose. Just keep everything for yourself and never a hello or goodbye or kiss me foot for anyone else.'

'You could eat your tea off the floor.' The head remained at the window.

'That would be her, her and all her little airs and graces. You could thrash her till you were blue in the face and she'd never give up.'

'I wouldn't give you tuppence for her kitchen.' The shadow had gone now. Sylvia must be climbing down the ladder. 'I'd have something bright in there. I'd have it looking something. She can keep her kitchen and her dead-and-alive colours.'

'That's right.' The other head was bobbing round to the front door again. 'You tell her.'

The old cat struggled to sit up, licked Louisa's hand.

'Oh Bunny,' said Louisa. 'I do love you, Bun-Bun.'

'Louisa,' said her mother from the front door, 'was the biggest little sod of a kid in the creation of cats. You could thrash that child, you could thrash her and thrash her and she just looked at you as if you stank. You just wait till Dad hears about this. Just you wait.'

'If you thought you were going to get a buckshee afternoon tea out of her you had another think coming, Mum. I'll just shove a note under the door. That'll give her a shock when she gets home.'

'Let her stew in her own juice — spooky old place gives me the willies, anyway.' In the old voice was a relic of former days. Where's the little pest? Where's my stick? What's she gone and done now? 'We'll go back downtown and get our own nice afternoon tea. I feel like something really squashy and sweet.'

'I'm going to have something chocolatey and delummy.'

'Sylvia's the clever one,' her mother used to say. 'She's got a real bent for words. She's invented another one — delummy. It means a cross between delicious and scrumptious.'

'I'll just do her a note.' The opaque glass of the front door gave a grotesque view of a large figure requiring chocolate, the arms scrabbling wildly in a handbag. 'I'll just get a pen. What shall I say?'

'Say, long time no see. Say, thought you were smart but we tracked you down from your photo in that magazine. Say, just blew in for a big afternoon tea, sorry you were out.'

'Oh Bunny,' said Louisa from an unassailable position on the stairs, 'I think they're going.'

'Hurry up and get your silly note finished, Syl. We might as well get back downtown.'

'Keep your hair on. Hold your horses, don't get off your bike, I'll pick up your pump.' The note flicked under the door. 'What a shame. I was really looking forward to seeing her go white as a sheet when we came barging in.'

From the upstairs landing Louisa and Bunny watched the departure, watched those two faces stare back at the house, each head as narrow as a magpie's. The old lady seemed to be pointing at some of the larger trees.

'Oh Bunny, she's saying she'll get the axe into those.'

They climbed out of the car at the gates, slammed them with a jeering insolence that frightened all the birds again, then turned into the stream of traffic like scavengers seeking a wider, richer shore.

'Oh Bunny,' shouted Louisa, 'they've gone, they've gone.'

Much later, when the blazing afternoon was dying into early evening, they stepped out on to the front verandah. The old cat went first, like a loyal guard, and walked stiffly on bowed arthritic legs.

'I'll hose this all down tomorrow, Bunny,' said Louisa. 'There isn't time now. Uncle Philip's coming home soon.'

Together they coaxed Sergeant back through the gap in the hedge.

'Poor old chap,' said Louisa. 'Poor old boy. Did they frighten a poor old chap? Did they throw things at an old sweetheart? You come here and let me tickle your chinny-chin.'

It was then that she found them on the side step, two waratah flowers wrapped in metal foil. They were stiff and unyielding flowers, blooms that would look the same dead or alive, flowers that possessed no generous abundance in scent, beauty or number.

The two cats, waving their tails gently, led the way to the back of the garden and turned every few steps to make sure she was following.

'It's all right, treasures, I'm coming. Don't worry, Bun-Bun, Mummy's coming,' and the silver paper flashed in the last of the sun as the bunch described a wild arcing flight to the rubbish heap, the foil glistening like the polished blade of a scimitar as it descends upon a neck.

ALBERT WENDT

Daughter of the Mango Season

'It's June 1894, and I'm fifty-five years old today,' Barker said to Mautu as they sat in cane chairs on the store verandah overlooking the malae. As usual Peleiupu, Mautu's daughter, sat on the floor beside her father's chair. They were having a breakfast of strong tea and cabin bread. 'Fifty-five is old, isn't it?' Barker asked. Mautu nodded as he dunked his cabin bread in his mug of tea. 'Not many people here or in England live beyond forty,' Barker continued. 'I've been lucky. Haven't been seriously ill, ever — ' 'Aren't you going to eat?' Mautu interrupted him.

Barker said, 'I'm not hungry.' Paused. 'How old are you?'

'Nearly forty-five.'

'The oldest man I've ever known was a Chinaman we took aboard in Hong Kong. About eighty he was. Small fist of a chap but very, very tough. Never said anything, not to me anyway. Bloody pagan he was. So you see, Mautu, we don't need to be Christians to live a long life.' Mautu, who was the village pastor, refused to take the bait. 'The next oldest was a Hindu. As black as midnight and at seventy-something years old not a wrinkle on his face. Another heathen. In fact the longest living people I've met were *not* Christians!' Mautu refused to reply. 'If old age is proof of the gods' blessings, then the pagan gods are more powerful.' He paused dramatically and, gazing at Mautu from under lowered bushy eyebrows, added, 'Perhaps *your* God doesn't exist!'

'Going to be good mango season,' Mautu said in English as he gazed up at the mango trees that shaded the store. The high, sprawling trees were pink with blossoms and buds. Peleiupu wanted her father to offer their friend some consolation, an answer to grasp at. Mautu pushed away his food tray, looked at Barker and asked, 'Why is God's existence important to you if you do not believe in him?'

'It *isn't* important!'

'Then you not need to chase your own questions!' Mautu looked up at the mango trees again. 'Yes, the mangoes, they going to be a lot this season.'

'Why do you always talk in riddles?'

'It is you who deal in riddles!' Mautu replied. Barker looked away. Peleiupu timed it perfectly. Just before Barker could jab his frustration at Mautu, she jumped up and picked up her father's food tray. She stood looking at Barker's tray.

'Yes, take mine too!' he said, finally.

'But you not eaten!' Mautu insisted.

'It isn't the food of this world that I need!'

'Not even sweet mangoes?' joked Mautu.

For the first time that morning, Barker relaxed and, looking up at the mango trees, said, 'Perhaps the sticky juice of the mango can hold my tattered fifty-five-year old body together for a while longer!' When Peleiupu returned from the kitchen fale a few minutes later Barker said, 'Pele looks more like Lalaga than you.'

'Then she is not beautiful!' chuckled Mautu. Embarrassed, Pele avoided looking at them and sat down behind Mautu's chair.

'I wish my children were like Pele. The brats are total savages!'

'Like their father perhaps?'

'I'm not a savage!' Barker pretended to be hurt.

'You no believe in the English God. Or English civilisation. You not respect other papalagi, not even the missionary, so you are a palagi savage!'

'I do believe in other things!'

'What?' Mautu trapped him. 'What?' Mautu whispered.

'In many things!' Barker stood up suddenly and, turning his back to Mautu, recited, 'I believe in birth; I believe in death; I believe in thirst, hunger, pain, desire, joy, because I can experience all those. I believe in the earth, the sea, the sky. In birds too. And mangoes. Especially mangoes because I'll be tasting their delicious flesh in a few months time.' He wheeled to face Mautu. 'I have no need to believe in a supreme being, in a God. I don't need such a crutch!'

'But you continue for to search —'

'Not for God!'

'— across all the earth's seas and islands —'

'Not for God!'

'— why you search all these fifty-five years?'

'Not for God, I tell you!'

'Then for what, for whom?' Mautu snared him. Peleiupu suddenly thought of Barker's huge hands as helpless anchors dangling into the emptiness around him, and she wanted to reach out and hold up their immense weight of doubt.

'As I have said already, the things I can feel and taste and experience, those are enough for me!'

'If that is enough, then you not need to keep asking me. You not need anybody, my friend.'

It was as though the mellow morning light had solidified around them and for a long moment they said nothing.

'I not know what answers you seek,' Mautu said. He reached out and touched the back of Barker's right hand. Barker sat down again. 'All I know is you are a English lord who is shipwrecked on a island full of sun and sky and mangoes and need nothing else!' Mautu said, impishly.

'Yes, I *am* the civilised English lord shipwrecked in Paradise and have no need of the Christian God, missionaries, other white-skinned lords and crucifixes!' he laughed softly and clutched at Mautu's shoulder. 'I am a pagan in the midst of so much plenty! I am fifty-five years old today and I seek nothing and need nothing!'

'Perhaps just mangoes?'

'Yes, perhaps mangoes!'

As their laughter lost itself in the thick foliage of the mango trees, Peleiupu realised the two men had a profound need for each other, a bond so strong that one couldn't do without the other any more. They were so alike, this pagan papalagi trader and the Christian.

'Our annual church fono is to be held in two weeks time,' Mautu said in Samoan. 'Will you take us again in your fautasi?'

'Yes, but on one condition.'

'And what is that?'

'That you take Pele and Arona with you.' Baker winked at Peleiupu whose surprise was trapped breathlessly in her throat.

'Do you want to go?' Mautu asked her. Peleiupu nodded. 'You'd better ask your mother then!'

'We'll leave you and your party at Malua, and I'll take Pele and Arona into Apia.'

'I don't think so!'

'Don't you trust your papalagi pagan friend to care properly for your children?'

'It's not that,' mumbled Mautu. 'I don't like Apia.'

'Apia and the whole life that goes with it is here to stay whether you like it or not. Your children will have to live with it.' He reached over and ruffled Peleiupu's hair. 'And Pele can cope with anything, even Apia!' he added. 'She watches and learns and understands quickly. Don't you, Pele?' Peleiupu blushed. 'She is fortunate!'

Later as they walked away from Barker's store, Peleiupu glanced up at the mango trees. Their dark green foliage, now peppered pink and red with flowers, stirred lazily like slow spring water. She shimmered with joy at the thought of visiting Apia.

'Do you like Barker?' Mautu asked. She nodded. 'Why?'

She pondered quickly and said, 'He is a very sad man, eh?'

'Barker *is* right about you: you *do* watch and learn and understand.'

They walked in silence the rest of the way.

'Mautu,' she pleaded as they walked up the back paepae of their fale, 'I want to go with Barker to Apia.'

'All right!' he whispered. Lalaga was weaving a mat in the centre of their fale. 'But you had better ask your mother about going on the trip.' Before she could insist on him asking Lalaga, he escaped to his desk at the other end of the fale.

'How is the papalagi gentleman?' Lalaga asked her in English. (Lalaga had taken to referring to Barker that way but there was no malice in it.)

'He is well,' Peleiupu replied formally, thus undermining Lalaga's line of attack. 'Let me do it.' She sat down. Lalaga slid away from the mat and let Peleiupu continued the weaving.

For a while they said nothing, and as Lalaga observed Peleiupu's deft hands and fingers weaving the mat she experienced an upwelling surge of pride in her daughter. At fifteen Peleiupu was already an expert weaver of mats and highly skilled in other female crafts. Everything came easily to her, too easily, Lalaga had often thought. 'It is a gift from God!' Mautu had once allayed Lalaga's fears about Peleiupu. Even her English was now better than Mautu's. Yet Peleiupu always made herself appear less skilled than other people so as to make them feel more secure, safer, in her presence. For this Lalaga loved her deeply, knowing that Peleiupu would not use her gift, her superior talents, to harm others.

'What did your father and the papalagi discuss this morning?' Lalaga asked, expecting Peleiupu, as usual, to check if anyone else was listening before replying.

Peleiupu looked around the fale quickly and then said, 'Mautu says its going to be a very good mango season this year.'

Lalaga wasn't going to be distracted *that* easily. 'What did the papalagi gentleman and your father, the prophet, talk about?'

Shrugging her shoulders, Peleiupu said, 'The usual.' Her hands worked more quickly.

Lalaga waited but got no further enlightenment, so she asked, 'And what is the usual?'

'The search for God.' Peleiupu's hands stopped their furious weaving. 'You believe in God, eh?' she asked.

'Of course I do!' Lalaga protested.

'That's what I thought.'

'You *thought* so!'

'Lalaga, some people don't believe in God,' Peleiupu explained patiently.

Lalaga was frightened by what she felt she had to ask. 'Are you one of those people?'

Peleiupu's hands continued their nimble weaving. She said, 'Barker doesn't believe and I think many other papalagi are the same.'

'I knew that!' sighed Lalaga but, when she noticed the abrupt halt in Peleiupu's weaving she tensed again, expecting another devastating revelation of heresy.

'Mautu believes, doesn't he?'

'How can you ask such a thing?' Lalaga was almost shouting. 'Your . . . your father is a servant of God!'

Peleiupu ignored her anger and said, 'All I meant was that Mautu *sometimes* doubts.'

'Doubts what?' Lalaga insisted, angry with herself for allowing Peleiupu to question her belief.

'God,' was all Peleiupu said.

'Peleiupu!' Mautu called to her.

'Yes?'

'Get me a drink of water!'

Peleiupu scrambled up and out of the fale, leaving Lalaga grasping for meaning like a fish kicking at the end of a line. She continued weaving but Peleiupu's revelation about Mautu's doubt kept picking at her.

Peleiupu was soon back with a mug of water for Mautu. While raising the drink to his mouth, Mautu whispered, 'What are you and your mother arguing about?'

'Nothing!' she whispered. Mautu started drinking. 'I just told her that you sometimes doubt the existence of God!' Mautu choked and coughed the water out in a splutter. 'That's true, isn't it?' she asked. He wiped his mouth with the back of his hand and, trying to steady his trembling hands, drank the rest of the water slowly.

'Have you asked her about going to Upolu?' He handed her the empty tin mug.

She shook her head. 'Why don't you ask her?'

'It's best that you ask her,' he whispered. And before she could plead with him he added, 'Go now, I've got a lot of work to do.' He continued writing.

She hesitated for a moment, turned swiftly, and started hurrying out of the fale.

'We haven't finished talking!' Lalaga stopped her.

Peleiupu went over reluctantly and sat down beside Lalaga, confused by her mother's unexpected anger and her father's timidity and refusal to get permission for her and Arona to go to Apia. Everything was straightforward but adults, especially parents, made things complicated, stupidly unreasonable, she thought. She was only fifteen years old, yet she had to be ever so patient with their lack of understanding, their slow decision-making, and the eternal complications they made of their lives (and everyone else's!). Most of them were so *unwise*, yes, that was her description.

'Going to be a good mango season,' she remarked. She tried to dispel her confusion with the thought of fat, delicious, succulent mangoes, but couldn't. Beside her, Lalaga's presence was a solid rock pillar. She wasn't going to offer to do the weaving any more. 'Where are Arona and the other children?' she asked.

'I don't know!' Lalaga replied. She suddenly realised her daughter no longer referred to herself as a child, and it wasn't out of any pretence or arrogance. Peleiupu simply did not think of herself as a child. And, physically, she was quickly blossoming into a woman, tall and supple. Peleiupu wasn't self-conscious about this physical transformation either. It was as if, anticipating well beforehand every change in her life, she adjusted to them before they occurred.

'Very hot, eh?' Peleiupu commented, noticing the beads of sweat slithering down her mother's arms and face. 'Where's everybody gone?' All the neighbouring fale appeared empty of people.

'Working in their plantations or fishing, you know that!'

'Yes,' sighed Peleiupu, 'but where are Arona and Ruta and Naomi and the other children of our aiga?'

'Swimming probably. Now stop your questions! Here, you weave!'

When Lalaga looked out of the fale and saw that their mango trees beside the road were covered with blossoms, she heard herself saying, 'Yes, it is going to be a rich mango harvest.'

'Mautu was the first to observe that this morning.' Peleiupu paused in her work and, gazing steadily at Lalaga, said, 'Funny how you can make an important observation the property of everyone by just pointing it out to someone else who then points it out to someone else and so on. Of course it has to be an observation that is important to those other people. Like the other morning, while Arona and I and the other children were in our plantation collecting coconuts, I suddenly *heard* the silence in all that growth . . .'

'Heard it?'

'Yes, I heard the silence — it was deep and still, a huge kind presence all around us and in us . . . And when I heard it I told Arona to stand still, silently, and listen to it. He did. I told him to shut his eyes. He did. Then I asked him if he was hearing it. He nodded. Then we asked the others in turn to listen. And when we had all had a turn, we all closed our eyes together and listened as a group. And we all heard it and allowed it to become part of us.'

'What did you think that particular silence was?' Lalaga pressed her knowing that Peleiupu, as usual, had glimpsed a deeper meaning to it.

'It was the land itself,' she explained. 'The silence of these islands. It must have been here when God created our country. And has always been here.'

'But why is it important?'

'I don't know yet how to explain it,' she said. 'Perhaps it is important because if we refuse to hear it, or let it be part of us, we will become other creatures . . . I don't know. Arona knows better. He doesn't allow his thinking to get in the way. *He just knows.* He lets things become what they are in himself.' She paused and added, 'It is bad to think too much, Barker keeps telling Mautu. He is right . . .'

'But Barker does nothing else but chase his thoughts round and round! That's why he can't believe in anything!' laughed Lalaga.

'That's the palagi way, that's how palagi people are.'

'And your father?'

Aware that Lalaga had once again led her deftly to a discussion she wanted to avoid, Peleiupu said, 'May I go for a swim?' Before Lalaga could pin her down again Peleiupu called, 'Mautu, may I go for a swim?'

'All right!' he replied. And Peleiupu was out of the fale and running towards the pool.

Lalaga continued to weave her mat, refusing to ask Mautu directly about his doubts because he was, like Peleiupu, very adept at dodging her questions.

It was almost midday and the sun was snared in a smother of thick cloud that seemed to have oozed out of the sky's belly. Only the quick, soft squeaking and scratching of Lalaga's fingers against the pandanus strands disturbed the quiet. Occasionally, she heard Mautu shift in his wooden chair. Mangoes, she thought inadvertently, and then cursed herself for having thought that. Why did her daughter understand more than she? She had no right to, she was only a child!

On their way home from the pool, Peleiupu edged up to Arona and whispered, 'Do you want to visit Upolu?' Arona looked straight ahead. A brother, at his age, should no longer be seen displaying affection for his sister. 'Barker and Mautu will take us if we want to go.'

'Who said?' Arona asked.

'Not too loud!' she whispered. Ruta and Naomi and the others were too busy talking among themselves to hear anyway. 'Mautu and Lalaga and the elders are attending the church Fono at Malua. Do you want to go?' He nodded once, sternly. 'Lalaga hasn't said we can go though,' she added, hoping he would volunteer to persuade Lalaga. He said nothing. 'Did you hear?' He nodded once. 'Well?' she asked.

'Well what?'

'We won't be able to go if Lalaga says no!'

'You ask her then,' was his curt reply. He looked so aloof and baulky in the noon sun, with the droplets of water glistening like fish scales in his hair and over his body, that she hesitated from persuading him any further.

'You're her favourite,' she ventured onto precarious ground.

'I'll ask Lalaga!' Ruta volunteered.

'Ask her what?' Peleiupu snapped.

'Whatever you want me to!'

'It is not your concern!' Arona stressed, just like their father when he wanted quiet. Ruta shrugged her shoulders and resumed her whispered conversation with her friends.

They noticed that some of the older girls and boys were gathering in the fale classrooms behind their main fale for their afternoon lessons. Lalaga was still weaving.

'I'll ask her,' Arona said finally, and then walked away from her.

As usual, after lotu and their evening meal, Mautu conducted an English lesson with Lalaga, his children, and the brightest Satoa children. During these lessons, whenever Mautu didn't know the meanings of words or their correct pronunciation he got Peleiupu to explain them. However, he always rechecked with Barker later. Sometimes when Mautu couldn't take the class Peleiupu took it; and secretly, Lalaga and the others preferred her relaxed, democratic, patient style of teaching. Mautu also gave her all the students' assignments and exercises to mark.

After the lesson that night, Peleiupu and the older girls strung up the mosquito nets and soon all the children were in the nets and falling asleep. Instead of sitting up with her parents, Peleiupu got into the net where she slept with Ruta and Naomi and three other girls, pulled her sheet up to her chin, and pretended to be sleeping. Intermittently however, she would peer through her half-closed eyelids at her parents and Arona who were playing cards beside the lamp a few paces away, hoping to hear Lalaga's decision about their going to Upolu.

Like the sudden pulling back of a curtain, she was awake. It was bright morning and the other children were outside picking up the fallen leaves. She rolled out, untied the net quickly and folded it with her sleeping sheet and placed it on the lowest rafter, with the sleeping mats.

Arona and three of his friends were behind the kitchen fale scraping coconuts to feed the chickens, but because there were no girls with them she couldn't go and ask him. At the drums of rain water under the breadfruit trees, she filled a basin, washed her face and combed her hair, all the time keeping an eye on her brother.

As she helped the other girls in the kitchen fale cook their morning meal, she tried not to think of Lalaga's decision. Shortly, when she saw Arona strolling through the scatter of banana trees towards the beach, she got up and pretended to be heading for the lavatory that was located at the edge of the beach behind a thick stand of palm trees.

'What did she say?' she called to him. He was standing up to his thighs in the sea, his back to her, washing a coconut strainer he had brought with him. He continued as if he hadn't heard her. She moved up to the water's edge. What did Lalaga say?' she repeated. Raising the strainer with both hands, Arona squeezed it in one long drawn-out action, and the water dribbled though his hands like solid white smoke and splattered into the surface of the sea.

He waded back towards the beach. 'She will decide by tomorrow.'

'Tomorrow?' she cried, stamping her right foot into the thickly wet sand. He nodded and started to walk past her. 'But why?'

'Don't worry, she'll let us go!'

'She had better!' she snapped.

There was no one else in the main fale as she sat with Arona facing Lalaga who, she sensed, was avoiding looking at her. In the pit of her belly a ferocious beast was inflating itself outwards, threatening to fill every nook and cranny of her shape. She could hardly breathe; sobs were breaking up from her chest like huge bubbles about to burst but she swallowed them down repeatedly.

'. . . Arona may come with us,' Lalaga was saying, 'but you'll have to stay and run our classes . . .'

'I won't. No!' The choking cry broke out of her mouth. She slapped at her knees and she was sobbing.

'Don't you talk to me like that!' ordered Lalaga. 'No child talks to her mother like that. You hear me!'

'I want to go!' Peleiupu cried. She sprang up, fists clenched at her sides, her huge tears dripping down to the mat. 'I'm going!'

'I won't allow any child of mine to talk to me like that. Hear me?' Lalaga rehitched her lavalava. 'If you don't watch out, I'll beat you!'

Peleiupu scuttled across the fale. At the front threshold she wheeled, wiped her face fiercely with her hands, and called, 'I'm going and you can't stop me!'

'Get me the broom!' Lalaga ordered Arona.

Peleiupu jumped down onto the grass and started running furiously across the malae.

'You wait!' Lalaga threatened. 'You wait until I get you tonight!'

They watched Peleiupu disappearing into a stand of bananas and into the plantations. 'Go and bring her back, now!' Lalaga ordered Arona who rose slowly, glanced at her, and started ambling out of the fale. 'And hurry up!' she chased him.

For a while, Lalaga stood on the front paepae gazing after her children, then when she realised the neighbours were watching her she retreated to her weaving.

'I'll show her,' she kept repeating. 'She thinks she knows more than her own mother — the animal! Just wait. I've spent my life slaving for her. Just wait!'

A short while later, however, when she remembered how determined her daughter was, she visualised with increasing panic Peleiupu in a fragile canoe, paddling suicidally across the hungry straits which could inevitably swallow her up. Then, more frightening still, she saw Peleiupu up in a tree fixing a noose round her neck. She scrambled up and out into the classrooms where she instructed the oldest students to follow Arona and search for Peleiupu.

The undergrowth was a dense green sea sucking her into its depths as she ran, her feet making plopping, sucking sounds in the muddy track. 'I'll show her! I'll show her!' Peleiupu repeated. Ahead, the ifi tree was a massive mother with arms outstretched to welcome her. She jumped up, clung to the lowest branch, kicked up and landed on the next branch then, branch by branch, climbed until she reached a platform of interlocking branches, lay down on her back and cried up into the maze of leaves and branches and thin rays of light.

This was 'her tree', her refuge whenever she was troubled. When she had first discovered it five years previously it had intimidated her with its heavy brooding presence; an octopus, she had thought. Its rich, fertile smell of mould had made her think of supernatural beasts. However, one morning after a nasty verbal fight with Arona and Lalaga, she had found herself up in the ifi's protective shade, and, as she had lain on the platform, the tree's breathing and aromatic odour had healed her hurt. Soon after that, she had heard Filivai, the Satoa taulasea, say that certain trees in pre-Christian times had been the homes of some aitu and atua. After about fifty years of missionary conversion, aitu had become evil beings to be feared and there was only one Atua. Her ifi tree had an aitu, she came to believe, after hours of relaxing in its green healing. Her tree was also part of Nature, a spiritual force she kept reading about in English books. She wondered what ancient aitu lived in her tree and in her imagination tried to give form to that aitu. She tried her mother, then the taulasea Filivai, then a combination of all the women she admired. One day she even pictured her tree's aitu as one of Snow White's dwarfs; she tried the supernatural beings she read about in Barker's books — the Cyclops, the Genii, the Unicorn. None of them fitted, she decided. So she tried all the animals she knew. Then all the fish and other sea creatures. Her patient search was methodical and led her deeper into the rich depths of the garden of her imagination. Years later, especially in moments of crisis, she would realise that in her search for her tree's aitu she had explored and groped her way towards the wisdom of her imagination, to a faith that lay beyond logic and belief.

One overcast afternoon as she sat crosslegged on the platform, hands on her knees, her back straight, gazing motionlessly into the foliage, she let her thoughts settle into a still pool, so still a whisper could shatter it. She waited. She thought she was dreaming: she saw herself sitting crosslegged on the platform. She waited. Gradually, almost as if a slow melting was radiating through her pores into all the corners of her being, she inhaled the tangy aroma of the moss that covered, like a cloak, the bark of her tree. She relaxed with an ecstatic sigh, and the odour not only filled her but the sky and bush and all the creatures in it. Everything was drunk with it, and she *knew* that the presence of the moss's odour was the aitu of her tree, and it was in her soul, now.

When she surfaced from the spell, evening was starting to cover her tree like a black silk garment.

A few days later, when she began to doubt her faith in her aitu, she wandered to Filivai's home and played a game of lape with the children of Filivai's aiga. Halfway through the boisterous game she pretended she had taken ill and went into Filivai's fale.

Filivai was using a stone pestle to pound a mixture of leaves and coconut oil. The pungent odour of the potion reminded Peleiupu of her tree's aitu, as she sat down a few paces opposite Filivai. Because she was thought of by the Satoans as 'Mautu's very gifted daughter', she was welcomed in all their homes at any time. However, like almost all Satoans she was wary of Filivai because she was a healer not only of physical ailments but of ma'i aitu. Filivai's powers, she heard Satoans whisper, came from the Days of Darkness: Filivai was heir to an evil heritage which the missionaries and pastors had exorcised (and were still exorcising). But unlike other taulasea Peleiupu had heard about, Filivai was an earnest Christian who refused to heal ma'i aitu, unless it was absolutely necessary. And before performing such healing she always asked Mautu, her pastor, for permission to do so. Her father, Peleiupu remembered, had never refused Filivai, and she wondered why. Later in her life Peleiupu would observe that her people's belief in the Christian Atua, the Holy Spirit, was only the top third of the pyramid which included, in its three-dimensional body and belly, a feared assembly of savage aitu, saualii, sauai, and the papalagi-introduced ghosts, vampires, frankensteins, demons, devils, and Satan. Linked to this observation was the perception that all living creatures were part of a world inhabited by other beings who were both visible and invisible and benevolent and destructive. Now that they were Christians, the Satoans tried not to discuss, within Mautu's hearing, these other beings. From what Peleiupu heard and observed, she knew that many Satoans, especially the elders, sometimes met and talked with the spirits of their ancestors. At times they even suffered the wrath of those spirits, and were sometimes possessed by them. Even her parents, who professed unshakable faith in reason and the Bible, were not free of the feared menagerie which inhabited the murky depths of the pyramid. To her death Lalaga would deny verbally the existence of the menagerie, but Peleiupu knew Lalaga feared its existence. On the other hand her father, whose ancestors had been taulaaitu, would come to believe more profoundly and without fear in what he called 'that other reality' in which dwelled the banished spirits of his taulaaitu ancestors, their atua Fatutapu and all the other presences and spirits. Mautu would never reveal this to his congregation, but Peleiupu would love him more abundantly for it.

'How is your father?' Filivai greeted her.

'He is well, thank you.'

'And your mother?'

'She is well too, thank you.'

Filivai trickled more coconut oil into the potion and continued pounding it. Peleiupu watched her. Filivai was over sixty, one of the oldest Satoans, but she looked as young as Lalaga. Only the network of wrinkles on her forehead and cheeks and the looseness of her flesh betrayed her age. Her pendulous breasts, blue-veined around the almost black nipples, hung down to her belly and shook in rhythm to her pounding. She wore a stained lavalava and a tiputa draped over her shoulders.

'It's going to be a good mango season,' Peleiupu heard herself saying.

'If it rains heavily while the mangoes are in flower, there won't be many mangoes.'

'Why not?'

'The rain will break many of the flowers,' Filivai said. Peleiupu wanted more details but wasn't going to be impolite. 'Is it true you read a lot of books?' Filivai asked.

'Not as much as my father or Barker,' she admitted. Then, quickly perceiving the opening, added, 'Do you like Barker?'

'He's married to a woman of my aiga,' Filivai evaded her.

'He doesn't go to church or believe in God, eh?' Peleiupu sensed Filivai wasn't surprised by that.

'You didn't come to talk about the papalagi, eh?' Filivai's unexpected parry surprised Peleiupu who, for a pause, didn't know how to counter. 'I'll wipe my hands then we'll talk.'

Using a corner of her lavalava, Filivai started wiping her hands clean of the sticky bits of leaves and oil. 'How many years are you now?'

'Fifteen.'

'But your mind is much older!' Filivai remarked. Peleiupu wondered how Filivai had lost her two top middle teeth; there was a thin, white, perpendicular scar on her upper lip also. 'Your brain is much older.'

Flattery always embarrassed Peleiupu so she said, 'I must go!'

'Don't go! I am glad you came to talk with me.'

A short while later they were conversing easily.

'I have a tree,' Peleiupu said.

'What kind of tree?'

'A ifi. I remember you telling my parents that in the olden days some trees had aitu or atua.' Peleiupu paused. Filivai nodded. 'My tree has one.'

'Have you told your parents that?' Filivai asked, as if Peleiupu's revelation wasn't unusual. Peleiupu shook her head. 'You shouldn't let them know: they are God's servants and may not understand.'

'That is why I came to you.' No reaction from Filivai. 'The atua in my tree reveals itself to me through the odour of the tree. Is that possible?' Filivai nodded. 'It is a kind atua; it heals my pain, always.'

'It comes easily, doesn't it?' Filivai asked. Peleiupu didn't comprehend. 'You know, you see without knowing how you do it. It is a great gift,' Filivai said. 'From God,' she added hurriedly. 'Because of it most people will be frightened of you. Do your parents know about it?'

'If you mean I have intelligence, then my parents know I have it, especially my mother.'

'Is she happy about it?'

Peleiupu pondered for a moment and then admitted, 'Don't think so!'

'What about your father?'

'He knows but he is too busy with his books.'

'I knew a young girl once. She had the gift too,' Filivai said more to herself than Peleiupu.

'Were other people wary of her?'

'Yes,' Filivai emphasised. 'Yes, very frightened when they discovered she could see into the world of atua and aitu and other presences. A world outlawed by the Church . . .'

'What happened to her?' Peleiupu asked. She thought she could see tears in Filivai's eyes.

'She is alive. She is a simple healer,' Filivai said.

'And the gift?'

Filivai looked away. 'I must continue with my work.'

'I will go now,' Peleiupu said, rising reluctantly to her feet.

'You must learn to hide the gift,' Filivai said. Peleiupu glanced back at her. 'Don't ever try to destroy it. Or betray it. It is what you are.'

'May I come and see you again — if I need to?'

Filivai nodded once. 'I don't have the courage and may not be able to help you.'

'Thank you. I'll go now.'

'Don't expect too much from me!' Filivai pleaded.

Peleiupu walked out onto the malae where the scramble of children was still playing lape.

'Pele's in our team!' one of her friends called.

Peleiupu looked back at Filivai and found her gazing at her. Peleiupu waved once. Filivai nodded. Quickly Peleiupu decided what she had to do to survive, and skipped into the noisy game of lape, laughing and joking, a girl who appeared to be totally absorbed in the game.

The sun was setting. Two of the search groups had returned only to be instructed by a now panicking Lalaga to continue the search. (Mautu was due home from his fishing trip with Barker, and Lalaga didn't want to face his wrath.) Some of the old women came and consoled her. They sat on the paepae, looking hopefully up at the bush and hills and mountain range that darkened, like a fierce tidal wave, as evening dropped. 'She's too smart, she thinks she knows everything!' Lalaga kept saying. 'She's rebellious, disobedient, difficult!' They nodded in sympathy but didn't believe Peleiupu was like that.

Unexpectedly Lalaga saw Mautu by the kitchen fale, pulling his bush knife out of the thatching. She hurried towards him.

'I know already!' he called to her. In his softly spoken command she sensed an enormous anger. She stopped. He marched past her. She watched until he was at a safe distance heading for Barker's home. 'That's why she's like that!' she called after him. 'You always side with her!'

For a while, as the cicadas cried around her, she wept, more out of fear than anger. Then she wiped away her tears, returned and sat with the other women in the main fale and waited for Mautu and Barker and the search parties to return.

'Mautu and Barker told us to come home,' Arona informed Lalaga and the elders. They had their lotu, the young people served the elders (nearly all the old men and women of Satoa who hadn't gone on the search) their evening meal which they ate in strained silence, with everyone trying not to see the fear in Lalaga, then the young people ate, bathed, got into their nets and fell asleep easily, exhausted from tracking through the plantations and the bush.

Most of the elders tried to stay awake with Lalaga but fell asleep one by one as the night progressed. Beside the centre lamp, Lalaga kept her vigil. At times she prayed for forgiveness, asking God to save her daughter who she had mistreated. Every time she dared look into the darkness outside, unwelcomed images of a dead Peleiupu jumped into her mind and she would shut her eyes and pray more fervently.

The rooster's crowing unclenched in the centre of her head it seemed, and forced her out of her sleep. She was still sitting beside the lamp; the elders, wrapped tightly in their sleeping sheets, lay in rows around her; someone was snoring like a boiling kettle. Dawn was spilling out of the east and splashing across the sky. No Mautu. No Peleiupu. The raw touch of panic caught at her throat. She held back the cry. She staggered up, gripped by the most overwhelming sense of helplessness she had ever experienced. Her daughter, how she loved her! There were people washing themselves at the drums of rain water beside the kitchen fale. In the half-light she saw Mautu and Barker among them. Her feet started running, dragging her with them towards Mautu before she could stop them, and she watched them melt their quick prints in the dew-covered ground.

Mautu turned his back slowly, surely, towards her, dismissing her. She stopped. She looked at the other men. They looked away.

Barker stepped in front of her. 'Peleiupu is all right,' he said in Samoan. 'She is sleeping with her sisters.' Lalaga blocked her mouth with her hands, wheeled and started hurrying back to the main fale. 'She came back on her own. We find her in the net when we return this morning!' Barker called.

She was ripping up the side of the mosquito net and reaching down at Peleiupu. '*Don't you touch my daughter!*' Mautu's command stopped her. No one moved. Not a sound. As though Mautu's order had stilled everything. She again tried to push her angry outstretched hands down towards the sleeping Peleiupu. 'Don't!' Mautu's threat was final. She dared not disobey. 'Let my daughter sleep!'

Lalaga stumbled past him towards the beach. Mautu got a towel and, with Barker and the other men, headed for the pool. Once they were out of sight, the elders and their children dispersed to their homes, unwilling to face their pastor's anger. Ruta, Naomi and the other children made little noise as they put away the mosquito nets and sleeping mats and then went to the kitchen fale, leaving the spacious main fale to Peleiupu who was sleeping peacefully in the large net that was shivering, like a live white creature, in the soft breeze.

No one, not even Arona, would dare mention anything to Peleiupu about her rebellion. Not ever. They all sensed that Mautu wanted it that way. They also assumed, without asking Mautu or Lalaga, that Peleiupu and Arona were accompanying the elders and Barker to the Malua Fono and Apia. But from that morning on, they noticed that whenever Peleiupu needed to be chastised or disciplined — a rare occurrence — Lalaga left it to Mautu. 'After all, she is *his* daughter!' Lalaga told the Satoans.

RODERICK FINLAYSON

Flowers and Fruit

It happened just after Weston had been given the job, which came about this way. Fobister, the Resident Agent on Vaihana at the time, thought damn it, he'd better give the fellow a job. He would have to make it a sinecure. The man would never be worth his keep but he would go to pieces just brooding over his health, and there had been enough human wrecks on the island. A job might help to bring him out of himself.

Weston had come to the island with his wife some months previously thinking that the warm climate would do him good. Fobister remembered their arrival. A queer pair. Fobister had found himself guessing by how many years the man was younger than his wife. Was it *only* that lost lamb look and that pale fadeless hair that made him appear slightly ludicrous and juvenile? A second glance showed how deceptive his looks might be. Anyway she was a motherly type all right: short, plump, with happiness-club eyes and grey hair set in a businesslike perm. She must be used to looking after him. Emaciated and curled up and clutching his middle the fellow kept whining about a perpetual chill in his stomach, a pain in his guts. He said he hoped to escape the worst of the Wellington winter. He had no plans. He had had to show some money, of course, and his return ticket to New Zealand. But now the money was spent and his health, he said, was worse, and Fobister couldn't get him to leave the island. Always the argument went the same.

'Better take the next boat home, Weston.'

'Good God, Mr Fobister, do you want to sign a man's death warrant?'

And so he stayed — helplessly, not defiantly.

At last Fobister suggested a spot of work. He said moping about was bad for morale, and that they couldn't have a man beachcombing.

'What do you think I could do? Hard labour? Or run your office for you?' Weston, with feeble sarcasm, wanted to know.

'Look here, Weston, the fruit trade's coming along nicely. The administration wants to encourage horticulture and I have authority to appoint the necessary staff. You'd made a good fruit inspector, Weston. What do you say?'

'But I hardly know an orange tree from a lemon.'

'Oh, you'll soon learn. Routine work. Just watch out for signs of blight and condemn the unhealthy trees.'

'You've got me in a corner, Fobister. You know I'm often too ill ...'

'You'll get around between bouts.' Fobister was determined to remain optimistic. 'The salary will just about keep you and your wife comfortably. Better give it a go, don't you think?'

Weston shrugged, mumbled some sort of agreement in a resigned tone of voice. And that's how Vaihana got its first fruit inspector.

Weston's wife was delighted. She told him that it would do him the world of good, and that now they could stay on in that lovely climate on that beautiful island. Weston, incongruously clad in a dark overcoat and a white pith helmet, crouched stiff and silent on a camp stool beneath the palm thatch staring out the memory of a ruined Eden, the pain inside ready to paw him gently if he moved. But his wife was blindly cheerful now that she would have a house instead of this native hut; for with the job went a house on the other breezier side of the island, a house with white walls, wide verandahs and cool rooms.

As he listened to her chatter, Weston's lips pursed themselves and his eyelids drooped lower. But with an effort as though to shake off his old chilling bitterness and to share a little of the warmth of his wife's enthusiasm he roused himself. With a wry grin he said: 'Be like a late tropic honeymoon, eh? Just a bit late — but not too late, eh?'

'Oh, it would always have been a bit late with you,' she laughed. 'Or rather, always too early.'

She laughed again, her motherly laugh which irritated him.

'*You* need talk, *you* need talk,' he flared. Then clacked his tongue into impotent silence, and crumpled up clutching his middle.

All the same, the worry of having a job was *something* to let his mind grind on at night.

Their first morning in the house in the new district three children came with a gift of flowers. They stood quietly on the verandah only whispering amongst themselves until the Westons at the breakfast table caught sight of their shadows, long in the early sun, and called to them to come in. Then they appeared at the doorway. There was a little girl in a pink dress, her dusky brown hair long and crimpy, her face half hidden behind a big bunch of scarlet hibiscus. There was an older boy wearing only khaki shorts; his full lips curved arrogantly but his eyes were shy and gentle. And there was a girl in her teens in a sleeveless white gown, barelegged like the others, her long black hair plaited, and in her eyes all the gentle arrogance of the boy. In one hand she held a single blossom of the ginger plant.

They smiled without speaking. The little girl held out her flowers.

'Oh, how lovely!' Mrs Weston exclaimed.

'She bring you more if you like them,' the big girl said.

Weston got up slowly from the table, screwing up his eyes a little, his long pale face drained of age.

'Good morning, Mr Weston.' The girl turned to look at him, expectantly, almost eagerly. She had his name from the head man of the district.

He looked pleased, warm and pleased that morning. The boy held his eyes with his good looks and lithe proud poise.

'How you today, Mr Weston?' the older girl asked, drawing his attention.

'Oh, not so bad, not so bad, eh.'

Mrs Weston was bustling about arranging the flowers in a big blue bowl while she exclaimed at their loveliness.

'Yes, we bring your mother more flowers if she like them,' the girl said watching the short plump motherly woman.

Weston, gazing at the boy again, didn't grasp it for a moment. But his wife turned round amused, laughing at the girl's mistake.

'Why, didn't you know? I'm Mr Weston's *wife*,' she explained, still laughing.

But Weston had sagged against the table, suddenly haggard.

'Oh, he looked so *young*.' The girl twisted the flower and giggled, embarrassed. The boy, who hadn't said a word, looked sharply from face to face with the faintest flicker of a smile curling his lips.

'Have you children too?' the little one asked, unexpectedly interested.

'No, dear, no,' Mrs Weston said with a worried glance at her husband. She hoped he wasn't in for one of his bad bouts. 'But we love children . . . Here, I'll get you kiddies some cake.'

They stood tongue-tied again while Mrs Weston went to the cupboard for the cake; the solemn little girl and the lithe brown-bodied boy and the tall girl holding the ginger blossom cupped in her hands as though shielding its pale flame.

So young-looking, eh? Well, perhaps. But now he looked hurt, hurt and sick.

He flicked the flowers in the bowl beside him, breaking one stalk.

'What about the fruit crop here?' he demanded of the girl who stared back with a little disappointed pout. 'No bananas, no oranges, nothing for export this year?'

'Yes, not too many yet,' the boy said, speaking for the first time. 'But coming on pretty good.'

'We have plenty flowers though, all over the place,' the girl said, laughing a little, but haughty now.

As his wife came toward them with a large piece of currant cake he brushed roughly past the children and disappeared into his bedroom. They heard him fling himself upon the bed.

The children now cheerfully thanked Mrs Weston and at a sign from the older girl the boy took the cake and they went down the verandah steps, down the coral sand path under the pawpaw trees, the boy walking between the two girls, dividing the cake with delicate graceful gestures and sharing it with the others.

Before they were quite out of sight of the house the big girl looked back over her shoulder as she threw away her piece of cake with sudden distaste.

Weston turned restlessly on his bed, the cramp in his stomach abating a little.

'Did y'hear what she says? Flowers all over the bloody place. Ginger flowers and hibiscus flowers and all them great flaming trees and what not! It's them that sours the soil and carry the blight, sure. Sure, they give the blight to the fruit trees and stunt their growth. Well, I'm fruit inspector now, and I mean to do something about it. I'll have them all cut out. Burn the lot! Clean up this corner of the blessed island paradise! I'll get *something* out of this blasted wilderness.'

FIONA KIDMAN

Earthly Shadows

'What sort of an of is that?' The tone is ominous.

'It's existential,' says Jimmy O'Flaherty in a miserable kind of way. 'Or a Wallace Stevens kind of an of. A because of kind of an of.'

Marlon leans back in his chair and looks around the room. Jimmy's eyes follow his as if inspiration might be lurking, waiting to reveal itself, in one of the corners. He wants to be the first to see it. But it is a plain white box-like office, similar to a hundred or so others in the same building. Two large curling Penguin posters adorn the wall above him, one of Iris Murdoch looking worried, and the other of Paul Theroux bearing an odd resemblance in this pose, to an unlamented Minister of Education in the last Government. On the windowsill a poinsettia with yellowing leaves struggles to survive in a pot.

The producer seems in no hurry to further their brief acquaintance. He reaches out to pick an imaginary thread from his jeans then turns over a sheaf of pages on his desk with the sort of care that suggests there might be something nasty stuck between the pages. Marlon is a small sandy complexioned man with a crew cut. He wears a green striped shirt with a pink scarf around his neck, and beneath denim-clad legs his feet stick out, encased in pink, green and orange diamond-patterned socks and twinkling red shoes. Born plain Norman Jones, he changed his name to Marlon when he discovered, as he says with a reflective smile, that he was just a raging old queen. Though once darlings I was young, he is likely to add, not that he expects to be believed. It is clear, his manner suggests, that he has always been exactly and charmingly the same, and that with luck he will remain so.

Now he rests his gaze on each of the other four people in the room, returning at last to Jimmy O'Flaherty, the hapless playwright. 'Radio is an exacting art,' he says. 'Yet here before us, we have a play entitled *The Shadow of the Earth*. How, my pet, can there be a shadow *of* the earth. There are shadows of trees, there are shadows of houses, there are shadows of us poor mortal human beings, but earth is an ongoing flowing continuity, is it not, that cannot in itself cast shadows. Am I not correct, Fenella?'

He turns to a large woman who sits far down in her chair opposite him. Her eyes glitter. Her face shines like a hand-painted dinner plate. She loves script conferences. She loves young men who sit like plucked hens in front of her.

'Gross, darling, yes it does sound a little gross,' she says to Marlon. 'Of course,' she says, addressing Jimmy, 'you must take no notice of me, I have really no part in this at all.' Fenella comes from that long and honourable tradition of women whose fiancés were killed in the war and have kept broadcasting running ever since from the bowels of control rooms, where their shadows have fallen further over the hierarchy than Jimmy's earth could ever do. She is also the one person in the world, or broadcasting at least, who remembers Marlon when he was Norman.

'Are you a producer too?' asks Jimmy, for although they have been introduced, her role in the discussion is so far unclear.

'Fenella will present the panel discussion that follows the play, straight after it goes to air. Fen is the Voice.'

'You mean you're going to do it?' says Jimmy, who until this moment has been sure that his play is about to be rejected. He sits very still as if sudden movement might jolt the atmosphere. He has prepared so carefully for this interview, on the face of it could almost rival Marlon himself. He wears a French blue waistcoat under a worn salmon-coloured smoking jacket and he too wears a scarf, a plaid one which hangs all the way to his handmade leather belt with its silver studs. But the hands which hang between his knees are thick and chafed, and he has a slight rough cough, which might be from working on building sites in the cold (he has opted lately for real life experience as part of his apprenticeship for becoming a writer) or from too much smoking. His hand strays to his pocket now, hesitates over his cigarette pack, and drops. He tries to catch Georgie's eyes. She sits with one leg hanging over the padded vinyl arm of her swivel chair, and appears not to see him. He bites a freckled lip. He thinks she is responsible for him, yet she seems to be doing nothing. He could almost swear she was ignoring him.

'If we do it,' Marlon corrects himself gently.

Another voice speaks.

'Hills have shadows. Cliffs have shadows. They're earth. That what you mean, eh lad?'

Jimmy O'Flaherty turns his raw Irish face full of Catholic guilt about deceit and honesty, or whether to tell the truth or not, and blurts out no, before he can stop himself, and realises too late that he may lose an ally in the other corner. Though it is the first time he has had a chance to take a proper look at Brian, who he recalls is a talks producer. Presumably in charge of Fenella's department.

'Oh take no notice of him,' calls Fenella as if they were across a ballroom from each other, 'he adores playing devil's advocate, don't you, darling?'

With relief, Jimmy senses that it is not all bad news if he has, indeed, lost Brian. There is a silence which he suspects he is intended to fill. He flicks a glance towards Georgie May, looking for a cue. She is inspecting a scrag of fingernail.

'Georgie May or may not,' Marlon had said with a leer in his voice when he had invited Jimmy to come in and talk about the script. 'Like it,' he had added. 'She says it's interesting.'

'I'll be awfully grateful for a chat,' Jimmy had said.

'Can't promise a thing, dear heart, but we must follow our script editor's advice.' He was referring to Georgie.

'Don't you like it then?' Jimmy had asked, and known straight away that it was a bad question.

'Lovie, I haven't had an inch of time to actually *read* it,' Marlon said, 'but of course we do produce the odd little play now and then, despite the budget, and we do like to talk to the talent. You know how it is? So we can get acquainted. You do follow me? Well of course you do. Georgie says you're talent, and well frankly, my angel, there isn't much around at the moment, so when I've got a moment I'll have a peek at the script and we can talk about it when I see you. Hnnn?'

'Hnnn,' Jimmy had replied, and hung up on the silence when nothing more happened.

Now, it appears that he is deserted. While Georgie picks her fingernail, Brian takes off one of his roman sandals and unravels a sock from over his foot. He puts his heel up on the desk and takes a large pair of scissors from out of his lower drawer. It is time for him to attack his nails too. The scissors clunk together like hedge clippers.

'It's about the earth's influence over us,' Jimmy says. 'How we're prisoners to the land.'

Brian bangs his scissors on the desk. 'Oh. That. You Kiwis, you're always on about that, aren't you. The land. I am the salt of the earth blah blah blah. You should come from where I do. We don't have quarter-acre sections, and privilege. You think you haven't got class here, but you're all landed gentry. Some of you just have more of it than others.'

'Ee by goom, and I haven't got anything, oh God, oh poor me, oh Brian, why do I have to come to your office, I ask myself a thousand times.' Marlon clutches his head. 'And put that thing away, that foot, that misshapen toe, it's like a dog with its cock out for Chrissake.'

'I'll show you cock.' Brian throws the scissors down and jumps to his feet, his eyes bulging and a thick vein rising in the side of his throat.

'Oh Brian, you couldn't,' says Georgie, speaking at last.

Brian lays his hand on the scissors again.

We're for it now, thinks Jimmy, half rising to disarm him.

'Such angst,' says Fenella. 'Do sit down, Brian and tell the boy what line the panel will be taking.'

Brian is calmer but does not sit down, as if to prove that he is in charge. He walks up and down the side of the room, tugging savagely at his pointed black beard. He limps slightly in his one bare foot.

'But he cannot tell us what his play is about.' He jabs a thumb in Jimmy's direction.

'Tell us what the play is about, cherub.' Fenella yawns elaborately and in the space between them Jimmy catches a whiff of something rank, like onions. Or gin for breakfast.

'Oh surely not.' Marlon crosses his knees and swings away from them holding his head on one side. 'We don't have to go into all that. Please, not what it is *about*.'

Jimmy stops himself, just in time, from asking Marlon again whether he dislikes the play.

'I really like the old man in it,' says Fenella, compromising by talking about it herself. 'The one who wants to keep the land. It's about a family who're going to lose their farm,' she comments to no one in particular.

Marlon gives an exaggerated squirm. 'Yes, we know, heart, we know.'

'Well the old man is adorable.'

'But it is not about the old man,' cries Jimmy.

Fenella beams triumph. 'They'll always start talking sooner or later. I knew you'd tell me,' she says to Jimmy. She leans over and pats his knee. 'Everyone tells me things. Just pour it all out to little old me.' She adopts a listening pose, hand under her chin, head at a girlish angle.

'It's about the woman. She's the strong one. The one who runs the farm and finishes up saving it.'

'Oh dear. Oh dear me. Not feminism?'

'Well, it's based on feminist thinking.'

'My dear boy, you'll have to play that woman down, she's not a good role model for mothers. I mean, she has got a child, hasn't she?'

'But I would have thought. I mean you're a woman.' Although it is Georgie May whom Jimmy looks at, rather than Fenella. Georgie stares into middle distance, her eyes appear unfocused.

Brian has stopped his pacing and stands in front of Fenella, beaming down at her, his fly a few inches away from her nose. She swallows in a perceptible way.

'I sometimes forget what a sensible woman you are,' he says, rocking backwards and forwards on the balls of his feet. Jimmy notices that the bare one is covered with varicose veins. 'A woman's place is in the home.'

'Oh well, Brian,' Fenella remonstrates, wheeling her chair towards the wall. He follows her. 'That's not quite. Not quite what I meant.' Her voice is faint.

'No no. No, no. Married women. Married women.' He picks up a ruler from the desk and whips it backwards and forwards through the air. Fenella ducks.

'On their backs,' says Georgie.

Brian closes his eyes for a moment, walks to the window, stares out, clenching his fingers around the ruler as if it were Georgie's throat.

'He has had an unfortunate experience,' remarks Georgie, addressing Jimmy. 'I'm sure he'll tell you about it sometime when you have a few hours to spare.' She bites the worrisome fingernail. Her teeth are exact and white, maybe a trifle large.

'It is not my fault that I have never married,' Fenella is saying with deep careful enunciation. 'You can only love once. Deep in your heart. What a lot of unhappiness the world would be spared if more people understood that.'

'She's a strong caring woman,' cries Jimmy. Everyone in the room, except Georgie, stares at him in a perplexed way. 'The woman in the play.' He feels the interview slipping from his grasp. 'Like — like you, Fenella,' he says, inspired with great daring.

'Oh?'

'Like you would be if you had children. I mean, if you *were* married.'

Fenella picks up her purse. 'I can see I'm not needed here.'

'Oh heart,' says Marlon. His voice is tired. 'Do sit down. All this noise, I simply have such a raging headache.' He gestures to Jimmy, pushes himself across the floor on the rollers of his chair, and for a moment Jimmy thinks he will take his hand. 'I went to the pub last night and met an absolutely divine dancer. We won a competition. I won a bottle of brandy, wasn't that clever? Did I tell you I won a bottle of brandy?' He purses his lips and blows a kiss towards Fenella. She has subsided back into her chair, takes out a mirror and pats her nose vigorously with a powder puff as if the morning has already left its traces.

'Now look,' Marlon says in a reasonable way. 'We seem to be talking around in circles. Fenella says the play is about a man and you say it's about a woman?'

'It's about both. But the woman is a strong autonomous character who is a focal point to everyone in the play.'

'But that is a matter of perspective?'

We are getting somewhere, thinks Jimmy. His spirits begin to rise, and he and Marlon smile at each other.

'Surely it is ideologically unsound for a man to be writing about a woman as a central character?' says Brian.

'Exactly, Brian,' says Fenella. 'Personally I would have thought that was one of the first things that would have occurred to *you*, Georgie.'

'But you don't believe in feminism,' says Jimmy.

'Of course I don't, but we live in a world of political realities.'

'Rule Number One. Look after yourself first, second and last,' says Georgie. It looks as if she is about to be drawn.

But the phone is ringing. Georgie picks it up, and answers with her name. The call is for her, she listens intently, swings her chair away into her corner of the room.

'On the other hand,' says Brian, 'it is a perfect vehicle for a panel discussion on the sociological implications of land tenure through acquired wealth versus inheritance.'

'True, true. A consideration,' murmurs Fenella.

'The *nouveau riche* versus the squattocracy. Is there anything to choose between the two?'

'Oh dear.' Marlon looks pained again.

'It's a local issue, of course,' Fenella says. 'Leave it to me to handle.'

'Or, will the poor ever get rich,' cries Brian, ignoring her, and full of sudden enthusiasm.

In the corner, Georgie May has begun to cry, and Jimmy can see what a fragile little person she really is, even though she looks so tough and self-assured on the outside, dressed up in her gay tights and sweater, with her black hair falling like straight silk over her ears. She pushes it back and twines it round in her fingers. Her ring finger has a vulnerable white line around it, where a ring has recently been removed. Her tears are silent but they cover her face. Suddenly she leaps to her feet and rushes out of the room.

Fenella raises her eyebrows. 'Sports or newsroom?'

'Probably both together,' says Marlon.

Fenella's ample bosom quivers and she lets out a snort like a tidal wave.

'That's what happens to married women who play around,' says Brian.

'Divorce.' Marlon is watching Jimmy's stricken face. He cannot take his eyes from the doorway where Georgie has disappeared, as if through concentration he might will her reappearance. There is something regretful about the way Marlon looks at Jimmy.

'Well, separated, so far. Unless she sees the light. Your Mrs May has a varied sort of life, Jimmy.' Fenella comments. 'But then you'll know about that.'

'They never do. Learn. Don't want to.' Brian is sinking into late morning depression. 'You see, she'll come out of it all right. They always get the money. Women do. It's a scheme, they have it from the beginning.'

'Brian's been to his men's group again,' says Marlon.

'So have you, haven't you, darling?' Fenella is enamoured of her own wit and snorts again. She glances from her watch to Jimmy and back again. She too has noticed his longing eyes follow Georgie out of the room.

'So you are going to do it?' Jimmy ventures, feeling that a resolution is in order. He knows he should be asking about the fee, and tries to remember what the Writers' Guild has said about contracts — he won't be able to face the meeting on Thursday night if he is not business-like straight away, sees his invitation to join the committee slipping through the cracks.

He takes another deep breath, flexes his thumbs in a pattern like a cross between his knees. 'I'm so glad you like it.'

Marlon looks at him blankly.

Jimmy laces all his fingers, working the palms rapidly backwards and forwards from the wrists, so that he pops out a noise like the awful underarm squelch that boys at primary school make to disgust girls, and blushes. 'The play, I'm so glad you like the play.'

Marlon wrinkles his nose. 'Like it?'

'I thought you did,' Jimmy O'Flaherty murmurs without looking at him. 'It's a very important work to me. Seminal. It's my life.' He puts his hand on his breast, without thinking, without affectation, and is overcome with fresh and deeper embarrassment.

'Darling heart, I'm sure it is. You've a great career in front of you.'

'I do?'

But there is foreboding in the air. Fenella and Marlon have drawn closer together, almost in a physical way, bound by the old unbreakable ties of knowledge, which pass for, might even be friendship, and anticipate the outsider.

'Writing soapies, I think you'll be exquisite.' Marlon lights the cigarette Jimmy so badly needs and feels he has renounced.

'They'll love you in telly,' murmurs Fenella.

'Oh yes, lucky old chap, they will, won't they.' Marlon flicks ash with care and accuracy towards a distant ashtray.

'But.' Jimmy seeks words. He is in love with words. Like Georgie, they have eluded him.

'Sorry, sweetness,' says Fenella, '*Coup de grâce*. Mind-bogglingly crapulous. Terrible shit.' Her vowels are round and delicious, fluid behind her full red mouth. 'We should have brought spoons to eat it with. Really, positively vulgar.'

'All that sentiment. Sheer humanism, I'm afraid. In spite of the of.' Marlon smiles with great warmth at Jimmy.

Jimmy stands up, sure he is going to weep just like Georgie May. 'A misunderstanding. I thought you were going to do it.'

'But we are, ducks,' says Marlon.

'But why?'

'Fills a gap. Hole in the schedule,' says Brian. He has taken a barley sugar which has gone sticky from out of his drawer and is delicately picking staples off it before he puts it in his mouth.

Marlon removes a shred of tobacco from the tip of his tongue. 'You're not taking this personally, are you? Oh dear.' He looks helplessly at Fenella, who shrugs, and sits up straight with her purse on her knees. 'You know, I've no objection to giving people what they want. I don't mind doing crap if it makes them happy.'

'Makes *who* happy?' Jimmy hears the note of pleading in his voice. It is a sound he knows will come back to haunt him.

'The people, angel. They'll love your *Shadows on the Wall*.'

'*Of the Earth*.'

'Oh. Earth. Yes. Of. See how confusing?'

'You ain't gunna do it.'

Fenella rolls her eyes. 'Standards. A university boy too.'

'You're . . . not . . . going . . . to . . . do . . . my . . . play.'

'Bless you, heart, you'll never get on if you don't get on top of all this subjective emotion,' says Marlon. 'It's one thing for the soapies but it'll never do in real life. Of course we're going to do the play. Now run upstairs and tell them to fix you up with a contract. The money's lovely, pet, it's just gone up again.'

There is a rushing in Jimmy's ears. Far below, he hears the sound of traffic. 'Thank you,' he says.

'I've just remembered,' says Brian, when Jimmy reaches the door.

'Well,' Marlon says, 'what a consciousness-raising morning. Treat us to your memories, Brian.'

'What about the Maoris?'

'Maoris? What about the Maoris?'

'There aren't any. In the script.'

'Oh dear. No. Neither there are.' Marlon rubs his nose.

'We don't have to have them,' says Fenella.

'You ought to,' says Brian. 'With the land, and that.'

'La, look who's talking.' But Marlon is worried. He turns to Jimmy. 'Can you do us a Maori?'

'I guess. I don't know.'

'On the other hand,' Brian's voice is lugubrious, 'maybe he'd better not. Ideologically unsound. From his point of view, that is. They're bound to phone in and complain.'

'But they'll complain if he doesn't.' Marlon pulls his nose in genuine bafflement.

'I could do you an Irishman,' says Jimmy.

'I'll bet. No, let's be devils, we're in the business of taking risks. Make it a Maori, or even a couple if you can manage it, Jimmy my sweet.'

Fenella sighs. 'I can always get rid of them on the panel.'

Jimmy closes the door behind him. Georgie May walks down the corridor towards him, her face composed, if a little pale. There is no trace of tears.

'Well, that went all right, didn't it,' she says brightly.

Jimmy O'Flaherty scowls. His heart is clenched with envy. 'Sports or newsroom?' he asks.

She glances at him. Hesitates. 'Newsroom. I'm going back to my husband, you know.'

'Of course,' says Jimmy.

'You didn't let them worry you, did you?' She nods in the direction of the office he has just left.

'Nah.' His fingers curl round the cigarettes.

'You shouldn't, you know. You're a real writer now.' She plants a feathery kiss on his cheek. 'You can take me to lunch when you get your cheque.'

But her step is purposeful as she heads back towards the office.

Jimmy leans on the lift button. He is uncertain whether or not he is supposed to be happy. He waits to be taken away.

CRAIG HARRISON

Eye Contact

NZPA: The only good news they found in Bhopal was the word from Auckland that he had won an award for the best camerawork of 1984.

SOON TO BE RELEASED ON VIDEO with Dolby Valbazen: The Diderot Encyclopaedia Co. in conjunction with TransAustralia Corp. PRESENT

caption	*WORLD OF DIFFERENCE*
EXT DAY BHOPAL	: For NewsFocus at Nine
MCU	: Children foreground
CUE MUSIC / *Quiet please*	: Pan to Joyce Melville /
okay Joyce go ahead	: The dimensions of tragedy are hard to measure, as impossible perhaps as the fixing of a price on a human life, and yet there are those who

Sorry / CUT / Bob there's too much shadow, I know, but if we reflect light from here it's still too bright unless she wears the sunglasses so could

> *No glasses* John we've been through all that

I know okay we agreed but

> It comprises eye contact, it implies barriers against reality it says rich tourist, polaroid, dishonest

If she faces this way
We don't get the factory in the background and Dave has to pan round about one-eighty degrees
Well suppose Joyce walks from here to here

No John what's the motivation?
it suggests awareness of camera
presence, no way

We'd get our shadows in the shot then, so —
Okay but maybe the hat could be more to one side and back a little
yes thats better

Makeup? I need another pin for
this hair

Simon Simon darling could you move those kids out of the shot, no
those on the left the ones who keep smiling

The dimensions of tragedy are a
heap of shit Warren I can't say
this stuff I mean for christ's sake

Okay everybody take five
Pure visual medium they'll be looking at you love not listening to the
soundtrack look they love disaster lap it up insatiable morbidity
suburban boredom who knows? we provide a service cater demand do
what we can within the fuckin system I mean

EXT EVENING   The camera pushes aside the long grass moving
                lightly forward over the field so easily carrying a
                million eyes and a percentage of minds, strokes
                the surface of the car slides the reflections
SOUND FX: Tui, something like that.
Intro music / Vivaldi
VOICE OVER / female   *Holden . . .*
                        Such stuff as dreams are made of
                The sky climbs the sides of the metal
                        Power at your fingertips
HAND ON GEARKNOB / female
crescendo Vivaldi / CUT /   John that was fantastic

Essential to the process, selectively consulted,
thick ticks in boxes

DO WE | sometimes | | infrequently | | scarcely | | not at all |

          see ourselves young for ever ever rest content in
          rooms white as western teeth. where spills wipe
          clean the stuff of dreams, statistical ghosts.
          holograms of randomly sampled desires.
          Actually look quite beautiful, perfectly real.

Warn The Soviets That We Have Never Failed to Pay The Price Of Freedom

The ability to fail to communicate instantly with anybody you choose, anywhere on earth, by the miracles of microprocessor POWER

AND THE WINNER IS

(the manicured fingers on planetary hookup start to depress a button or unnerve a manila envelope —

As a Hindu all my lives I am thinking have been leading up to this moment I should like to begin by thanking last of all my father and my mother without whom

A billion lives are being wasted, *now*.

Well I think the strangest thing he ever said was when he asked me to look at it from another angle altogether, he asked if I realised that at any given moment out of an audience of one billion there are bound to be people out there, I forget the exact figure he quoted, who have actually died of natural causes whilst just sitting watching this programme, and nobody knows. That seemed to me to be, a, uh, disturbing conceptual parameter.

It certainly is. And now, some music from Henry Mancini.

I'm tired Helen. I'm tired of trying to sustain this pretence in front of Joanne day after day. And I'm worried when I think that these very words are being beamed out, irrevocably, for ever, to the most distant galactic systems in the universe, a massive expanding circle of electronic pulses carrying our images for billions upon billions of years open to any interception. Have you any idea what this could do to Joanne if she finds out?

Listen sweetheart. This is another fine mess. MaydayMayday

What a glorious feeling, I'm happy again

Heavy rain later spreading east

God I hate this stupid senseless war. What will you do when it's over?

Do it to Julia.

Eat a peach.

The necessary murder.

Your starter for ten. Starting NOW

Diderot. He reached out across the table and said to his wife, I wonder if I dare eat a peach? Then he slumped forward and died. In medium close-up. The camera does not move. This is a deep focus shot. The lights fade on the still life. Richard suggested some Albinoni in the background, provided we can get it played on the authentic instruments of the period. But they've been using it on Channel 2 for those Sunday discussion progs. So I don't know. The only certainty is that the Lord's final judgment is being prepared at this very moment, and that Jesus saves. In fact your savings can earn you fifteen per cent per annum on unsecured deposits. American lawyers hope to gain substantial damages of which they will retain a percentage of the gross, the ultimate irony, the obscenity at the heart of this darkness

---

Methyl isocyanate is corrosive when combined with the moisture of the human eye

---

EXT DAY / Long shot / Man weeping over bodies
CAPTION December 1984
CUT to / INT DAY American lawyer in swivel chair
 behind large oak desk
Bob, I think here zoom in on the cufflinks, maybe we could jump cut with shot 17 to hammer this whole thing about exploitation, right? Who loves ya baby.
CUT TO: EXT DAY Funeral pyre
The Muslims bury theirs, so we need some shots of the mounds for balance
   Well for the 8.30 slot so far we have Watties
Holden Cadburys BNZ Valbazen Moro KentuckyChicken Toyota K-Tel Pizza Hut CookieBear KerridgeOdeon
   Made it quite clear the food industry won't pay ten thousand bucks for thirty seconds slammed right next to these hard-edge famine pix or whatever, see it from their point
   Social awareness costs
   I'm proud of this I really
   World of difference between honesty and shock for its own
sake I'll have the porc au gratin
   Much more relaxed atmosphere I do appreciate
believe me Introduce you to Roy at the Film Commission
   Sure there's no basic disagreement, we do want this to go
as much as you   Finance for next

PAN ACROSS   Flames
DISSOLVE TO   Mounds
FREEZE FRAME / FADE TO BLACK
ROLL   CREDITS
                      EDITED BY /
        Julian wanted to roll the credits over the moving
pix but lesson one is your viewer always gives priority to picture
never words and I'm sure we all want to get a teeny bit more from
this than ten days of the shits and possible hepatitis B are you with
me?

        Could possibly realise the absolute intensity
involved in this, the total commitment, the power of the medium,
which I find totally overwhelming. Of course words are inadequate.
We live in the twentieth century. Verdun, Belsen, Dresden,
Hiroshima. Of course they are. What can you say? The images count
for everything. Trust them. The dimensions of tragedy can't be measured any other way. This is a highly personalised self-referential
medium, producing immediate responses. Those responses reaffirm
our common humanity.

        When we get holograms with Dolby you won't
be able to tell it from the real thing. I don't see any limits to what
we can't do.

        I don't see any limits.

IAN WEDDE

Circe and the Animal Trainer

The man across from her at the garden table wasn't good looking but he was sympathetic. Having worked for some years in Geneva she'd probably have preferred to use the French word *sympatique*, without however being able to explain clearly the different shade of meaning. She'd have said, 'You know what I mean.' Such assumptions were typical of her. She had a queer unconscious knack for flattery. A woman of experience, she assumed others to have been likewise exposed to the more glamorous vicissitudes of life. It wasn't on the whole an assumption that people resented. In fact, as often as not, they'd find themselves thinking, 'Yes, I *do* know what she means.'

She was well above average height, for a woman. He was about as tall as her, which made him unexceptional in this respect as in others. That is, he was about average height, with a squarish 'pleasant' face. His hair was thin and well trimmed. His cheeks and chin were shiny because he'd recently shaved very close. Yet there was nothing cosmetic about him. He was clean and plain. His dress was simple and almost clerical: he was wearing an old pale grey suit, a cream shirt, a dark blue tie with some sort of monogram on it. His hands were large, square, and white. His expression was somehow stern and amused in equal parts. There were no nicotine stains on his fingers, no purplish maze of capillaries in his cheeks. Yet he showed the usual signs of wear and tear: his teeth were poor, his waist somewhat thickened.

As a young woman she'd been strikingly beautiful: dark, tall, slender, brown-eyed, soft-voiced. But what had provided her with an altogether extraordinary charm was the following combination: she was wide-hipped, and she was clever. So that having recovered from the first wounding discovery, that her elegance was by no means austere, you got as it were the second barrel: her intelligence. The combination was lethal. She'd left in her wake an army of vanquished pretenders to her heart. And yet she gave the impression of being quite unaware of this carnage. No doubt she assumed, even then, that her suitors understood 'how things were', and would be able to view their feelings with a certain amount of ironical amusement, not to mention, at a more terminal stage, disdain. It never occurred to anyone for a moment to suggest that her apparent facility with the adroit management of passions, hers and others', might have had little or nothing to do with will or *savoir-faire*, and everything to do with an infantile inability on her part to follow the fragile thread as it wound its way back into the maze of human feelings, at the centre of which, in a dark court paved with bloody flagstones, each man had to reduce the Beast to his own scale — or rather, an inability on her part to offer any such way out, even to realise that some such means of escape was going to be necessary, and that she was going to have to provide it. So that she must often have wondered at the flicker of animal reflex as it drew back, for a moment, the lips and brow of her lover: the bray, the whinny, the growl, the roar, the grunt, the snuffle. 'Can't men be pigs,' she'd sometimes say to her friends.

Mind you, there's no reason why you should assume straight off that her apparent *savoir-faire* in fact concealed this failing. It's just that intelligences with a certain talent for logic often fall down on contingencies. And her intelligence, in the full sense of the word — her *élan-vital* — was faultlessly logical.

. . . and it's also that you are, if you're honest, invariably tempted to keep types as types. You're tempted to say, for example, that every man must have his Ariadne before he can have his Circe. That goes by way of definition. The one follows the other, in life if not in myth. She — she must be one or the other. And the lady in question, because of the kinds of affairs she'd had with men — she must be Circe. So you're tempted to say.

At this moment she'd paused in her talk to the friend across from her at the table. She was sitting back in the sunshine, her legs crossed, one foot swinging idly. Her face wore its customary expression of alertness and pleasure. Yet he'd sensed that she was about to tell him something out of the ordinary. Her manner was, as ever, faintly seductive. Now that she was approaching middle-age her former elegance tipped over frequently into more ample gestures: smiling, she rocked back in her wrought iron chair, looking at him from beneath the frankly cosmetic perfection of her dark eyebrows. He faced her quietly, his hands clasped together on the white-painted iron table top next to his spectacles case and his empty coffee cup.

She was thinking that her friend was like an animal trainer. Somehow he was able to understand with different senses from most people. She'd said nothing out of the ordinary, yet she realised that he'd anticipated her desire to do so. She found this placed a certain restraint on her. He always made her feel exposed. And yet she was well aware of her usual powers: he'd been in love with her for years. And so, of course, she was instinctively trying to disarm him by these means. But it was all too familiar. It was almost like a parody.

She was thinking that he'd called to her so often he was almost deafened. Then how did he hear her? It was those other senses, those other powers. What did he dream of? She imagined him sleeping, exhausted, deaf with whistling. Outside in the yard his chained loves twitched their dreaming paws.

'What do you dream about?' she asked.

He smiled, unclasped his hands, and spread them.

'I dream,' he said, 'that I might be allowed to cease faring upon the seas and to stay in your palace forever.'

It was a little routine they'd repeated more times than either of them could remember. She found herself wanting something different. Yet she'd started it, this time as others. Of course it was he who'd coined the nickname.

She realised it was now time for her to start talking. He was making no attempt to conceal the fact that he was listening, waiting.

'Listen, John,' she said. 'I want to tell you something but I don't know where to begin. . . .'

'. . . *at the beginning*,' they said together. If they'd in fact been sharing their lives all these years they couldn't have had the patter off any more glibly.

'At the beginning,' she repeated. 'But listen, I don't know where that is. I know, John, that you're going to think this is pre-menopausal melancholy, but it's not. I don't know how to tell you what I want to without producing a wretched string of clichés. I just can't think it out. I'm really very unhappy.'

'Well, you must have had *something* specific to tell me, or you wouldn't have called me. And I wouldn't have come. You see, I do keep hoping.'

She smiled, for form's sake. But her manner had changed.

'I trust you to understand more than most people do or can. I want you to explain to me what I'm saying. I suddenly remembered something the other day. It upset me very much. I don't know why.'

She lit herself a cigarette and looked away from him down the garden. In all the years he'd known her she'd never quite dropped her guard like this. There had always been ways of coping: little games, little routines:

'Knock knock.'

'Who's there?'

Now that she was off-guard, her former elegance seemed to have returned. It was as though, of late, her conscious attempts to retain her grace had become effortful, almost clumsy. Now he found his heart swelling again at the sight of her, as much with a fresh access of affection as with pity. Her expression, as she considered how to start, was thoughtful, almost serene. Yet her fingers trembled where she held the cigarette. 'You are a lovely, lovely woman,' he thought. 'You were wasted in this role.'

He reached over and put his hand on her arm. She continued to look away across the garden. She'd had a successful career. The garden was large and well planted, with nothing fussy about it: the kind of garden which looked after itself, with the chief exception of the grass, which she cut herself, energetically, using an old push mower. The shrubs had grown up and tangled together since she'd been there. Some of the trees had even had to be taken out to allow space for the others. The lawn was speckled with the first fallen leaves of autumn, yet, at the far end of the garden, a mandarin bush was just coming into its blaze of symmetrical fruit. There was a small dark gazebo overgrown with a choko vine whose fruit hung in pale green heavy bunches. And there were ginger plants still in flower, the garden filled with their cloying fragrance.

'No hurry,' he said. 'Today I don't have to be there till the afternoon.'

'What I suddenly remembered was this,' she said, still looking away towards the blazing mandarin bush. 'When I was a little girl we lived here, in Auckland, in Epsom. Medicine's always been in the family. Both my brothers are doctors. I'm a doctor. So were my father and grandfather. My father was an ambitious man. As children we were always given this sense of solidity and permanence in our situation. We were aware, from early on, that there was a tradition in our family for hardnosed dedication to a demanding profession. As I remember it, life was very full and active for us children: we always went somewhere for the holidays, we kept lots of pets, there were endless excursions. There was always something to do. Idleness, in play as in work, wasn't really tolerated in our family. We were encouraged to speak our minds, to be direct, to be clear, to be curious. This is the background, you see . . . We were confident that things were where they were. We were confident children.'

He knew all this already. He'd often listened to her reminisce, with affection and gusto, about her childhood. It had become a formula for him to say he envied her, although at his age he no longer had any particular feelings about his own very different childhood.

She was still looking away from him, seeming to squint slightly at the bright end-of-morning sunshine which fell in shafts through her trees on to the mandarin bush, and on to the dark overgrown gazebo where he'd once, long ago, had to do battle with the Beast and then find his own way back. Since then he'd worked, married late, been happy and — the word made him grin — successful.

'We're both so *successful*,' he said. 'What are we doing sitting here clutching each other like children who've lost the way?'

'Oh John.'

She had in fact brought her other hand round to hold his where it lay on her arm. Now she turned to look at him. He saw that her eyes were full of tears, her lips quivering. A wee dewlap by her chin was trembling also.

'My dear,' he said. 'I'm sorry. Please go on.'

She said, after pausing to push the tears away with the back of her hand, 'Remember how I've told you about our pets? Oh, we used to have everything. We used to put guinea pigs on the table at opposite ends of a long piece of grass and see what happened when they met in the middle. Daddy used to buy day-old roosters and tell us they'd escaped just before Christmas. We had endless Scotties. They were so smelly and mangy. I loved them. And then there were the Paradise Ducks . . .'

She'd managed a laugh of sorts, smiling through her tears. He knew the story about the Paradise Ducks. Though he rarely smoked, and never in the mornings, he reached across and helped himself to one of her cigarettes. Against his will he was beginning to feel irritated.

'John, I'm waffling on,' she said. 'You've heard all this a million times. But the point is, it's as though I've always left something out. You know,' she continued, after pausing to put on a pair of dark glasses, 'a moment ago I thought of you as an animal trainer. I thought of your tamed creatures running in their dreams. We all leave something out, John. Because I haven't got your gifts I can only guess at your secrets. But you can look into my eyes. You can see right through me. That's why I trust you to listen to what I'm telling you. That's why I'm asking you, John, not to pretend you don't know what I'm talking about when I get to the point.'

'All right,' he said. He was thinking. 'What do you know about compromise?' He was also thinking, 'In that case why have you put on your dark glasses?' He clasped his hands again on the white table top.

'The other day,' she said, 'I suddenly remembered how our street in Epsom had plane trees in it. It was actually an avenue. I don't know why I've never remembered this before. I've told you everything else . . .'

'Go on,' he said.

'Well, I got lost once. I was very tiny. Perhaps I'd just been to primary school — one of the first times I was allowed to go by myself. I'd always known our street by the plane trees. This day I couldn't find them. I couldn't find it. I couldn't find the trees. I don't remember how I finally got home. I guess someone must have found me crying. What had happened was this: while I'd been away at school or wherever, the Council had been around pruning the trees. They'd cut them right back to the trunk, you know how they do with plane trees. Pollarding. There were no lovely shady trees left in the street. Only these ugly rows of huge knotty clubs. That's what I wanted to tell you about, John . . .'

She stopped abruptly. Behind the modish dark glasses her face was white. In telling the story to him she'd understood herself what it meant. Throughout her entire busy successful confident life, all those things which had come to seem familiar and solid had, at a certain moment, been changed. Everything, everybody, one person and one thing after another. She'd been lost again and again. Only *he* had somehow never changed, or been changed. He was the same John.

'Oh John, my dear John,' she said. 'You know what I'm asking you, don't you?'

He got up from his chair and stood by the table opposite her. He looked as though he was about to deliver one of his lectures at the university: his square fingertips resting lightly on the table top next to the spectacles case and the empty coffee cup.

'I've understood your story,' he said. 'I've known you for a very long time, and I think I've always known that about you, though I've always wondered whether *you* knew it.' He was looking straight at her, speaking very deliberately. Then he sighed loudly and sat down again. 'You know,' he went on, 'how I've always liked to mix my myths — how I've even done that for my students.' He smiled slightly. 'You see, you've even got into my professional life. I've always said that Theseus and Ulysses and the rest of them stand for aspects of the one man, and that Ariadne, Circe and Penelope stand for stages of initiation. Silly, trite stuff. And yet year after year I've told my students this, and thought of you. You see, the most distant point of Ulysses' journey home was in Ithaca. Home may not be where you are, but it's certainly where you're going. It's where you're always going. How can I come here when I'm here already? And when I'm always going somewhere else?'

He stood up and walked around the table to where she sat motionless staring down the length of the luxuriant early-autumn garden at the dark gazebo and the blazing mandarins. She hadn't looked at him once since he'd begun to talk. She was sitting like a gauche schoolgirl. There was nothing he needed to say. But he went on, anyway, standing behind her chair, looking in the same direction as she was.

'My dear friend,' he said, placing his hands on her shoulders. 'It's much much too late for you to offer to be my Ariadne and show me a way out of the maze. And I already have a Penelope.' He leaned down to speak close to her ear. 'All I ever wanted,' he said, squeezing her shoulders gently, inhaling a perfume like gardenias from her neck, 'all I ever wanted was to be changed, to be changed by you, Circe. That's all I've ever wanted. And that's not what you're offering now, is it, my dear?'

'And now,' he said, leaning still closer to kiss her cheek, 'I have to go. I've work to do. Down among the little animals at the university.'

He walked back around the table and picked up his spectacles case.

'I'll ring you later,' he said, 'when I have some time to spare.'

He walked across the patio to the door.

'*Au revoir*,' he said.

'*Au revoir*, John,' she replied, without turning around. '*Au revoir*.'

Of course, it was the expression she'd always used. Of course he knew that.

JANET FRAME

You Are Now Entering the Human Heart

I looked at the notice. I wondered if I had time before my train left Philadelphia for Baltimore in one hour. The heart, ceiling-high, occupied one corner of the large exhibition hall, and from wherever you stood in the hall you could hear its beating, *thum-thump-thum-thump*. It was a popular exhibit, and sometimes, when there were too many children about, the entrance had to be roped off, as the children loved to race up and down the blood vessels and match their cries to the heart's beating. I could see that the heart had already been punished for the day — the floor of the blood vessel was worn and dusty, the chamber walls were covered with marks, and the notice 'You Are Now Taking the Path of a Blood Cell Through the Human Heart' hung askew. I wanted to see more of the Franklin Institute and the Natural Science Museum across the street, but a journey through the human heart would be fascinating. Did I have time?

Later. First, I would go across the street to the Hall of North America, among the bear and the bison, and catch up on American flora and fauna.

I made my way to the Hall. More children, sitting in rows on canvas chairs. An elementary class from a city school, under the control of an elderly teacher. A museum attendant holding a basket, and all eyes gazing at the basket.

'Oh,' I said. 'Is this a private lesson? Is it all right for me to be here?'

The attendant was brisk. 'Surely. We're having a lesson in snake-handling,' he said. 'It's something new. Get the children young and teach them that every snake they meet is not to be killed. People seem to think that every snake has to be knocked on the head. So we're getting them young and teaching them.'

'May I watch?' I said.

'Surely. This is a common grass snake. No harm, no harm at all. Teach the children to learn the feel of them, to lose their fear.'

He turned to the teacher. 'Now, Miss — Mrs — ' he said.

'Miss Aitcheson.'

He lowered his voice. 'The best way to get through to the children is to start with teacher,' he said to Miss Aitcheson. 'If they see you're not afraid, then they won't be.'

She must be near retiring age, I thought. A city woman. Never handled a snake in her life. Her face was pale. She just managed to drag the fear from her eyes to some place in their depths, where it lurked like a dark stain. Surely the attendant and the children noticed?

'It's harmless,' the attendant said. He'd been working with snakes for years.

Miss Aitcheson, I thought again. A city woman born and bred. All snakes were creatures to kill, to be protected from, alike the rattler, the copperhead, king snake, grass snake — venom and victims. Were there not places in the South where you couldn't go into the streets for fear of the rattlesnakes?

Her eyes faced the lighted exit. I saw her fear. The exit light blinked, hooded. The children, none of whom had ever touched a live snake, were sitting hushed, waiting for the drama to begin; one or two looked afraid as the attendant withdrew a green snake about three feet long from the basket and with a swift movement, before the teacher could protest, draped it around her neck and stepped back, admiring and satisfied.

'There,' he said to the class. 'Your teacher has a snake around her neck and she's not afraid.'

Miss Aitcheson stood rigid; she seemed to be holding her breath.

'Teacher's not afraid, are you?' the attendant persisted. He leaned forward, pronouncing judgement on her, while she suddenly jerked her head and lifted her hands in panic to get rid of the snake. Then, seeing the children watching, she whispered, 'No, I'm not afraid. Of course not.' She looked around her.

'Of course not,' she repeated sharply.

I could see her defeat and helplessness. The attendant seemed unaware, as if his perception had grown a reptilian covering. What did she care for the campaign for the preservation and welfare of copperheads and rattlers and common grass snakes? What did she care about someday walking through the woods or the desert and deciding between killing a snake and setting it free, as if there would be time to decide, when her journey to and from school in downtown Philadelphia held enough danger to occupy her? In two years or so, she'd retire and be in that apartment by herself and no doorman, and everyone knew what happened then, and how she'd be afraid to answer the door and to walk after dark and carry her pocketbook in the street. There was enough to think about without learning to handle and love the snakes, harmless and otherwise, by having them draped around her neck for everyone, including the children — most of all the children — to witness the outbreak of her fear.

'See, Miss Aitcheson's touching the snake. She's not afraid of it at all.'

As everyone watched, she touched the snake. Her fingers recoiled. She touched it again.

'See, she's not afraid. Miss Aitcheson can stand there with a beautiful snake around her neck and touch it and stroke it and not be afraid.'

The faces of the children were full of admiration for the teacher's bravery, and yet there was a cruelly persistent tension; they were waiting, waiting.

'We have to learn to love snakes,' the attendant said. 'Would someone like to come out and stroke teacher's snake?'

Silence.

One shamefaced boy came forward. He stood petrified in front of the teacher.

'Touch it,' the attendant urged. 'It's a friendly snake. Teacher's wearing it around her neck and she's not afraid.'

The boy darted his hand forward, rested it lightly on the snake, and immediately withdrew his hand. Then he ran back to his seat. The children shrieked with glee.

'He's afraid,' someone said. 'He's afraid of the snake.'

The attendant soothed. 'We have to get used to them, you know. Grownups are not afraid of them, but we can understand that when you're small you might be afraid, and that's why we want you to learn to love them. Isn't that right, Miss Aitcheson? Isn't that right? Now who else is going to be brave enough to touch teacher's snake?'

Two girls came out. They stood hand in hand side by side and stared at the snake and then at Miss Aitcheson.

I wondered when the torture would end. The two little girls did not touch the snake, but they smiled at it and spoke to it and Miss Aitcheson smiled at them and whispered how brave they were.

'Just a minute,' the attendant said. 'There's really no need to be brave. It's not a question of bravery. The snake is *harmless*, absolutely *harmless*. Where's the bravery when the snake is harmless?'

Suddenly the snake moved around to face Miss Aitcheson and

thrust its flat head toward her cheek. She gave a scream, flung up her hands, and tore the snake from her throat and threw it on the floor, and, rushing across the room, she collapsed into a small canvas chair beside the Bear Cabinet and started to cry.

I didn't feel I should watch any longer. Some of the children began to laugh, some to cry. The attendant picked up the snake and nursed it. Miss Aitcheson, recovering, sat helplessly exposed by the small piece of useless torture. It was not her fault she was city-bred, her eyes tried to tell us. She looked at the children, trying in some way to force their admiration and respect; they were shut against her. She was evicted from them and from herself and even from her own fear-infested tomorrow, because she could not promise to love and preserve what she feared. She had nowhere, at that moment, but the small canvas chair by the Bear Cabinet of the Natural Science Museum.

I looked at my watch. If I hurried, I would catch the train from Thirtieth Street. There would be no time to make the journey through the human heart. I hurried out of the museum. It was freezing cold. The icebreakers would be at work on the Delaware and the Susquehanna; the mist would have risen by the time I arrived home. Yes, I would just catch the train from Thirtieth Street. The journey through the human heart would have to wait until some other time.

JOY COWLEY

Going to the Mountain

'This winter I'll take you to the mountain,' his father said. While the boy knelt on the chair at the window, watching the grey lines of rain angle in against the hut. Which was very strange, because although the boy's eyes had been fastened open by the monotony of the rain, he'd been thinking about the same thing. It lay there behind the wetness, behind the water-filled bootprints at the back door, the axe, the fire-wood heap, the dripping fences, behind the paddocks full of grey sheep, a vision of a marvellous mountain with snow as dry as sugar.

He thought of it often, this mountain. It seemed to be always somewhere within him, a peak of perfect whiteness in a clear blue sky, and now his father, unknowing, had struck the hollow of its hiding place with a blow so precise that it opened right out, spilling whiteness into the room. With a rush it came, all of it at once, snowflakes as big as dinner plates, scissors-cut, icicles chiming in the cupboards and under the beds, drift upon drift whirling inside and out until the entire hut was sliding away in an avalanche with him kneeling at the centre, frozen rigid to the back of the chair.

'What do you say?' his father said. 'A train trip to Ruapehu? See some snow?'

The boy had no breath for answer. The feeling of cold was intense on his back and there was a melting in his eyes which blurred his sight. His father shimmered in the orange light of the fire, and the boy wanted to get past the snowdrifts to reach him. There was no fear of his father at that moment. He wanted to hook his arms round his father's neck and squeeze, shouting, 'When? When?' But the cold had locked his hands on the back of the chair and, although he fought it as hard as he could, he knew from the sliding away that the thing was happening again.

When he woke up, he was lying on a sack in front of the fire. The sound of rain was everywhere and his father's feet were close by, flat on the floor and unmoving. He stared at the socks, wrinkled khaki stuck with hay seeds, stared and quietly wept. He didn't hurt any-where but the thing always left him with a feeling of sadness and so tired that he could have been walking across the paddocks for miles in a gale force wind. He lay with his thumb in his mouth, his forefinger round his nose, and cried until his father nudged him with his foot.

'You wet yourself,' said his father. 'You'd better get changed.'

He sat up slowly, touching the dampness at his middle, then he crawled on his hands and knees to his bed and the box beside it which held his clothes. His father didn't look at him while he changed his pants. He put on some old grey shorts that Ro had given him last year, no buttons on them, her brother's cast-offs, she'd said. Then he went back to sit at the fire. His father gazed at the flames and worked his jaw from side to side as though he were eating his own teeth. The boy watched him for a while. 'When are we going to the mountain?'

The man stopped the jaw movement but didn't look at him. 'What'd you say?'

'I said, when are we going to the mountain to see real snow?'

'Oh. Soon. Pretty soon.'

'Tomorrow?' said the boy. 'Next week?'

'I dunno,' said the man. 'When the weather clears up. When I can manage a few days off. You change those britches?'

'Yes.' But the boy couldn't let it go at that. He stood up, clutching the front of his shorts where the buttons were missing, and went to the wall calendar. 'Next week's sure to be fine. Not much work now until lambing starts. Feeding out — Mr Grant could do that. Dad, what about next weekend?'

'Maybe,' said his father. He looked at the boy, then turned away again to the fire. 'Hang your britches out in the rain,' he said. 'Go on. Don't leave them on the floor to stink the place out.'

They didn't go to the mountain that weekend or at any other time. The boy was too young to realise that the promise had been a gift in itself, quite detached from any intention of fulfilment. Like the talk of a pony or a new wireless set, the offer had been prompted by guilt, for although the man was known to be harsh, he wasn't a vindictive person, and when he caught himself loathing his son, he would extend some generous words in atonement.

But the boy didn't know this. Each fine winter's day brought its own hope, and when the next weekend passed without mention of the trip, he fastened on the weekend after and all the others following it on the wall calendar.

He was eager to tell Ro. He watched for her and ran to meet her, grabbing her hand and swinging on her arm. 'Dad's taking me to the mountain!'

'Hey you, take it easy,' she said. 'Don't go getting all up.'

'We're going to the mountain. Dad and me. I'm going to make a snowman.'

'When's this?' said Ro, stopping and holding both his hands to make him face her. She was wearing a red skirt that made her look fat and she had red ribbons in her black hair. She never wore shoes. Summer or winter she came across the grass barefooted to clean their hut, do their once-a-week wash, all from the goodness of her heart. Ro had a heart as big as a barn, his father said. She was also very pretty.

'How long you going for?' she wanted to know.

'Couple of days, I think. Dad says as soon as he can get time off.'

'Oh yeah. Well, you stop jumping up and down like a rabbit or you know what. Your Dad, he's working right now?'

'No, he's inside.'

Ro laughed and put her arm around his shoulders, drawing him close until his head was against her red skirt. 'I'll go and make us a cuppa.'

She didn't greet the man, nor he her. She put the kettle on the fire, then got the boy to stack dishes while she pumped water into the tin basin.

The man had a newspaper on the table and was waterproofing his boots on it, greasing them with a rag dipped in mutton fat. He said to her, 'That one had another fit last Wednesday.'

Ro went on pumping. 'You belted him.'

'Didn't lay a finger on him. Didn't so much as raise my voice. There was nothing started it — that right?' he looked at the boy. 'He just set off by himself.'

The boy stacked the dishes carefully, knowing that if he was quiet, they would forget about him. Ro went to the table and leaned across it. 'It's not good for him here. He should be at school.'

'He does his lessons.'

'He needs more than lessons. He needs other kids, a bit of decent care.'

'Can't afford it,' said the man.

'Course you can. You're a miserable so-and-so. You treat him like one of those dogs. You don't talk to him unless you get mad at him or want him to fetch something. You're real rotten.'

The boy stood still, holding a plate to his chest.

His father pointed to him. 'Just as well he isn't my dog. By jingo, if a dog did that to me, I'd put a bullet through his head.' He winked at the boy and laughed, pleased with his own joke.

The boy laughed too, looked at the floor and giggled, the plate grasped in both hands.

Ro couldn't see the funny side. She grabbed the boy and held his face against her stomach, saying, 'Don't you listen to that useless no good. He's just talking a lot of big fat stink. Just pretending, eh. Just rubbish.'

His father went on laughing, a deep and rare sound. He stood up, his hands on the table, and said, 'Let him go, will you? Time he went for a walk.'

The boy looked up at Ro for support, but none was coming. She ruffled his hair, took the plate away and gave him an empty billy tin. 'Go down to the creek and get some watercress for tea.'

'I thought you were making us a cuppa.'

'Later on,' she said. 'You know, for when you get back.'

He glanced at his father, then dragged at Ro's arm until she bent her head to him. Holding her hair away from his mouth, he whispered, 'Tell him. Ask him. About taking me to the mountain.'

She straightened up. 'All right. But don't you be in any hurry to get back.'

'Okay.'

He closed the door behind him and waited on the steps until he heard the scraping of the bolt inside, then he went out through the gate, past the dogs that barked and leapt on their chains, past the hen-house and towards the creek, and it seemed to him that every step he made left a print in fresh white snow.

Perhaps Ro believed there would be a trip to the mountain, or perhaps she simply augmented the promise to please him. He never knew. But for the rest of that winter she knitted him a jacket from the fleece of a black sheep. To wear in the snow, she said.

The knitting made the journey a certainty for him. He sat at her feet while she pulled tufts from the fleece and rolled them into yarn against her thigh. Then she hooked the thread into the garment with sharpened bits of fencing wire.

His father would come in from the lambing round, cold, wet, in a bad mood. 'You still doing that? What about a feed?'

Ro would say calmly, 'Don't you come at me with that bossy stuff. I'm not your fancy woman.'

Only Ro could talk to the man like that without making him

angry. She would go on knitting and the man would slump in his chair and close up his face.

The boy used to say, 'It's getting near the end of winter.'

And Ro would answer, 'Got to wait till your jacket's finished, eh.'

That was how he remembered it in later years, and although as an adult he saw half the mountains of the world, he was always deeply disappointed. Not even the majestic peaks of the Himalayas could meet the expectation he had carried with him from his childhood. It seemed to him that every part of those years on the farm with his father, the hills, the dogs, the shepherd's hut, the ribbons in Ro's hair, everything whispered messages of snow, everything pointed to a mountain too rare for the world.

At a time in his life when he could no longer relive or even remember the excitement of that exquisite anticipation, the dreams of the mountain began. The first came soon after his wife died. He was in a glass bubble, a cable-car of the type he'd seen in Switzerland, slung on a cable track, doors at either side, full of people dressed for skiing. To begin with he didn't know why he was there, then, as the cable-car swung through the clouds, he felt a joy so keen that it stuck in his chest like a knife blade. He was going. After the years, he was finally going.

And oh, the indescribable pleasure of recognition as the cable-car broke cloud and he saw in front of him a wall of white ice as smooth as marble. He pressed his hands against the glass and absorbed the chill of it until he was tinkling and sparkling with frost.

'It's as I've always known it!' he cried, his breath exploding in fine crystals. 'How could there have been any doubt? Ro! Ro, do you see it?'

Ro stood amongst the people, smiling politely as though embarrassed by his lack of control.

'We're almost there!' he shouted at her.

Then he realised that the car was not slowing down. Indeed, its speed had increased and now it was travelling so fast that the ice face was a blur.

'No!' He beat on the glass doors, tried to kick them apart, while the other passengers watched, and Ro still smiled, her head on one side.

'Stop! I want to get out!'

It was too late. The temperature increased as they plunged into cloud again and in a moment there was nothing outside but a thick oppressive greyness.

Still, he did retain something of the journey. For days afterwards there was something like a wound in his chest where he'd suffered near-perfect ecstacy.

After that his dreams took him near the mountain a number of times, but in a lesser way, on foot and guided only by the expectation, that silence in him which was the hush of snow, or else the smell of snow in the air. It could happen on any kind of road and in the height of summer, a walk interrupted by something which quivered in him like the needle of a Geiger counter, and, sniffing the air, he would turn off through some orchard or lawn, forest or ploughed field, following the instinct he'd learned to trust. They were never easy, these journeys in sleep, especially that last slope where his feet became cramped and heavy and each step was a struggle through thick dark scrub or knotted grasses. But when he got beyond that and saw the vast white expanse in front of him, the discomfort would leave him and he'd be filled with the sweetest yearning.

That feeling of longing, like his sense of snow, did not exist for him outside of these dreams; but the remembering of them in waking hours did build a bridge directly to his childhood. It was a marvel to him that memories of those harsh years with his father could give him more satisfaction than the comparative comfort of adult life. Childhood was the time of snow.

Ill health forced him into retirement at fifty-eight. He sold the house and bought a small cottage a few streets distant from his eldest daughter who liked to manage him. She was a good soul like her mother, but noisy and efficient. She, her husband and their three children had all been blessed with loud voices. Sometimes, when he saw them coming, he locked the door.

One night, a week after his sixty-third birthday, he went to the mountain in an aeroplane. It was a DC10 and he was sitting with a crowd of people on a flight that could have been going anywhere, he didn't know; but when the air in the cabin became suddenly, inexplicably cold, he felt a small pain of hope. A few minutes later he was certain. The cabin lights dimmed and went out, the rest of the passengers disappeared. He was sitting alone with his face against the frozen glass, his heart beating out loud with the jubilant sound of new-year bells.

The wing-tip stirred the ink-blue universe, scattering stars so that they spun away from the leading edge in showers of silver dust. Inside, everything glittered with frost. The tops of the seats were ridged with white and luminous in the dark. In the rack above his head, his felt hat glistened like a wedding cake.

The bells tolled about his ears with greater vigour, reaching a fullness as the mountain came into view. It was not beneath him as he'd expected but bigger, higher than he'd seen it before. It reached above the aircraft, a tower of ice so close he marvelled that the wing did not touch it. How beautiful it was, glowing in its own white light, and how immense its coldness. While the wing-tip skimmed that sheer white wall, he felt powerful with rapture, and when at last the mountain receded into the night, he knew better than to weep with disappointment.

The next morning he felt the need to talk to his daughter, to have a conversation that went beyond housekeeping and pills, to find out, if the truth be known, just who his daughter was. He phoned and invited her over but she said she was busy. She was always busy. He said he needed to talk to her. She said, go ahead. Messages, he said. He needed some messages done. She told him, you should have said that in the first place, and later that day she sent her eldest son over with a jar of marmalade.

The boy was nine years old and had a bullying stare. He walked right in and helped himself to an apple from the sideboard.

'What are you doing here? I asked your mother to come.'

'She can't,' said the boy. 'She's got her work to do.'

'I don't want you. Go back home.'

The boy stood his ground. 'She said I had to get you your messages.'

'I don't want anything. Please go back and tell my daughter I have something to say to her.'

The boy bit the apple with a wrenching sound. 'She won't come.'

'All right, tell her this. Tell her I've had a bad turn.'

'But you haven't. Have you?'

He thought for a moment. 'No.'

'You're wanting me to tell lies,' said the boy.

'Is that so?' He tried to match the boy's insolence. 'And what will you be when you've finished chopping down cherry trees? Tinker, tailor, beggarman, thief?'

The boy was either too clever or too stupid for sarcasm. He shrugged. 'Don't know yet. Probably a lawyer like Dad. What do you want me to get at the shops?'

'Nothing. I told you — not a thing. Wait a minute, boy.' He

stepped in front of him and put his hand on his shoulder, felt softness, fat over bone. 'Did you know that my father — your great-grandfather — was a shepherd? I grew up in a one-roomed shepherd's hut, no hot water, no stove. Did all the cooking on the open fire — '

The boy's face went blank.

'I was ten before I went to school. Know that? Such education as I had out there, came from the correspondence school in Wellington.'

'You told me,' said the boy, wriggling to free himself. 'Thousands of times.'

'Stand still when I talk to you! and look at me! That's better. Tell me this — have you ever been to the mountain?'

'Sure.'

'When?'

The boy frowned. 'You know.'

'Damn it all, boy, do you think I'm asking for the fun of it?'

'You do so know. Aw, Grandad, you came up with us once. Skiing with Mum and Dad up Ruapehu.'

'Not that! I don't mean one of your heaps of trampled confection — ' He stopped, forgetting what he was going to say. It didn't matter. The boy couldn't possibly understand. He released him and waved him towards the door. 'There's nothing I need. Thanks for calling in.'

The boy shrugged. 'Mum says don't let the marmalade get mouldy.'

'I won't. Tell your mother she's very kind and I'm grateful.'

He went a little way down the path and watched his grandson saunter down the street, eating the apple. The child was solidly built, large backside and thick straight legs, blond hair like his father.

He turned and went back to the house.

By the front porch he stopped, hand on the railing, to look at a geranium bush which had grown large with bright red flowers. Grasping the railing firmly, he leaned over until his face was against the flowers, and he was surprised to discover that already, they smelled of snow.

MARGARET SUTHERLAND

A Letter from the Dead

What an unpredictable climate it is, thought Mrs Lake as she watched the surface of the pool pit and water pour off the tropical vines. The rain stopped just then and steam began to rise from the terrace tiles. Mrs Lake wiped her neck with a handkerchief.

The dog which had barked all day still barked. It did not like being tied up. Each bark was as clear and expectant as the first.

All the town grew noisy at that home-bound hour. The horns did not sound impatient so much as determined. Each one implied a house and garden and waiting family beyond the working world. Mrs Lake enjoyed that time of day. She had so many landscapes mounted in her mental album of people, mountains, harbours, buildings, trees, birds, cities, strays: so many airports, waiting rooms, hotel rooms in her life: she liked the thought of family life with its untidy warmth and hoarded past and the hangers-on.

Don will soon be here, she thought, and was glad. They would sit outside a while, sipping sherries, sharing the day's news. She would smile or commiserate until he settled back, his gaze on the harbour, enquiring. What about you, Amy? A good day?

All her days were good. Unlike the dog, she had the sense to know complaints were rarely worth persisting with after a certain time. She felt it was up to one to be happy, and so she was.

Mr Lake looked depressed and hot when he came in. Gratefully he kissed his wife, who in standard hotel accommodation could somehow create an illusion of lamplight and drawn curtains, and swallowed his sherry fast.

'Did any shipments get away today?' asked his wife, who followed his work closely. She was raising a topic inclining her husband to coronaries, and tipped the sherry bottle with a placating look. They both knew a serene fatalism towards Mr Lake's third-world contribution was sensible. They had spent fifteen years moving from one economic problem to the next: this time he was to find effective ways to distribute emergency aid supplies and fuel to the numerous out-lying islands devastated by the recent hurricane.

'Today, yes, I did manage to discuss the problems with some of those who take an interest in such things.' He nodded to the bottle. 'The Ministers of Finance and Economic Development are still at loggerheads — their business being money, they want to control all the funds. The Minister of Rural Development has his views, the villagers being the ones most affected after all. Before lunch I was interviewed by the Minister of Food and Agriculture. He expects a say, naturally. Then the Minister of Works and Transport considers his department should take over distribution but, as fuel's involved, the Minister of Energy disagrees. Tomorrow we all meet over lunch, probably to drink too much and set up a committee to commission a study. Meanwhile the rice rots and grafters siphon off petrol and stockpile the tinned goods to sell off on the quiet.'

'They don't want to implement your recommendations at all?'

'Be lucky if they read them, much less implement them.'

'Remember Kenya, Don,' said Mrs Lake calmly. She kept their past postings on file. Like an excellent secretary she knew exactly where to lay her hand on former near-disasters which, at the eleventh hour, were resolved.

'Kenya was a picnic compared to this place,' he grumbled, but she saw the lion in his breast was ready to lie down.

Above the harbour and the town, the sunset flung itself to the perimeters of the low, hump-backed mountains.

'Those hills remind me of a dinosaur, plodding on, searching for a mate,' said Mr Lake in his reflective mood. 'Poor old boy — no hope for him here.' The passionate sky made him sigh. 'God, these places are lovely. Amy! Would you ever see a sight like that in England?'

She had heard these ambivalences often and found them comfort-ing. Things repeated were reassuring, she found. She wasn't a house-wife in a suburb, who could predict the milkman would deliver at seven o'clock and the collectors would take away the rubbish on a Wednesday. Her life was an endless adjustment.

'A quick swim before we eat?' she suggested. He reached over and stroked her arm. 'Amy, you keep me sane.'

'And what would I be without you?' She went inside to change and turn down the camp oven. They carried it with them wherever they went and she made simple meals, saving restaurant fare for special occasions. Mince pie had an essential ordinariness in their rootless life.

Walking between wild orchids and hibiscus folding at day's end, they followed the path to the pool. He was a little taller than his wife, and she a little broader in the hips than he. Their stride the same in length, they went side by side down the pool steps and struck out at the same moment. Wide, slow ripples began to lap the edges as they proceeded in breaststroke to the end and back. Mr Lake turned over and floated, his face to the still-brilliant sky. Mrs Lake, who did not want to wet her hair, bobbed up and down, testing the bottom with her toe-tips and pulling up her shoulder straps which had a way of slipping since she'd lost weight. Recently her husband had put on two or three kilos; the same amount she'd lost. He looked rotund in his shorts as they went up the pool steps hand in hand. A large frog hopped along the path and a bat swooped. The air smelled of rain and some perfumed shrub.

The casserole wasn't quite tender. After they had changed, they sauntered down the hill and along the main street of town. The creek which crossed it, an oily, tidal inlet, was edged by an arched and colon-naded walkway — a South Pacific hearsay of Venice. All day birds perched there; now the last flight wheeled away, the rush and clatter of their wings like a supernatural breathing.

Mrs Lake stood still, gazing, her neck taut as a girl's. 'Oh Don!' she cried. 'The pigeons!' Nostalgia etched every line of her, and Mr Lake stood quietly, understanding. He knew the way of it — some idiotic little thing could jolt him back to England as easily.

'Where are we off to?' she enquired; coquettish, as though not a moment before she'd had the look of a child whose balloon has gone forever. They wandered on, their pace and interest suggesting there was nothing new and nothing expected from the surroundings. It was briefly cool, and the mosquitoes hadn't yet arrived. As the street lights came on, they turned by mutual consent and went back to the hotel.

As Mrs Lake came from the shower that night, fastening her cotton robe, she said to her husband, 'Do you find me attractive still?' He said, 'Of course I do. It doesn't change. You look the same to me.'

'Do I?' she asked, very surprised, for he did not look the same to her. She did not believe him, though she was pleased at what he said. Their lovemaking that evening was fond and unspectacular. Mr Lake found to his dismay that his worry over the next day's ministerial luncheon was interfering with his carnal interests. Fortunately his wife knew him well enough to effect a happy conclusion for them both.

'I love you dearly, Amy,' he said before he settled to sleep. Though she would have liked to stay, it was far too hot to think of cuddling up and she went back to the other bed. She checked the time and wound her folding traveller's clock; she had bought it in Hong Kong, years ago, and it was still as good as new.

Mrs Lake preferred the early hours. She felt most alert then as she went quietly on her own to attend to letters or do a little study on the terrace still wet from night showers. That peace established the routine of her day. After she saw Mr Lake off to his ministerial manoeuvres she did her housework which, in one room, did not take long. She had no windows to wash, no spring-cleans, no seasonal wardrobes to sort or appliances to have serviced. In the opinion of her relatives at home, she was a person to be envied.

She filled the hand basin and whisked suds to a business-like froth. She never let anyone else handle Mr Lake's laundry. She rinsed and rinsed till no trace of soap remained. She carried the washing, wrapped in a towel, to the terrace. There she fastened the expanding clothesline to the two hooks she'd fixed and pegged out, smoothing wrinkles, picking off lint, untangling the long socks.

Beds made, dishes done, Mrs Lake set off for town. The walk was a familiar one and she smiled at the taxi-drivers lounging by the rank and waved to the Indian vendor who sold sweetmeats on the corner. She went to the market and bought two avocado pears, a pineapple, a pawpaw and a handful of beans from her favourite stall. The owner wrapped her shopping in newspaper and she reached into her handbag where forethought catered for a range of eventualities (a folding rain-bonnet, a collapsible straw hat, a dome-away carry bag). She took out the kit, undid the domes, packed away her purchases and paid. She dropped the change with a rattle in the tin of a blind beggar who squatted at the market entrance and went on to the supermarket. There she clicked her tongue at the price tags of tinned salmon and olives, bought a bag of sugar, a bottle of vinegar and a loaf of bread. The kit seams looked stretched as she returned to the accumulating heat. She should have done her lighter errands first, she thought. Her face felt wet. The local women in their bright cottons maintained an air of freshness — she had no idea how.

Wearing the straw hat and trudging a little, she queued at the post office, despatched her letters home and finally walked to the news-paper office at the far end of town. There she made a donation to the fund for the children whose parents had died that week, rescuing their family from a house fire.

She was glad to head back to the hotel. She shifted the kit from hand to hand. There was a funeral at the Methodist church and she stood in the sun, her bag on the ground, waiting while the bearers carried a cloth-draped coffin down the steps. She watched quietly, making one of those journeys people do make, in the blink of an eye, when some passing event detaches itself from generality and plunges like a sword. The hearse drove away. She lugged the kit up the hill and gratefully opened her door. She drank two glasses of water, went to shower and change all her clothes and put away the shopping. That's that, she thought, with a sense of accomplishment. It was not quite ten o'clock.

The dog which yesterday had barked was barking still as she organised herself and her study books on the shaded terrace. Its energy and faith were boundless. I expect they are training it, thought Mrs Lake, who had an Englishwoman's horror of unkindness to animals and a lot of experience that not all people shared her feeling. With effort she detached herself from the barking and opened her text on Japanese script. In Tokyo last year, en route to a World Bank conference with Mr Lake and anticipating temples, lakes and gardens, she'd had to come to terms with skyscrapers and hurtling trains. The disappointing fragments did not deter her. She bought a *Teach Yourself* language course and the Penguin edition of Japanese verse. Asia was nothing if not patient — and she had time to spare for the search.

Memorising the *kana* and tracing the *kanji* in prescribed stroke order were peaceful disciplines. For basic mastery a reader needed to know two thousand *kanji*; the Chinese aspect of the script. Mrs Lake had now learned sixty-two ideograms. The pursuit of such a goal, even its unlikely attainment, somehow pleased her, aligning her with a child's perspective where each moment has its own permanence. When she tired of study she would imagine Japanese children, their hair cut straight, gazing out of schoolroom windows at the endless sky.

Now she scanned her book of verse. The words were spare and approached the blank page with the hesitant self-disclosure she imagined of the Japanese.

> *Was it that I went to sleep*
> *Thinking of him*
> *That he came in my dreams*

MARGARET SUTHERLAND

Had I known it a dream
I should not have awakened.

There is an attitude of acceptance even in loss, thought Mrs Lake. Still the dog barked.

As she cut open avocados and sprinkled them with salt and vinegar, the hotel receptionist tapped on her door and handed her an envelope with English stamps. 'A letter from home, madam,' he said, smiling wonderfully. She recognised her sister's handwriting. A premonition invaded her. She sat down to slit the envelope. Inside there was a letter, and a Christmas card which enfolded a linen bookmark embroidered in cross-stitch; grubby, like sets of table linen she'd worked herself as a girl, laboriously picking and restitching. She read the message on the home-made card. *Dear Auntie, thank you for the green silk pyjamas. They are the right fit. Mummy has made the cake and we are icing it today. We have a super tree. I'm sorry our present is late but french knots take ages. The stamps from the Philippines are stuck in and look very nice. When are you coming for another visit? Love from Althea.*

Her sister's note was as brief. *We have only just brought ourselves to sort through Althea's things. The enclosed was meant for you, Amy. I send it, as a keepsake, though I expect for you, as for us, reminders of grief are of doubtful value. It is too soon for me to look back acceptingly. She was a lovely little girl. I miss her every day. You were here with us this time last year. The church is a mass of lilies but I'm afraid this year the message of Easter is lost on me.*

Mrs Lake sat there, a bookmark and an open letter in her hands. How can I believe Althea is dead? she thought. I know it's true. They sent a cable. I opened it and read of the accident, there in that bright foreign city. I still have it as proof. But was there really a funeral? Could they have buried Althea? What flowers were there in December? I tried to pray for her of course but prayer needs an image and how can I imagine Althea under snow when I see her so vividly, running on the lawns of Greenwich, her cheeks so rosy, her fair hair tossed about? We went through the Royal Observatory and laughed at the funny old instruments for viewing the stars. We saw the shell of the old oak where Elizabeth the First used to play as a girl. We ate our picnic near the river where the *Cutty Sark* is moored. Althea asked me to send her stamps from the Philippines and I promised I would. We shared our sandwiches with pigeons.

Oh! thought Mrs Lake, it was wrong — wrong! — that I wasn't at her funeral.

A feeling of displacement and anger moved her and she picked up the telephone and demanded a connection to her husband's office. A detached receptionist explained Mr Lake was at lunch. Mrs Lake remembered the ministerial meeting and put back the receiver.

There was a knife and a spoon and a glass in the sink. She rinsed and dried them and put them in their proper places. She fetched in the washing, removed the clothesline and put away her books. Then she sat, quite still, like a painting framed by walls. She had the art of managing small spaces but today a vacuum threatened. Others had homes, babies, a place in the community — at least a friend to telephone. Where is my world? she thought despairingly. I am dependent and waiting, no better than that poor wretched dog.

Mrs Lake snatched her bag and went out into the slaying day. She strode down the hill towards the town. 'I am capable of walking,' she said rejectingly when the drivers smiled and offered their taxis. She ignored the sweetmeat vendor and pushed through lunch-hour shoppers, elbowing her way. The store windows appeared to offend her. Their owners, hovering in doorways, eyed her and did not invite her inside. She crossed side streets without looking and drivers blasted horns aggressively. She marched straight on.

She saw two local girls come out of the arcade. They wore knickerbockers and brief tie tops and their lips were coloured purple. Confused, feeling her anger rearrange itself, she stopped, thinking, don't imitate us. It was very hot. She felt in her bag for a handkerchief to wipe away the sweat on her face. Just then a boy darted out from the arcade and held a garland out to her.

Cutting him short, she said brusquely, 'I don't want it.'

'Fresh beautiful *lei*,' inveigled the boy, waving it under her nose so she saw the browning blossoms and smelled their sickly scent.

'I don't buy dead flowers,' she snapped, exhausted by beggars everywhere who thrust their claims at her.

'Fresh this morning!' he argued, used to tourists with fat wallets and uncertain resolve.

Mrs Lake snatched the *lei* and shook it in his face. 'Look at it! It's dying. You push your dying wreath at me and expect money. Do I look such a fool? Do you think the English wave dead flowers at strangers? Why are you here? You ought to be at school. Don't you go to school? And don't tell me a pack of lies . . .'

The boy, staring as though she was mad, pressed through the shoppers and was gone. Breathing fast, very flushed, the hot pavement dragging fluid to her aching feet, Mrs Lake stood and people stepped aside to avoid her. The flowers, so carefully strung, expired their foreign sweetness. Their cool, browning touch had the texture of death and she let the *lei* fall. It was all he had to offer, she thought: what am I doing here?

CHRIS ELSE

The Sphinx

'You!' said the Caterpillar contemptuously.
'Who are *you*?'
— Lewis Carroll, *Alice in Wonderland*

Otto Hueber was the official interpreter because no one else in Honigsbach spoke English as well as he did. He was thirty-five, short, scrawny, red-faced, with blond, thinning hair, blue eyes, mouth curved in a determined grin. His right shoulder sloped awkwardly and the empty sleeve was turned inside out and tucked away in his jacket. Like Harris, he had been a soldier. Neither of them wanted to talk about the war.

'So, from London, from the Institute of Applied Biochemistry,' he said 'You are the biochemist?'

'Entomologist,' Harris told him.

'What is that?'

'Insects. The study of insects.'

'Ach!' Otto sounded cynical. Perhaps the study of insects seemed absurd in a world which had just killed so many people. Harris made no comment. Insects were important to him.

'It is a mystery,' Otto said, shaking his head. 'The Bureau tell me that you are here to look after a plant because it might have chemicals of value. You, you say you are the insect man.'

It was warm at the wooden table outside the inn. Harris took off his jacket.

'What is this chemical?' Otto asked.

'We don't know. An alkaloid of some kind. Like nicotine, cocaine, morphine, strychine. They're all derived from plants. I'm over here to look for a particular variety of mandragora which only grows in Honigsbach.'

'For nicotine?' Otto was clearly sceptical.

'No. We don't know what it might be. The common mandragora produces atropine, like belladonna, but there are stories, folktales that some sort of larva feeds on the mandragora here and that people used to eat it and . . .'

'Lava? Volcano?'

'Caterpillar,' Harris said.

'In Honigsbach they do not eat caterpillars.'

'This was a long time ago.'

'A long time ago they were all crazy.' Otto laughed.

'I guess that's where I come in. I did my PhD thesis on the digestive system of the European Dung Beetle.' Harris lit a cigarette and found his hands were shaking. He was not used to talking so much.

Otto was staring at him and nodding slowly. 'Why is a raven like a writing desk?' he asked and laughed again when Harris did not understand. 'Your Lewis Carroll, with him I like. He knows the world is crazy.'

In the centre of the sunlit square was a stone plinth which might once have held a market cross and on the farther side there were red brick buildings with tiny, squared windows and huge, steep-pitched tiled roofs. A peasant woman with a heavy basket over her arm was making her way along the wall. The basket was covered with a red and white checked cloth. She was old and leaned painfully on a gnarled stick. The sky was blue. A lark sang.

The innkeeper was old too. He brought them more wine. His face was very wrinkled, brown and bristling with white stubble. Otto explained about Harris, why he was staying in Honigsbach, how he (Otto) was appointed to look after him and translate for him. Harris knew enough German to get the gist of the speech. He took the drawings out of his briefcase and showed them to the old man.

'The Devil's Fruit,' Herr Kruppel said. Otto translated.

'That's right,' Harris told him. 'The Arabs have a similar name. Satan's Apple. Does he know where to find it?'

Otto asked.

The black eyes disappeared for a moment amid the wrinkles. Herr Kruppel sucked thoughtfully at the stumps of his teeth.

'The Führer was here one time,' he said. 'He sat right there. Where you're sitting now. He drank my wine. My forty-one. It was a good vintage for the forty-one. Ten years ago now.'

Otto translated patiently. Harris stared at the drawings.

'We must build a new Germany, without such things,' Otto said.

'You like the wine?' the old man asked Harris.

He understood. 'Yes,' he answered.

Herr Kruppel stared at him with bright, glittering eyes. 'Hitler,' he said. 'Kleek!' he drew his finger across the flabby skin of his throat and laughed. Otto smiled and shrugged his one shoulder tolerantly.

'Apfel von Teufel?' Harris asked, tapping the drawings again.

Herr Kruppel turned and waved his finger to the north, to the slopes above the town. 'There are places,' he said. 'Ask the alraun.' Otto translated but had trouble with the last word.

'It's German for mandrake, mandragora,' Harris told him. 'What does he mean?'

Otto asked, and listened, and then explained. It must be a superstition. He talks of the Hanging Bastard. There is a story that the plant you look after grows under the gallows only. Do you know this?'

'Yes,' Harris said.

The old man spoke again, waving his skinny arm to emphasise some point.

'He says there's a goblin and that he saw it one time out there in the square,' Otto said, grinning apologetically.

'Is that the Hanging Bastard?' Harris asked.

Otto translated.

The old man laughed and drew his finger across his throat. 'Kleeek!' he said, screwing up his eyes.

Acherontia atropos, of the family Sphingidae, the Death's Head Hawk Moth, so named because of a curious mark resembling a skull on the back of the thorax. Its forewings are rich brown, beautifully mottled and banded, with a pale dot in the middle. The hind wings are yellow, with two black bands. The caterpillar, too, is yellow, sprinkled over with minute black dots, with seven oblique blue stripes on each side. The horn on its tail — a characteristic of all sphinx moths — is rough and bent downwards but turned up again at the tip. It feeds on the deadly nightshade, the potato, and similar plants and is commonly found in the month of August.

In all stages of its existence, whether as caterpillar, chrysalis, or perfect insect, *Acherontia atropos* has the power of uttering a distinct cry or sound. When disturbed, the caterpillar draws back its head very quickly, making at the same time a loud snapping noise, which has been compared to a series of electric sparks. The chrysalis, too, squeaks when it is about to turn into a moth: but it is the sound made by the perfect insect which is the most remarkable. Kirby and Spence describe it thus:

When it talks, and more particularly when it is confined or taken in the hand, it sends forth a strong, sharp cry, resembling that of a mouse, but more plaintive and even lamentable, which it continues as long as it is held . . .

This noise, coupled with the insect's startling appearance, has been the source of many superstitions and general feelings of awe and terror among the peasants of the countries in which it is found.

The most efficient plan would have been to interview the local people and so gain information which might narrow his search. Instead, he spent the day wandering in the woods above the town. He needed to be alone, away from buildings and the German language, in a place where he could forget the things he did not want to remember. A restless energy drove him, a need to keep on walking, as if by doing so he could leave his deepest fears behind.

The clearing was not marked on his map. He stumbled into it by accident. It was fifty yards long and twenty wide, knee high with lucerne and grasses, foxgloves, pink and yellow, cow wheat and buddleia. Above the flowers, in the rippling heat of the air, were clouds of butterflies. Admirals and whites, peacocks and painted ladies, strong-winged fritillaries which had drifted in from the wood, other species which he knew only by Latin names; they whirled and fluttered, settled, probing for syrup with their curling tongues, their wings spread languorous and rhythmic, pumping, flick, rising, twisting, scatter. Thrilled by the sight of them, he paused in the shade of a big elm tree, gazing at their rich profusion until he became entranced, his agitation stilled, calm.

Dry twigs crackled beneath his feet. The smell of seeds and flowers drifted to him, the hum of bees. The insect life about seemed to stir and rustle. The ants and beetles, grasshoppers, thrips and flies, the slow, teeming surges of death and regeneration seemed to draw him forward, out into the sunlight until he was wading through the heat, the grass, the drifting scent of flowers. The butterflies rippled out of reach and he felt himself suspended, as they were, a floating fragment in the warm currents of the air, his senses open, thirsty; long lost summers when he wandered in his sticky grey flannel shirt and short trousers, spindle-legged through the clearings of his boyhood. And the soft-winged fairies lifted Little Tom above the woods, above the town. And Herr Kruppel, who had seen a goblin in the square.

'There is a new guest to stay at the inn here,' Otto said. 'He is from America. Maybe you will like to talk with him.'

Harris thought it unlikely.

'We will drink wine,' Otto said.

The American joined them for dinner. He was fresh-faced, self-confident, amiable, wearing a suit and tie. His name was Stone. Otto was very solicitous towards him, shaking hands with his left palm, thumb downwards, ushering him to the table, introducing Herr Doctor Harris with due deference. Stone smiled, amiably.

'Glad to meet you,' he said, shaking hands. 'It's kind of nice to be talking English again. I'm almost out of the habit.'

'You speak excellent German, it is so,' Otto said, pouring wine. 'Like a native.'

'Not so good,' Stone said.

Otto winked at Harris. 'But he is a native. He was born in Dortmund.'

'I'm an American,' Stone smiled but his tone was firm enough to create an awkward pause. Harris lit a cigarette.

Between Dortmund and Paderborn was a village whose name he could not remember. Corporal Cunningham, his face white, eyelids screwed tight shut, his lips pale. Jesus, he said. Sweet Jesus.

'You like culture?' Otto asked the American.

Harris drank. The wine tasted bitter. He deliberately thought of the wood, the butterflies in golden sunlight. He remembered wind in the pines.

'I like music more than painting,' Stone said.

'You play?' Otto asked.

'Piano.'

'Carnegie Hall?'

But the pines weren't here. They were in Belgium. Then.

'Not yet.' Stone looked boyish, embarrassed. Carnegie Hall might be a real ambition.

Otto laughed cheerfully and poured more wine.

'Carnegie Hall!' he said, raising his glass.

Herr Kruppel's daughter, blonde and solid, served them roast lamb. She had cut Otto's into bite-sized pieces to save him trouble. Stone smiled at her. She blushed.

Her cheeks red, blonde hair, like the SS officer, cold in the pine wood, the grass underfoot was wet, the wind moaned and the grey uniform rippled against the hard muscles. Sturmführer Keppel. Why had he blushed like that?

'Do you like Honigsbach?' Otto asked.

'Sure. It's very pretty. Everything my mother promised,' Stone told him.

'Your mother knows here?'

'She and her sister used to come for holidays when they were kids. She always said it was the most beautiful place on earth.'

'Ah, mothers!' Otto's eyes were misty as he gazed into his wine.

Stone turned to Harris. 'And what brings you to this neck of the woods?'

A blushing neck? 'Not my mother,' Harris said.

Stone grinned. 'Military, maybe?'

'Not as far as I know. Not this time.'

'The Herr Doctor is here for work for the British Government, our allies,' Otto said. 'We will co-operate for many things. And with America also, of course.'

'It's a new world,' Stone said.

'We have many Americans, many English in Germany today. (About the Russians I say nothing.) Some people say we have the Army of Occupation. For me, it is the Army of Friendship. Everything has changed.'

'It sure has,' Stone said.

'Were you a soldier?' Otto asked him.

'I wasn't old enough.'

'Herr Harris and myself, we have been soldiers. Tweedledum and Tweedledee. Why do we fight such a war? So many have died. So many are destroyed, Hitler was crazy.' He poured more wine and beckoned Fraulein Kruppel who was sitting on the other side of the room beside the empty fireplace. She came with downcast eyes. Otto ordered another bottle.

The object of his search had been in the clearing all the time. On his second visit he almost stepped on it. A clear space in the grass at his feet, a circle about three feet across which was almost filled by a star of five dark green leaves. Each leaf was a foot long, six inches wide at the base and running to a point. They lay flat on the ground, radiating outwards, and from the conjoined centre there rose three stalks, about four inches high, topped by three single blooms the shape and size of a primrose which had bell-shaped corollas cut into five spreading segments of deep purple. As he bent down to look at it, the smell wafted up to him, rich and rotten, like old apples, dead flesh. It was so strong that he turned his head aside and found himself looking at four more purple flowers on little stalks not a yard away in another circle of shortened grass and beyond that he saw, as he stood up again, a third plant and a fourth, a long row of them parallel to the side of the clearing, as if they had been planted deliberately, as if the glade itself had been cut out of the wood solely to give them the perfect balance of light and shade.

He looked about him and saw for the first time, not the brightness of the sunlight, but the black, solid shadows beneath the trees. He sensed presences, eyes watching him, waiting. The heavy smell of the mandragora floated round him in the buzzing heat. The butterflies swam on it. The flowers and grasses were suspended in its foetid ripeness. All the life of the clearing now seemed steeped in the sweet odour, tainted and nourished by the soft exhalations of the purple flowers and the pointed leaves. He felt giddy, intoxicated, his pores clogged with sweat, his skin crawling with the palpitations of the air. He blinked, shook his head trying to clear it. He tried to breathe but his lungs felt numb, cramping in his chest. A listlessness dragged at his muscles so that he had to force himself to turn and walk back towards the elm tree, his signpost, while the air sucked at his heavy limbs to hold him, to draw him deep and drown him in its sweet viscosity.

Slowly, step by step, he drew away. As he gained the shade of the tree the air grew cooler, less suffocating, and he breathed more easily. He knew he should go back and look at the mandragora. His mind was very clear on that point. He should take notes, and measurements, and photographs. Yet somehow, when he reached his rucksack, which he had set down between two large roots, he did not pause but simply picked it up and kept on walking. He was not afraid, of course. Why should he be afraid? He just needed the shade, the cool for a little while. In fact now, walking down the narrow path beneath the high arch of the branches overhead, he felt a new lightness, lucidity, a fresh precision to his logic, as if he had the power to analyse and render plain any situation which might present itself.

Had Keppel been afraid in that Belgian wood? The thought struck him so suddenly that he stopped and looked round as if someone had spoken to him. Then, gently, his mind drew into focus an image of the tall trees, dark, the grey autumn sky, the rutted road. The slow soughing of the wind, the crunch of pine needles underfoot, and wet grass, and Keppel in his grey-black uniform with the double runic S of the Schutzstaffel on the left lapel, skin pale, white, his hair like straw, like spun gold stirring in the air as he walked, with hands held high, a pace or two ahead of Cunningham's sten gun. All right, Corporal, Harris said and, drawing his revolver, he stepped forward, ordered Keppel to halt, moved in front of him so that he could see into his eyes like opals, chalk blue, staring at the trees. Harris raised the gun to the prisoner's temple. We are a forward patrol, he said. Prisoners make things difficult. If you have useful information I can send you back to headquarters under escort. You must prove to me, in English . . . He stared at Keppel's stiff jaw, pouted lips, as if the staring might bring out the words. I will have to kill you if you do not give me information. Twitch, the jaw, the muscle. Safety catch clicked off. For the last time, Harris pleaded. And slowly, from the centre of Keppel's white cheek a rosy blush spread and outwards to his ear and down over jaw bone to the base of his slim neck. His skin flamed, nostrils tensed. His eyes were misty, far away. What did a man think of that he blushed like that at the point of a gun? Harris turned and walked away, holstering his revolver. He glanced at Cunningham. The sten gun roared. Good fuckin' riddance, if you'll pardon the expression, sir, Corporal Cunningham said when the echoes had died.

On a sun-dappled bank beside the path, Harris sat staring at the palms of his hands. Gunfire reverberated deep in his mind, the distant boom of explosion, the smell of cordite and blood. There had been many battles, it seemed, too many to remember distinctly. Why was Keppel more important than any other prisoner shot in the back?

He stood up, slowly, shouldered his rucksack, and set off down the hill towards the town.

The square and the inn were filled with music. Harris stepped into the dusk of the hallway and looked though the lounge room door. Stone was sitting at the old piano, straight-backed, head cocked, fingers ripping through the arpeggios of what must have been a Beethoven sonata. The piano sang and trembled. In the far corner of the room stood Herr Kruppel's daughter with a feather duster raised against some brasses on the wall. She did not move. Her head was bowed, intently listening. Her cheeks flamed with the passion of the music. Stone had his back to her. Jaw set, eyes fixed on a distant point, he was lost in concentration. His body shook with the effort. Two strands of brown hair hung down over his forehead. He was young, talented, and proud. As he hammered home the final chords, he flung back his head and turned, in the dying echoes, to where Harris stood leaning against the door jamb. He had a look of triumph in his eyes. The silence boomed. Memories, like insects rustling under dead leaves, stirred in Harris's mind.

Stone sighed and said, 'It was a nice instrument once, but now
. . .' He tripped a high note with his right forefinger, repeatedly, to
show how flat it was. The feather duster began to fly across the surface
of the brasses.

'Did you have a good day?' Stone asked.

'Yes,' Harris told him.

'Find what you were looking for?'

'Almost.'

'Me too. I've been hanging around talking to people. Haven't I,
Greta?'

Fraulein Kruppel turned, enquiringly. Stone asked her a question
in German.

'Ja,' she answered and blushed to the roots of her hair.

Stone smiled.

'Well,' he said, standing up and closing the piano, 'that's enough
Carnegie Hall for one day.'

At dinner he was cheerful, more amiable than ever.

'Are you interested in folklore?' he said, turning to Harris. 'Or is
it just bugs?'

Harris shrugged.

Stone continued, 'I learnt an interesting bit of ritual today. And
then I remembered my mother mentioning the same thing. About the
harvest festival in Honigsbach. You'll know this, Otto.'

Otto was busy with the bottle of a new wine which Herr Kruppel
had recommended to him. He poured a little, sipped, and smacked his
lips in approval. 'Good. Very good.' He filled the three glasses. 'What
is this story? A new gossip?'

'Not new,' Stone said. 'Old. Thousands of years, maybe. Every
harvest they used to make a dummy out of straw and carry it round
the town. Then they'd bring it to the square in front of the inn here
and hang it like it was a criminal. Apparently, the guy who did the
hanging, der Henken, as they called him, used to be a kind of priest
in ancient times. He'd get hopped up on something and go into a
trance and then make prophecies and predictions.'

'A drug?' Harris asked.

'I guess. Nobody seems to know what it was.'

'Has this got anything to do with the Hanging Bastard?' Harris
asked Otto.

'The Hanging Bastard?' Stone was eager, curious.

Otto waved his hand dismissively. 'Nonsense. All nonsense. Superstition. The Nazis used to play with such stories. They thought they would bring back the pagan times. But in Honigsbach we are modern now, scientific.'

'Do you mean the Nazis organised a Hanging Festival?' Ştone asked.

'Maybe. I do not know. I did not live in Honigsbach for many years. I was with the army.'

'Why didn't you tell me about this festival?' Harris demanded.

Otto was flustered, embarrassed. He looked from one to the other helplessly. 'It is a stupidity,' he said. 'Nothing for a person of science and intelligence. Come, drink some wine and let's be friends. It's very good, I assure you.' He patted Harris on the sleeve. 'One day,' he said, 'we will go to Augsburg. I will show you a library which is very old with many books. There will be everything about all the useless things you want to know. Perhaps Herr Stone will come to see the cultural places.'

Stone shook his head. 'I've got too much to do here.'

'Ah!' Otto said, knowingly, and raised his glass. 'Your good health!' He winked.

Stone blushed.

There were seventeen mandragora in the clearing. On nine of them the flowers had begun to fall, revealing small purplish green nodules which would grow, over the next few weeks, into the blue-black, apple-scented fruit. Harris took a selection of photographs and then drew a sketch map, marking the positions of the plants and the distances between them, which he measured with a tape. On seventeen consecutive pages of a field notebook he listed their statistics: number and dimensions of leaves, number of footstalks and the condition of flowers, approximate hours of sunlight according to position. Careful observations of the relative growth rates and maturity might prove useful correlations with the level of alkaloid concentration in various parts of the plants. He also needed samples to send back to England for analysis. He would take one plant to begin with but he had not decided which. Perhaps, if he chose well, he might find a caterpillar in the root. There was certainly no sign of insect damage to the leaves. Probably there would be no caterpillar. He had never had much faith in it.

When night fell, he took from his pack two lamp traps, set them in the clearing about thirty yards apart and sat down under a tree to eat his supper. Crickets chirruped in the gathering darkness. From somewhere down the slope beside the stream a frog began to croak. The two lamps glowed blue-white. Each consisted of a funnel of frosted diffusing glass with a battery powered mercury vapour globe at the base, hidden in a light metal chamber with a glass bottom. Night-flying insects attracted to the glow would land on the funnel, crawl down towards the greater brightness of the globe and become trapped in the chamber. They were not the best traps but they were all that the institute had provided. Harris checked and emptied them three times before the temperature began to drop and the night flyers became more subdued. He found no large moths or beetles, nothing uncommon. Eventually, he got into his sleeping bag and lay, gazing upwards through the massed shadows of the tree tops at the stars.

Warm and cold, black and white. Everything divided, clear, distinct. The silence, the great void of space, was made up of tiny fragments, sounds, like pinpricks, stars, like the tiny dots of a newspaper photograph, so absolute beneath a lens but grey in the light of everyday, uniform with the double runic S of the Schutzstaffel on the left lapel. The death's head cap badge.

He blinked awake, startled by the image. The night sounds, silence, hummed about him, settled into furtive stillness, inaudible, peace, the ultrasonic reverberation of the war he did not want to remember. He thought instead of the inn. Maybe Otto and Stone were still awake, still drinking, with Greta, quiet as a mouse, between them. Stone, smiling his white teeth. Otto, moist-eyed, red-faced. Have some more wine, he might be saying. It's first class. Really. And Stone with his blue eyes, from Dortmund. Near Paderborn. There was a little country village with little white houses. And a dead horse in the street and a cart with one wheel. I'm dreaming, Harris thought as he slid gently into his dream. It'll be all right this time. And the platoon moved forward carefully, checking out the deserted houses. Anderson and Peters leapt the little fence, stepped through the ravaged garden to the door. They crashed it open. Silent in the dream. No noise. But he could smell the dead horse, warming in the sun. And Anderson fell backwards with four bullets in his chest and Peters, flat on his belly, lobbed a grenade through the open door and blew out both the front windows and the guts of the German infantryman inside. I shall dream it carefully, Harris thought, and then there will be no mistakes, no noise. Except that he could already hear the moaning.

He was awake again, alert and listening in the moon-pale night, straining his ears for the sound. Or was it in the dream? He had heard the low, plaintive cry of someone in distress, an animal maybe. Like the call of the dog fox except melancholy, soft. An owl? A dream. The German had been left in the village because he was wounded and could not walk. Now he was dead, like Anderson. So who had made the noise? Again, yes. He could not mistake it this time. Someone had sobbed, pale, keening, animal. A beast in the dark. He listened, still as a stone, until he could not hold his breath any longer. And all the time, in the back of his mind, a skein of images kept floating. It wasn't just Keppel, a small voice said. Keppel was the least of it.

At dawn he checked his traps again and stowed them away in his rucksack. Then he chose a medium-sized mandragora and, with a long narrow trowel, began to loosen the soil around its base. The root was brown, unbranched, travelling straight down into the ground like a parsnip. It was at least a foot and a half long. He took about ten inches, together with the leaves, flowers and fruit nodules. There was no sign of insect damage, no insects at all. He packed everything away and walked down through the woods into the dew-wet valley.

In Augsburg Harris arranged for the despatch of a progress report and of the mandragora samples to the institute in London. Then Otto took him to the library. It was an old two-storey house tucked away in one of the back streets of the city, ten rooms filled with tall glass-fronted bookshelves of blonded oak. The librarian, Herr von Ritter, explained that the library had begun in this building as a private collection of a fifteenth-century burgomeister named Wallen and that, after four hundred years during which it had been moved several times and had grown to its present size, it had been returned to the place of its origin when the city fathers received the house as a bequest in 1873.

Herr von Ritter was a small man with a big, domed, bald head fringed with white hair. He had a heavy white moustache, yellowed with nicotine, and gold-rimmed spectacles. Sitting down in a big leather chair in the little room which served as his office, he lit a black pipe and began to answer questions about the history of Honigsbach. His knowledge was extensive. He knew of the Hangenfest, the mandragora, the caterpillar. The latter, he said, had been called the Worm of Knowledge. People used to eat it to receive wisdom and enlightenment, although there were some writers who claimed it was the devil himself come to tempt man in the form of a serpent as he had done in the Garden of Eden. Did he believe the tales of eating caterpillars to be historical fact or were they merely folklore? It was hard to say. For one thing, what insect could it be? Such a big caterpillar that some writers called it a snake. Harris mentioned *Acherontia* but Herr von Ritter shook his head doubtfully. He had never heard of such a moth. Was it common in the region? Harris knew it was not. He asked if there was any connection between the caterpillar and the ritual of the Hangenfest. The old man puffed slowly on his pipe for several seconds before answering. He could not say that there was although the parallels were clear enough. He put down his pipe and stood up slowly, beckoned them to follow him.

In a nearby room he took a little ladder and, refusing offers of assistance, shakily climbed the four steps so that he could reach up to the highest bookcase. Slowly, arms trembling with the weight, he took down a large leather-bound volume with a spine ornately tooled and stamped in gold. Otto translated the title as *Curious Stories of the Plateau*. Herr von Ritter turned the thick pages carefully until he came to a large steel engraving. It showed a man wearing a hooded robe with a single horn, curving backwards, on his head. He was standing on a flight of steps which led up to a little stone platform, his left foot on the platform itself, his right two steps below it. His right hand was raised above his head in a kind of salute while in his left he held a two-handled cup which rested on his knee. Below and about him was a crowd of people reaching up to him in eagerness and pleading. Beneath the picture were the words 'der Henken'.

Herr von Ritter found the appropriate place in the text and read slowly as Otto translated. For two months before the festival of the hanging, the Hangman lived in the woods where he ate insects and berries and drank only wine which he also mixed with various herbs according to a secret recipe. As the time for the festival drew near, the wine became stronger and stronger with the herbs and der Henken's visions became more and more inspired until he was ready to utter the great prophecies which the people demanded. He might tell them of a new age to come or of terrible disasters about to befall the world. Then he would hang the straw man, the criminal, as a sign to all whose spirit was not at one with the festival. It was not known whether der Henken was truly able to foretell the future or not as no accurate record of his predictions existed. Harris asked if any mention of the mandragora was made in the book. There was none, although Herr von Ritter pointed out that the wine of Circe was supposed to be infused with the plant so it might be possible. He also thought that he had seen a reference to the local mandragora as a means of detecting witches. He could not be sure. Would it be useful if he were to compile some sort of bibliography and selected references for Herr Doctor Harris? He would be very happy to do so and also to allow translation of useful passages if that would be helpful. Harris thanked him. Yes, any assistance would be much appreciated.

'Do you care to see the old places of the town?' Otto asked when they were in the street again.

'No,' Harris told him, 'I'd like to get back.'

The sun was setting as they drove along the narrow road beside the river. The sky above the hills was red like a burning city.

'Such is glory,' Otto said, staring into the distance.

Harris thought of the clearing in the woods above Honigsbach, butterflies whirling in a light red with fire. Beneath the trees around the glade the shadows were black, alive, swaying like dancers. What did der Henken prophesy? A Reich to last a thousand years?

'With our friend Daniel do you speak much?' Otto asked.

'With who?'

'Herr Stone. Has he talked with you why he has come to Germany?'

'No,' Harris told him.

'With young people today there is no morality,' Otto said with a sigh.

Harris didn't answer. He was only half listening.

'He makes with Fraulein Kruppel too free,' Otto went on. 'It's not good in a place small like Honigsbach.'

'Makes free? What do you mean?'

'How do you say?' Otto clenched his fist and short-jabbed his arm upwards. 'For sex.'

'Oh.' Harris did not care much either way.

'Clean. We need a clean world. I think, maybe, people are the same all over all the time.'

The dancers flickered in the back of Harris's skull.

He had not sent all the mandragora. One slice of root, a cross-section the size of a florin and about half an inch thick, he kept for himself, intending to prepare slides for microscopic examination and to make one or two crude chemical tests. The light in his room was too poor to make slides in the evening. He had only a single lamp with a low-wattage bulb on the little work table beneath his window. He decided therefore to try the analysis and took out his rack of test tubes, his pipette, his supply of reagents, his distilled water, his spirit burner. Then he placed the sample on a glass slab and began to cut tiny pieces from it with a scalpel. The tests did not tell him much. The root contained an alkaloid of some kind, possibly atropine, possibly a similar substance, possibly something quite new. There was no way of telling which.

He sat pondering the problem, staring at the creamy-white disk which was flattened at one side now where he had cut his test samples. A drop of moisture, crystal clear, had oozed from the fresh surface, gleaming in the light of the lamp, clean like a mirror. If he looked close enough, he would see in that tiny globe an image of the room, minute, bulging out of shape. He held the disk up to his face, concentrating, cross-eyed. Bright, transparent, the drop of moisture sparkled like a tear. He had known his chemistry would fail. With the primitive equipment at his disposal, the drop was unfathomable.

Slowly, aching with a tension which gripped his jaw, he slid out his tongue, touched the drop with the tip of it, squeezing with his fingers to get the most juice, as the muscles of his mouth quivered with strain, as he felt a tingling sensation, burning. He snapped it back into his mouth. Drown it in saliva. Spit. No, he should have spat but somehow, instead, he was working his tongue back and forth across his palate and his salivary glands were gushing. He swallowed, skin-numbed, and panic gripped him. Whatever this stuff was, it could be deadly. Jesus, sweet Jesus. His head was buzzing, cold sweat, vision blurred, dancing with spots of red light.

Yet despite his fear and against his will he was already beginning to relax. A sluggish warmth suffused him. Starting at his throat it flowed downwards through arms and chest, through belly, groin, and legs. His fingers felt thick and clumsy. Leaning forward with his elbows on the table, his head bowed, heavy, his hands like swollen sponges, he felt himself sinking into a drugged sleep. He could not move. Everything drifted downwards except for a single drop of clarity, like the tear of the mandragora, a bubble in his mind which floated free, expanding slowly. As it grew, pale and gleaming, his concentration focused on it until, like a planet drifting towards him, it seemed to fill his field of mental vision, growing, bursting so that it showered down upon him bright slivers of light and icy cold through all the flesh which sleep and heat had numbed in him.

He saw with startling clarity how Anderson was dead, how he and Corporal Cunningham were crouching beneath a window, a white wall, their boots in the soft earth of the flowerbed. He could hear the noise inside the cottage, the scrape of metal on metal, clink, scrape, and he could see the grenade in Cunningham's hand, their wordless understanding, clink, scrape, and the pin being pulled. Their hearts' thump counted one and two and he, half-standing, smashed the barrel of his revolver through the window above him and Cunningham lobbed the grenade through the broken pane. Flat on his belly, hands over ears. The wall beside him trembled, vibrated. Dust and smoke spewed out of the shattered window frame. Glass showered down around him in bright splinters, slowly, sparkling, he could see it, just as he could see once more into that shattered room where the children were. Two of them dead but one, a boy about eight years old, was still breathing, slumped among the shredded furniture with his skinny legs at an absurd angle. His back was broken. Eyes stared wide, moved slowly, rolling. Jesus, sweet Jesus, Corporal Cunningham said.

Harris in his room in Honigsbach, his head slumped, focused inward in his own brain, watched himself commanding self and his own broken boyhood twitch as the shock subsided and began to scream in pain. His corporal, right-hand man, struck helpless, watching the black mouth open, scream, and choke, and bubble blood. Poor little Tom, thought Harris, and poor little Alice too, and little baby. They will never run again. They will never dance like butterflies and catch the goblin in the square. The screams dropped to a whimper, a plaintive keening, and Otto's face, bewhiskered, streaked with the soot of battle, hung like a moon and tears welled up in the corners of his eyes and ploughed twin runnels through the grime of his cheeks. A scream again. There was a revolver in the rucksack underneath the bed. It was the same revolver. If he could reach it, he might stop the noise. For Christ's sake, said Cunningham, his eyes screwed tight, for the love of God. He had the revolver in his hand. He held the muzzle close to the boy's head, to his own temple. He pulled the trigger. Snap. The screaming stopped.

He was standing in the middle of his hotel room with the empty gun in his hand. The lamp on the table in the window cast a yellow pool of light. The glass slab gleamed. He put the revolver back in the rucksack. His pulse was slow. He was breathing gently. There was a bitter taste in his mouth. He went out to the bathroom at the end of the hall and washed it away, gargling, and spitting many times into the white sink. He wiped his mouth on a towel and examined his tongue in the little square of mirror fastened to the wall. There was a blister, pinpricks of numbness still. He felt unafraid, unworried, calm. His vision was sharp, hard-edged and clear. Back in his room, he looked at the test tubes, the bottles, the slice of root, which were still on the table. It was a stranger's room, abandoned suddenly by its occupant. He put on his jacket and, closing the door after him, went downstairs.

Stone was in the lobby talking to Greta. Harris walked past them and out into the darkness of the square. There was one street lamp burning to his left. He set off towards it.

'Wait!' A voice behind him.

He paused. Why did he stop? He should have gone on. Stone caught up with him.

'Is it okay if I walk with you?' Stone asked.

Harris didn't answer. Why didn't he say what he felt? Stone fell into step beside him.

'I needed an excuse to get away,' he explained. 'Just say the word if you don't want me along.'

Harris said nothing. There was a faint buzzing in his head, a tingling, like cold air breathed on a frosty morning.

'Greta's gotten to be a pain, these last few days. It's hard to shake her off.'

'Perhaps you shouldn't have made free with her.'

'That's a weird sort of expression, "made free".'

'It's Otto's.'

Stone laughed. 'Our friend Otto's a weird sort of character,' he said.

It was a warm night. There was no sound except their feet on the cobblestones as they crossed the square and began to make their way down one of the narrow, winding streets on the further side. The river was below them, far below.

'Did you know he was a Nazi?' Stone asked.

'Who? Otto?'

'He's not from Honigsbach at all. He's a Berliner. His father was a diplomat in London. A Nazi diplomat. With connections like that our friend was a sure bet for intelligence work. He spent several years in the SD, Ausland Division, under Schellenberg.'

Harris said nothing so Stone continued.

'There was some problem, some disagreement. He got shuffled sideways. At the end of the war he was in Frankfurt. A tank ran him down, tore his arm off.'

'How do you know all this?'

'Greta told me. At least, she gave me the last clues to link up Otto

Hueber and Reinhardt Baumgartner. When he got out of hospital and they'd given him some new papers he decided to stay in the south. There was no reason to go back to Berlin.' Stone laughed. 'Pathetic really.'

'You came all the way to Honigsbach to track down Otto?'

'God, no. He's very small fry. We just like to keep an eye on as many as we can, that's all.'

At the bottom of the hill, the street joined another in a T junction. There was a lamp on an iron bracket jutting out from the brick wall of a house. The air about it was cloudy with moths, their shadows flickering over the pool of light it cast on the flagstones of the footpath and the cobbled roadway. Crickets were singing.

'And who's the big fry?' Harris asked. 'Anyone?'

'Sure. I found him too. Except that he got wind of it somehow. He's run for cover. That's why I'm leaving tomorrow.' Stone beat away the moths with motions of his right arm.

'The most beautiful place on earth,' Harris said. He crossed the street away from the light. There was a brick wall, about four feet high, with trees and darkness beyond. Stone followed him over to it.

'There's almost a sheer drop from here, nearly two hundred feet, to the river. You can hear it if you listen,' Stone said.

Harris listened. From somewhere below, faintly, came the sound of water. Falling, wheeling over and over, his body through the tingling air.

'The strange thing about Greta is that I really like her,' Stone said. 'I don't know, this country makes me feel weird somehow. Like I was a kid again. Do you know she believes in fairies? She says there's one comes into the town at night and takes food if you leave it out for it.'

'It's a goblin,' Harris said.

'Don't tell me you believe it too.' Stone was grinning.

'I once knew somebody who looked a lot like you,' Harris said. 'Same height, same build. Same age. Maybe he even played the piano.' He paused, looking at Stone whose hair shone yellow with the lamp light behind it. 'He was a prisoner. I had him shot.'

'That was the war,' Stone said, after a minute or two.

'Is that all there is to it?'

Stone did not answer.

Harris pitched his tent at the southern end of the glade, rolled out his sleeping bag, unpacked his equipment, his supplies, his notebooks, his cooking utensils. He cut the grass and lucerne in front of the tent so that his little primus stove would not set the clearing alight. Then, after he had checked the mandragora and fetched a can of water from the stream, he sat down cross-legged with his back to the tent pole and watched the butterflies. With nothing to do but think, he thought of nothing. There was no need to remember Stone with his suitcase packed and his fresh-faced eagerness to take up the cause of justice, nor Otto standing in the morning sunlight and watching his two foreign visitors leave in opposite directions, a short, stubby man with one shoulder and a face red with wine and sentiment. Here there was only heat and summer and insects. Mindlessness. No future, no past. He stared, unseeing, at the butterflies and at the heat rising like fumes. Was it possible to live like this, as if the past had never been? To sit in the sun and have the reek of it evaporate from his flesh?

A thrush was singing somewhere in the wood. Harris raised his head to listen and, as he did so, he caught a movement on the far side of the glade, a brown shape, humped, bobbing over the grasses, a shadow, a crouched figure. He scrambled to his feet, staring after it and for a moment his eyes met those of something, someone, over the distance between them. Then, a twitch, a shadow flickering, a rustle of leaves. It was gone.

Harris began to run, thrusting himself, wading, through the grass towards the spot where the shape had been. With one arm raised to protect his face, he plunged into the bushes in a roar of leaves and crackling twigs, forcing his way through the undergrowth and out into the twilight of the woods. The shadow was in the distance, dancing, it seemed, down a winding path between the trunks of the trees. He set off after it, tripping and stumbling over twisted roots in the crunch of oak mast and dead twigs, his breath rasping, but his quarry was too nimble. It drew further away from him at every step. At last, he slowed to a walk, breathing hard, his ears ringing, telling himself to be careful, he did not need to get lost.

The wood was silent, cool. Above his head the leaves were dazzling green and all about him the thick, black trunks of the oak trees thrust upwards. The ground between them was clear, bare except where a shaft of sunlight had coaxed a tuft of weeds out of the soil. Nothing moved. No birds, no butterflies. His own footfall sounded huge and crashing. He stopped, listening to the silence. He was an intruder, alien. The turmoil of his memories was as great a violation of this place as his clumsy body. Leaning against the trunk of a big tree, breathing deeply, he waited for his pulse to slow. Behind his eyes his anger and his guilt jangled like iron harness in the stillness, loud and strident. He longed to dissolve himself in the cool emptiness of the wood, to move like an inhabitant of his own dream, a shadow merely, flitting among the ancient trees. Nothing, it seemed, which was not thought or driven by thought could destroy the peace of the forest, not even the dead man hanging by a rope from a branch a few yards away.

Harris stepped forward and looked up. The corpse was middle-aged, balding, cropped grey hair, a pair of gold-rimmed spectacles still on its nose before its dull, dry, bulging eyes. It wore an SS uniform, black, with three silver oak leaves on each lapel, three double-plaited silver threads on the shoulders, black leather buttons, black tie, black Sam Browne belt, black breeches and black jackboots. On the third finger of the right hand was a silver ring bearing the death's head insignia. An officer's cap lay upside down in the grass beneath its feet beside a leather suitcase. A fly, buzzing softly, circled in the stillness and settled on the blue-grey lips.

The man had been dead for two or three days, had hanged himself, Harris guessed, by standing on the upended suitcase and kicking it over, thick legs thrashing, treading air, as the branch above jerked and rustled. And held. Harris pulled the suitcase away and snapped open the brass catches. Inside was a suit of clothes, white shirt, tie, all neatly folded and packed away with a pair of brown shoes. There was also a shaving mirror, a comb and a clothes brush. In the inside pocket of the jacket Harris found a wallet with several thousand Deutschmark and papers bearing the name of Helmut Klippe. The fly buzzed slowly. The rope around the branch creaked. Harris looked up and found he was being watched.

It was a child, an adolescent, thirteen or fourteen years old. It was lean and brown, grubby, and wearing a shirt and pants of ragged, dirty canvas. Its feet were bare. In its right hand it clutched three stalks of the mandragora topped by half-ripe berries.

'Guten morgen,' Harris said. His voice boomed aloud. The child flinched and said nothing, its mouth fixed, its eyes wide. Slowly, Harris stretched out his hand. The child shrank back, clutching the Devil's Apples to its breast.

'Geben Sie mir. Ist nicht gut.' Suddenly, he remembered the word for poisonous. 'Es giftig.' He beckoned for the fruit. The child did not move. Harris reached further and it took a step backwards.

'Was ist dein Name?' he asked.

'Rauber,' said the child. 'Wer ist du?'

Harris, kneeling, dropped his gaze and stared at the ground in front of him. A single leaf from the tree above spiralled downwards and landed in his field of vision beside a tree root. Close to where it fell was a tiny ant, bronzed and shining, labouring over the twigs and fragments of dead bark in its path. Harris watched it as his own huge weariness and loss welled up inside him. When he raised his eyes again, the child was standing closer. It stared at him curiously and then, slowly, raised a finger and touched the tear which was running down his cheek.

Its hand was warm and smelled of earth and apples.

J. H. BENTLEY

Mersey Tributary

Pedestrian

He hovers outside a cakeshop on K. Road, eyes narrowed against the sun, and my problems begin in our beginning. For I had meant to avoid parochialism by giving the street name (a cloak of) anonymity, employing only the initial 'K', perhaps, initially. But, not to say alas, Karangahape Road is often referred to colloquially, in a manner of speaking, that is, as 'K. Road', anyway. I saw the approaching traffic, took, as I thought, evasive action, and tripped over the kerbstone.

C.O.D.

I have already made use of the dictionary (what splendidly mnemonic initials, by the way), although I might have done better to refer to the first secretary of Manchester's Portico Library.* For instance, 'employing' should perhaps be 'providing', or merely 'using', but there *was* a rare, compensatory glimpse of the late Sir Julius Vogel, if I wasn't dreaming, when I was 'looking up' *videlicet*. (You see the dangers of parochialism?)

John Lennon and the Old Joanna

Outside a cakeshop, then, and the darker-skinned brethren, Polynesians, perhaps (and no money from me on the proposition that they weren't Melanesians, even at one hundred and thirty against, say, or Micronesians, though I might take five to one, there, with an atlas brought into the affair), browner skin that me, certainly, gazing, *per contra* in this as in other matters, into the adjoint fish shop window. Another problem here, *per contra* coming up from the wells of inspiration accompanied by *per cuncta saecula*, the last remembered

---

*Peter Mark ROGET. Here I make my first Manchester/Liverpool connection, for the Portico's constitution owed much to Liverpool's 'Lyceum', although architecturally the temple of Pallas Athene at Priene is the chief creditor.

shred of a Latin hymn learned, what was it, over thirty years ago, at Old Hall Lane, and if the then J.W.L. played football too there's a distinct possibility that during the season, what, September to May, when we played against Quarry Bank . . . I'll enquire about that, have after deliberation left a question-mark on my notes to that purpose, and will in addition ask the little girl to give the right notes from the old joanna, though some might consider both exercises, at least, supererogatory.

? There.

Glaze Gloss

Pearl Fisheries. That had musical connotations, too, he realised. Now window-gazing with glazed eyes and the fish too glazed of aspect, if not in aspic. (Double-glazed windows then, at least metaph. if not lit.) A festival for the eyes was offered, a harvest from the sea, and each, whole creamfish, mullet, trevally, flounder, snapper, bearing its tale. The snapper (a stronger spirit might admit the variation 'schnapper'?), the snapper to be had also in steak form, as were hapuku and kingfish. Long pieces, fillets, he thought, on trays, of trevally, gurnard, and lemonfish. 'Catnip' in bowls, small pieces for the cat, he surmised. Now, as you may have surmised, gazing into that same fishmonger's window at, you may have surmised too, well, certainly not bowls of the scented leaves or purple-spotted white flowers of the catmint plant. Bowls of smoked mussels, though.

Equine Amity

He still remembers, can actually write down, as I, now, six of the ten piscatorial varieties, when in the friendly, neighbourhood Totalisator Agency Board building.

(J.W.L., by the way, was born on the ninth of October, 1940; christened, perhaps, named certainly John Winston, then. Winston for the hero of Their Finest Hour, I wonder.)

Recording his ichthyological *aide-mémoire* on the paper provided, one imagines, for betting transactions ('One imagines'! He knows full well.), and headed PLEASE CHECK FOR SCRATCHINGS BEFORE ENTERING YOUR BETS, viz., 'Whole: creamfish, mullet, trevally, flounder, snapper, smoked mussels'.

Adding, for verisimilitude if not out of habit,
'John Winston, Future Legend, Beat All, Tribute' (race-horse names,
you have guessed), as the fancy took him. Check, if you will, that
these horses were indeed scheduled to race on the tenth of December,
at T_____, (T.A.B. code number: 8). Though it
will take some sifting of the archives to get the dusty answer to that
one.
Was he tempted to 'bet on' any of these horses?
Yes.
Which?
The one represented by the word 'Tribute' — scheduled to 'run',
gallop, canter, or, better still from the investors' point of viewing the
matter, pace or trot from barrier position number seven in the eighth
race 'on the day's card'.
How much money was advanced?
To what extent was 'tribute' paid? One dollar, Queen Elizabeth to
the fore, was advanced on the tacit proposition that the horse and
accompanying sulky, driver, and other accoutrements would be
'placed' first, second, or third in the race.
Equine amity?
Her majesty, a well-known admirer of horse flesh, passed from hand
to hand with her accustomed equanimity.

Bone Idyll

The cakeshop, too, was a temptation. Two iced buns were purchased
here, purchased, and the soft pith containing a rare raisin or sliver of
candied peel soon consumed in, of all places, you might have said, the
cemetery. His back pressed against the warm tombstone, under the
oak trees' mobile shade, leaves green on this side of the summer
solstice and affected noticeably by the (stiff) breeze. Verdant crabgrass,
the iced buns (pink, sugary icing), the nearest gravestone 'In Loving
Memory of dear sister Ethel who died Nov. 15 1885 aged 5 years'.
Iron-railed through two world wars, he wonders, remembering war-
time, 1940 certainly, collection of aluminium saucepans for Spitfires.
A wheelbarrow, too, under the trees, containing grass, weeds, the
detritus that gathers — empty bottles, for instance, among the tomb-
stones' drunken disorder. Wooden or metal, the wheelbarrow, a spade
too, and a transistor to, he decides, wile away the time. The paper bag
for the iced buns is crushed and thrown on to a heap of branches and

weeds. That's where the wheelbarrow load of dead stalks, dried reeds, tussocks, and debris will be going? Order, if not symmetry, cemetery-wise.*

Moving Words

Do you see that I have 'got going'? I 'had my work cut out' initially but now things are moving like the white cumulo-nimbus clouds scudding across their summer sea. At this rate you might anticipate sex (rearing its ugly head) at some page in the near future, throbbing pen(is)es, say, then she undid her dress, perhaps, cruelty and greed kept Carol to a life she hated, that manner of thing. Make do with

John and Yoko at the Heartbreak Hotel

I J. and his inamorata lived and loved quietly in a secluded suite of the remote Heartbreak Hotel/lithe limbs and warm with the softly radiant glow on their fullness

II Despite (or because of) his bookishness, J. had a peripatetic nature/ the rich bloom of drowsy flesh, the heavy eyelids, the lusty heedless love in the still afternoon

III On the other hand, Y. was widely acclaimed for her improvisations on historical instruments/her fulgent eyes, strong limbs, the faint blush suffusing her cheeks

IV Invocations to native deities were her speciality/her avid and thrusting mouth, soft down brushing lightly against his own skin, his stomach muscles flattening and contracting.

A sacrilege for those who knew him? The alternative being to pay tribute (again) to a hundred or so million dollars' worth of real estate? Is that the choice?

Please hand this slip to the seller Please check your tickets

I crush the slip into a ball as I earlier, through my *Doppelgänger*, crushed the paper bag (sticky inside from the icing), used and to most intents and certainly to the original purpose now useless. A breather

---

*Order, at a price. The mina-birds, and their see-saw song, have been omitted for want of an adequate description. And the opening sentence originally read, 'His next goal was the Bon Accord cake shop.' The parochialism has gone, but so has the pun.

here. A stock taking PRIOR TO CLEARANCE SALE. EVERYTHING MUST GO. Leaseholder losing patience.

Dwellers All in Play for Time

'What's big, warm, & friendly and full of great ideas?' The question is (in)scribed on a bookmark supplied free, gratis, and unsolicited by the menials of the public librarian, and full justice done to the ampersand — derived, as I should like to demonstrate to you, from 'Et', as perhaps,

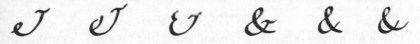

noting how it becomes, gradually, more 'laid back'. Something of the such which, as my father might have said.

Time Wasting in Fact

The answer to the question is supplied on the verso — 'Right! Your library!' Were you right? I find also written on this bookmark two phrases, one from a magazine, 'a pregnant lady, carrying all before her', and, from a novelist's final work, 'the checker was a chubby little thing'. Perhaps you too will appreciate these pleasantries (I am a little concerned that they might not have travelled well), and will find no less pleasant 'All irrelevances here are genuine irrelevances', a guarantee I intended to sooner or later place in front of you, with or without split infinitive.

I Know what (Word) You're up to

and you're no doubt raring to go on, as indeed I am, anxious to lug the guts into the neighbour room, to dismiss quickly, to subsume with despatch under the heading 'present influences' the sounds, of a bus changing gear, of the electric sewing machine sorority, of an explanation *in re* of the Carter–Reagan inter-regnum, and of the little girl now entering,
'Mummy, we have to do folk-dancing in front of sixty people,' recorded as I switch attention or have attention drawn from one to another,

' . . . back with Patel to start a new over . . .'
and a susurrus, too, as of the rustle of leaves in a breeze, with
'That sounds like my . . .'
voiced of the now girl playing in the courtyard or drying-ground
which serves the flats,
(The gold medal of the Institute of Architects of _____ for 1936
was awarded for the design of this building)
her long hair, blonde, flowing in the wind, it *is* leaves rustling, and a
dog whimpering, earlier over-looked, now almost over-heard.

Describe an Arc

Playing with three other children and a dog (the two bicycles propped
against each other) a game involving a child gripping one end of a rope
and swinging the rope through an arc of about one hundred and
twenty degrees at a level foot above the ground. What a difficult feat
this appears, in retrospect! The dog drifts away, the children try to
jump the moving rope — an unsuccessful attempt seems to lay one
under the obligation of a turn at rope-swinging. Their screams and
shouts are more easily recalled. The blonde girl is ten or eleven. Of
the others one, a girl, is perhaps the same age, and the other two
children, of one sex or the other, are younger. They are all at the far
end of the courtyard which, incidentally, holds three circular drying
lines. Should the courtyard be called a drying-ground? At this distance
it is hard to see their 'features' clearly; are they (the two smaller, perhaps younger, children), Polynesian (Melanesian, Micronesian) or
Asian? Certainly these children have browner skins, and at this stage
of relationships — her first week in this 'block' of flats — they are
calling the blonde child 'girl'.

The wind is getting up now.

The children played until about six-thirty, the clock face at 'Arms
downward place!'

And all inadvertences here are genuine too. Had you noticed that the
'point of view' changed, after a short struggle, from 'third person'
back to the original 'first person'?

A breeze blowing at Perth, too.

Followed by our sporting roundup. You can imagine what happened
with 'Tribute', can you? Though 'John Winston' and 'Beat All' and
'Future Legend' performed profitably.

He was shot by then, by the six p.m. time signal in fact, and the radio station playing 'Imagine all the people, living in the world'. A brief extract.

Acronychal Chronicle

'What a lot of class he's got, that guy.'
'Incredible charisma.'
'He's quite sensitive, too.'
Whose praises are being sung here? Not J.W.L.? That would require a past tense?
'Where's the can around here?'
Can! They're Americans!
'The kitchen's an absolute disaster.'
(What hotel was it? The 'Algonquin'?)

I meant to say how he might have enjoyed (seeing) the children together, 'every creed and race/gathered here before Thy face', but the voices from above (see above) and the radio still unstilled . . . 'troops defeated in Chad . . . Soviet trawler factory intercepted . . .', and the girl writing 'Hello, how are you? How come you always write stories with no meaning?' and the radio . . . 'brief appearance of Chairman Mao's widow. . . . shot five times outside his home in New York . . .', too much intruded.

(Can you trust this specious explanation? Here's the music I half-pie promised, by the way:

per cuncta saecul — a   )

Lunatic Fringe

Out of doors the moon shining silent, clouded, in its tarred sky. No signs of his death in the concrete canyons, and more in the empyrean or at the Empire, Now Showing *Malibu Beach*, Forthcoming Attraction *Bedside Dentist*, to meet the eye, that in the emporia, Friendly, Fair, and Courteous Advice and Frost-Free Fridge-Freezers notwith-standing. An off-shore wind brings the wail of a departing ship from the estuary to K. Rd, where this window refrigerated for our customers' convenience keeps the smell and taste of the sea. Trevally and mullet to clear, flounder now five for a dollar, the packet's plastic, the price elastic, and here we are, in St Kevin's Arcade, the *Star* with 'How Killer Stalked Lennon'.

(Threw his spanner in the works of God
And struck a spark.)

As far gone* as the Lovin' Spoonful, Pastrami Malted, the androgyne quaternities' deep elation (trance outlandish) echoing Mersey-less with music only in the clatter of their clogs, the old chimeras traded in, we're going to get along without them now, the Liverpool *Echo* a few pages tossed up near the Royal Liver Building, 'City Agonises' floating by the Perch Rock lighthouse.

(But that was in another country.)

Here, a motorcycle leaves behind its angry exclamation mark to the loving coupling's brief sentence.

(And, besides, the wrench.)

He's dead.

*Although the Bon Accord Cake shop (remember Arbroath 32 Bon Accord 0?) became the Penny Lane Bake Shop. So Life nods to Artifice.

JENNIFER COMPTON

An Unusual Spiritual Experience

I don't get a chance at the morning paper very often where I live (or keep a mirror, the dresser windows have to do for vanities). One Saturday morning Rosie brought it down for me to read (or start the coal range) from the big house on the hill above us where she works of a morning or whenever they need her. She was off up country now to visit her family for the day — and a very beautiful day it was too, being mild, still and bright but with that ever shifting strength of light that can make all the familiar objects in the valley become new and strange in a moment.

She walked around the little dark house we share packing up a pot of the new gooseberry jam, picking silverbeet from our garden, and I tried to tell her the thought that had come to me as I was biking back from town the day before, Friday, about Bob Dylan's imagery. I take that man very seriously and we now had his new album, *Desire*, to play loud as we wanted lacking complaining neighbours. Well, lacking any neighbours at all really. She stopped as she walked past me (pushing the magpie aside with one foot because she will talk over the top of us and never listens) and I waved my hands but bicycle thoughts are often hard to recover and all I could say was that I had had a perception and that if I listened to the song again I was sure I could grasp it but that I couldn't even remember which song it was — her grey eyes looking at me because she takes me seriously — and that I might have to wait until I was on the bicycle again with my legs going round and round but that I couldn't guarantee it.

After she had gone off up the track (the magpie flying in front of her as far as the gate) in her car with leather seats and the doors that open towards you instead of the way they do now, I sat on the back step, with the cool house open against my back and the bright sun on my feet, reading the paper. Headlines, weather report and horoscopes. Mine said — 'you will have an unusual spiritual experience.' Well, that's a lot of people having unusual spiritual experiences. One twelfth of the world? In New Zealand alone — well! But because things had been coming and going on me and not just Bob, because a paper was a rare thing and this one had arrived by chance and for a purpose, I thought — 'I'll keep an eye open for that one and an ear too.' For I am prone to the experiences spirituelle, hear voices, etc., which is one of the reasons I live down here in this valley in case it was the neighbours. It wasn't.

I sat on the back doorstep for a long time. Watching and waiting for the voices in the head, the frogs crawling up out of the grass with a word for me.

'But if it is to be an unusual experience I won't know what it is — what it is going to be. It won't have happened before. I don't know what to look for. The signs.'

I closed the back door. So nothing could creep up on me.

Did some weeding. Not too much. I don't like killing plants.

I went down to the river and had a look at it. It was pretty much the same.

Came back, made a cup of tea. Felt at a loss.

'Let's hear from Bob Dylan again. I'd like to reclaim that thought.'

But before the record-player had raised its old arm to come down on *Desire* (I'd given the arm a little push so it could fall anywhere because if you don't know what you're looking for you might as well start anywhere) before the needle fell into any old groove I needed to know the time. And why live down here two miles over a gravel road to the nearest bottle of milk if you can't obey yourself, so lacking a clock or a watch I went through to the common room and switched on the radio and a voice said '. . . three minutes to four . . .' and that was very satisfactory so I turned it off and Bob started singing in that moment. 'Isis'.

(As I write this in my friend's leadlight workshop I can hear a woman saying '. . . that's more turquoisy . . .' which will amuse you later on if you stick with me.)

I listened to Bob, drank tea and it was satisfactory but not revealing. 'Nothing was revealed.' As the man said.

So the sun went elsewhere, our free and friendly magpie came down out of the sky for me to turn stones over for her (woodlice, spiders, worms) and then went up to roost in the eaves, and Rosie came home. I could hear her car coming down the track across the fields as I put the frypan on the coal range. We ate dinner, put the dishes together on the cheap tin tray for later, stoked the coal range. Then, as we settled into the night, as the night settled in —

'A strange thing happened today,' said Rosie.

I said nothing, started listening. What I had been waiting for all day could belong to Rosie and that would be fine by me.

'I started singing "I was thinking about turquoise, I was thinking about gold" — from that song "Isis" — and Mum turned round to me and said "Why did you sing that?" She'd seen a programme about Aztecs last night . . .'

'Turquoise and gold!' I said.

'. . . about Aztecs last night on telly and she was thinking about their ornaments, turquoise and gold, and I went and sang it.'

'What time was that?' I asked her.

'Funny thing, I don't usually want to know the time when I'm at home but I suddenly did so I went through to the kitchen and it was just before four.'

'Three minutes to four?' I said.

'About that,' she agreed.

I explained it to Rosie of course and she said — 'I thought it was strange enough anyway, but this!'

And then I said — 'I've often wondered about received things, if they take time to travel as it were, but it seems that, sometimes at least, they happen all in a moment.'

'If you're talking to someone in the same room it takes a moment.'

'And thirty miles cross-country don't take no time at all.'

Next Friday we were going up to the pub in town, and while Rosie got her washing out into the late low shadowed sun I put *Desire* on and gave the arm a little push out of sheer naughtiness if you like, and perhaps it was exactly the same little push but — 'I was thinking about turquoise, I was thinking about gold.'

Rosie put her head round the bathroom door where the washing machine was doing its duty but with the odd little scream.

'Put it back.'

I was grinning like an idiot, didn't know what she meant.

'Put the needle back a bit and see what comes before.'

Rosie is very clever in her own way. Because when I obeyed her and slipped the needle back — 'I said where we're going? He said we'll be back by about four.'

I looked into Rosie's serious grey eyes and beyond. And she looked into my eyes whatever they look like, for we don't have a mirror down here in our valley except the dresser windows which show us only the silhouette of our vanity, and she looked into my eyes whatever they look like.

And Bob sang, 'I said that's the best news that I've ever heard.'

So Bob, wherever you are, we can hear you. You're getting to us.

But that's not the end of turquoise and gold, because towards the end of that summer Rosie went to live on the other side of town. It still seems strange to me that we parted, but it became inevitable and it wasn't like us, Rosie and me, having that quarrel, it was a scene from a play that had been written a long time ago. Somehow as the words and actions unrolled I looked into her eyes and beyond and she seemed to be standing apart and gazing at me with great regret.

I drank cider in the sun with the record-player up loud enough to hear from the bottom of the garden, and to shake the dust from the little dark house I lived in, loud enough to lay the old ghosts while I got used to being alone again. I drank cider in the sun at the bottom of the garden planning to paint the old house, planning to fence the vegetable garden.

A car came down the track across the fields. The local fencer come to quote me and brought the wife and kids to enjoy the late low shadowed sun. The wife had been here before, oh a long time ago when people had lived in the house before its long emptiness before I came here (and Rosie had come and gone). She had found in the river, she held out her wrist to show me how she always wore it, always had, a bracelet of turquoise and silver. I told Rosie about that when I went up to collect the horse to graze my overgrowth from the big house where Rosie still worked of a morning or whenever they needed her. I met her in the courtyard with the warm horse's body between us. I showed her the place under the horse's delicate ear where the bridle had been rubbing and told her about the bracelet of turquoise and silver found in the river twenty years before.

It grew colder and I moved back into the house. And where Rosie was living was even colder for my little valley is strangely mild, doesn't seem to get the frosts and the wind blows right over the top of me. I lent her a blanket. She said it was just enough and now she was quite comfortable. I painted the cheap tin tray. I had a pyramid of tins of paint given me by people who didn't have the time to watch them separating in a corner of the garage into amber oil and a skin like elephant ears just under the lid. I seemed to remember there had been a turquoisy blue and a small tin of silver. But no — it was turquoise and gold. I painted the cheap tin tray, left it to dry while I went with buckets to see if the pine plantation had fruited again. And the magpie came down from her winter home on the top of the tool room door and I met her at the back door talking at the top of her voice, gold oozing between her toes and behind her a fussy circle of bird's feet.

She died soon after that while I was away for the day. She died of anger, flew up to the big house to Rosie with string on her feet as if some kids had tried to trap this free thing and she died of anger without a mark on her.

That night I dreamed she died in my hands because a woman living in a bright blue house refused to take her in.

(As I am listening to *Desire*, to the song 'Isis' that is the instigator of this farrago, I find that it might not be finished with even yet for the lines before the lines before are — 'I gave him a blanket, he gave me his word.')

Rosie still has my blanket — though it is summer again.

I'm still planning to paint this old house.

And it isn't finished with even yet because this story has just made a return journey from a magazine with this note attached.

'One thing that gets to me about Spiritual Experience — which I couldn't help but be impressed by particularly as I was listening to, you guessed it, *Desire*, at the moment I first picked it up — I think he sings — "We'll be back by the fourth", damn it!'

The argument hasn't even begun.

The beat goes on.

MICHAEL MORRISSEY

Beethoven's Ears

When Ludwig van Beethoven died on March 26th 1827, his ears were amputated by the eminent anatomist Dr Joseph Wagner and placed in a jar filled with spirits of wine. Beethoven had slowly been going deaf since 1801 and Wagner wanted to examine his ears and try to ascertain the cause. In his autopsy report, Wagner noted that 'the external ear was large and irregularly formed, the scaphid fossa, but more especially the concha, was very spacious and half as large again as usual'. He also noted that the great composer's liver had shrunk to half normal size and was of a 'leathery consistency beset with knots the size of a bean'; the spleen was double normal size and the excretory duct of the pancreas 'as wide as a goose quill'; the stomach was 'distended', and the body 'much emaciated'. In short, Beethoven was a mess.

However, on examining the brain, Wagner found its convolutions to be 'remarkably white' and 'very much deeper, wider and more numerous than ordinary'.

But to return to the ears. They sat in the spirits of wine filled jar for several weeks, but before Wagner could complete the examination, the jar mysteriously disappeared. No one is quite sure what happened to the jar, but it is thought to have been illegally sold by Wagner's servant to an English doctor and smuggled across the English channel into the sceptred isle. Having been fruitlessly examined by the English doctor (the syphilitic cause of Beethoven's deafness then being unrecognised) the ears were returned to the jar and placed on display in his living room for the curious scrutiny of dinner guests. In 1843 an urchin chimney sweep stole the jar and sold it to a pawnbroker who eventually persuaded a baronet from Kent that they were indeed Beethoven's ears.

When Phineas T. Barnum made his triumphal tour of Great Britain with Tom Thumb and the mother-daughter team who had won American hearts by playing Topsy and Little Eva in Uncle Tom's cabin, the baronet offered the colourful American entrepreneur the ears for ten guineas. Barnum accepted the offer. So Beethoven's ears joined the Feejee Mermaid, Chang and Eng (the famous Siamese twins), Lionel the Lion Faced Man and General Tom Thumb, the world's most famous dwarf. When the general lifted one of the ears from the murky preserving fluid and placed it over one of his own diminutive organs and pretended to hear messages from beyond the grave both of the Fat Ladies would invariably shriek — to a duo of thigh-slapping delight from the Siamese twins.

The ears subsequently went underground (as it were) and were not seen or heard of again until the World Fair in St Louis of 1904. Soon after they fell into the hands of the Great Tosca, a turn of the century hypnotist and mountebank, who claimed that 'the ears of the great German composer Beethoven had peculiar psychic properties'. They could, said the Great Tosca, hear a person's innermost thoughts. Tosca, a tall bearded man weighing eighteen stone, would stand blind-fold on stage with the jar balanced delicately on his head, and reveal the embarrassingly private thoughts of his largely female audience. He would tell people what they had in their handbags, where they had been in the previous week, and what they had eaten for supper. These spectacular feats would produce thunderous applause and Tosca's assistant, a French girl from Marseilles, swears that on good nights 'the ears would undulate ever so slightly' in appreciation of this crude symphony of hand clapping.

But now the fate of Beethoven's ears takes a forked path. According to the European theory, the ears were sold to an eccentric, an unsuccessful composer called Erasmus Windhover. Windhover was the creator of several leadenly dull choral works and a large body of chamber music that had never been performed (though he would often hum these opuses aloud for the benefit of Beethoven's ears).

Six months later, Gustav Mahler received a visitor claiming to have in his possession the Tenth Symphony of Beethoven and would he care to conduct it? Mahler was sceptical but accepted the score and studied it closely. An hour later Mahler called Windhover back into his study. He said it was always a pleasure to meet a representative of the nation that had produced Purcell and Elgar. Then Mahler coughed and said that though the work did indeed appear to be in the style of Beethoven, the third movement was almost identical to the third movement of the *Eroica* and the concluding movement was very similar to the concluding movement of the Seventh. In short, the Tenth Symphony of Beethoven was a fake. Enraged, Windhover swore that he knew the symphony to be 'a true and original work of Beethoven', for had he not taken down every note, line by line under the dictation of the great composer himself? It was typical of Mahler, an Austrian, to be jealous of Beethoven a German, etc., etc. Mahler bowed and said curtly, 'Goodday to you, Herr Windbreaker.'

Undeterred by Mahler's scepticism, Windhover returned to his pastoral retreat near Salisbury Plain, where he composed an eleventh Beethovenic symphony. Out-Mahlering Mahler, he called it the Symphony of the Ten Thousand. It called for two thousand musicians (502 first violins, 502 second violins, 240 violas, 240 celloes, 200 basses, 80 flutes, 80 oboes, 20 clarinets in E flat, 60 clarinets in B flat, 5 bass clarinets in B flat, 8 bassoons, 4 double bassoons, 27 horns, 10 trombones, 5 bass tubas, 6 harps, 3 celesta, 3 sets of tympani, 3 cymbals, 3 tambourines) and eight thousand singers. The local parish priest was 'deeply impressed' by Windhover's dedication to the craft of choral and orchestral music but inquired politely of Windhover how it was they could accommodate so many visitors in their village of three hundred? 'The Lord will provide,' Windhover replied. But the Lord, it seemed, was intent on turning a deaf ear to this posthumous masterpiece of Beethoven. When Windhover met with no interest in London musical circles, it is said he went to the famous circle of stones at Stonehenge and buried the ears under the largest stone. Some now claim that Beethoven's ears transformed Stonehenge into a gigantic listening device. Others maintain that the famous black magician Aleister Crowley dug them up and hung them around his neck, deriving much of his horrible powers from having them so close to his villainous heart. It was rumoured that The Great Beast nailed the ears above a table near the door of of his infamous Black Magick restaurant, where strong men were weeping into their daemonically hot curries. The ears, Crowley said, greatly enjoyed the peculiar atmosphere of sexual decadence and diabolic incantation, as well as the sound of strong men weeping. When Crowley died, the ears were cremated and co-mingled with his ashes and placed in an urn on top of the Rock of Cefalu, where they remain to this day.

The alternative or 'Colonial' theory is that the ears passed from the Barnum show to a theosophist, who gave them to Annie Besant. When Besant visited New Zealand in the nineteenth century, she bestowed them upon the local branch of the Order of the Golden Dawn. After the First World War, they appeared once more on the shelf of a Mrs Eleanor Spencer, a Dunedin music teacher, who said 'they could always detect false notes'. It is said that they are in the possession of the most musical of Mrs Spencer's eighty-seven grandchildren, but, according to another account, they re-entered show business . . .

In 1905 the Fuller Brothers toured with Cleopatra, 'a fearless snake charmer'. Cleopatra, who caused 'strong men to experience a strange shuddering thrill' and women to 'shriek in horror' at her skilled handling of boa constrictors, anacondas and black snakes, swore that Beethoven's ears kept her from being bitten. When Cleopatra was approached to donate Beethoven's ears to a time capsule, she agreed, even though parting with them was going to put her life in jeopardy. Where the time capsule is buried, no one knows, but it was rumoured to be secured under the Largest Wooden Building in the World. It is feared that, should the time capsule be excavated it will be as corroded by water as the time capsule retrieved from a well beneath the former District Court in Auckland.

There is even a post-Colonial theory concerning Beethoven's ears (especially espoused at the University of Auckland). According to its exponents, Beethoven's ears never existed or if they existed 'we as ex-Colonials have no need of them. We don't need European ears anymore; we have our own.'

It is uncertain, perhaps, whether Beethoven's ears still lie beneath Stonehenge or with Aleister Crowley's ashes or with one of Mrs Spencer's musical grandchildren or buried in a Wellington time capsule. It is certain, probably, that the ears will be in some way listening to human endeavour through all eternity and that many of us will believe — and who can do otherwise? — that throughout the aeons to pass they will listen to the sounds of new civilisations as well as their collapse, which will be heard by those ever alert organs as a strange, exciting but somehow orderly music.

APIRANA TAYLOR

Hera

Hera sat on top of Pukenui and watched the sun go down. From the hill's summit she saw the empty settlement of Puketapu. Hera was the last living person in the valley. A year ago the Manuwaka family lived in Puketapu but they moved to Wellington — looking for work.

The Waikino River flowed between Puketapu and Hera's house. In 1910 the river ran close to the village. It was now 1978 and over the years the river's course changed so that each year the river flowed closer to her home.

Almost on the river bank was the grave of her long dead husband. She was sixteen when her grandfather arranged for her to marry John Waimana who was forty-two. He was a strong silent moody man. Hera loved him. In this wild lonely country there were few people to love.

For fifteen years they lived together and worked raising a family. Each year Hera became pregnant. Some of the children lived, some didn't.

When she had eleven children and was pregnant for the fifteenth time John died. The Waikino got him. In the middle of winter he made a mistake at a time and place when lessons learnt from mistakes made were cruel. He tried to cross the flooded river on horseback. They found his body two days later. The river had taken his life and left his body mangled and twisted in the branches of a tree.

Behind the house was a small vegetable garden and at the side was a rose garden. In the curled wind it was a swirl of colour. Blue, violet, yellow, green, red. A plot of domestic beauty in the wilderness.

The hill, Pukenui, sat like a giant overlooking the house. Behind Pukenui, steep slopes slanted into mountains that made the hill look like a small child.

Hera thought of the mountains and hills as living beings. Just as she thought of the river as alive and having a spirit. Her grandfather, Te Kapua, had taught her all the old myths and legends about the river maiden and how in days of the old mountains were giants who fought each other for the right to sleep next to the river maid.

The house was a small building with two bedrooms and one large room in which there stood an old wood-burning stove. Hera's bedroom overlooked the river but she no longer slept in her bed. She preferred to wrap herself in a blanket and sit on the clay floor next to the stove. There she sat for hours before falling asleep. She often wove flax mats and kits, singing to herself as she worked.

She spoke English but Maori was her mother tongue and she preferred to use it. Sometimes she read the Maori version of the Bible. She felt what was not written, for she saw in the unwritten words something she already knew. We are part of all living things she decided, thinking of the river maid and mountain giants.

When the light from the kerosene lamp was not strong enough to read by she would close the Bible, put more wood on the stove, and stare into the fire as she fell into a light sleep.

Hera breathed deeply. She looked down to the foot of the hill. She saw her garden wedged between Pukenui and the house. All my life I have lived here. My husband was a strong man. We built our house at the foot of this hill a long way from the Waikino River.

There were a lot of people in Puketapu then. She counted. The Manuwakas, Chief Morehu, the Kereopas, Taipanas, Kamaus, the Irishman, the minister and his family and the Kellys. Lots of people over fifty.

I have lived here all my life. John and I had a garden big as a field. We had corn, kumara, potatoes, pumpkin, kamokamo, plenty of food. A big family, no money, but always plenty of food. And now my husband has been dead for many years and nobody lives here.

Everybody has gone. All my family lives in Wellington. Each year the river flows closer to my house. The garden, once big as a field, is now just a small patch beside my home and I am sixty-nine years old. Growing old is when your life gets smaller and you can't do anything about it. She looked at her garden.

Each year my children come home for Christmas saying to me: You're too old to live here, come back to Wellington with us. Always I say: Yes, next year I'll come to Wellington. I've been to Wellington; I don't like that place. In Wellington they build houses with the toilet right next to the kitchen. That's not clean. Here my toilet is out in the bush, an outside toilet a long way from the house, where it should be.

Why should I go to Wellington? This is where I live. If I go to Wellington and stop living the way I have that will be like dying before I'm dead. Nobody should die twice in one lifetime. She looked at the garden again. The little I can do gets harder to do each day. But I carry on and will carry on till I stop.

From beneath her jersey she pulled a sack which she spread on the ground. She withdrew two barbed hooks from the sack. One hook was made of whalebone, the other she had bought when she went to Wellington. At the bottom of the sack was a torch and a ball of string. In the old lady's breast pocket were six batteries. In a sheath strapped to her thigh was a butcher knife.

She held the whalebone hook in her hand and looked at it. Te Kapua gave me this hook before he died. What a man he was! They say when he was a young warrior he ate people. He was a chief and if he didn't like you he killed you and ate you. He didn't say the rumours about him were true but neither did he say they were untrue. If people asked him did you eat anybody, he just laughed, smiled and showed a set of strong white teeth.

He was a tohunga, a chief with great power. He chased missionaries away from here, saying we didn't need them. Then when he saw missionaries trying to stop his people from drinking whisky like the whalers he welcomed the missionaries as friends. He did not like his people to drink.

Te Kapua knew all about the land — hunting, eeling, fishing — and the Gods. The missionaries said there was one God. Te Kapua said: Yes that's right. Does it matter what I call them?

He brought me up. He taught me all I knew. Before he died at the age of a hundred and two, he gave me this hook saying: I have made this hook for you. My mana has gone into its making.

She knew the hook was not magic, but because Te Kapua made it she valued the hook and regarded it as a link between her and her ancestor. Te Kapua taught me to recite a thousand years of tribal history without making a mistake. More than that he taught me how to live.

She sat cross-legged on top of Pukenui. As the sun went down the moon turned red. Then the sun was gone and the moon was yellow. Again she looked at Puketapu, the Waikino, John's grave and the little garden.

I'm wasting time. As I grow older I waste more time, though I have less of it to waste. She put both hooks in the sack, then stood frowning. I'd best be going now.

The moonlight cast long, thin shadows. In the dark hills in the forest, so thick the ground beneath it had never felt the moon's rays, Ruru, the morepork called. Morepork, morepork.

A mass of clouds loomed on the horizon. Hera made her way down Pukenui heading towards the hill country and bush. She made for the creek that came down from bush-clad hills and eel-like flowed across the lowlands before joining the Waikino River. The moon made it easy for her to see. She walked quickly. Almost with the step of a twenty-year-old.

When she reached the creek she crossed it and kept heading into the hills. Bright moonlight is no good for me tonight. I will not waste time looking in the creek here. It rained last night and this morning. There are clouds on the horizon. If I'm lucky the clouds will cover the moon and perhaps bring a little rain. Before the clouds hide the moon I'll make my way to the creek. If the clouds come. I want a dark night with no moonlight. Eels like dark nights and a little rain. Tonight the air is warm and heavy. If it gets darker many eels will come out from their holes under the banks.

Te Kapua taught me about eeling. Don't be greedy. Never kill more than what you need to eat, except maybe people. To live you must live with what you live on. We are part of all living things. Therefore, if you see a small eel, don't kill it; leave it. If you kill all the small eels in the creek, there will be no big eels. Then what will you eat, how will you live? Do you understand, e Hine? She nodded yes, but in her youth she did not understand. Now she was sixty-nine.

This part of the bush brings back old memories. Many years ago I had my first child. I remember the time. I was working with my husband in the field. John, I called. He looked at me. Not here girl, we grow our food here, he said. Leave this place you are unclean.

I was only sixteen and with my child trying to get out of me, I walked all the way into the bush. It was here somewhere I had my first son. Cousin Mary was with me. We stayed here for two days. My husband brought me food but he would not come too close to me because I'd just had a child. I was unclean.

When I brought my son back I was not a girl of sixteen. I was a woman. I was equal to Te Kapua and all his wisdom, equal to my husband and all his strength. I'd done what they could never do. I was not dirty or unclean. It was painful. I don't care what anybody says: I was proud to have a baby.

I had fifteen years of being pregnant, as I worked in the field or hunted when I could. In all those years there was never one of me. There were always two, me and the baby in my belly. I liked my life then, though I got tired sometimes.

The clouds hardly moved across the sky. The moon spread pale light across the land. Once, gangs of scrub-cutters worked here. Clearing the land, cutting down the trees on the forest edge. Then they left. The land was too rough, too wild for farming.

She kept making her way towards the track. Small clumps of manuka grew on either side of her. She entered a wide belt of manuka trees. She found the track. A black tunnel cutting through the bush winding up into the hills and mountains. Now she was surrounded by manuka. They grew thick on either side of her; above her head their branches joined together. It was dark. Fingers of moonlight could not pull back the leaves and reach through to the forest floor.

She made her way upwards. How dark it is. I won't use my torch though. The batteries are weak. I must save them till I need them. I've been here during the day but at night the bush is different. It feels as though there is something in the bush, something unseen that awakens only at night.

Morepork, morepork, screeched Ruru as he flew up into the sky. There was a rustle in the undergrowth. Ah, I should not think of such things or I will frighten myself.

Gradually her eyes became used to the dark. She could see a little way in front of her. For a quarter of an hour she followed the track up into the hills. How good it is to be out. She breathed deeply. The bush has a smell of its own. Earthy moist. The stench of decay, rot, water, earth — life smells. Ah, the bush makes me feel strong.

I have always taken my food from the land, the bush, rivers, creek and sea. These things give me food so long as I'm strong enough to eat it. Tonight I feel strong, but not as strong as when I was young. Tonight I will catch my eels. If the clouds cover the moon and I am lucky. I hope it will rain a little. I'm sixty-nine, but I don't feel old.

As she rounded the corner the trail became steeper and narrower. It led almost straight up a cliff-like bank. She paused, looked up. She could not see the trail's end.

On the lowlands the Waikino flowed. It cut through mountains, it bled like a vein down stark, black rock and fern bush slopes. In its belly it carried melted snow from the sacred mountain all the way to the sea. Each minute the river ran closer to her house.

For five minutes she moved slowly upwards. She leaned forward, taking as much weight off her feet as possible. Still, she could not see the end of the trail and the track was getting steeper. Her legs ached.

For a while the track was so steep it was easier for her to crawl. She used her hands to grab branches and haul herself up. She felt her strength leave. She called on her mana.

Strength oozed through her veins like fire. The track went up and up and up. The fire in her veins became cool, then cold. Unable to go any further she sat down. Her lungs demanded she breathe in chestfuls of air. It took ten minutes for her to recover. She sat on the trail.

I've been here before, but only during the day. It's hard to tell where you are at night. I don't know whether I'm at the top or whether I still have a long way to go.

She stood and kept walking. Five minutes later she sat down again. She kept climbing and resting. When she rested she found new strength, but each time she sat down her strength took longer to return and there was less of it.

Finally, she sat down and thought: Enough! Perhaps I should return home. She stood. Looked down the trail. When I was young this was easy for me, but not now. She glanced behind her. Thirty steep steps away she saw the end of the track. She turned, began to climb.

It will be a long time before the clouds hide the moon, she thought, I'll keep moving upwards through the forest. The moonlight makes it easy for me to see. Before the clouds cover the moon and it is dark I will move to the left and find the creek. Then I shall start eeling.

Before walking into the forest she reached out and grabbed the branch of a small manuka tree. She twisted and bent the branch downwards. Te Kapua said there was one God, what did it, ahh, matter what he called them. She pulled the branch down. I now understand what he meant. Here in the forest the God is Tane, King of the Jews. Ha! The branch snapped. Hera laughed. I have never worried much about Gods. I know this much: sometimes I pray for rain. Sometimes it rains, sometimes it doesn't. That's what Gods are like.

She pulled Te Kapua's whalebone hook and some string out of the sack. She tied the hook on to the manuka branch. Now I have a fine gaff she said. With Te Kapua's hook I will catch many eels.

The trees cast strange shadows. Branches became arms and twigs looked like fingers. A warm wind swept the forest floor. The trees waved their arms. The forest was alive.

This hook, she thought, has never let me down. It's as though all Te Kapua was and all he knew went into the hook. So I have his knowledge with me always. And I have my own knowledge. I hunt with my ancestor close to me. She looked at the hook. It glinted in the moonlight. I am strong as whalebone. I know many things. Few eels escape me. All I need is a strong hand and a quick eye.

Ruru spread his wings across the moon. He circled then swooped through the forest. On the creek bank a water rat sniffed the air. Clouds sailed on the night wind.

She kept walking. She looked up at the sky. The clouds are coming. I don't think I've been this far into the bush before, not for many years anyway. Perhaps now, I should make my way towards the creek. No, I won't. It will be a long time before the clouds cover the moon. I like eeling when there is no moonlight, for then many eels come out from under the banks to feed. I will keep walking deeper into the bush. But I must watch those clouds. If I get caught in the bush with no moonlight I could easily get lost. . . .

From above her head the old lady swung her gaff down at a leaf lying on the ground. The gaff cut through the air with a swishing sound. She missed the leaf. Swish, she swung the gaff again. She looked at the hook. The leaf was caught on the barb.

Ah, I'm still good with a gaff. I'll get many eels tonight. People don't know much about eels, she thought as she skirted a big tree. All I know about eels comes from sixty years trying to catch them. They can live to a very old age. They are cannibals, for I've often gutted eels and found smaller eels inside them, and like sharks they have rows of teeth.

I've been bitten by an eel. One night I was walking in the creek. There were steep banks on either side of me. I didn't want the eel to fall off the hook and into the creek. I didn't throw the gaff far enough. It landed halfway up the bank and with the eel twisting and turning, the gaff rolled back into the water. I dived on top of the eel. I felt something grip and tug my stomach. Through my jersey. Its teeth sank into my belly. There was no pain at first but the eel would not release its grip. I tried to force its jaws open. Nothing worked. Finally I had to cut the eel's head off with my knife. I saw why I couldn't get it off me. It had rows and rows of little sharp teeth that angled back. When an eel bites, it bites for good.

She looked around. Continued walking. She moved carefully for there were many branches strewn about the forest floor. Clouds hung low in the sky, halfway between the horizon and the moon. It'll rain heavily tonight. I wanted light rain to bring the eels to the surface to feed. Heavy rain is no good; that makes the water murky and I won't be able to see.

Hera found herself on a small clear hillock. Although the moonlight made it easy for her to see, there was not enough for her to see anything at a great distance. The night's darkness blended in with the yellow moon and the forest's greenery. She looked ahead searching for a trail along which she could walk. She peered across tree tops, looking for a gully or a thickening of undergrowth that could mean the presence of a stream. She listened for the sound of water.

In ten, twenty minutes, perhaps thirty, those clouds will cover the moon, she thought. I must try to reach the stream long before the moon is behind the clouds. I'm sure the creek is less than twenty minutes in that direction. She peered into the darkness. I must hurry, she thought. She moved down the hillock and was soon in the forest again. The land was flat but the ground itself was uneven. Gnarled tree roots reared up through earth twisted and curved along the forest floor. The air smelled of damp moss and decay. Broken branches lay beneath giant trees as if unevenly scattered by a giant's hand. Moonlight cast undulating shadows.

Hera wanted to move quickly, but she had to walk slowly, carefully picking her way between tree roots and branches over which she could easily trip.

Everything became black; she could see nothing. She looked up. It became light again. The moon emerged from behind a cloud. So that's how dark it will be when the others come. The cloud moved across the sky. It was only the vanguard behind which followed a large grey mass.

The old lady moved quickly now regardless of forest debris. When young she found she could move quickly through bush if she bent low and ran in a kind of loping jog. I'm too old for this now. Okay when I was young, but I can't keep this up. I hope I am close to the creek.

Darkness covered the land. She looked up. The moon emerged from behind clouds. Then disappeared, not to be seen again that night. She stopped, sat down, waited for her eyes to adjust to the darkness. After five minutes she found she could hardly see more than two yards in front of her.

The first light drop of rain hit her on the cheek. The second trickled between her sagging breasts, as she groped and grappled her way through the bush. She kept moving. Sometimes quickly, but usually with small cautious steps.

I must not sit down. I must keep moving. I know what can happen to people who sit and do nothing. Fear grows in their minds. That fear kills them. She walked a little quicker and with less caution.

Alone in the bush with no light, she lost sense of distance and time. How long have I been walking? she wondered. How far have I come? Perhaps a long way. Perhaps not. Where is the creek? As she walked her left leg got tangled in the twigs of a broken branch. She bent down and untangled her leg.

I've got three batteries in my torch and six in my pocket. Should I use my torch? No. All my batteries are weak. I've used them before. I must save the batteries. If I find the creek I'll need all the light I can get to see the eels.

Wind blew through hills. Rustled through the forest, boughs creaked. Rain fell; earth, air, sky and tree sang the sorrow of ageless sadness. The forest has many voices. They all sing the same song. It is a sad song. The call of hunter and hunted. The living and dying.

Ruru spread his wings and flew across Hera's path, flying deeper into the forest, though in the darkness she did not see him.

Rain fell, light and steady. For about a quarter of an hour she walked until she heard the sound of water falling on rocks.

Hera forced her way through a thicket of manuka and found herself standing at the foot of a small waterfall. She looked about. I don't remember ever seeing this part of the creek. Tonight I've come further than ever before. 'Tuna tuna, hara mai konei,' she sang. She shone the torch into the water and walked upstream along the creek bank.

The rain fell heavily; the torch did not penetrate deeply beneath the water's surface. It was hard to see the creek bed, though the water was not deep.

She kept moving her torch across the water. Swarms of sandflies hovered above the creek. Good. Eels like dark rainy nights. The tuna will feel safe to come to the water's surface to feed.

The ground levelled out. She shone her torch around. She was no longer completely surrounded by bush. That's one blessing. Now I won't worry about bumping into trees. I can keep my mind on eeling. The rain beat down on her face. She walked for a long time without seeing an eel.

When my husband died it rained like this. How I missed him. It was as though half of me had gone away. Two of us no longer worked in the field, hunted, fished or gathered watercress. My house seemed empty. I had no one. It was not until he was not there that I knew how much he meant to me.

Then the first year of sleeping in the big double bed all by myself. Sometimes I wished he was there to do those funny things to me that made me pregnant. More than that I missed having someone lying next to me. I didn't think I would ever feel like that because often at night when he was alive I hated him. He was dirty and rough. Sometimes I felt he wanted me for one thing. I used to watch a bull in the paddocks. He was like that.

I had fifteen babies: four died. Two were born dead and two burnt to death when the church caught fire. I spent all my time caring for my children with no husband. Slowly all my children went to Wellington. Then one morning I woke up: there was no one to cook breakfast for. No one to do anything for.

For years I have cleaned my house, worked in the garden and hunted my own food. My own this, my own that; all these years I have been alone and . . . Splish!

Hera shone her torch upstream. She saw the flick of an eel's tail. She held the gaff half-raised in the air ready to swing down and hook the eel which swam slowly towards her.

For a moment fingers of moonlight broke through the cloud and glinted on the hook. 'Eel, you are too small,' said Hera. 'I'll let you live.' The eel swam beneath the hook's barbed tooth. Hera wanted to swing at the eel, but she didn't.

You are lucky little eel that Te Kapua taught me the laws of hunting. Let the children of the land, rivers and creeks live. If you don't the land will close its heart to you and you will die.

The lay of the land began to rise. The stream flowed down in a series of small pools and waterfalls. A corner of the old lady's eye caught a glimpse of grey and silver. She swung the gaff above her head and brought it down. Splash! Missed.

Shining her torch into the water, she ran down downstream. She saw the eel race towards a small waterfall. Eye, arm and hook moved in one graceful curve. She swung, and hooked the eel under the belly. The eel wriggled and squirmed. She ran from the creek with the eel on her gaff. She ripped the hook from the belly then put the eel in her sack. The eel was about two feet long. You're big enough to eat. She walked back to the creek.

Rain fell hard as stones. Raindrops hit the creek. The once clear stream clouded over. Hera knew with weak torch light and murky water it would be difficult to see. She changed the torch batteries. The ray shone down into the water and reached the stream's bed. This is better. Still I must keep my wits about me. My eyesight is not as good as when I was a girl. Though then I didn't know what I now know about eeling. The knowledge in my head must now make up for weakness in my eyes.

She came to a steep slope. A climb of about thirty feet. The ground was slippery but she struggled upwards. Slithering and sliding she finally reached the top. Here, the creek was about thirty feet wide. It must be deep here. I can't see the creek bed. Her ears caught the sound of water falling. Not the trickle of a small waterfall, but a great roaring, rushing, plunging.

She could no longer see the opposite bank. I must be on the edge of a big pool. She shone her torch around and saw, about thirty yards in front of her, a torrent of water falling, cascading from a height of about a hundred feet. This pool is like a black lake. There will be big eels here. But unless they are in shallow water I'll not be able to hook them.

Behind her grew a gnarled old tree. She leaned against the trunk and shone her torch along the pool's edge. She saw, near the bank, a submerged log.

Morepork, morepork, called Ruru. She almost dropped the torch in fright. Spun round. The bird was perched on a branch, sitting almost on her shoulders. His saucer eyes stared unblinkingly straight at her. Hera felt her skin go cold and hot. Her flesh felt as though it were melting from her bones.

Ruru, the people of our tribe often think of you as an ill omen, the death messenger. They say if you enter someone's home and call there will be a death. But you have not come to my home; I have come to yours.

'Go away,' she spat. Ruru swooped off the branch and followed the creek downstream. 'I'd kill you if I could,' said Hera as she watched him fly away.

She shone her torch back into the pool. She moved the light back across the water to her right and then to her left. Her forehead creased in a frown. Where she'd seen a large log, there was now nothing. The log had disappeared, leaving a swirl of mud behind. She approached the water's edge, held the gaff ready to swing, and with straining eyes followed the light which she moved about the pool.

She could not see what she was looking for. A log does not disappear.

Lightning cracked across the heavens. Thunderblasts, like the belch of an ancient God, rolled deep and gutsy across the sky. Rain fell heavily hard as stones.

She shone her torch towards the middle of the pool. The eel's eyes were cold, lifeless. It swam with its mouth half open, crossing the path of the torch light. Stately as a chief, it let itself glide slowly through the water. Its head was almost as wide as Hera's body.

I've never seen such a big eel. 'He taniwha tenei,' she said. Look at it. She watched the eel swim past. She counted, one two three four five . . . six . . . seven. Still the eel's body had not completely passed through her torch beam. Eight, nine. . . . It must be so old, so big that it has not been able to return to the sea as do its kin. Ten, eleven, twelve. Eel, with Te Kapua's hook and my strength I'll catch you, old though I am. Thirteen, fourteen. The eel was so big, so long that in all this time its tail had not yet come into sight.

Hera switched the torch off. I must save my batteries. I don't think the eel will come close to the pool's edge and I don't want to wade out and get it. It looks to be at least twice as long as me. She sat thinking. There must be another way. No there is no other way.

The eel was about ten feet from the pool's edge. She took her first step into the water. Her left foot sank a little into the mud. She took another step, then another. One more step and I'll be close enough to strike. She fingered Te Kapua's hook. I'm ready, I'm ready.

The eel was motionless, looking straight at her. Hera lifted her foot and placed it on the pool's muddy bed. Her foot sank. She waited for it to settle on a firm surface. Her foot kept sinking. She heard a sucking sound. Air bubbles rose the pool's surface.

Quicksand, she thought. Her right foot started sinking. She could not move either foot. The eel turned and swam away from her. Then it circled and with its mouth half open swam towards her. She raised her gaff. She saw the eel's head about a foot away from her left leg. She swung the gaff. Te Kapua's hook bit deep.

The eel raised its head with the barb buried deep in its gaping jaw. Higher the eel raised its body out of the pool. Then it fell back, slapping the water with its tail. Crack. The gaff snapped in two. The eel disappeared in a cloud of mud.

Quicksand sucked. Hera felt herself go down. From the pool's depths the eel swam towards the shore. In darkness it swam up to Hera, passed between her legs and sent a wave rippling across the water.

Hera threw the torch on to the shore and twisted her body towards the pool's edge. In darkness her fingers found a root of the old gnarled tree. She pulled. Still she found herself sucked down. Again she pulled. A wave of water passed between her widely spaced legs. The mud gripped and dragged her down. She strained. Inch by inch she dragged herself out of the mud.

The rain beat down. She sat on the ground. It can't rain harder than this. My hook is gone. I have lost Te Kapua. There is another hook in my sack. I can't catch the eel from this side of the pool. I'll go to the other side.

She stood up. She looked at the two banks on either side of the waterfall. If I climb up there I may find a space where I can cross over and make my way to the other side. She looked down from on top of the bank into the water. The eel swam close to the surface. She looked at the eel's head, searching for Te Kapua, her lost hook. It was not there. At the bottom of this pool lies my hook. As far away and as dead as Te Kapua. Now there is just me and you, eel.

E tuna, how big and fat you are! So ugly, yet beautiful. You swim strongly and gracefully. The eel dived. Its tail broke the surface as it swam to the pool's edge. Just where Hera hoped to hook it.

She felt tired. Ah, eel how slowly you swim. You must be very old. I've caught many eels but none large as you. Nearly all the big eels I've caught were slow swimmers. Many of the large eels never tried to swim away from me. I think it was because they were so big and old that unlike small eels they were afraid of nothing. You, e tuna, are the biggest and oldest eel; so I'm betting you won't be afraid and swim away.

An old totara lay where it had fallen across the creek. It rested on both banks like a bridge. She crossed and made her way back down to the pool. From her pocket she pulled her remaining length of string and fastened it on to the second hook. She fashioned the free end of the string into a loop into which she put her right wrist. She entered the pool.

Here the bed was hard flat rock. She knew she would not sink this time. She stood waist-deep in water. Almost on top of the eel. What a monster, over twelve feet at least. She leaned over. Slipped the hook into the eel's belly. Her arm was yanked upwards as the eel leaped out of the pool and fell back into the water.

Now I have you, but I'll need both hands to hold you. She threw the torch on to the bank. Tried to reel the eel in. The eel dived. Hera was pulled forward and down. She could not free herself from the string. Down went the eel. Down went Hera beneath the water. She pulled her butcher knife from its sheath and cut the string.

Lightning flashed from Rangi the Sky God's armpits. Thunderblasts and more lightning searing across heaven. Rain drummed into the mountains. The earth giants, strong and eternal, mighty great mountains, laughed. The old lady sat next to her torch on the pool's edge.

Next to Hera was a broken branch shaped like a club. There is not much I can do now, she thought. Look at my torch; the batteries are almost dead. She switched it off and sat in darkness. I've lost both hooks. I'll go home. She shone the torch into the pool one last time. E tuna, I would like to have caught you.

Splash! She shone the torch to where the sound came from. Five feet away a water rat emerged from the pool, and sat on its hind legs sniffing the air. Hera raised the club-shaped branch. Whump! The club fell smack on the rat's head. She raised the club again. Whump, whump, whump! Squashed, flattened, the rat tried to crawl away. Whump! The rat lay dead.

I did this once when I was a girl but will it work this time. She picked up the rat and looked at it. Ah, big and fat. But blood, there must be lots of blood. She fingered the sharp edge of her knife.

She cut fifteen strips of flax from the bush. These she plaited and tied end to end until she'd made a rope. Then she shredded the end of the last length of flax. Quickly she gutted the rat and pushed the shredded flax into it and up till the flax stuck out the rat's mouth. She pulled the rat down the shredded flax to the knot which joined it to the next strip of flax. Eel, I'll try for you one last time, she thought. She made sure the rat was firmly fixed to her line. She walked across the pool and threw the rat into the water.

She shone the torch into the pool. Will the eel bite? She switched the torch off. The eel may be hungry. I wonder how long, e tuna, you have lived in this pool. It will be better for you if I kill you. There is a hook in your belly: the rest of your life will now be painful.

'Tuna tuna, hara mai konei,' she sang. 'Tuna tuna, hara mai konei.'

The eel could smell spirals of rat's blood in the water and swam up from the depths. Its jaws closed over the rat. Hera felt a twitch on her line. Then a tug. It has bitten.

'The eel bites,' called Hera. Bite deep, e tuna, she thought. She felt another hard tug. The line went taut. She ran into the pool till the line went slack. Eel, you must not know I've caught you, otherwise you may struggle. I must keep the line slack and go wherever the eel goes. I'll try to take the eel down into shallow water where I can kill it.

She stood in the pool. Water lapped around her knees. The eel moved on the end of her line. 'Come with me, e tuna.' She walked downstream and could feel the eel move down with her.

The eel chewed the rat and the shredded flax got tangled in the eel's teeth. Firmly fixed in the eel's mouth the line held better than a hook. Unlike the hook the flax brought no jagged pain. The eel didn't know it was caught, and allowed itself to be taken slowly downstream.

The eel is coming with me at last. I must go carefully. If the eel struggles in deep water I may lose it. If I can get the eel into shallow water I'll kill it with my knife.

Lightning cracked. A deep gutsy rumble erupted in the sky's belly. Rain fell harder than stones. Pelting the land, making small holes in the earth. Turning clay into mud. Filling ponds and rivers. The creek level rose. Hera felt the line tighten. She ran into the water, then kept walking downstream. Hara mai, e tuna, hara mai.

When we near shallow water perhaps the eel will struggle and try to turn upstream. I think an eel this size will feel safe only in deep water. If the eel turns there will be little I can do except hope my line doesn't break as I try to turn the eel back downstream. Both of us hold an end to the line. Who has caught who?

She made her way out of the water and walked downstream along the creek bank. The eel swam a little faster forcing Hera to increase the length of her stride. Sometimes Hera led the eel and sometimes the eel led her. She didn't notice the rain or the creek rising. She knew only herself, the water, and the eel.

Hera shone her torch and saw the eel's head almost at her feet. Its mouth was wide open. Tangled in the teeth she saw her shredded line. What a big eel! You are the biggest eel I've ever seen. You are the biggest in the world. With a grace and mana only the powerful have, the eel moved its body, slowly swished its tail and lazily rolled one wave upstream.

You and I have lived a long time. Now we both go downstream. How old are you eel? There's as much life in you as there is in me. You'll die soon, e tuna. The eel moved upwards. For a second its mouth broke the water's surface, then it dived.

She watched the eel go down. The water here is very deep. If the eel goes down too far what can I do? The line will run out. The eel will struggle, pulling the flax tight till it breaks. The eel dived deeper. The old lady almost fell into the water.

She regained balance and pulled hard, reeling the line in a little as she did so.

Again the flax rope was almost pulled from her hands as the eel dived. The line held. Hera pulled, reeling in. Pulling hard, slowly reeling hand over hand, she strained till she saw the eel's head almost at her feet.

Surging, twisting, the eel rose. Its body half out of the water, like a great snake the eel towered above Hera. Again it dived, almost yanking the line out of her hand. The eel twisted, lashed its tail through the water. With a shuddering jerk the line jarred as the eel pulled the rope to its full length. The line held.

Pulling, straining, Hera walked downstream. Strength against strength. Old against old. The eel pulled harder forcing Hera to enter the water. There she stood straining. The more she pulled, the more strength she used, the more strength she lost. It was as though her mana flowed from her along the line and into the eel. As she weakened the eel seemed to grow stronger.

Hera felt a pain as though someone had thumped her in the chest. Thump, she felt it again. The pain went away. Somehow, with line in her hands she made her way out of the water. She tied the line around the stump of a tree and sat down breathing heavily. It was a long time before she could breathe easily enough to think.

Now when I was young, life was hard but we enjoyed living sometimes. But always we struggled. The eel rose out of the water, twisted its head, and dived again. Always my husband, my children and I struggled. We wondered: will the crops grow? will the rain come? Or: I hope there is no rain tomorrow. Now, for my children, it's different. They live in Wellington. They go to the shop and buy potatoes. They don't ask, will the crops grow. They ask, will the shop be open? They don't get their food from the land. They get their food from the money in their pockets. They struggle, but their life is different from mine.

I remember once as a young girl I went fishing with Te Kapua. He said something I did not understand. I remember the words for I now know them to be true. We are like fish on the end of a line, he said. Always we struggle to live, till one day we tire and the line is reeled in. That is the end of life here.

The eel broke the water's surface. Swishing its tail, yanking the line, splashing water over the old lady. 'Soon, e tuna, soon.' I feel tired. This morning I was sixty-nine and young. Now I feel sixty-nine and old.

Hera stood up, looked at the eel. What a monster! So old and ugly. The eel opened its mouth. She untied the line from the tree trunk and rubbed her chest as she did so.

Ruru had not eaten that night. Through the rain his eye glared searching for food. Without knowing, Hera and the eel passed under the tree in which he sat. He twisted his head. His eyes followed Hera as she walked downstream.

Look how slowly the eel swims. It must be tired. A big eel like this does not often travel far. It stays in its pool growing old and fat. Perhaps the eel will turn and try to swim upstream. She rubbed her chest. I wonder what it's like down there. Can the eel see me? Perhaps, e tuna, you think you have caught me.

How far must I go before I kill you? I'd like to be at home in bed. Tomorrow I'll weed the garden. Of all the things I've grown it's the roses I love the most. They are beautiful, red and golden. All around the roses, wild things grow right where the wind and birds planted them. From these hills right across to the lowlands the country is wild except for my little rose garden. Wind and birds did not plant the roses, I did. It's such a little garden. Each year I grow older, the garden gets smaller. Soon I'll have no garden. It is true, a person does not grow older, they just get smaller. I'm too small, she smiled.

The eel tugged on the line. Hera switched the torch on. She saw the creek had narrowed. She laughed. Soon I'll be in shallow water. Eel, your creek gets smaller and smaller. Soon, e tuna, soon.

As the creek narrowed, the current flowed faster, carrying the eel with it. Hera increased her pace to keep up with the eel. Again she felt a thump in her chest and pain as though her heart was being ripped apart. Morepork, morepork, called Ruru.

Surely I've covered a lot of ground, but I'm moving down hill. I'm not out of the hills yet. I still have a long way to go, but I should be in shallow water by now. What has happened? She looked at the creek. She saw the fast current and the rising water. Swirling, rushing, the current gathered speed and strength from the rain.

How stupid I have been. The creek is flooding. How can I kill the eel now? There is no shallow water. No wonder the eel moves so quickly and I've had to move so fast with my bad chest. No wonder the eel has not tried to turn upstream. The current is too swift and too strong for it. If it could, perhaps the eel would turn. If the eel turns I must try to keep it moving downstream with the current. When my chance comes I must move quickly. But I feel tired. Again she felt the pain.

Hera looked into the creek. The eel was trying to turn. The current was too strong. On downstream went the eel. Hera followed walking fast. 'Aue, taku ngakau,' she called. My heart, my heart. E tuna, this creek is too fast for both of us.

Eventually they reached a point in the creek where the current flowed slowly for a hundred yards. Still the eel did not turn upstream. Perhaps you are tired, thought Hera. We will both rest here. She sat down. The eel remained close to the bank, almost motionless.

On the first day I was married my husband came home from the field riding his horse. All day I'd been waiting for him. When I saw him I ran out to meet him, laughing. I was happy. He smiled, then stopped. He didn't smile much, but his eyes often laughed. How strong he was. With an arm almost wide as my waist he lifted me easily, but gently. I felt my feet lifted off the ground. I hung in mid-air. His eyes twinkled. Then quickly with his big arm he raised me and sat me in front of him on the horse. My heart went whoops. Ha ha, Hera laughed at the thought. I was only a young girl. Only sixteen.

We rode home. I talked and chatted. John hardly said anything. His eyes spoke for him. Often his eyes were cold. Sometimes they burned. Sometimes they laughed. I could read his eyes. A hard day in the field, they were cold. In drought, they burned. If something was funny, his eyes laughed. Hard work, drought, jokes. He did not have to speak.

We arrived home. Put the horse out to pasture. We walked into the kitchen. He looked at me. He looked at the table. 'Kai whea taku kai e hine?' he said. On my first day married I forgot to cook tea. With a fist big as my face he hit me twice. I got two black eyes.

He never hit me again. In the field he was boss. In the house, I was boss. I told him what to do. E John, go and get more wood. Quick, I want more wood. And away he would go. But I didn't have to tell him much, nor him me. We just knew what was what. When the children came he was gentle and kind. A big man I wondered how he could be so gentle.

A year before he died, he chopped a tree. The tree fell wrong. Landed on top of him. Squashed him into the ground. For the first time I heard him scream. But it wasn't a scream. He sounded more like a bull roaring. I tried to lift the tree. I couldn't. I ran to get the horse. When I came back John had lifted the tree and pushed it aside.

He got better, but after that he was not the same. A big man suddenly withered, small and weak. His strength was gone. Then the river flooded. Don't cross the river, I said. But he was drunk. I watched the Waikino drag him from his horse. Yes, the river got John. We found him two days later. There were big pieces missing from his body. Eel bites, I think.

The eel pulled Hera's line. She looked into the water. The eel circled, turned, then dived. 'Ah tuna, you won't give up your life easily, eh? I'll not waste strength trying to pull you downstream. I'll let the current do my work.' The eel began to swim upstream against the swirling water.

Hera walked upstream. 'E tuna, soon the current will drive you back.' She looked into the creek, but could not see the eel. The line moved in front of her. Somewhere in mid-stream the eel was swimming

This is a strong eel, it should have been washed downstream by the current a long time ago.

The eel leapt almost right out of the water landing with a splash. It did not dive, but kept close to the creek's surface. Hera watched the eel move through the water.

Whirlpools sucked, arms of water pulled, waves twisted its body. Still the eel swam on. Sometimes the current held the eel in one spot, but the eel struggled onwards.

'If this keeps up, e tuna, you'll swim right back to your pool,' said Hera. She pulled the line. The eel kept swimming. She pulled with all her strength. The eel surged ahead dragging Hera with it, upstream against the current.

It was as if her life ran along the line into the eel. The eel found new strength.

Thump. The pain in her chest grew. Thump. Thump thump. The pain subsided. Aue, the eel will swim back to its pool, back to safety. She pulled the line. The eel kept swimming. 'E tuna, how hard you fight. You deserve to live.' Thump thump thump. 'Aueee aueeeee.' She stopped pulling the line.

What can I do? Cut the line. If I do the eel will live and so most probably will I. But that's giving in and I can't do that. Other people do that, but not me. I will not spend my few remaining years giving in.

This eels swims easily against the current. If I turn its head the current may catch the eel side on and wash it downstream. She walked level with the eel's head. She pulled the eel sideways, jerking the head to the left. She yanked the line.

The eel tried to dive. Then it twisted its body and rose out of the water. The current caught the eel side on. They found themselves once again moving downstream.

The eel and Hera were driven towards the lowlands. Sometimes rushing, sometimes moving slowly, but always they went down.

The eel had no strength left. It allowed itself to be driven by the current. Hera did not move her legs. It was the creek, the strength of the current that forced her muscles to move as she held on to the line. If they could, Hera and the eel would have stopped where they were. The creek gave them no rest.

It must be about two o'clock in the morning. It feels as though the rain has eased a little. It will be a long time before the water runs calm. This swollen creek joins the Waikino River. Surely the river has flooded.

The last time the river flooded I thought the next time this river floods its waters will rise and take my house and garden. Perhaps that has happened. Perhaps all has gone. Eel, perhaps all you and I have left are our lives. I feel I should let you go, but something within me says no.

Ruru had not yet eaten. It seemed as though in taking refuge from the storm all life evaded his beak and claw.

In a long swoop he glided over the creek, above the eel. Tilting his wings, he circled and landed on a branch just above Hera's head. She did not think him an ugly bird, nor an evil one. To Hera he was the bird of the long night. Of the distant and ever reaching night.

Alexandra and the Lion

Not long after midnight the lions begin to roar. Maybe they feel the cold. They temperature has dropped to almost zero. Pacing distractedly backwards and forwards in their confinement, they vent their fury at the full moon.

A mile away, Alexandra tosses and turns restlessly in her sixth-floor bed. Effortlessly, she absorbs the sound into her dreams. Falling, falling deeper into cold velvet depths. Above her, waves smash and roar their way to a waiting shore. Her arms flap and flounder as she thrashes her sheets into knots. Inadvertently a flailing hand strikes Narron as he sleeps tidily beside her.

Sleeping the sleep of the dead, his eyelids barely flutter. A gentle breath escapes his mouth as small, perfect teeth sink into a fleshy rambutan. Followed a second later by a hiss, as the rambutan dissolves into a limp butterfly struggling to be free. Deeply asleep he spits, desperate to rid himself of the taste of dry leaves which suddenly fill his mouth to the brim.

A gob of spittle falls on Alexandra's face and she plucks anxiously at it, trapped by a sheet which has wound itself about her with the tightness of a shroud.

A cloud passes. Released, the moon shines brightly into the room. Alexandra wakes abruptly, her heart thumping. Gradually she becomes aware that the roaring which fills her ears has not abated. Not only that, but the sound appears to be getting both louder and closer.

She shivers with the cold and untangling the mess of sheets and blankets huddles closer to the still form of her tiny husband. Only his face registers his dreams. His body remains immobile. Narron gives off little body heat and there are no soft flesh hollows in which to nestle.

Wrapping her arms tightly around her chest and bringing her knees up almost to the level of her chin, she burrows deeper into the bed. Very soon she submits to sleep.

The lions pursue her into dreams. Relentlessly she strides with them around the absurd prison. Her own throat opens to emit a shout.

A call of anger and dismay. A cry for the banished earth and sky. The wind blows and dulls the roars to a whisper.

A sudden draught and a door silently swings open. A dozen dark shadows leap into the void and disappear.

A solitary shape remains. From opposite ends they stare and then with one accord move towards each other. Without making a sound, a diminutive Alexandra climbs upon a firm broad back. She has barely grasped handfuls of rough woolly mane before he jumps.

Velvet paws swallow miles. A sharp intake of breath and with a lunge they're cloud bound. Over the monument at One Tree Hill. Past a volcano. Near an island. By a sea. Past a ship with winking lights. Lime-green eyes shining and red hair flying, Alexandra is transported swift as thought.

Alone in an apartment Narron waits. At the foot of the bed a heater, freshly activated, warms an ice chamber. Slender olive fingers drum against the mattress. He turns over onto his side — and there she is. He has not heard her return, but she is there.

Tentatively Narron reches out a hand for reassuring flesh. Upon contact, he flinches, scorched from the touch. Alexandra is burning as if fevered. He nuzzles against a long red curtain and smells damp strands of salt water and sea air. He lifts himself up onto one elbow and gently brushes the hair away from her face. He looks down at her closed eyes, knowing better than to ask where she has been.

In the morning they perch doll-like upon their breakfast stools and consume bowls of cold brown rice, sprinkled with a selection of chopped nuts and slices of hard-boiled egg. Narron liberally drenches his with a dark sweet sauce.

Alexandra is buried in a manuscript for a new novel her company is planning to publish. She is chief editor at a large publishing house. Half-heartedly she picks at her rice with her spoon, keeping one eye on the clock and another on a typewritten page.

Narron thinks already of his orchids, waiting for him in his glasshouse on the roof garden. Today he has an important client coming to visit. He is accepting bids for his new award-winning hybrid, which he has named 'Singing Swan'. No one but Narron knows why he names his orchids as he does. He expects to receive up to $800 for the rights to 'Singing Swan'.

He has a great deal on his mind. Usually he is completely absorbed by the maintenance of his huge greenhouse and his other great passion — cooking. He runs a catering business in Indonesian food as a sideline.

Now, however, there is the mystery of Alexandra's nocturnal disappearance and — more worryingly — 'The Book'. Alexandra has asked him, on behalf of her company, to write a book on his especially rare orchids, as well as detailing growing techniques. She is to edit it and Narron's good friend James is to design and do the photography for it.

Alexandra has told Narron that whenever he feels so inclined he is to speak into the miniature tape-recorder she has given him. He wears it around his neck and most days he feeds it a few sentences, usually while he is in the throes of cooking a meal. Away from the demanding presence of his orchids, he seems somehow to be able to think of them more clearly.

Alexandra has no memory of the night before and wonders why she feels so exhausted. Narron anxiously notes the smudges of mauve under her eyes. 'Tonight we will be very warm,' he promises her. You will be so warm you will not vanish again, he tells himself.

That night the temperature drops further. Unprecedented low temperatures for that time of the year. Coldest June for fifty years, headline the newspapers, radio and television.

Narron is in the kitchen preparing the peanut sauce for a simple Sumatran-style gado-gado. He quickly fries the crushed onion, garlic and shrimp paste together and then tosses in the ground peanuts and red chillies.

Alexandra is also in the kitchen — all but sitting on top of the heater. Her long red hair is spread fan-like around her to dry. She finds it comforting to watch Narron as he cooks. He is very neat and economical in his movements. Unlike Alexandra, who sketches the air with wild extravagant gestures, and often leaves a litter of chaos behind her, Narron always stacks his pots and dishes into formidable piles ready for her to wash after each meal.

'And how is "Singing Swan"?' she enquires.

'It awaits the right owner,' he replies, adding a pinch of salt, a generous squeeze of lemon juice and a small amount of brown sugar to the swirling mass.

'And who is the right owner?' she enquires mischievously, raising an eyebrow.

'I'll know the person when I see him. Or her,' remarks Narron cryptically. Swiftly he pours in coconut cream. 'Now don't interrupt me any more, or I'll burn the sauce,' he says, momentarily exasperated.

Alexandra trudges wearily into the lounge, dragging the heater behind her. Narron has complained of the excess heat in the kitchen.

She notices immediately Narron's tape-recorder lying neglected on the sofa. Curiously she picks it up and winds it back.

'. . . The Paphiopedilum family is found not only in Indonesia, but also in India, China, Burma, Malaysia and New Guinea . . .' emerges Narron's thin reedy voice.

Alexandra switches the tape on to fast-forward and quickly listens to random pieces in order to assess Narron's progress.

'. . . Man-made crossings between the species and/or hybrids have been produced in the Paphiopedilum family for more than a century. The Paphiopedilum hybrids today are very different from their delicate exotic parents. The plants are stronger with larger, fuller flowers and their colours are richer and better defined. Their appearance, which seems glossy, almost lacquered, is very distinctive . . .'

'Well, what do you think so far?' enquires Narron, appearing suddenly in the doorway.

'I like it. It seems to flow quite well. I especially loved the bit about the "delicate, exotic parents". Keep going, you're doing well,' she enthuses.

Narron, resplendent in large white apron, takes a bow. 'Dinner is served, madam.'

Alexandra drops the tape-recorder and, very much like a child, hastens to the table.

'Selamat makan!' She grins at him.

Narron takes a swallow from a glass of cold water and observes Alexandra with pleasure as she greedily spoons up her dinner. Alexandra adores her food piping hot, whereas Narron prefers his slightly lukewarm and gains his heat from extra chilli. Finally, he serves himself some gado-gado, a little salad and *lots* of rice.

'Mmmm. I'll never, never tire of your cooking, Narron,' comments Alexandra enthusiastically, her mouth full.

'And I'll never tire of you doing the washing-up,' replies Narron with equal enthusiasm.

After dinner, Narron watches the Tuesday Documentary — 'The Wandering Company'. He is a great fan of Ruth Prawar Jhabvala's novels and he is interested to hear of her partnership in films with director James Ivory and producer Ismail Merchant. He dreams of one day visiting India.

Alexandra divides her time between her book and the television. Before the documentary is finished she rises, yawning and rubbing her eyes, muttering something about having an early night. Narron is glued to the set and doesn't respond. It is only later, when he has plunged the television into silence with the portable remote-control, that he remembers Alexandra's words.

He swiftly turns off the lights and makes for the bedroom. In the darkness he can see only the glowing red spot on the Goldair heater. It whirs away comfortingly, drowning out any sound of human breathing. Narron cautiously prods the bed till he makes contact with the sleeping form of his wife. Reassured, he begins to undress. He dons a pair of fine red woollen long-johns and a baggy red T-shirt. He climbs, flinching, into the cold bed.

Alexandra is curled into a small foetal ball in the middle. He gently rolls her off to one side and then hops out again to pull on an old sweatshirt — also red.

He curves his body around Alexandra's and waits for sleep to claim him. 'I must buy an electric blanket . . .' is his last conscious thought.

The clock strikes midnight. As if on cue, the lions once again begin to roar. How they howl. The wind blows more and more furiously, but does not succeed in drowning their sound. Windows rattle and open gates swing crazily backwards and forwards on their hinges.

Alexandra stirs, but she does not wake.

At about one o'clock the noise reaches a crescendo and Alexandra sits bolt upright in her bed. She stares straight ahead — her eyes wide open in the darkness, straining towards she knows not what. She only knows that she is filled with a terrible sadness, which becomes a great yearning. Though she is awake, she gets up with the jerky movements

of a marionette and puts on a violet, velvet dressing-gown. Mechanic-
ally, she adjusts the quilted satin collar and tightens the belt. She twists
the handle of the door gently and silently closes it after her. Behind
her, the small lump of flesh that is Narron releases a soft snore. In his
dream he is reliving his first sighting of Alexandra.

Narron is in his second year studying for a Bachelor of Commerce and
hating it. He has in addition been sponsored by a New Zealand
family. Narron is not in the least bit interested in his degree but his
country needs qualified people so desperately, and his parents over in
Jakarta have put enormous pressure on him. If he could decide on an
appealing alternative he would forfeit it all — but his background has
not allowed or prepared him for the luxury of choice.

In order to take his mind off his worries his sole friend James, a
Malaysian student, has dragged him to see the annual university
capping revue at the Maidment Theatre. Most of the humour floats
easily over Narron's head. It is not until Alexandra appears on the
stage in the guise of Cinderella that it absorbs a great deal of his
attention.

It is a humorous parody of the old fairy-tale and the audience is
soon shrieking with laughter. Narron alone is completely silent — his
lips parted sightly in disbelief. His entire concentration is directed
towards a tiny red-headed figure in centre-stage. He is deaf to all
sound. He can only drink in the sight. So does a starving man look
at a banquet. The rest of the performance passes by in a blur. He
stumbles into the night half-dazed.

In his sleep, Narron permits himself a small smile.

Alexandra, meanwhile, is already in the lift, swiftly sinking to the
ground floor. Through the lattice-work of the metal gates, she can see
a ghostly blue flicker of light as she passes each floor. She is not afraid,
for she believes that she is dreaming.

As she emerges she glimpses a powerful dark shadow waiting
silently, through the glazed double-doors of the foyer. She feels no
shock or surprise. She knows exactly what she must do, as if she has
been rehearsed a dozen times.

With practised ease she slips the lock on the front door and glides
through. A great draught of cold air rushes up at her. She is oblivious.
She has eyes only for the familiar, oh so dear shape attentively
nuzzling at her hand. Trustingly, she grasps a clump of mane in one
hand and resting the other on the broad tawny back, lifts herself up

onto the beast. No sooner has she settled herself astride than with a heart-stopping leap they are swallowed up by the thick fog.

Narron fights against the waves of sleep which threaten to engulf him. All is not well. Slender fists batter cool, stiff sheets. To no avail. Overcome with weariness, he drops back into a dreamless slumber.

Alexandra is many miles away in the far north. The storm increases as she journeys further. Yachts drift from their moorings and smash into a thousand fragments against the rocks. Mandarins and lemons are flung helter-skelter into the air. A shower of sparks pierces the blackness as a large old tree spontaneously combusts. Alexandra droops low over the lion's head as a volley of citrus fruit is hurled at the leaden clouds.

Then — as suddenly as it had begun — the storm ceases. The absence of sound is almost as frightening as was the storm itself. The air smells sweet and fresh and the lion, in an abrupt about-turn, heads for home.

Alexandra is almost unconscious. She drifts in that state between wakefulness and sleep. Her petal-like face collapses over its fragile neck, combining to unbalance her torso, which nose-dives into the lion's mane. Her spirit rushes to get temporary oblivion.

Closer to home they pass over a deserted park. The swings whine and squeak in the breeze. Discarded beer cans litter the ground. Over the road the Market's brick chimney looms large. Alexandra's dangling feet brush within millimetres of it.

The sudden silence as the storm abates in the city at last brings Narron to his senses and to the realisation that he is alone. With a shrill cry of panic he flies from the bed. He wildly searches the apartment, calling Alexandra's name.

Desperately, clad only in his red bedclothes, a barefoot Narron rushes to the lift. Dancing with impatience at what seems an impossible slowness, he finally reaches the ground floor. Flinging aside the heavy metal grille with almost Herculean strength for his tiny frame, he lunges towards the front doors. A few persistent droplets of rainwater plop intermittently from the roof onto the concrete steps.

Narron is inconsolable. Dawn is still an hour away and he peers frantically into the garden from his vantage-point on the steps. His eyes narrow. A slight breeze has caused a dull piece of cloth to flutter under the lemon tree. The cloth continues to flap about bravely, as the wind playfully tosses it this way and that. Hardly daring to hope, Narron makes his way over there.

A sodden, discarded bundle has been placed as an offering to the heavy old tree. With a cry of horror Narron runs towards the crumpled figure. He gently eases her onto his back. The rag doll's arms flop over his shoulders and swing crazily onto his chest. A slipper falls and an icy white foot is exposed.

Even rag dolls can become a dead weight. Narron crawls over the garden at a snail's pace, terrified of dropping his precious burden. He heaves a reluctant form up the steps and, pausing only to draw breath, once more tackles the cumbersome metal grille.

Back in their apartment, Narron with a beating heart directs a spotlight onto his beloved's face. Not a cry escapes his frozen throat as he gazes at Alexandra under the harsh glare. There is no time to be lost.

After wiping the perspiration from his forehead, Narron quickly switches on a couple of heaters and relieves Alexandra of her garments. He briskly towels her dry with sure, even strokes and wraps her up in the warmest clothes he can find. Afterwards, he seals her firmly in the bed. She utters a low moan.

Concerned, Narron bends over Alexandra and her eyelids snap open. There is no sign of recognition in the glance she gives him. Soon, her eyes drift shut again and her breathing resumes its normal rhythm. Scarcely relieved, Narron bustles about, rearranging the heaters and then dealing with the wet garments. He remembers Alexandra's drowned hair chilling her head on the pillow and, grasping a blow-drier, attempts to dry the soaked tresses. Despite the drone of the drier, Alexandra does not reawaken.

Narron sits on the bed beside the still form. He keeps watch on her till daylight.

Every hour he brews up a fresh pot of strong, thick coffee. His little face is grey and pinched with worry. He plans to ring a doctor at 8.30 a.m. In the meantime, he ponders over Alexandra's nocturnal activities. He is too astute to attribute them to mere sleepwalking.

His mind in a turmoil, Narron is eventually driven to phone James. It is many years since student days and Narron and Alexandra both have a wide circle of friends. Yet James, his first friend, has remained, aside from Alexandra, his closest confidant. In a halting, confused sort of way, Narron relates the events of the past couple of days. James paces up and down his lounge. He jabs at his cigarette, stubbing it out in the ashtray.

'Possession,' he states. 'Something or someone has some sort of hold on her.'

It all makes sense to Narron. He frowns and pulls at his lower lip. 'What do you suggest?' he asks.

'You say you found her in the garden. Have you searched it in daylight to see if there's some sort of clue as to how she got there?'

'No,' replies Narron with excitement. 'No, I haven't.'

The problem assumes more tangible proportions. They hasten downstairs.

They both notice at once, as they prowl about, that several smaller shrubs appear rather battered. One or two seem to have been completely crushed.

'These bushes could have been damaged in the storm, though,' Narron reminds James.

James gives a sudden shout and Narron rushes over to the lemon tree again. James is pointing to a muddy area at the very base of the tree. An animal's footprint can clearly be seen.

'The sort of animal that made that mark would be pretty heavy,' speculates Narron.

'It's the print of a lion,' replies James quietly. 'I'm absolutely certain.'

A piece of the jigsaw silently clicks into place in Narron's mind.

Thoughtfully they return to the lift. They have managed to discover only one other footprint. More blurred than the first, but nevertheless made by the same creature.

'You know what you must do, don't you?' says James. 'You must not let her out of your sight for the next few days. You'll have to lock her in the apartment and hide the keys.' The thought seems distasteful to Narron, but he can't think of a better idea.

'I'll be back this evening, though. I'll even stay over and keep you company if you like.'

Narron accepts James's offer with gratitude and persuades him to swallow a quick breakfast.

A long day looms ahead of Narron. He checks on Alexandra. Her face appears bloodless against the black sheets. The doctor comes and goes. 'Warmth and rest, warmth and rest,' she assures Narron heartily, patting him on the shoulder.

'Don't let her get up too soon. We don't want to catch pneumonia.

Ring me if there's any change for the worse.'

Narron phones the publishing company and speaks to Alexandra's secretary, who asks if she may visit. 'No, no,' replies Narron, horrified at the very idea. 'She is much too sick. I will phone you again.' The secretary, puzzled, slowly replaces the receiver.

The hothouse is out of the question for the day, so Narron seeks to divert himslf with his tape-recorder.

'. . . It is difficult to grow the hybrid Paphiopedilum satisfactorily without a glasshouse.'

Narron sighs deeply and then recommences.

'. . . Ideal ventilation often incorporates a fan system and maybe perforated polythene tubing. Any rapid drying out which occurs can be counteracted by . . .' Here Narron pauses, momentarily losing the thread of what he was about to say. With an effort, he takes a grip on himself and continues. 'Counteracted by automatic foggers or vapour jets . . .'

A shrill series of rings punctuates the air. Narron jumps.

'Is that Narron's Indonesian Catering Service?' enquires a recognisably eastern suburbs voice.

'Yes,' replies Narron listlessly.

Undaunted by Narron's seeming lack of response, the woman rushes on, 'Would you be available to cater for ten people this Saturday? I know it's short notice being Wednesday already — but could you . . . ?'

'I think so,' replies Narron dolefully. He takes down the address and phone number and they discuss menu details. Narron requests a deposit in advance and the woman promises to mail a cheque to him that very day.

He shuffles into the kitchen to retrieve his large diary and transfers his phone notes into it. Out of habit, he methodically checks his stock of spices and ingredients and begins to make a list of the items he will need to purchase. He observes that he has run out of terasi (shrimp paste) and also kemiri (candlenuts).

His business details thus arranged, Narron once more attempts some recording. It's a slow process. He regularly tiptoes into the room to look at Alexandra.

A weak and sickly sunshine gradually begins to filter through the windows. This cheers Narron somewhat. After his last phone call he has activated his answer-phone and when the rings pierce his concentration for the second time that morning, he is able to sit back and listen to his recorded message. James's comforting tones penetrate the room. Narron jumps up and quickly switches off the machine.

'James, James, I'm here after all,' he says.

'I'm just phoning to see if Alexandra has woken yet,' explains James.

'No, not yet,' replies Narron.

They discuss the situation for some moments more and then James rings off. He is not having a good morning. He has a presentation to a major client in a couple of days and there is still much to be done. He has put an amount of work out to free-lancers but there are some aspects of the advertising campaign which can only be dealt with by himself. He doodles onto his layout pad with his felt pens and the shape of a lion emerges. He tears the drawing off the pad and places it under a fresh sheet of the thin paper. He traces over his first drawing and extends the legs so that the lion appears to be running. He draws the small figure of a woman on its back. Long red hair streams behind her. The woman's eyes are firmly closed and she has a beautiful smile on her face. Threadlike fingers grasp handfuls of mane and the lion's eye appears to burn. James erases the mouth he has drawn and replaces it with teeth that are bared in a terrible grimace.

James stares at his drawing for some moments and then he reaches over and picks up the phone book and looks up Auckland Zoo.

He doesn't have much luck with his phone call. He can tell that he is viewed as a crank. Nevertheless he has, through his persistency, established that yes, all lions are present and correct, they're all sleeping now but have been unusually restless over the past few days. James suddenly taps his head excitedly and dials the same number again. He discovers that the zoo has only recently brought in a new lion from Central Africa — one of their largest lions in fact. When James thinks back, he does actually recall glancing over a small article in the *Inner City News* about the new arrival.

He picks up his two drawings and carefully places them in his briefcase, wedged between the pages of a magazine.

Narron is finding it progressively more difficult to concentrate on his dictation. His heart is simply not in it. He has just re-entered the lounge from yet another check on Alexandra. He has managed to spoon a little warm orange juice and honey down her unresisting throat.

Narron decides to cheer himself up by making a sop kembang

kubis, or cauliflower soup. All this worry and excitement have made him hungry.

Soon he is quite absorbed as he boils up some chicken stock, onion, cauliflower, black pepper, nutmeg and salt. He stirs dreamily and remembers back to how he finally got to meet the Cinderella he saw on stage all those years ago.

His studies were neglected for a few days as he loitered about the university grounds, hoping for a glimpse of Alexandra. After a couple of days, his patience was rewarded and he espied her in the student cafeteria. She was laughing with a group of friends. Her hair thrown back over the chair, exposing the slender white column of throat. Narron swallowed nervously.

He sat down at the next table and stared, not even bothering to camouflage his activity behind a screen of sipping coffee. She didn't notice him and when she got up to leave, Narron followed behind at a discreet distance.

It was not difficult to discover the pattern of her lectures and movements. Narron pondered as to how he could actually meet this glorious creature. She seemed totally unapproachable, always surrounded by friends.

'Do you know anyone vaguely connected with her who could introduce you?' James had suggested.

'No,' admitted Narron in despair. 'It's hopeless.'

'Don't give up,' comforted James, 'there must be a way around it. Somehow.'

Alexandra acquired a faithful shadow. On an edge of consciousness she sensed an intense concentration directed inexorably to her. Signals indicated the presence to be benign. She waited. There was an inevitability about the collision.

On a crisp autumn morning patience was rewarded. A slight figure, walking for once towards her, glanced up. Discomposure. He tripped and fell, literally, at her feet.

A freckled white hand pulled him to his feet with a surprising strength.

His thoughts, like birds, flew right out of his head. She took the initiative.

'Don't you think it time you introduced yourself?'

Narron smiles as he tosses noodles into the steaming broth.

Alexandra wakens very weak and Narron spoonfeeds her some soup. He doesn't wish to upset her by clamouring for explanations at this point.

Her gaze is clear and open, expressing only gratitude and love. She displays no curiosity or memory of the previous night. Soon she falls asleep again.

Narron is relieved a few hours later, when James cheerfully arrives.

'You look a bit washed out,' he comments as he bounces in and throws himself on the sofa. He points to the bedroom and mouths, 'Is she okay?'

'Not sure,' replies Narron and he makes a seesaw gesture with his hands. 'It could go one way or the other.'

'I've brought you a drink,' says James and passes over a bottle of chardonnay. Narron brightens. 'I'll fetch some glasses.' James attempts to divert Narron and launches into an hilarious piece of gossip about one of his clients. In spite of himself, Narron begins to smile and look a little more cheerful.

'. . . He was wearing a crotchless spiderman's outfit,' continues James, 'trying to climb on to the wardrobe in order to jump off it, when the thing overturned and fell on top of him, breaking both his legs . . .'

Narron's eyes gleam. He pours them both another drink. 'And then what happened?' he encourages.

'Well!' replies James. 'His wife, meanwhile, was still tied to the bed, so *she* couldn't do anything . . .'

Narron laughs, imagining the expression on the neighbour's face after he had responded to the cries for help.

Narron turns up the heat and stretches out full-length on the sofa. A wave of exhaustion sweeps over him. For a brief moment he closes his eyes.

The ever-observant James get to his feet and offers to cook dinner. Narron smiles in anticipation. Each has tried to outdo the other over the years in creating spectacular culinary delights.

Alexandra lies perfectly still in the bed. Only the feverish fingers plucking at the bedclothes betray her inner turmoil.

She is in a dimly lit movie theatre, seated in the front row of the lower level. Two enormous golden plaster lions flank either side of the screen. Their cavernous eyes are lit from within by fierce red bulbs.

Alexandra becomes mesmerised as the eyes flicker on and off, on and off.

In that blurred dimension of dreams, she is both watching herself in the seat and at the same time tentatively reaching out to touch the gleaming muscular flanks. There is a swift intake of breath as her hand encounters the chilled surface of the statue. She explores further. Seen from a distance the skin appears smooth, satin and wonderfully modelled. To her dismay, however, some of the plaster falls away in her fingers. The rippling flesh is an illusion. Gold flakes attach themselves firmly to her hands. An icy buttock peels away and crumbles onto the stage.

Frightened and tearing at her hands to remove the gold foil, she finds herself once more in her seat. Slowly, the great head swivels and a fiery eye fixes her in its gaze. Alexandra's teeth are clenched with fear. Her breath comes in short gasps.

Mercifully, the creature finally averts its eyes and once more faces its twin. Rhythmically they flash signals across the stage.

Alexandra tosses and turns then, as the darkness grows deeper. She doesn't hear James clattering about in the spare room. She doesn't feel Narron's pliant little body slip quietly in beside her.

The moon is at its zenith. Despite having vowed to keep awake, both James and Narron quickly fall asleep as the wine takes its toll of their bodies.

All night long, sure footsteps pad softly around the small apartment block. A velvet shape rests briefly under the lemon tree before resuming its regular circuit. Daylight advances stealthily.

It is the milkwoman who first observes the trespasser and raises the alarm.

Up on the sixth floor, Alexandra's consciousness faintly begins to stir. The lion on her right slowly stretches and emits a huge yawn. Alexandra scarcely dares breathe. A burning look passes between them before it begins to cross the stage towards her. The audience, which until now she has been unaware of, breaks into a confused babble all around her.

Alexandra grips the seat tightly with both hands and clamps her knees firmly together. Her heart is beating so hard it drowns out all the noise. The beast is almost upon her when suddenly all the lights are turned off and the theatre is plunged into darkness.

She screams.

A loud cracking sound splits the air. Two human cannonballs hurl themselves at the door of the top apartment and negotiate the stairs in a series of leaps and bounds which take them to the ground floor and finally to the front lawn. A small crowd has gathered around the body. In daylight the teeth appear yellow and tarnished. The splendid mane, a tangle of matted twine. In spite of himself, Narron's heart contracts.

James and Narron, remembering Alexandra, leave the scene of all the excitement down below and rush back to Narron's apartment. They peep around the bedroom door and see Alexandra beaming and rubbing her eyes.

'I've had such an odd dream . . .' she murmurs.

HUGH LAUDER

The Stone Collector

That morning I woke in silence, the washing machine had stopped in mid-cycle.

Other things happened in that same period between dawn and dusk. For example, I met a young woman throwing stones into the village pond. At first it seemed she was throwing them at random, blue stone after yellow stone, purple after green but it soon became clear she was throwing them according to an ordered sequence. I thought perhaps she was a sculptor and the stones and the water her medium. I also wanted her to love me.

In the morning I attended my father's funeral and in the evening I spilt coffee on the white mink carpet.

Her hair was russet coloured, deeper than blood-red sheets, brighter than my father's last purple face. I tried to catch the stones to interrupt her concentration. And then I tried to catch the stones because I realised they were a part of her. By chance or because she understood about the silence and the washing machine, about my father and the coffee, she lobbed a stone in my direction. Catching it I closed my eyes and brushed my finger over it — feeling where it was smooth and where it was sharp. I walked away with the stone in my pocket. At home I put the stone in the terracotta dish where I kept all the other stones.

He contemplated the stones in the terracotta dish; he was beginning to feel comfortable with the world he was collecting. It was not, of course, the real world, in fact it was only barely recognisable as a world at all. Nevertheless he was beginning to trace a faint line at an angle from the real world in which he could feel at home.

After all his mother had done the same thing with her collection of Dresden dolls. She had begun to feel the same sense of place he was now feeling, in Dresden in 1939. In the event in 1944 his mother transubstantiated into a moth. It was a relatively painful process — all that was required was the removal of the 'e' and the 'r' and she was able to dance the exquisite minuet of the moth while her porcelain figures burned.

When he looked out that evening at the Southern Cross and saw the stars fall away and die he applauded their aerobatics. And when the next night he saw the paw of the bear fall off he was saddened by its leprosy. And so he lived and presumably died in the space it takes a stone to be thrown into the water all the while thinking that in Dresden the shop always, and only sold, dolls.

MICHAEL HENDERSON

Rutherford's House

-sko-ool
— Rutherford's last word

Sprig marks like goat hooves. Side-line flags scungy as Dangle's nosks. Spaghetti-white worms. Larval appetites waiting to drag him down. Decomposing mice. Deliquescent forms relapsing into formlessness. An insatiate ditch — no, a lake of death, never enough life to slake it. If he hadn't been through the muck so many times, he'd have thought the maggots were lifeless too, but he knew they were not dead, only helpless. Like Simone's mother when they burnt her alive. Like Adriana under that squirming bastard Astarita, worming his way into her.

Sk-ool, sk-ool for evv-uh!

The maggots wallowing and heaving with Scobe on the footy-field in their light and dark blue were larger, but just as helpless. Not dead, but good as. Dead from the knees up. Ox with scrum-pox.

On the ball 'til the daylight flees!

'Till I flee! Empedocles emerging from larvae, he thought, as he fled thorugh the mud above the smouldering Dump, a charred copy of *Siddhartha* safe from the latest bundle of confiscated books, enough of the first page left to find an echo of his own name in *Om* — *this wor of words, to ay it wardly with   ake of   ath, he reathing out with a   oul, his   ow rad ng*

In ache of *breath*? *Inslake*? of *death*? *Worm* of words? *Th'unfetter'd Muse, many a holey text around she strews!* Exacting meaning from mud and murk was insane. Meaning was a vanity he was better free of.

He fought a limp as well as dyspnoea, fanning away the Dump's fallout with Coomaraswamy's portrait of the Buddha still visible on the scorched cover of the book. Not another *Woman of Rome*, there couldn't be another Adriana, but it'd do for today.

If he climbed the forbidden terrace to the pedestal he'd be off his rocker but he'd be out of the stultifying puddles in which the Lord showed-off with headstands, bedecked with soot and drizzle, sur-

rounded by the mute audience dumb drowned worms and bloated
maggots, gobs of blood and goob awaking an image of dead Arthur's
bier and reminding Tom of the elegy he had to hand in by third
period tomorrow if he wasn't to end up even more of a crash down
Jerp.

Scobe's voice drooled in steamy exhalation and the Men in dirty
blue harrowed the field with drony phonation to prove they weren't
dead.

We'll play for evv-uh, no foe shall make us bow!

Forked, split, aped by the surface I appear on, a bigeminal baby
arriving on my head! Re-born puddle by puddle, baptised in black
water (hence foorth I never will be a Romeo!) with maggots, worms,
mice, an uncorked Australoid in skin, hair, face, limb, condemned to
ape uncondommed Dad, homo erectus for whom birth did not
expunge the crude concussion of the eely womb.

Baby eels! Transparent leaves fallen from what family trees?
Impure organism or pure spirit, doomed to turn into evil eeldom for
evv-uh! Are those white strands eely *worms* or wormy *eels*? What can
I, who can tie nifty double overhand knots, loops, bends, hitches, and
make a narler eel or setting sun out of a cradle of string, make of *them*?
Are those globby clews maggotty mice, putrefying owl food, or grotty
goob hoiked by Scobe's merry Men? Do I, an aged Romeo (thirteen
years down the drain, Benvenuto!), know anything about the upside-
down bookworm I make in the mire at the edge of this maelstrom?
Is *he* right-side-up? Am *I* upside-down? Treading water in — or over
— hell, which is caricature: me or my ghost?

Free of scaffolding at last, taller than the goalposts, outreaching the
clock-tower, rising like a rocket to snatch lightning from heaven, the
statue eclipsed what was left of the sun, but the mire still mirrored more
brightness from the sky than there was on earth. And there he was,
Tom Gray, dwarfed by the Lord's statue, socks at half-mast, dragging
the school colours in the mud with the reflections of Centenary
bunting looping around the end of the field, beyond the rifle-range, the
gym and the morgue until the distant lights of the Bin formed a halo
around the ay-over-kay Lord, a nimbus in which Tom strung an elegy,
Die letzten Tage der Menschheit —

> should this son sink
> in contagion
> of horror risen

let me go down
silent as the glow
which burned to grow me

the surface is
not enough
to stand on;
a hoik
of whooping cough;
air
caving in

the surface is
my face, my will
to surface again

Let Jerp make head or tail of that! — waffling on about Phaethon, the bastard suicide, dribbling on about the sons who amassed at Eden's Suez side.

An' nothink in life shall sevv-uh, the chain that is round us now.

Chain reaction, thought Tom, out-of-bounds on the pedestal where, all ready for the Unveiling, the marble implored the Lord's due:

LORD RUTHERFORD
First Baron of Nelson and Cambridge, O.M.
1871–1937
Eripuit caelo fulmen
At rest in Westminster
with Newton and Faraday
Bless'd For Ever, For Ever Bless'd
Old Boy 1887–89
First XV 1889
Inventor of the Scrum-machine
and Torpedo Kick
FATHER OF NUCLEAR ENERGY
First Man to Split the Atom
No end of fun
With matches begun
Erected by fellow Old Boys
to mark the Centenary of His Going Forth
from their School, the Best For Ever
For Ever the Best

Th'unletter'd Muse, many a jolly text around she spews!

Gulls snooped and drooped for Dangle to plug with his catapult from behind the Armory prefabs.

From here, the unblinking Lord, whitening with gull slime, could supervise the dutiful Jerp heaping up the books in the Dump, busily putting Beehive matches to novels, librettos, codexes, manuals, broadsides, albums, anything Italian and Greek! — a virtuous Titivil swearing the condemned words to hell, a Housemaster of Misrule smug as Shih Huang Ti burning up books even before Jesus Christ, Angela Brazil, Carter Brown, Mickey Spillane, Fallada and Gadda came along, not to mention the greatest Greek, Italian, wop or whatever she was, graceless Metalious.

Tom put the remains of today's book in his shirt, and with a runaway hum fit to restore Del Shannon, got out his string and made a couple of turns around the spar of his favourite knee scar, capstan barrel or windlass drum, for it was weather for a lark in an ark. Scobe had cowed 3Pl with visions of solar-smelted polar caps. Life was dear when you'd already splurged your childhood, and although your armpits and groinpit stayed bare, hair grew long in your nostrils, a-quiver to the alternating treble and alto below.

Thales was right, said Scobe. All things are made of water. But Jerp plumped for Heraclitus and fire.

Flood'd be the only way to put the Dump out, for it burnt deep underground, heading towards Spain with a heart that the winter rain could not reach in any gust or spasm so long as Jerp's daily confiscations fed the conflagration.

That fire said there was no end to fun with matches begun — durries up the Gramps! Guy Fawkes bangers! Joan of Arc sizzling at the stake! all the public urnings, starting with the House of Njal! caliph Omar burning the Library of Alexandria! inspiration of Mau Mau and Hau Hau! Rosenburgs rosy on their wedding anniversary! Belsen collage! Mount Arthur's bush seared across the bay, country hicks up to tricks with splinters tipped in red!

Black and white but read in bits, page 15 joined antiquity's fragments as he plunged back into the ashen remains of Hesse's dreams
— *ear after ear I have quest ed the Brahmins*
     it ould have been equally good,   *ever and holy, if I*
d questioned the rhino (were there any *left*?) or   *chimp*

     the

     owl has no worse enemy than the man of knowledge,

Red returned to trouble Tom on page 17, *no ore in the   bled ream of forms.*

But now the drizzle became a spit, dripping, dropping on to his neck like seed from the heavy public parts of the statue, then scattering across the puddles over the field, dampening the Dump, dousing fiery fragments, holey texts alighting in chance flutterings from the sky, Svejk's shriek assailing staid stucco along the dormitory wings, Van Oudshoorn's unpured Dutch defiling this other Zeeland along with more and more of Moravia's ravings! What if Jerp, or even the Lord himself, was to get an elegy to burnt books, not just a grizzle but a spit, *J'irai cracher sur votre tombe —*

> what's expressed
> can be suppressed!
> *but* Truth, safe from fire
> in the safe
> of the inexpressible,
> safe from Jerp's Safety Matches
> in Mt. Horeb's bush,
> safe as the salamander —
> invisible eel or worm
> that Benvenuto saw
> when he was five,
> that Empedocles dived alive
> into the lava for,
> that the sallow Simone survived
> her holocaust for,
> gold and silver
> unchanged by flame
> just as Scobe's Men, 30 true
> stay changeless through
> the heat of the game,
> for there's no end to fun
> with matches begun:
> but Truth suppressed
> has *been* expressed!

The daylight had not fled, it had simply abdicated to Jerp's pyre, which warmed the Lord from his calcified toes up, and gave a glow to the reflections and the things reflected, for weren't they helplessly the same, all made of water, or fire, or ether, or 'toms helpless as the yelping whelp the Men had hanged from the crossbar for lifting its leg with morbid instinct against the goalpost padding, helpless as Adriana with that vermiform Eyetie bastard Astarita worming his way into her.

Amicus Plato amicus Aristoteles magis amica veritas. The truth, that glacial, unmeltable ice-cap, was that the Dump, smouldering away night and day, kept him here as much as Simone with her caverning hair. That fire, that crucible-tongued volcano, that alembic of this hell, distilled Hašek, Wedekind and Moravia, *his* dirty blue men, his Vallejo, Céline and Dagerman, *his* thirty true men, his superchaux!

He deciphered the ash of Hesse's trash as the *phlump, phlump, phlump* of Simone's iron came from the House to belabour him ear by ear in the smutty air, no respite here or anywhere, stringing her invisible screams around his throat, panicles of panic setting in as he did House Matron fatigue, sorting nosks and snot-rags into the eighty-eight lockers of the Clothes Room while she folded the ironing with unrelieved goose-flesh, saying that as smoke her mother rose to the sky, and as water fell. He couldn't sever the rain that bound her now.

In his Lab, Scobe'd say, spouting away, that air is composed of a couple of gases, one which helps things like Joan of Arc to burn, another which won't let anything burn, not even Jews like the Matron of Rutherford House. Not that we need bother about Simone Salamon and mephitic vapours if we remember that bodies *like* to seize and combine in cheerful chemistry with fire gas, producing more than enough heat to stay alight, like the Dump, since the combustible gas oxygen is the gas of life, which adorns the fact that *matter can be neither created not destroyed by human agency*, the elements are supreme, and there you have it, sir!

The coals in the Dump became skulls as Scobie's Men, thirty true, crouched and grouched in the mud on the dead ball line.

Cockalorum in the plumage of his waistcoat on his be-flagged dunghill, Scobe crowed *We'll kick and we'll follow* just as a good coach should for the hundredth year since the Lord's XV of '89, the first scrum-machine, the infallible torpedo kick, and the unforgettable team talks and hakas in the old bathroom and boot-house, attended by roaches, crucibles, bunsens and beakers as the Lord's first appliances and chemicals arrive in baffling disarray from Sydney. It was a never-ending dag that the headgear, shoulder-pads and shin-pads which the prodigal Lord had mischievously invented to lull opponents into a false sense of security were still worn by gutless hooas, hockey players, and piker and poobah Collegiates which had never yet produced more than a couple of lesser All Blacks or VCs, let along a Lord of their own.

The shimmering mudscape dimmed. The mud had lapped up the sky, searchlights bevelled in the Bin, nocturnal howls said owl-light was light enough for Dangle's pot-shots, even if it was too dark to read by. Tom soothed singed Siddhartha inside his singlet.

The bellowing oxen came again, *We'll run, pass and collar, As· we shout the same merry refrain! ON THE BALL 'TILL THE DAYLIGHT FLEES!*

From here it didn't matter if the rings of spaghetti, invisible at last, were eels, or worms, Astarita's sperm or just plain salamanders sick of sprigs and spittle and the rush of falling stars. Tom felt the presence of Newton, who yearned to burne his stepfather and mother, and the house over them. How'd he survive the day he was born? Faraday's candles of tallow and spermaceti, so breefe, were done at both ends for a bookworm immersed no more in the pages of the puddles. Newton is my friend, Faraday is my friend, Rutherford is my friend — the smouldering Dump breathed in and out with the owls — but my *best* friend is — *strike!* Floodlights flashed on at Tom's feet, shrinking the black-backed gulls to moths frazzled in the pursuit of light, flapping their flannel like boarders beaten by the bell, like looneys binned.

Was he in the gun! Scobe and his maggotty Men, even Dangle, suddenly saw Tom Gray plain as day, a cracked telamon, an undraped caryatid despoiling their Lord's entablature, an escaped looney, not lifeless masonry, but helpless putty ready for them to pummel, for Tom was all ankle pain asking for it in the rain. They'd belt the living daylights out of him, knock him to smithereens! Boy, would Gray do a paper! He had it coming to him, it'd serve him right, the chinless wonder, the piking yellow belly with books down his shirt!

-sk-ool, -ool, unsuppressed, a moping morepork declaimed the elegy that had always been its own. *For evv-uh! evvuh more!* It didn't give a hoot for anything but its hoot.

Be still, friend. You crave the night; it falls.

Two Clues to Mrs Mooney

The Bullet Hole

Mrs Mooney comes out into her back garden and hangs a towel on the washing line. She notices a shiny snail trail on the path, and follows it to the flower bed, where she finds a family of snails of all sizes under a dahlia. She leans over and looks through the hole in the corrugated iron fence. This hole she calls the bullet hole. The edges are peeled back and jagged, from a big nail. The iron is rusted, violet and brown. She sees that a spider has thrown a line from the tip of a clematis leaf on one side to a purple fuchsia petal on the other. It glistens. She is so close, she can see little irregularities in the thread where the spider has stopped for breath, an instant. The line bisects the view, and vanishes when she changes focus to the lawn, the brick path, the edge of a flower bed, a delphinium, and the corrugations of a similar fence on the other side of the garden. A hose snakes across the lawn to a sprinkler sending up an inverted cone of fine spray, which sends sparkling drops to fall just short of the leaves close to her eye. Now and then the spray swirls in a breeze, a flurry disturbing the cone's symmetry. One drop has reached the spiderweb, and clings. It slides to one of the tiny irregularities, gently bouncing until it hangs still, like a pearl on a string. Mrs Mooney looks right through the drop of water. The garden on the other side of the bullet hole is microscopic and inverted. She can see the tiny white pyramid of spray which has cast on to the spider's line the drop she is now looking though.

Mrs Mooney's Poppy

Mrs Mooney is fond of the large poppy plant which grows outside her kitchen door. The serrated leaves unfurling from its strong round stalks have a milky sheen that rubs off under her thumb to reveal a darker, shiny surface, like a cabbage leaf. The dull pink petals darken to purple at the centre. When she picks off a spent head, white juice wells up to make a round white ball at the top of the broken stalk.

One morning she comes outside, and sees fine earth scattered on the path, and a hole where the poppy was the day before. Who has done this? She looks around, but the garden gate is still padlocked, the rest of the garden undisturbed. Then she notices a footprint in the dewy grass, and then a whole trail, right across the lawn to the back fence. The prints are clear green: from the fence to the poppy and back to the fence, leaving a trail of roots and earth. Mrs Mooney is puzzled. She goes into her kitchen and makes a cup of tea.

When she comes out again, the sun has dried the dew but the foot-prints are still clearly impressed on the grass. She examines them. Blades are bent, and daisies flattened among crushed clover. She measures the prints against her foot. Much bigger: a man's boot. In the soft ground near the fence are heel marks where the intruder has jumped down, steadied himself, and walked straight over to the back door. Somebody has been in my garden while I was asleep, thinks Mrs Mooney. About six feet from my bedroom window.

What did she dream of last night? A grove of miniature orange trees. She was standing on the wide verandah of a house, looking out over fields and hills. The grove of dark green trees was on the sloping lawn in front of the house. The trees were heavily laden with ripe oranges: she walked among them in peace.

When she woke up, she was pleased to see sunlight brightening the curtain. She went outside as soon as she was dressed. Then she saw that the poppy had disappeared.

She imagines herself hearing a noise in the night: the back fence creaking, a thud on the lawn. She lies still, listening hard. Slow, deliberate steps come across the lawn. She gets out of bed and looks through the gap between the curtains. A man, all in black, is standing in the garden. A long shadow cast by the moon stretches across the white grass, from his feet almost to her window. She backs away from the curtain, takes her dressing-gown from the end of the bed, goes through into the kitchen and lays her hand in the darkness on the handle of the poker in the bucket beside the coal range. She listens at the back door. No sound but her breathing. Her feet are cold on the linoleum. She goes back to the bedroom window. Outside, the moon is pouring down. There's nobody there.

Already the clover is standing up, in jerky movements freeing one leaf and then another. The footprints of Mrs Mooney's visitor are fading. Even the heel marks are slowly springing back from the soft earth. A fat worm emerges and slithers across into a hole. She looks up at the fence from which the visitor has jumped, and sees small marks where the toes of his boots have scrabbled up again. But why should it be a man? wonders Mrs Mooney. It might be a woman with big boots on.

PHILIP MINCHER

Träumerei

Aunt May lived with my grandparents in the twilight zone between two centuries. In the beginning, in the oldest memories of my grandfather's house, she was a classic beauty with striking bright eyes in the sitting-room photo with my father and her other brothers. The old man and my uncles all had clean young faces you had to look hard at to recognise, and Aunt May was a beautiful young woman looking right at the camera. The young men stood grouped around their sister seated at a desk, and you could tell they were a close family.

In those early days, visiting my grandfather's house, I didn't see much of Aunt May because of her being a business woman and working for a big firm in the city, whereas my other aunts were always at home during the day. Then too for each of my other aunts there was an uncle, and that must have added to the fascination she held for me. I guess I must have fallen in love with my Aunt May before I even knew her, or rather with her classic beauty in the picture from the other side of my world.

Then when I knew her she was a gaunt grey old lady who was always going somewhere else and never dropped a syllable from my given name. She was generous from a distance, with a range beyond Christmas and birthdays. Once she bought me *The English Struwwelpeter*, and that must have come out of the past too:

> The door flew open, in he ran,
> The great, long, red-legged scissor man . . .

She wouldn't have known about the nightmares. For balance, there were a couple of Bonzo books, and I remember a magnificent tin sword that would have put Wilkinsons to shame. But there was so much more.

For Aunt May, bless her imperishable soul, gave me music.

Her room was a velvet and lavender inner sanctum as old as her picture. There was a smell of musk and lilac like the inside of handbags, bric-a-brac and lace from another age. And there was a wind-up Brunswick gramophone standing silent in the corner.

199

One Sunday morning I was parading my cigarbox insect collection for my grandfather. We were engrossed in the study of wetas, sharing the magnifying glass over fierce heads and barbed legs and gleaming armour-plate, when somebody began to play a piano on the other side of the world. The notes came gently on the still morning air, pervading that other passion, charging our halls of science with the new energy of art.

Hearing and sight fought for mastery, the pinned wetas stared back at me with black soulless eyes. I looked ever so carefully and there was my grandfather listening too and not with his mind wholly on science. The record machine had been silent for so long.

The theme filtered mistily through the walls and down the clinging corridors of time. I didn't know what it was. I hadn't, consciously, even heard the name of Robert Schumann, and a title like *Träumerei* from *Kinderscenen* would have meant even less. But a wordless message crept into my soul, infusing utterly, a cipher for all time. And then there was silence again and the warming sun shimmering through.

I had to know.

'What would that tune be, Grandad?'

'I don't know. Pretty piece.'

'Is it old?'

'Ah.'

That was my lot. The tune was old, 'pretty', nameless. To his glory he'd given me the natural world; in this dimension he was deaf, mute. I was on my own in a new galaxy and my touchstone was a sad song, a message of loss and longing from Aunt May's record machine.

After a while my aunt came out of the silence on her way to church, with her grey gaunt beauty and her formality with my given name.

'What have you there, Philip?'

'Wetas.'

'Wetas!' She made a face. 'What are you doing with the lad, Albert?' She always called my grandfather 'Albert' and my grand-mother 'Eliza'.

'That's all right,' my grandfather winked at me. 'This is for men only.'

'How are your people, Philip?'

'Fine,' I said. 'Aunt May — ' I groped for the question, roughshod on holy ground. 'Could you tell me please — what was that music?'

I felt her eyes checking me out.

'Music, now? That's an advance on bugs, anyway.' Then she named Schumann's *Träumerei*.

I put the two names away for safe keeping.

'Do you have a gramophone?'

'Ours is busted,' I said.

That was all. I never heard music from my aunt's room again and she never even mentioned the subject until the day she gave me her gramophone and record collection. Looking back on it later I guessed she must have been watching quietly and waiting for me to grow up, and that we never got back to talking about it because she was always going somewhere else.

By that time there was only the slightest hint of the classic beauty thing, a cosmetic whisper of the past a stranger would have missed. But my eyes always saw the same Aunt May.

'How goes it with music,' Phillip?' She caught me unawares fresh from my grandfather's other Eden of English wildfowl and Damascus shotguns.

'Oh,' I groped for words to justify her interest, 'I heard *Light Cavalry* on the wireless last week.'

She came to the point without fuss.

'Would you like my gramophone?' Her words struck a magnificent chord. 'You'll have to ask your father, of course.'

'Aunt May, do you mean — your records too?'

'Oh, yes. You'll add to them when you grow up, of course. Wireless might be a great thing but you can't choose what you want to hear.'

I wanted to ask her in that case what if she chose to hear her records again, but she was getting ready to go out and had already put the matter aside.

We went back next weekend in my Uncle Jim's car and I had that feeling of a first fishing trip, or even going to buy a microscope. Uncle Jim was my uncle on the other side and not Aunt May's brother and she said 'How are you keeping, James?' and ushered us in through the sitting-room with the old clocks and the memories. We went quietly and respectfully into her room and took away her gramophone and all that ready music in the faded paper covers. We lashed the machine on the carrier and stowed the records carefully inside and even when I said my piece to Aunt May you wouldn't have known she was giving away anything that mattered. She said 'Cheerio, Albert' to my old man and 'My love to Winifred, James' to Uncle Jim and we drove away.

At home there was the usual turnout when we put the gramophone in place in my room and everyone had a look as if the record titles meant something to them. I promised to consider other people with the sound, and then I just shut up and waited. My mother touched the top of the machine and said 'Poor old May' and they all looked as if they understood what she meant by that and went out for a cup of tea. And at last I was alone with Aunt May's gift.

The titles made their own music: *Träumerei* of course; *Pathétique*; *Humoresque*; *Andante spianto*. The lyric poetry of the arias sang for me before they were played: *M'appari tutt' amor*; *Che gelida manina*; *Ah! fuyez, douce image* . . . Even the artists' names made their own exotic poem: Schnabel, Kreizler, Gigli, Korjus . . .

Cataloguing was one thing, playing was another. The new-found dimension was a box of foreign sound to my people. Music meant songs like *Waggon Wheels* or *Honey, you play in your own backyard*, or military bands on the *Diggers' Session*: if you couldn't sing along it was noise. So I chose my times to venture into the uncharted territory Aunt May had given me. Exotic voices sang for me alone, transcending language. Unseen fingers bridged chords of time and sonatas crept into my soul.

The catalogue included what you might have called extras — light songs I scarcely noticed at first: *Santa Lucia*; *Beautiful Dreamer*; *Ah! Sweet Mystery of Life* . . . These were to acquire meaning as my demand became less severe. One day I examined them more closely and brought into the light a vintage ten inch of Grace Moore singing *Whistling Boy*. There were four words written on the jacket in a florid hand. They said: 'Good morning, Miss May.'

The message was faded and only the tidy storage of the record covers had preserved it. The four words confused me beyond truth, half-meanings burst in my brain like those vague adult passages that worried me in films. A whisper of excitement trembled in my blood.

I turned the disc, searching. The flip side was Grace Moore again, with a song that should have been corny: *One Night of Love*. I listened with a new awe, a first sensual stirring. The vision burst in my brain like a movie flashback: a classic beauty with long dark hair, in a perfumed room on the other side of life. I was crushed utterly on a theme of longing, a soundtrack of loss.

I probed for clues with more stealth than Charlie Chan. Did Aunt May play the piano? Sing? My mother looked back for the controlled answer. 'No, dear. She used to have a friend who was very musical . . .'

I never knew the truth. Her song had been sung before I came, I shunned the sterile murmurings of critics. My mind was too clean for old maid jokes, my love unsullied by time. I never knew why she chose silence. Afterwards when she went deaf the silly adult world lamented out of sequence: 'Poor dear, her music would have been such a comfort.' As if they knew.

Over the next couple of visits to my grandfather's house the likelihood of Aunt May being home took on a new wonder. There was a blend of wanting to see her and needing to be careful about the way I looked at her, and then each time disappointment to find she wasn't home. But finally she was there.

She came in on the latest display of specimens, the old Sunday morning pilgrimage to my grandfather's kitchen table. There was a mixed haul and my grandfather was geting up to find his other glasses.

'Good morning, Philip.'

'Good morning . . . Aunt May.'

She came closer to examine the display, blending her aura with the glories of my other world: a baby octopus in an Agee jar; a mouse's skin tanned in cold tea; trout ova in formalin; a pickled embryonic rabbit. If she laughed . . .

She didn't laugh.

'So you're going to be a scientist?' She touched one of the jars.

'Yes.' I wouldn't have believed in anything capable of preventing it.

'Not a musician, then?'

'I . . . don't think so.'

'You've got a violinist's hands, Philip.'

So. A violinist. I couldn't look at her eyes.

'I've got a friend who plays the violin,' I said. Don's hands were smaller. He'd shown me how to hold the thing and the truth was my joints had ached from just trying to look the part.

'And you wouldn't want to learn?'

'I don't think I'd be any good,' I said.

There were so many things. I had a fear she was thinking about lessons and I wanted to save her the disappointment.

'Aunt May.'

'Yes?' She was looking at the jar with the sleeping unborn rabbit. I wanted to cry.

'Thank you for the gramophone.'

'Oh yes. What did you like best?'

'I think — the violin pieces . . .'

I felt her eyes searching, longing for that lost era. I loved her back through the melancholy facade of age. Beyond propriety, once and forever, she took my hands: lifted and looked long. My hands were my nakedness, my eyes welled truth. I flew to her classic beauty out of sequence, pressed to her pilgrim spirit out of time. I sobbed against her dry breast.

'Hush, child. What is it?' But she knew. She held me with tenderness unbound, her gaunt cheek wet against mine. 'We'll just go out on the verandah for a while, then. We don't want to worry old Grandad, do we?'

I sobered rapidly in the sunlight, almost ashamed. Melancholy bells shimmered on the morning air. Aunt May waited quietly at the old distance until I was all right.

Back in the kitchen my grandfather had his other glasses on and was studying the baby octopus. After a while I stopped feeling conscious of my hands. When I looked up Aunt May had come in from the verandah and I guessed she must be getting ready to go out.

Finally the sweet sad violin in my head lifted into silence.

JEAN WATSON

Ali Leaves For Delhi

Amie was sorry she didn't have a camera.

She wanted to capture the scene forever.

Something changes and everything goes on the same.

Everything changes and yet goes on the same.

A stone is dropped into a current of flowing water, for an instant the ripples are disturbed, change shape, then resume the same pattern again. In this ebb and flow, this disturbance and resumption of intricate patterns — the themes with their variations — she can see the arrivals and departures of friends, and from a further point of detachment, her own.

It is eight in the morning, Amie sits at the houseboat window. Behind her in the lounge Saffi the houseboy is sweeping the carpet with a straw broom; he sings as he works.

To the left of the ghat stands a clump of three willows, they lean toward the lake, to the trunk of the foremost one is attached a cable which leads to the houseboat where Amie is watching from the window.

On the right of the ghat is a narrow two-storeyed house, from a fire behind it wisps of smoke drift slowly across the roof towards the tops of the willows. In the background is a larger group of willows.

The lake is still. But reflected by the lake water, the light is moving, waving to and fro, delicate and potent on the trunks and among the branches of the willows. Between the willows and the concrete wall is a mound of dirt and broken bricks.

At the top of the ghat the road begins. It passes through the tiny lakeside village and, a mile later, joins the main road to town.

Now two cars are parked on the road at the top of the ghat, a black one and a grey one, both striped yellow along the body above the doors. An English couple are getting into the black one.

The sunlight catches the bumpers, dazzling. In the foreground the trunks of the three leaning willows cut across the bonnet.

Saffi approaches the back door of the black car, he is carrying a wicker lunch basket and a blanket, he hands them to the couple in the car and closes the door. He waves as the driver backs, turns, and disappears along the road. A group of quacking ducks wanders from among the willows in the background onto the concrete steps.

Underneath Amie's window, two little girls paddle past with a shikara load of lily leaves.

'Hello what's your name?' they call.

Among the willows, a small boy is rolling a single bicycle wheel.

An elderly couple are going out onto the lake in their shikara, the old man kneels in the bow paddling. He is talking loudly all the way, the old woman sits in the centre smiling and nodding, saying an occasional word.

On the bottom step a woman sits washing clothes with a slap, slap, slap sound. Next to her sits another woman washing a samovar.

Two tourists, one in a bright pink dress, walk past the remaining grey car and the willows. They stand for a few minutes among the ducks and then move out of sight.

A willow trunk hides one of the headlights of the grey car. There are two suitcases on the rack. The driver, dressed in a grey checked sports coat, is polishing with a red cloth, first the bonnet then the windows. In the background a woman walks past, she is wearing a turquoise head-dress and carries a copper plate upside down on her head. The sunlight catches it as she walks past the grey car.

The grey car is waiting for Ali, to take him to the airport in town. He is catching the plane to Delhi today.

Two brown sheep wander down beside the concrete wall.

Now at last two people are approaching the grey car. One, a thick-set tourist wearing a navy jacket with a red handkerchief in the pocket, the other, Ali.

Amie is trying to fix the scene in her mind, as if taking a colour photograph.

A photo would be square, the edge of it cutting off all except the grey car, the willow trunks, the top step of the ghat and the two standing by the car.

A photo would be still and cold and harshly lit.

Now the tourist gets into the back seat, the driver closes the door after him. Ali stands a few minutes talking to the driver. Ali is thin and dark brown, he is wearing a bright red and yellow striped jersey and dark glasses.

Just that — a few seconds, Ali standing by the grey car talking to the driver. Now he gets into the front seat, the driver closes the door and walks round to the other side, opens his own door and sits behind the wheel, a sharp slam as he shuts the door. He starts the motor, backs the car, turns and drives off through the little village along the road to town.

Shifting sand, swirling foam on the ebbing and flowing tide.

Ali has left for Delhi.

Smoke drifts from behind the house on the far side of the ghat, it drifts down among the willow branches.

A crow sits black among the green willow branches.

A duck at the water's edge rises and flaps its wings, surrounding itself in a mist of spray.

A row of men sit on the concrete wall talking.

A small boy hurls stones at the water.

The light moves delicate and potent on the trunks and among the leaves and branches of the willows, reflecting the almost imperceptible movement of the lake.

The two sheep are now standing on the mound of dirt in front of the willow trunks.

The elderly couple are returning from the lake in their shikara. They have a large bundle of weed tied up in sacking. The man is still talking at the same rate and the woman still smiling and nodding. They pass right under Amie's window, they smile at her, the old woman's smile is gentle and friendly, the man's smile more hesitant and a bit wary.

They reach the shore, the old woman hoists the bundle of weed onto her head and nimbly jumps out of the shikara, walks up the steps and towards the village. The old man dawdles behind talking to the men who are still sitting on the wall.

Two boys bring a pushbike bumping down the steps, rest it on the bottom step, and begin to wash it.

A blue kingfisher sits in the willow branches.

A group of children climb into a shikara and paddle towards the middle of the lake / the car has gone / the activity on the water's edge continues / Ali has left for Delhi / closes over his departure / continues / as water in a lake closes over a falling stone.

GRAEME LAY

The White Daimler

Four o'clock in the morning was a barbaric hour to arrive in a country, he thought, even if it is a tropical island. Behind him the other passengers oozed from the 747 like toothpaste from a tube: ahead, on the far side of the runway, was the profile of a vast range of serrated peaks. The mountains, black against a just-lightening sky, and the thick, warm air gave him a feeling of exhilaration, in spite of his tiredness. He passed through Immigration and Customs without difficulty, and carried his two cases out to the front of the small terminal building. In spite of the hour, smiling, open-faced Polynesians were milling about, or placing fragrant leis around the necks of the other arrivals. John Beretti stood to one side. There were no garlands for him. Apart from Edward, he knew no one here. And Edward was nowhere in sight.

A decade ago, they had shared an apartment in Kelburn before each had married. Edward and Joanne were divorced a year before Jan had been killed in an accident on the Hutt motorway. Shortly after the divorce, Edward had come to the island to edit the government-owned newspaper. They had corresponded sporadically, and in his last letter Edward has assured John that he would be at the airport to meet him.

He stood in a pool of light beside a large hibiscus bush. Further along the forecourt, mini-bus drivers were loading cases into their vehicles, while their European clients stared out at the darkness, their faces a mixture of jet lag, apprehension and determination to have a great time. John both envied and pitied them, then, as the buses pulled away, envy won out. Of course it was a hellish hour to ask anyone to turn out. He looked vaguely around for a taxi. There were none in sight. The last mini-bus moved off. Above the mountain ridge, the sky was fading faster.

He was about to move off to try the Tourist Bureau when a very long white car emerged from the shadows to his right. A saloon model, early fifties, with running boards. A Straight 8 Daimler. It drove a little way past him, then pulled up sharply. The driver jumped out.

'Johnny!'

'Edward . . .'

They shook hands. He was dressed in a pale green safari suit, and was stouter than John remembered. He was effusively apologetic for his lateness, caused, he explained, by a malfunctioning of the alarm clock. He put the bags in the boot and they moved off. John had forgotten how cavernous cars once were. The bench seat was worn, but real leather, and a little light by the glove-box showed that the dash-board was walnut.

'What do you think of the car?'

'Terrific. Where on earth did you get it?'

'Belonged to a trader here for years. Chap called Davis. He died a few months ago and I bought it at an auction. Beautifully comfortable, don't you think?'

They swept along a narrow, unlit road lined with thick bush, past the slim, spectral shapes of palm trees, and occasionally, close to the sea. The powerful headlights lit up mangy dogs which trotted confidently but perilously close to the wheels. They talked of old friends, but neither of them mentioned the divorce or the accident. The car skirted a small harbour basin where there were silhouettes of yachts and small cargo vessels, then Edward turned the Daimer off the main road.

'My place is just up here.'

'You must think of the island as home now, I suppose.'

'I do. I've had to make a few adjustments, of course, but I get on well with the local people. I fit in.'

The house was set in the centre of a large section, surrounded by tall, spreading trees. Edward parked the car in the drive and they went inside. The walls were stucco, painted cream, the floor was covered with seagrass matting. In the centre of the lounge ceiling a large fan revolved languidly. The furniture was cane, and one wall was completely occupied by wooden shelving which housed books, carved Polynesian artifacts and a modern stero unit. John put down his case.

'This is nice. Very nice.'

'Comes with the job. Plenty of room, peppercorn rent. No air-conditioning, but I prefer the fan.'

He still had the same self-assurance, the same air of authority. But the physical changes were there. His face was fleshier, more rubicund, his hair tinged with grey. On the top of his head his hair was damp and plastered down untidily, as if he had brushed it without the aid of a mirror.

'It'll take you a day or two to get over that bloody awful flight. Have a good sleep in the morning. Your room's through here . . .'

A high passage led from the lounge to the spare room. In places the cream paint was peeling from the walls, and near the ceiling on one side a brilliant green lizard clung to the plaster like a brooch. In the room was a dressing-table, single bed, chair and a large window covered with insect-proof gauze. John looked gratefully at the bed. He felt soiled, weary.

'Thanks very much for putting me up like this, Ed.'

'No trouble. The bathroom and kitchen are at the other end of the passage. I work tomorrow — today I mean — so call in and see me at the office. It's next to the courthouse, in the centre of town. Oh and I've got a cleaning woman who comes in the afternoons. Her name's Tuaine, but she doesn't speak much English, so don't expect any meaningful dialogue with her.' He smiled. 'Have a good sleep.'

He did, though his dreams were accompanied by a fanfare of shrieking roosters. It was two in the afternoon when he woke, and the room was pleasantly cool. From the passage came a slow, clunking sound. He got up, wrapped himself in a towel and went out. A woman was sweeping the floor with a soft wooden broom. She was about fifty, short and dumpy, with black hair tied back. She wore blue pareu and jandals. She stared at John and he nodded.

'John Beretti. I'm a friend of Edward's.'

It was difficult to tell if she understood. She went on staring at him. Her round, fat cheeks were thickly pitted with a crimson rash, and the whites of her eyes were shiny yellow, like polyurethane. 'A friend of Edward's,' he repeated. She nodded, dismissively, and went back to her sweeping.

He walked the half mile into town, past unpainted huts surrounded by lush gardens, under breadfruit trees with their vivid green, oval fruit, past the palm trees lining the lagoon. High above the island a few clouds clung to the bush-mantled mountains, and the air was thick with humidity. Local people strolled about, or rode past on mopeds. All grinned as they passed, some waved. He could feel the air of warmth and amiable indolence soaking into him. He liked it. This seemed a good place to forget grief, to throw off the hounds of the past. He thought he knew why Edward had made it his home.

He reached the town centre. There was a roundabout with a flame tree in flower on it, the courthouse, a post office, corrugated-iron picture theatre, and on a corner, a low, sprawling, verandahed building, painted brown. Everything seemed closed, and the tiny nation's flag hung limply from a pole in front of the courthouse. He found the office of the *Island Times*. It too was shut, and Edward's car was not outside, but as he walked back to the waterfront he noticed the Daimler parked behind the brown building. He crossed the potholed street and entered the building through the front door. Above the entrance was a hand-painted sign. *Tangaroa's Place.*

The building was like a large, decaying colonial homestead, with a central hallway floored with bare boards. As he walked down the hall he peered into the rooms that led off it. Each contained a few formica-topped tables and chromed chairs, where groups of Polynesians sat drinking and playing cards.

At the end the hallway opened out into a large room with a sunken dance floor surrounded by more tables and chairs. In places the yellow ceiling sagged, and there were several large holes in the walls. Lionel Richie's voice wailed from a 1960s style juke-box in one corner, and at the other end a group of men were playing darts. The place reeked of beer, sweat and smoke. Along the rear wall was a bar, and there, sitting on a stool, was Edward, surrounded by a group of laughing Polynesian men.

When he saw John he tipped his head back, grinned, and got down off the stool. He introduced John to the group amid a confusion of names.

They were all quite young, at least two looked to be only in their teens. One tall, slender youth had no iris in one eye, so that it moved in its socket like a milky marble. The mouth of another hung open, as if he was partially retarded. Two were Rastafarians whose heads looked as if they were becoming unspliced. All wore T-shirts and jeans, except Edward, who still had on his safari suit. He remounted his stool.

'There aren't too many places like this left in the Pacific now. Somerset Maugham had a few sessions here, they say.' He swivelled round and called to the barman. 'Hey, André, come and meet an old friend of mine. And get a bottle of Vailima while you're about it, you little lala.' The other men roared with laughter at the word and the barman, who blinked and rolled his eyes in mock coquettishness. He wore a blue and orange Hawaiian shirt, and his plump buttocks were enclosed in tight blue velvet jeans. He brought the beer over and held out his hand to John like a lady being helped from a carriage. The others hooted again as the visitor took it. When the mirth subsided he said: 'Is this your regular watering-hole?'

'Yes.' He paused. 'A lot of ex-pats just drink with each other in the big tourist hotels, isolate themselves totally from the locals. These chaps . . . ' he nodded in the direction of the others . . . 'are a bit rough, but they're terrifically amusing.'

John nodded. Ed had always valued amusing company, no matter who it was. If you could make him laugh, you were his friend. As he sipped his lager John noticed the cleaning woman, Tuaine, enter the bar and join a group of women sitting near the juke-box. As she stared in their direction he nodded back at her, but Edward appeared not to notice.

'Did you finish work early today, Ed?'

'Mmmm?'

'I thought you said you would be working.'

'Oh, no. I packed it in about twelve. It's a quiet time. Not a hurricane or a political scandal in sight.'

'How many have you got on your staff?'

'Depends what the fishing's like.' He laughed, and added: 'Six.'

'What are they like?'

'Better than they used to be. I delegate a lot now.' He chuckled. 'A case of See You Later, Delegator.'

John laughed. He had never known a man who could get away with what Edward could. As he finished his lager, Edward held out his hand for the glass.

'Have another one, old chap.'

John shook his head.

'Not just now thanks, Ed. I thought I'd take a tour, see the rest of the island.'

The briefest flicker of annoyance passed over his face, before he put his glass to his lips, tipped it up, drained it. He set the glass down, swallowed hard, and without looking at John said tersely:

'I'll take you.'

'No, it's quite all right, I can get a bus.'

Waving John's protestations aside, he slid off his stool.

'No trouble, no trouble . . .'

They drove with the front windows open and warm wind whipping at their faces. The Daimler sped past laughing, waving children, strolling women, and once, a vast matron on a moped with a struggling pig lashed across its carrier. The island was a mass of brilliant green bush, emblazoned with blooms of hibiscus, poinsettia and frangipani. Small gardens of arrowroot, pawpaw and beans could be glimpsed behind rampant hibiscus hedges, and bright ginger chickens scuttled out of the path of the car. Edward drove with one hand, saying little apart from pointing out items of interest. A break in the reef, a motu, an icing-white church of coral stone, the island's highest peak, soaring from a kris-like ridge a thousand feet above them. John reacted to the physical beauty enthusiastically, but Edward seemed to have lost most of the bonhomie he had displayed back at the pub. He seemed tired, no doubt from having to get up so early. They rounded another bend, and a large low building occupying a flat promontory came into sight up ahead.

'What's that?'

'Lagoon Lodge. Tourist hotel.'

It came more clearly into view. The complex was built of dark stained wood, roofed with thatch. The central building was surrounded by a constellation of units, linked by covered walkways. John leaned forward. It seemed a good chance to repay Edward for the inconvenience he had put him to.

'Let's stop off for a while. I'll return that drink.'

Edward put his right hand on the wheel, eased himself up on the seat and squinted in the direction of the hotel.

'All right,' he said, 'why not?'

Mellifluous Island music flowed through the carpeted foyer. Edward led the way up some broad steps, past the duty-free boutique and into a large lounge bar furnished with sofas, chairs and low, glass-topped tables. Through the landscape windows there was a vista of lagoon, reef and blue gloss enamel sky. American accents drifted across from three couples sitting in a corner. The two men walked up to the bar.

The barman was carefully skewering stuffed olives onto tooth-picks. He had a broad, sallow face and frizzy hair, and wore a white shirt, bow tie and cummerbund.

'Takai,' said Edward, casually.

He looked over at the door, then back at Edward. He swallowed, put down a toothpick, picked up a cloth and began wiping his hands vigorously. John moved forward.

'Two Vailimas please.'

The barman's dark, startled eyes went round the room like a pair of searchlights. They came to rest momentarily on John's face, then went again to the door.

'I'm sorry, sir. Mr Van Staten said . . .' His face had deepened in colour, and when he spoke his voice was thick and slow.

'My friend said two Vailimas, Takai.'

The barman's throat bounded. He looked over to the door once more, then turned quickly and opened the sliding door of the fridge. As he poured the drinks his hands shook a little.

They carried their glasses over to the window. Edward glowered at the glass.

'What was that about?' said John.

Edward sipped his drink.

'There's a new manager here. A Dutchman. Thinks he's running the Dorchester. We had a bit of a disagreement recently.'

'What over?'

'The time the bar should close. It was all a typhoon in a teacup. That's why I prefer Tangaroa's. The only Polynesians you meet in here are servants.'

So, John thought, he hadn't shed the anti-colonial convictions they had shared in the old days. He certainly couldn't be accused of elitism in his choice of pub. Edward nodded in the direction of the sea.

'Anyway, Johnny, here we are and there it is. Palm trees, beach, reef. The whole cliché.'

The lagoon, with its coral heads, was a chiaroscuro of the pale green and brown. At its outer edge waves reared suddenly into enormous tubes, then exploded on the reef in a line of brilliant white, like a lasso around the land. In the strong sea wind the palm fronds moved like ostrich plumes. There was not another person or building in sight.

'It's stunning. I used to think that Europe had a monopoly on beauty. You know, cathedrals, medieval villages and all that. But this . . .'

Edward nodded.

'And here there's an added bonus. You don't have to put up with Europeans.' He paused before muttering: 'Except for pricks like Henni Van Staten.'

There was silence again. He continued to stare out at the sea. He seemed in a kind of reverie, looking outward, seeing inward. After a pause John said, quietly:

'How long do you think you'll stay on the island?'

Not turning his head, he said:

'Me? For life. I fit in here.'

He finished his drink.

'Another one?' asked John.

'No, no,' He turned away from the window, visibly snapping back into the present. 'I thought we could drive on and have a meal in town. What do you say?'

Darkness came quickly, after a swift, spectacular sunset glimped through the palms. The Daimler swept majestically on, its headlights picking up, then abandoning huts, dogs, mopeds, groups of strolling people. In the dark, commodious car, the talk turned to women.

'Have you met anyone else yet?'

'No. I'm not really interested at the moment. It's only five months since . . . What about you?'

He chuckled.

'Getting a woman here is about as hard as finding a ripe mango. After you've been here a while you can understand why they mutinied on the *Bounty*. They're incredibly beautiful.'

'Yes. Have you got anyone particular?'

He laughed again.

'Hell no, why settle for one? Even when I've got a bird in the hand, I'm still thinking about the two in the bush.'

Although he laughed, John had a sudden disconcerting thought. Perhaps by staying in the house he was interrupting Edward's delicious routine. Yet when he had replied to his letter he had made no objection, and they had been friends long enough for him to be able to do so if he had needed to. Even so, he did seem different. He seemed to have created a shell round him that even their friendship could not penetrate. The only time he had been as John remembered him was when he had come across him at Tangaroa's. Still, he told himself, everyone changed. They passed the brightly illuminated airport, then the harbour. They had come right around the island.

Deep in the heart of Polynesia, they dined at a Mexican restaurant run by Chinaman. Chang's Cantina was a small, square building on the main road, overhung by breadfruit trees. A curtain made from strings of shells hung in the doorway, and inside were a dozen tables and a small bar. They drank Châteauneuf-du-Pape with their enchiladas. By the time they were on their second bottle Edward's manner was expansive.

'The wine lists here are better than they are at home. There's no duty, so they import all sorts of stuff. But they've really got no idea. A few months ago they were selling case lots of French burgundy at half price, because it was old stock . . .'

They were still laughing when three people entered: two Polynesian girls of about twenty and a European man, tall, perhaps ten years older. The girls were tall and loose-limbed. They both wore pareu and frangipani flowers in their long, glossy hair, and their bare arms and shoulders were very smooth and brown. As they entered, both girls glanced at Edward but did not speak. The man did not look in their direction. He was fair, with an auburn moustache and well-cut, casual clothes. He led the girls to the table at the far end. As John ate he noticed that Edward was clearly distracted by the attractive trio. Several times he turned and looked over his shoulder at the trio, and between glances he drank and ate quickly, saying little. John poured the last of the wine.

'Another bottle?'

He nodded, then glanced around again. The Chinese waiter was pouring the others champagne. When he passed their table John ordered another bottle of red, then asked Edward:

'Who are they?'

'Who?'

'Those three over there.'

Staring at his plate, he said:

'The girls are dancers. Part of a troupe. The Regal Polynesians. They go all over the place. Tokyo, Manila, California. They make a lot of money.'

'Who's the chap?'

'A Yank. Tiare — that's the one in blue — met him in Los Angeles. He lives there now, with both of them.'

'Both of them?'

Through a mouthful of tortillas, he nodded. For a few moments he went on chewing, staring down at the table. Then, abruptly, he got up and strode over to the table where the others sat. His voice carried easily across the small room.

'Good evening,' he announced.

The girls exchanged glances but did not reply. The man's look was hostile.

'What do you want?' he said icily.

Edward was looking at the girls.

'My friend and I wondered if you would like to join us.'

'No way,' said the American. 'Everyone's had a gutsful of your behaviour.'

Edward's eyes narrowed.

'I didn't include you in the invitation.' He turned back to the girls. 'Tiare? Katarina?'

The darker of the two lifted her chin a little, and smiling slightly through closed lips, shook her head slowly. The other girl did the same, without the smile. Their condescension was unmistakable. Edward stood staring down at them for a few more moments, then he turned and came back. Without speaking or looking at John he swallowed a glassful of wine. His face was crimson, his blue eyes glittered.

'That Yank-kee bastard . . .'

'Don't worry, Ed, it's not . . .'

'I knew those two before they went away. They were all right then. He's corrupted them, screwed up their lives.'

This curious interpretation of the rejection made John again recall Edward's anti-Americanism of twenty years ago. But the rebuff had been demonstrably personal, not political. Acutely embarrased for him, John said:

'Look, Ed, I'm still pretty tired, I think I'll go back and get some more sleep, all right?'

Still staring at the table-cloth, he made one swift affirmative motion with his head. John called the waiter and paid the bill. As they went through the shell curtain light laughter could be heard coming from the corner table.

He drove without speaking through the blackness, under banyans and palms, past shuttered roadside stores. It began to rain, torrentially, and the car was enveloped in sheets of water, but he did not slow down, and water roared against the Daimler's floor. Then, on the out-skirts of the town, the rain stopped as suddenly as it had begun. They came to the roundabout. A light glowed on the verandah of Tangaroa's. Edward braked and they slid to a stop outside.

'There's a band playing here tonight, let's go and have a drink.'

'Not for me thanks, I'll have an early night.'

'Mind if I do?'

'Of course not. I'll walk back to the house.'

'All right, it's not locked. I'll see you later.'

There was a full moon, and the blotches of black cloud stained the pale sky. The silhouettes of the palm trunks soared above him like racks of black scimitars, the air was warm and heavy with the scent of sea and tropical growth. As he walked he thought of little else except Edward. Edward, talented, urbane, witty, whose company everyone sought, who had been editor material from the day he had first set foot in the *Dominion* office. Now he seemed like an island upon an island, as misplaced as the outlandish vehicle he drove. Where were his friends? His colleagues? The lovers he picked up like fallen mangoes? Why did he frequent that dump in town? How had he offended the people in the restaurant? None of these were questions that he could possibly put to Edward. He reached the house and walked across the lawn to the door.

He made himself a cup of tea and sat in the lounge, the big fan above him creating welcome whorls of air. Tomorrow he would see about doing some scuba diving. He went over to the bookshelf and pulled out a big blue hard-back. *Hemingway: A Biography*. The top was covered with a layer of dust. He put it back and ran his fingers along the side of the other books. The dust was as thick as fur. Above the stereo was a heap of newspapers. He picked up the top one. The *Island Times*. Eight pages of A4, the columns typed on to a gestetner stencil, printed on cheap newsprint and illustrated with fuzzy photos. He flicked through it. Reports of twenty-first birthday celebrations, an interdistrict rugby match, a three-paragraph editorial lauding the government's policies in encouraging the export of vegetables. The Miss Hibiscus contest, a centre page story on the guerilla war in Afghanistan, reprinted from *Newsweek*, classified and airline timetables on the back. He put it back. It made the *Dominion* look like the *Christian Science Monitor*. He scanned the rack of tapes above the stereo, Charlie and His Volcanic Eruptions, The Nashville Rustlers, The Sea Cucumbers, Michael Jackson. Michael Jackson. At home he had never missed a classical or jazz concert. Still, when in Rome . . . He washed his cup and went to bed, covering himself with just a sheet. In minutes he was asleep.

Nobody wants to play rhythm guitar behind Jee-sus . . .

The music detonated his dreams. He turned over, wondering for a second where on earth he was.

Nobody wants to play rhythm guitar behind Jee-sus . . . Everyone wants to be the lead singer . . . in the band . . . The noise was coming from the wall behind his head. He turned on his back and pressed a button on his watch. 1.57. The singer's voice came again, sounding as if it had a hole in its muffler, the accompanying guitar reverberating in his ears as if the stereo speakers were only millimetres from his head. Then an Indian whoop, and a series of parrot-like screeches came through the wall, louder even than the song itself.

He sat up, befuddled by noise and shattered sleep. If it was Edward on the other side of the wall, why the hell hadn't he warned him that he was going to have a party? He certainly wasn't going to get up and join in, feign amusement at being woken up so rudely. He lay on his back in the semi-darkness while the appalling song went on, rattling the louvres in the bedroom window.

By the door of the room, something moved. He stared. A tall shape, a tall human shape. As it grew thicker, John tightened his fists. Its hands hung at its sides, the bare feet scuffed the stone floor. John's heart began to pump wildly. Then, as the man came closer, he shouted:

'Who are you? What do you want?'

The intruder went completely still. Then his head turned slightly and the white of an eye gleamed. John heard short, deep breaths. He swallowed, then shouted again: 'Get out! Go! Bugger off!'

At the last two words, the man glided away. Cursing, John flicked back the sheet and struggled into his trousers and shirt. His head ached from noise, wine and jet lag. He stumbled down the passage to the door of the kitchen, which was brightly lit by an unshaded bulb hanging from the centre of the ceiling.

The two boys with the Rastafarian hair were taking it in turns to drink from a large bottle of whisky. Their singlets were wet with spilt liquor, and behind them was an open cupboard which contained more spirit bottles. They took no notice of John. The shorter of the two took the empty bottle from his lips. He held it out in front of him, staring at it for a few moments. Then he tossed it over his shoulder and it shattered on the slate floor. Steadying himself against the wall, the other youth reached up into the cupboard, groped, and withdrew a full bottle. There were cyrillic letters on the label. Vodka. He unscrewed the lid, put the bottle to his lips and tipped it up high, holding it there for a full minute before passing it to his friend. John turned away, walked down the hall and stood in the doorway of the lounge.

There were about a dozen people in the room, mostly young men, many of whom had been at Tangaroa's earlier in the day. And as at the bar, liquor and laughter were the main forms of communication. A youth with an Afro was leaning against the bookcase, caressing the shoulders of a thick, buck-toothed girl in orange and white pareu; in one corner the barman was dancing slowly with the youth with the milky eye, cupping his buttocks in both hands as he nuzzled his neck. The short fat youth whom John had thought retarded had passed out and was lying beside the cane sofa. The rest were sitting around the room, drinking, laughing, shouting encouragement to their host, standing in the centre of the room.

Edward was thrashing the strings of a ukelele made from a half coconut shell, in an attempt to keep up with the guitar music pumping through the stereo. His head was lolling about on his chest, and somewhere along the line he had shed his shoes. As John stared at the inebriated tableau the song ended and the tape switched itself off. Edward's head snapped up. He threw down the ukelele, strode over to the bookshelf, picked up a glass and swallowed the contents. As he did so the buck-toothed girl broke away from the boy with the Afro, and with one breast exposed, ran across the room and into a rubber plant. She and the plant fell over. Everyone else shrieked with delight, except the barman and the youth with the milky eye. They were pressed against the wall, their bodies and lips locked together.

Edward pushed another tape into the stereo. There was a pause, then a burst of slit drum beating like a round of machine-gun fire. He raised his arms, jiggled his hefty hips and began to clang his knees together. As he shuffled his way back to the centre of the room the movement of his knees grew slower and slower, until he ended his dance with a defiant and suggestive outward thrust of his pelvis. The others yelled gleefully and raised their bottles to their lips. Edward stood panting, his mouth open, his chin on his chest. Then he looked up, and saw John. He walked over then threw his arms around him.

'Johnny! Come in, come in . . .'

'Who are these people?'

He rocked back and waved at the room.

'This is . . . the team.'

'What team?'

'The team.'

'Your friends?'

'Friends, yes.' He searched for something lodged deep in his mind. 'Others come up here, they stick together, they think their ordure has no odour. These are the real people of this country. We have a lot of fun.' He nodded triumphantly. 'I fit in, you see, Johnny.'

From the kitchen came the sound of more breaking glass. Edward's smile grew wider. 'A lot of fun.'

John kept staring at the collection of human wreckage. It was like a portrait of an asylum, run by a demented doctor. He put his hand on his friend's shoulder.

'Okay, Ed,' he said, and turned away. He went into the passage towards the bedroom, pursued by the hollow, unrelenting beat of the drums. The door of Edward's room was open, the room was lit by a light above the head of the double bed. John stopped. There was a naked, unconscious woman spreadeagled on the bed, an empty gin bottle beside her right hand. The skin of her full round belly hung in folds, her puffy cheeks flared with the scarlet rash. Tuaine.

He packed quickly and left by the back door. He walked across the front lawn, past a shirtless youth lying face down under a flame tree, past the white Daimler parked crookedly in the drive. He began walking in the direction of the Lagoon Lodge. Some minutes later he stopped and looked back. The Daimler gleamed in the tropical night. He walked on. It was another twenty minutes before he could no longer hear the sound of the drums.

Makawe

The blade cut, sliced, clean, gleaming greenness flashing in the rising sun's light; ropes of hair flung like torn kelp, and the red spray. An arch of blood against the pale sky, droplets glistening like stained foam.

Again, the blade came down, the fierce roundness of its edge neatly cleaving.

Enough. He'd had enough. Of her, of the killing. Of her body, of the early morning hours. He scratched the line along his cheekbone. Kowhiri. It never healed. It festered. Hot, sore, and itchy, like the growth between his legs. He touched that, too, then fingered the blistering curve on his face one more time.

Turning his back on the crumpled body, he looked towards the waters of the lake. Shapes floated and bobbed clumsily on the murky wavelets, glutting the space between the canoes. At the island's edge, corpses choked and heaped amongst the weeds. Some might be his.

Caressing the cool stone of his weapon, he moved towards them. Somewhere a dog barked. The stench of blood and fear and burning mingled with the faintest whiff of ngawha from the mainland — *their* smell, this people's smell — rotten, he mused. Like the bowels of the land; reeking and rotten.

He clawed at his cheekbone again, closed his eyes, and drank in the memory of the woman, and her blood. Red, fanning a rainbow against the dawn sky.

He flicked his hair, combed it carefully, shaping the front. Applied more mousse, another flick. Yeah, that was it. Ran the orange plastic teeth through the wavy mass again, then smiled. Not bad, he thought. Not bad at all. Might even score tonight, if I don't choke on the sulphur stink of this place. Gross, the way the stench here rose out of the earth, formed a dense fog all around. Clammy, yet warm, sweetly warm, like a drunk's breath. He leaned forward, peered again into the mirror. Yep, he was a winner. Like their group — the first ever from the north, to swoop down, and stun the judges at the

National Finals, to claim that grand competitions trophy, massive totara that swirled like serpents around a proud shield. To take it home, on the bus, away from this damp, smelly place where winter really rained like winter; to take it home where, even in July, the ocean moved warm across the sands. Too much going on to feel homesick. Shoulders back, he strode out the bathroom door. The night invited him. And that girl — out there, waiting, somewhere.

Her face was somehow achingly familiar; the hair, falling in thick ropes down her back, and the dusky hollow at her throat, a velvet brown. She was standing by a huge arrangement of flax blades and flowers, very still, watching only him. Only him, he was sure of that. With eyes so black they glowed and glittered hungrily. She was watching him haka, and a faint smile flickered at the corners of her darkened lips. He noticed her moko, perfectly drawn, the effect gouged. Almost the real thing, it could've been. And he wanted her, all that attention, all that beauty. So his muscles flexed, his eyes bulged, his mind went blank, and he hurled the first call of the haka at his men, snarling. Snatched from the tight hollow in the small of his back, the mere pounamu sang green in his hands, and through his pounding blood and passion they took the haka section, then the final trophy. They won.

He'd looked for her in the crowd afterwards, watched out for the almond eyes and long hair — there was no one like her, and he felt secretly that she'd helped them score, and win the competition. The magic of her being there, beside the performing area, watching from the flax. Watching him.

He had a feeling he'd see her again, before the night was out.

'Hey, man. Your hair . . .'

'Whatcha done to it, eh?'

'Mousse.' Bored reply. 'Just mousse, man, that's all.'

'Y'mean that sticky stuff? Like what girls use?'

'Nah. Just stuff to keep the style in, man.'

'Oh yeah?'

'Yeah.'

Sometimes his cousins made him sick, they were that dense. Real country bumpkins. This trip was the greatest moment in their teenage lives, they raved on and on. Something really choice, worth the long bus ride — and coming first just crowned it for everyone. Wow. Sweet victory. They'd be the toast of the whakangahau tonight, and they all knew it. The big last-night social, with three bands, a massive supper and dancing till two, and drinking till even later. The cousins twitched at the thought of it — the winning group, they'd be sure to score some local talent to take them for a bath in one of the pools; who cared about the stink. They were winners, and the night was young.

They walked along the road, following the lake side. Everyone else had gone on ahead. Music clamoured through the open doors of the brightly lit dining room, which stood surrounded by a colourful clutter of buses, cars, trucks, vans, and jostling, excited people. Bottles clinked and guitars moaned. Doors slammed and money crinkled. Hands clasped and noses pressed. It was going to be a great social.

He shoved his way through the crowd, the cousins following, boisterously possessive. Aware that he was being stared at, he fingered the discoloured birthmark on his cheekbone, pushed on through. Out there, the surge of people and the odour rising with the fog, made him feel uneasy. And she was more likely to be inside.

Yet another bracket of dances, and she still hadn't turned up. He made another round of the hall, nodding at proud relatives and supporters, feeling like a chief, like a hero, knowing that *his* performance had won them the trophy to take home. Ha. If they knew what had made his jaw stretch and tongue dart and stab, what had peeled the lids off his eyeballs, what had enflamed his blood, making his mere dance, a green demon slashing in his hands. He knew.

He ran his fingers through his hair. One wave was not quite right; the curl sprung out like a pikopiko. Gotta fix it. He headed for the large ablution block outside next to the building. Fresh cold air, and a big mirror, and no drunks. He liked to be vain in private.

Ten minutes later, the curl under strict control, he sauntered slowly from the concrete outhouse. Rain had just fallen, suddenly, harshly, and the vehicles jamming the carpark and marae shone in the dim lights. Billows of steam lurked in the air like ghosts, alert and aware. Clouds of fog parted, revealing hired vans and canoodling couples, parked cars and snuffling dogs, then closed again swallowing the whole scene.

He leaned against a fence of dewy ponga, fronds tickling his neck. Whether or not to go back inside or take a walk and check out some action in the carpark, or see what the kids were doing on the buses . . .

She was there by the flax. It had to be her. Alone, too. Looking at him. Directly at him.

Too amazed to do anything else, he walked towards her, passed the cars, the vans, the trucks, and the buses. She seemed to be lifting her arms, opening them, widening herself, asking him in to her body.

And yet, at the same time, she seemed to be moving, silently, noiselessly backwards into the veils of steam. He was too entranced to notice — locked into the glittering darkness of her eyes, hooked onto the indigo barbs of her moko, clutched within the promise of her shining skeins of hair.

The cousins reckoned he must've scored and taken off with a girl from home, so the bus left without him, trophy up the front, next to the driver. He must've gone home, because his great-grandfather's mere was missing from his pack. Just the mere — seemed weird at the time, but he never moved without it.

They didn't find him until three days later. One of the local weavers was about to soak some flax in the pool, Hinakohuru. Then she noticed something funny about the smell. It was the scum, floating on the surface of the ngawha, curdling beneath the steam. 'It was just like mousse,' she said.

YVONNE DU FRESNE

Farvel

You know, all today they have been here. In my house. A door opens by itself. A hand raps on the window glass like the crack of winter ice breaking up in the old country. A hand touches my shoulder and I turn ready to hear somebody say,

'Use the new jam for lunch. It has set so *nice*!' There is nobody there.

Somebody touches my hair, absentmindedly, as they used to, gazing out of the windows, looking at the sky, at the land. Our land. It speaks, you know. Or a voice sings. Suddenly. And you must listen, every sense alert.

Who touched my hair?

The door shut with no wind to do that.

The house is full of them. I hear tag-ends of words, laughter. Then a wind pounces on the garden, the trees. Grass, leaves, shiver, ripple with silver, with laughter, with calling voices.

'Hoy!' I call to them in Danish, 'you come now to your nice lunch!' As if they *need* lunch, those ones. They have no desire for this world's food any more. They are with God now.

Then I hear that one living voice from a month ago. Calling from her farmhouse drive, with its trees leaning from a lifetime of the north-westerlies. She as bent as her trees, out on the Tainui Line.

'Farvel, mit eget kaere barn!'

'Farewell, my own darling child!'

I turn in the road. I know that cry. I call, with a laugh, you know?

'Nej — nej. You are not saying farewell to me forever. No death for you yet!'

But she is not laughing. Again comes that cry, bleak as the wind —

'Farvel, mit eget kaere barn!'

And then she looks at my face. She is learning it all over again. She is leaving us. Soon. She will know the time. She is warning me.

'Nej!' I call. 'Not yet.'

I look at her face, not just her face, but all the faces that one by one have gone. I see her stand, out in the road, watching me as if she

226

can never have enough of looking. Not just my face, all our faces. We look the same, you see. So I do my part. I wave. I shout.

'Farvel! Tante Helga Westergaard, you are *great*!'

She knows. She breaks into a broad smile and waves. I go, but the figure left behind on that road never moves, never blinks its sea-pale eyes from fear that they miss one last, small glance.

She is being drawn back into that other country. From the first breath I took, I heard its music; the men and women singing. Remembering too, you understand, the thin soil, the howling winter weather. But, being so young, I only thought of that great multitude of our left-behind people, their faces shining with love, singing in a world filled with light. And that was Europe to me. That was my Denmark. There were the singers, and the sacred dancers, moving rank on slow rank. And now they come to claim her, those dancers, and she goes to meet them, her hands outflung in greeting, so tall, walking so softly.

The wind still blows.

'Ah,' I say to the voices in the rooms, to the laughter in the trees, in the sky, 'you be quiet now. I have to think. I have to be with her.'

Our language was spoken in a rapid, cold stream, like the water rushing in its courses over the moors, and gleaming so still in the marshes where we lived in Jutland. I was always part of a group, a frieze of women, very tall, in the long grass of a paddock, or looking out of a window. Always standing, once or twice in the busy day, one hand on the hip, the other used to help the meaning along — coming delicately down to rest on certain words that mattered. They talked as they danced, the movements spare and ceremonial, leaving things to be understood. Taking in, breathing in, the messages of the land and sky of the Manawatu. I learned the spoken words, and with my skin, my eyes, my senses, endlessly took in the signs, the changing light of sun and colour, and water, the line of hills and plains, the movement of birds. The signs were the magic signs learned by our people long ago in Denmark. They had the power, my Bedstemoder said, to see them, to use them in the new lands. They knew the secrets of food-growing, the places to find water, how to build shelter, and the patterns of the seasons. We learned all that so that our bodies and our spirits could grow, side by side. And they had the power to change themselves into the shapes of birds — the swan, the wild geese, the eagle, the falcon.

The first people here, said my Bedstemoder, had the same powers. Here it was that the sea birds and the ghost-herons became the souls of the people who had died. Who journeyed back to their home, to the sun at their death, as we do.

When I first saw those people, the Maoris, at the Recreation Ground in a huge gathering, long ago, I knew she spoke the truth. There they *were*, standing under the soft thunder of the macrocarpas. They wore the long mantles, and the birds' feathers, sweeping back in their hair; half men, half birds. As certain men and women in Denmark changed to swans, eagles, so did they. So I always saw that race and ours, able to read the signs, to haunt the sky on wings, an irresistible sweep of wings; sky-walkers.

Tante Helga is loosening the cord. Coming into my ears is a voice.

'My child, I need Thee.'

So I go and put on a more suitable dress and wash my face, making myself neat for Tante Helga. I brush my hair in front of the mirror, not looking into it, and then I do. I see the face of an ageing woman; the lines, the bones of my people. They have stamped me with their image forever. But also on it, the squint-lines of our summers here; the ridges and hollows left by the sun and dust of the new country, *my* country.

I go to the verandah and lean over. The sun beats down. The river is shrunken, its black banks glitter with mica that my Bedstemoder said was treasure, dragonfire, here as in Denmark.

Then, like a sigh, up the drying river bed flies a heron, that one that lives on the little island. A grey heron, but today changed in the flat light to black paper, a soul, starting its journey to the sea. That is my sign. So I walk out into the beating sun, to the fence that borders the paddock, that reaches to the river.

I stand and look at the land. The ghost-heron has vanished. And I *cannot* stop my grief, my tears that turn down my wind-furrowed face. I look at our land, and the river, and I cannot make sense of it, or hear Tante Helga's voice. All I can remember are her cheek bones, the blue northern eyes of our lost people. I weep like a little child. Out of my shameful gaping mouth I call,

'Tante Helga. Tante! We are lost forever.'

And her voice comes, deep in my ear, loosening the cord, but still gossiping on, as she did, one summer afternoon, on the lawn behind me.

'There your Bedstemoder, Abild Westergaard, lay on the second day of her death, in her room, in this house. And your Moder and I peeped out of the kitchen window into the farmyard and saw the Maoris, and she said,

'"Helga, they are here."

'And they were. Some sitting, some standing, and the Chief standing looking out over the land. They were quite still; warfalcons at rest.

'Your Mother gripped my hand, so *tight*.

' "They are from the pa," she whispered, "where Moder went. She loved them all. Come now." '

I stood in front of the Chief, the one with the long feather sweeping back from his head. We looked at each other. I greeted him in Danish, he greeted me in Maori. Then we turned and stood with his people, our neighbours. We touched their faces, in their way of greeting, and we stood here. Our hair blew about, but we stood so still with them, helping Abild Westergaard begin her journey to sun-fire. It was a great honour they did us that day.'

The old lilting voice dies away to a murmur, to silence, in my mind.

Who are left now? They and us, changed a little, but still knowing who we are. Using our old knowledge, and our new.

I look over the paddocks at my neighbour, Rangi Katene. Her house looks at me through the trees. I often stand in them in their circle of ancient trunks, and the wind hisses through their leaves and combs the grass at my feet. Sacred trees. Their roots reach down to underground rivers, dragonlairs. The house and Rangi know those messages from the dark.

And now, you know something strange? The wind has dropped. There is a golden light, that light when the sun is spent, when the dust motes turn to golden bees in the air. Every grass blade in the parched earth you can see, golden wires. The head-dresses those ancient dancers wore in the Jutland festival, they were made like wheat-ears, red-gold, quivering over their still faces. Faces that knew everything. Like my Tante Helga. Somehow, the power of the Old Religion slipped into the New Religion in Jutland. God and the Old Magic mixed together. I have worked out that truth, by myself.

The golden bees of the sun swarm over the paddocks. It seems to me not a trick of light, but a gift from God that I see those Maoris and Danes and English, now clear, now blurred, standing facing their lands. My house, like Rangi's, reaches its roots down to the heart of this land. Our roots are the same. We have our people, living and dead, round us forever.

Canoe, Viking ship, foam-necked, set out together on the last journey north, over the sea-roads to world's-end.

So I let go of the fence post I am gripping, scrub my face dry with a knuckled fist, and lift my eyes to be blinded by the light that welcomes Helga Westegaard at the end of her journey.

Oh, my brothers and sisters, see how our hands join together as we farewell our great Dead.

Farvel. Farvel.

JAN KEMP

The Golden Couch

She'd grown fat. It can't be denied. There was something definitely carnivalesque about her figure. The picture of Spassie resplendent in a bath of champagne, dressed with ice-cubes, caught Smithie's eye. It has been taken on her birthday, the inscription on the back had said, in the middle of winter and was her answer to a dare. One of her women friends had kept her barefoot balance on either side of the tub looking down and had snapped Spassie from above. Spassie's face shows the shock of cold, champagne notwithstanding, on her skin. She gazes down between her enormous breasts at her lush body, some of it submerged, some of it soft, creamy islands above, let's say, champagne level. And it *is* champagne. Tiny, frothy bubbles collect around an emerged knee or bubble at the edges of the plump stomach where a few ice-cubes jostle.

Whoever took the snap had a natural sense of composition or it was one of those accidents that make art question all its sweat, Smithie thought, smiling to herself. The photographer had inadvertently taken her own foot and pantaloon-leg, the latter of purple silk in a paisley design that flowed out over her arch and drooped in a curve. It exactly off-set and complemented Spassie's nakedness. She looked like someone who'd escaped from a harem with a few veils.

Who could not love Spassie for providing these loud images redolent of a voice-box she'd use at sergeant-major pitch until Smithie would wince and cover her ears; oh sorry Smithie, I'll turn it down a few decibels, she'd say in that mocking and yet utterly apologetic tone she'd assume if she knew she'd offended. The tone which showed the truth of her confession that she loved. And love she did. Ardently.

Smithie still had a little chest of Chinese lacquered drawers, pearl earrings, a bracelet and if she started to go through the filing cabinet, she guaranteed the billet-doux would fall out. And yet, Smithie could not return her love, not in the same way.

'Know what, Smithie?' Spassie sniffed and clutched at her duvet. They were in her half of the house.

'I dreamt of you last night.'

'Of me?' Smithie laughed.

'No, I mean, really dreamt. I mean of your body too!'

So that was it. Her hooded, lingering looks desired Smithie's body. Smithie's first feelings were of revulsion. To have Spassie's spatulas, as she called her fingers, probing into her, trying to please her and, Smithie imagined, Spassie's hard, quick, little kisses smothering her mouth and tongue made her jerk back, though she was careful to cover herself by pretending she was re-settling the cushion in the wooden rockingchair where she sat near Spassie's bed. Spassie had the flu.

'But, Spassie, you know I'm . . .'

'. . . heterosexual.'

'Yes. And I don't think that will alter.'

'Do you know how I've sat, clutching Black Rock, riding the night and having the stars spit on me?'

'Don't be so dramatic.'

'My love for you is like the song of a bird dying as it sings.'

'A thorn bird.'

'Okay, I know it's an Australian cliché. My love's like this, then!'

Defiantly, she leapt out of bed, nearly tripping on her long, wincyette nightie and set the stereo at a selected track. The solo voice of an English choir boy pierced the hallowed ground of top A and came down to rest like a bird in a polyphonous flock. Spassie stretched to the top of her five feet and stood triumphantly near the Gustav Doré etching that hung on the wall above her cello leaning next to the folded music-stand.

'See? My love for you's like that.' She gestured at the stereo.

'It's very sweet of you, Spassie,' Smithie began, 'but . . . I'll make us some tea.'

Ten minutes later she returned carrying the teapot in its cuddly cosy, a small jug of milk and some mugs on a tray.

'It's in my horoscope, Smithie,' Spassie said, looking trustingly up at Smithie. 'Whatever, whomever I love, I love. There's no sexual discrimination. I'm like John the Baptist in Leonardo's painting holding up his finger and smiling a secret smile.' She imitated his pose, balancing on her knees next to the disarray of cushions and pillows. I'm ambidextrous,' she said as coyly and sacrilegiously as possible. 'Before, it was my cello I loved and now it's you.'

'Spassie, don't you see, for me, this can't be the most romantic of confessions, I just can't . . .'

232

'I knew you hated me anyway,' Spassie said and rolled back into her duvet and dragged it up to cover her face.

Smithie made herself avoid getting stuck in the treacle.

'Maybe you should find a woman who suits you?'

Smithie patted the shape of the bed-socked foot that was thrust out near her.

'No one asks anyone to love anyone. *Love* chooses,' Spassie said and flung back the duvet. 'I love you!' she said, arms out, imploring.

'Spassie, I don't know what to do. Don't you see? I love you too, you know I do. But not in that way. It's not instinctive for me, you see? I'm as helpless as you are.'

Spassie got up to hug Smithie, and Smithie let her wrap her arms around her. And held her. Spassie let go all the venomous tension then and just sobbed.

'The tea's cold. I'll make us some more,' Smithie finally said, gently.

From Spassie's kitchen window you could see the inner sweep of the bay with the tide out, leaving the mangroves like a caravan of little green animals making their way over the muddy sand. It was a clear, bright day. And you could see right over past the single, white-painted tower of White Heron Lodge on the next headland, this side of the harbour, to the clusters of little wooden houses that were Devonport, their roofs glinting white in the sunlight; and even further too, past the Devonport Heads to the channel by Rangitoto Island, where their ship had come in and gone out, their sailors' ship, Spassie's and Smithie's, last summer.

Spassie had been in Lewis Eady's music shop when she'd met Jeff browsing over the sheet music.

'Play anything?'

'Flute, ma'am.'

And there'd followed a long conversation about music between the friendly, chubby, cello student and the American sailor, which Spassie recounted word for word over tea when Smithie got back from the department that evening.

'And I told him that my friend on the other side of the house was a real New Zealand composer.'

'Oh Spassie, you didn't. I'm just a music tutor.'

'I showed him the score of your children's opera. It was there on the shelf. I hardly needed to lift a finger. He bought a copy. And you need promoting, Smithie.'

'That was nice of him. And you.'

'He's coming here tonight with his buddy for dinner. I know you've got to go to rehearsal, but you can come in afterwards for drinks. I told him they could meet you about ten o'clock. D'you want to come?'

'But Spassie, you don't even know them. Who are they?'

'One's a geophysicist, that's Jeff. And his friend Hank's a navigator. They're going to Antarctica on an ice-breaker.'

That was it. No more discussion. Spassie was adamant.

'Go on, Smithie,' she'd said and punched Smithie's arm. 'You've got to come.'

Smithie was there at ten. Spassie grabbed her sleeve at the door, pulled Smithie to her and hissed, 'I want the one on the bed.'

'Okay, okay, Spassie,' Smithie said, shaking her off, her sense of propriety piqued. She hadn't even seen the guests. But no one was on the bed. Or near the bedroom. They sat in the elephant armchairs where they all always sat in the living-room — which was the advantage of Spassie's side of the house, a proper living-room. As well as the view from the kitchen window. Spassie threw herself back into a technical discussion about a cello concerto with Jeff and left Spassie to talk to the navigator with the trim blond beard.

By midnight, Hank lay down on the couch in Smithie's tiny front room saying, 'I think I'll spend the rest of it here.' Smithie admitted to herself she was drunk. She admitted too that she'd airily invited them all over to see her half.

'Stay the night. We've plenty of space, haven't we, Spassie?' Smithie said magnanimously.

Spassie caught up with her in the kitchen. Shoved her back against the sink bench. 'You always get what you want, Smithie, don't you? I told you I wanted the one with the beard. And look what you've done. You've got him. He's lying on your couch in your living-room.'

'Beard? Bed? Oh no, Spassie, I misheard you. Take him. I don't care. Take him. I don't want either of them. Love's not like that. Send in the other one. He can sleep on the couch.'

Spassie said, 'As if he'll come.'

'Yes,' Smithie said. 'How can you force people to your will? I'm sorry, Spassie, I . . .'

Then Jeff came in and led Spassie away, his eyes alight, his arm around her shoulders, gentle, protective. Smithie crept to her bedroom. Why couldn't she better help her? Was she so selfish? Then Hank came in. 'I should like to stay with you,' he said politely. And

Smithie let him turn the dimmer-lamp right down and get in beside her.

'I'm glad you got him,' Spassie said. 'He was heavy-duty. I'd never have coped with his talking about that girl who died.'

Smithie switched off the boiling kettle and as she poured the water into the pot, face averted so as not to be enveloped by the hot steam, she thought again of his girl who he'd made love to every day, every morning and every night for a year. Then she'd died in a car crash. And he'd joined the ice-breaker and gone to Antarctica for the first time, and she'd come too, like an albatross.

'Real Ancient Mariner stuff!' Spassie said, her eyes nearly popping out. 'And my Jeff was so beautiful.' She laid out the four mugs. 'He knew I was scared. That I'd never really done it much before. Well, you can't count my brother,' she said devastatingly, 'or Uncle Ned's nips at my tits. Though you could count the bassoonist at the Cambridge Music Festival, couldn't you? The one in the tent?'

Smithie nodded. 'Yes, that sounded more like it,' she said, pouring the milk into the mugs set out on the breakfast trays. Spassie was absurd. She could reduce a thing to its most common denominator and still retain a sense of awe when discussing it. 'Oh stop being so prissy, Smithie,' she'd say when Smithie's look of disdain came on her face.

Their sailors stayed a second night. Hank said, 'You're warming me, you're warming me.' They didn't get out of bed until Spassie and Jeff came and tapped on their window.

That evening they went down to Jellicoe Wharf like ship-girls, Spassie cute in her green corduroy dungarees and Smithie in her denim skirt and jacket with her red tights. They'd been aboard the ice-breaker in the afternoon and had seen Jeff's columns of glass filled with wet rock samplings from drill-cores on the sea-bed, Hank's bridge with all the brass equipment and the fantail deck where Jeff and Hank met and talked and smoked cigarettes at sea. 'Nothing nuclear, eh?' Spassie had joked as they sat in the canteen below decks. 'No, nothing nuclear,' Jeff had said, 'we're a research boat.'

They waved at them. Hank saluted from the bridge. Jeff waved. The real ship-girls tottered along the wharf on their high heels, one of them, her teased long hair flying, waved a scarf.

'I think they really meant it,' Spassie said, as she turned her tearful face to Smithie's, 'just like us.'

They raced in Smithie's Morris Minor over the Harbour Bridge and beyond Devonport town to Marine Parade. They poised Spassie's camera on the high wooden railing at the edge of the cliff that over-looked the beach. They could just make her out as she came sliding into the channel in the dusk-light — the USCGC Iceberg 453, her peculiar rigging was set against the darker looming shape of Rangitoto Island like a huge mechanical insect, their radar equipment, Hank had said. Spassie and Smithie stood, their arms round each other, waving, waving, their faces wet with tears, waving, waving, soft so soft inside they were, waving at their sailors in the near dark. 'Come back, come back,' Spassie had whispered.

Alone in bed again on her side of the house Smithie rolled into a cocoon to try to enclose her body, make herself whole, complete, the way she'd felt for those nights when Hank had been there. He had shuddered into her like a ship off the cradle into a choppy sea. She was contained, sealed up and freighted off south to Antarctica where green icebergs floated by and the soundless air muffled the voices of men in balaclavas.

And now he wasn't there, only the memory of his body imprinted on hers, the faint smell of his hair still in the pillow, in her nostrils and of his body in the sheets. She clung to her cocoon shape, recalling, squeezed her eyes tight, re-imaging, remembering.

Then the window sash went up and a body heaved itself over the low sill and fell in onto her bed.

'Smithie, I'm lonely,' Spassie's petulant voice said. She was drunk. Smithie could smell the whisky.

'Spassie, what's, what's, don't, please, what's the time?'

'About three.' Spassie's voice was high-pitched. 'I haven't slept all night. I've been thinking, thinking of them, thinking of us, thinking how they came like ships in the night, don't laugh, I mean it, veritable ships in the night. We gave them everything and now they've gone and we're left alone. Just left! I hate men. Don't you see, Smithie, all we've truly got is each other.' She burst into floods of tears.

'Let's go and sit on the golden couch,' Smithie said and wrapped a blanket round each of them and took Spassie back through the adjoining front doors into her half of the house. Spassie lay on the golden couch under the windows in the dining alcove while Smithie made tea in the kitchen. Spassie plumped up the cushions at Smithie's end of the couch and leaned out and dragged over a chair for Smithie to set the tray on.

'Not *on* the gold,' she said, meaning they might spill on the gorgeous velvet she'd so carefully upholstered onto the stripped and re-oiled wood of her ottoman. The ottoman as extravagant as Spassie's dinner parties of sour-creamed soups and legs of lamb.

Smithie sat at her end, poured two mugs of tea and carefully transferred them both to the windowsill. She smiled at Spassie. Her colour was back now they were doing something. Just as hers must have come when Spassie tended to her so gently, that night six months ago when she'd broken off with Peter. Neither of you will finish it, can finish it and it's destroying you both, Spassie had said, so I've finished it. I told Peter just now, never to phone again and not to write and that you wouldn't. You've just got to accept it, Smithie. He can't be with you. He's married. Spassie was right. Quite right.

Smithie's mind had caved in then like a mine-shaft. All she could see was a little platform where the light from the lamp on her helmet fell. It was gold. Beyond, it was only blueness, deep dark blueness.

'I want to sit on the golden couch and look at the sky,' she said in staccato, and like a zombie had clambered to the ottoman where she'd lain, her helmet fallen off as she racked her head back and looked and looked at the night sky.

Spassie said, 'You've been there three hours. Have some tea and a muffin, Smithie,' and had balanced a mugful of tea and one of her special raisin-bran muffins on a plate on the narrow sill. On the gold couch you were safe. Nothing could get you. Shoes off and feet up too and make yourself an island. You are inviolate. No hurt. No more hurt.

Even if she would never quite understand her, she'd never forget her, Smithie thought. She waited for the kettle to boil, looking at the photograph, stuck on the cork-board in the kitchen: Spassie in the bathtub, taken all that time ago, the year she went off to London.

Smithie turned to look out the window, to watch the light fall on the mangrove swamp, on the glinting sea, the white tower block and the winking roofs of the Devonport houses way over. Whatever their differences, Spassie had a lot of guts and an enormous appetite for life. Smithie set her cup on the windowsill and sat down on the golden couch and pushed the window a little further open.

And then she heard it. The first bar, drawn with three quick struts of the bow followed by the opulent imagery. Smithie leaned over the end of the ottoman, rummaged for a pencil and a manuscript notebook on the desk-top and then, sitting, feet curled up under her on the golden couch, began to scribble the notes. She could hear Spassie's voice under her own old windowsill by the little garden at the side of the house — the garden they were supposed to have dug together, which Smithie had left to Spassie to tend, sensing the meetings between the tomato stakes were charged with a strange, desirous flavour she'd rather not have to acknowledge.

'Never writes me a note of music, does she?' Smithie heard Spassie say to the seedlings. 'Writes scores for mentors and lovers, all male. Never writes a damn note for me. And who does all the weeding? Who looks after you marties?'

Smithie heard the *sproing* of the garden fork as it struck against the spade. Spassie was certainly a percussive gardener.

Well, now, at last something had come. She swiftly wrote the notes, hummed a first half-page, yes, it was coming and it was Spassie's, her very own cello sonata made with the kind of love Smithie could give her. When it was quite finished, after a week or two of cooling and editing, she'd write it out with pen and ink on her special manuscript paper, then send it off to Spassie in London.

GREGORY O'BRIEN

Karminrosa

He has always lived in the spaces between trees. Now he has taken a loft between trees and arranges tubes of paint along the window-ledges overlooking the park. The residence of a painter.

His first afternoon is spent arranging the return of his coloured pencils and eating avocado sprinkled with lemon and light from the window in the roof. He lifts the telephone receiver high into the spaces between trees:

— Gino, have you finished using my set of pencils?

— Sorry, I meant to return them. I haven't used them in ages, says Gino, with Pale Geranium Lake in his right hand.

Gino is busy designing a poster for his band *I Spartacus* — a four-piece group comprising guitarist, bass-player, drum machine and smoke machine. A review of their last public performance said the only piece of equipment that seemed to be working properly on stage was the smoke machine. Cloud upon cloud of smoke and the band nowhere to be seen.

Gino says he will deliver the coloured pencils to the residence in an hour.

The artist feels jealous when his forty-eight coloured pencils are away. It is as if the people who have borrowed them are having wonders bestowed upon them. But, rightfully, they are his pencils. His wonders.

There is a knock on the door of the residence in the park.

— That will be the coloured pencils, he says to himself.

— Sorry. I haven't used them in ages, says Gino, Pale Geranium Lake in his trouser pocket.

Forty-seven pencils and one empty space now make up the box of forty-eight. The artist inspects the points, noting which colours are to be sharpened, which colours are the furthest gone.

— Viridian. Raw Umber . . .

— You should visit me some other time when there is more time,

Gino, he says in the doorway. But not in the evenings. I work in the evenings.

Late every afternoon a novelist called Ada visits.

There is no milk delivery where he lives. There is a row of empty milk bottles on the highest shelf above the stove and there is a woman breast-feeding on a nearby park bench. But that is as close as he gets to the delivery of milk.

Strollers in the park notice the arrival of Ada each day. They can see through the window to where she is lying on the couch.

— She is a novelist resting between novels, they whisper.

The artist hears the sounds of construction inside his head. Tall cranes and front-end loaders are developing in there. Since moving into the park, his head has become inner-city real estate.

There are no neighbours despite the fact he lives in the middle of the biggest city of the biggest country of a very small world. Or else it is the smallest city of the smallest country of a vast world. Which-ever way, there is an orange tree beside a fountain beside another orange tree. And sometimes the artist feels at one with the oranges beneath. And with the sounds of construction inside his head. And the faint sound of an electric band practising across town. *I Spartacus* in a rehearsal room above a car yard. Sounds coming across in the spaces between trees.

Surveying an empty canvas, he sits balanced on the edge of a desk on the edge of a room balanced on the edge of a house on the edge of a park.

He is a painter resting between paintings. When the trustees of the residence come to visit he is always lying on the couch asleep. Or thinking.

About one woman.

In particular.

One day the trustees will arrive to the sound of paint on canvas — the purple, orange and green sounds. But for now he is a painter resting between paintings.

To tell the time of day he consults a clock of flowers five metres across in the park nearby. The two arms move around a bed of orange, yellow and pink depending on the time of year. A touch of green. Sometimes the hands travel across brown earth for days on end until the flowers arrive.

Once there had been a beehive near the residence and whenever guests arrived they would be surrounded in a vapour of bees.

From the bedroom window he can see a headless statue in white stone, a seagull where the head once was. And the statue's head can be found hidden in the long grass, as if laid there by a bird. A polished white egg.

— When your friends visit they must see how incompetent you are in the kitchen and want to weep, Ada says, her feet shuffling among novels at one end of the couch.

But he is too busy licking stamps to answer. The stamps have citrus fruit on them but taste nothing like citrus fruit. They taste a thousand miles away from citrus fruit. They taste of dusty bags full of lost mail on a broken-down trolley — all the mail misplaced except that which is found by mice and used subsequently to upholster the insides of old pots and pipes which are, respectively, the residences and limousines of mice.

— When are you going to draw me naked? she asks.

He laughs and turns his face towards the window where two fantails have just flown in.

— That means either good luck or someone has died, he says.

— That means *soon*, she says.

He opens the skylight in the roof with a pole designed for that purpose. The skylight is a square acre of sky and he holds it above his head on the end of the pole, changing the angle of the sky so rain cannot reach him.

Rain is his only neighbour. He talks to the rain while leaning over a hedge behind the house.

— Now you have your coloured pencils back, there's no excuse, she says. You'll have to draw me.

— What are you reading, he asks, noticing a book lying open across her lap.

— It's not a good book, she replies. A good book should take you away from yourself. But I'm still here.

— But a book will only take you out if it thinks you're desirable, he says. Books have different expectations. They're often let down.

— Anyway, she adds, it's a terrible book. And instead of taking me anywhere, it seems content to leave me at home looking after the children.

— You should leave the book.

— I shall.

Ada crosses the room, picks up a box of coloured pencils, and asks:
— Which one is me?

Her fingers running along the many colours.

— Here it is! Karminrosa!

Rose Carmine.

She closes the box, leaving the chosen pencil sitting on the lid for the artist to pick up when it is time to draw her.

Ada's first novel is called *The Avenue of Raving and Melancholy* and she suggested to the publishers that they approach the artist in his residence for a cover design.

— You could draw me naked and that could be the cover of the book.

He has already completed a design based on a medieval City of Wolves.

— The book won't sell anyway, she continues.

— Yes it will, he says. Because *we* will buy it.

Never having owned a double bed until now, he invites his friends to sit there among half-filled teacups and unread novels.

His friends can be seen through a window sitting on the bedspread among Turkish designs.

One in particular.

Lying there.

Towels and sheets hang from the rafters to dry. A field of clover descends from the ceiling and pillowslips dangle either side of it. Ada thinks she has seen the sheets before but cannot imagine where. She slips between them without a word.

She sits on the couch and says:

— Anyone would think you're running a Chinese laundry.

— Haiku, he says, sneezing.

Then it occurs to her the sheets hanging in the room are made out of the uniforms of Japanese sailors.

The artist looks up, surprised.

— I thought I'd seen them somewhere before. The sheets. And I have. The uniforms of Japanese sailors!

— Having you visit is like having a film crew in the house, he says and lies on the couch, his head in her lap. And her head in his lap.

Ada's novel is set in a laundry where miles of hot-water piping circulate around a very confined space. The air around the pipes is made of sheets and linen. It is completely white and the woman in the novel breathes only that air.

At night, cold water runs through the piping in the novel.

Ada is a woman who runs either hot or cold. Sometime in her past warmth was put out with the laundry and never returned.

When she arrives at the residence in the park, she touches the artist's face and he can tell at once: hot or cold. Sometimes he need only touch her hand to tell — or see her walking past the fountain beneath the window.

It is rumoured that one day the fountain will come to life, but for now it is empty and a source of wonder for strollers who cross the park to look at the plain brick appliance which has never spilt a drop of water since the day it was installed.

The closest the fountain has got to water is rain.

But even the rain will not go near it, lingering instead among the orange trees, taking the long way around to cross the square.

Dry as a bone, one day a dog might run off with the fountain. Ada passes in a flowing gown and the fountain looks enviously on. At a woman who runs either hot or cold.

This afternoon she is running cold.

He is lying on the bed thinking, and waiting to be thought about. Sheets curl around his legs. He remembers saying:

— If you sleep in the afternoon, what is left of the day?

(It was morning and she was reading a novel entitled *In the Morning*. Later that day he found her reading a novel, *In the Afternoon*.)

The artist is waiting for Ada to walk in among his drawings and he will prefer her to them.

Maybe she might even think about him, he wonders. And imagines, later, falling asleep and being unable to distinguish between the drawings and her.

— Nudes, she says as she enters the room where pencil drawings lie scattered.

— Whose nudes? she enquires.

He says he had her in mind, then drew her. Eleven times her.

Ada searches the drawings for herself. But cannot find herself there. Something is wrong. She examines the colours.

— Braunocker, Brown Ochre. Venezianischrot, Venetian Red.

Ada is running colder and colder.

— Hellgrau, Light Grey. Weib, White!

— None of them is me! she cries.

Then storms out of the residence, leaving a storm of coloured pencils in her wake. Her sight intent on seeing no one.

Night and then another day. He is without her. The following evening the construction noises he is accustomed to in his head cease. All that remains is the distant thrashing of an electric guitar and the gurgling of a smoke machine.

He remembers the woman saying the skylight was not in the roof of the residence but in the roof of his head.

— Nothing shall come between the skylight and his head, she said. We should avoid middle-men.

And later:

— There are too many men in the middle of everything.

He remembers talking to her about books, but seldom agreeing about music.

— That is not music. That is a sea-elephant having a fit, she said.

— You can't call that music. That's a nearby construction site.

He had a record which sounded like precious articles being broken on the floor. He listened to it often in the evenings until one night he found himself listening to it without having turned the record player on. Upon entering the lounge he found Ada breaking all the precious items in the house — crystal glasses and intricate statues, heirlooms and ornaments.

— This is not music, she said. This is not.

The following evening or the evening following that. He remembers the exact place on his shoulder where she last kissed him. Goodbye. Not the last time he saw her. Even if she was to return, he would continue to remember that place.

A breeze keeps touching him there.

It is a rare occasion — the dusting of the furniture and ledges, behind the television and the tops of books along a shelf. A cloud of unknowing circulates around the room, following the artist with duster. Finally he dusts behind the desk and a coloured pencil rolls out from behind a leg.

— Karminrosa, Rose Carmine, the pencil says, in silver letters on red.

— Karminrosa, Rose Carmine, he says.

— Karminrosa, Rose Carmine! he says, remembering Ada and her discovery of the pencil. And leaving it on the lid of the box, from where it must have rolled. And then remained hidden between the desk leg and the wall.

The telephone is a tiny piano. To ring Ada, he plays Schubert's *Trout* and on the other side of the city a telephone resounds, also with Schubert's *Trout*.

Small, delicate lamps light up around his house as he rings Ada. They illuminate the small hours.

— Who is it?

— Is it you?

Karminrosa.

— Rose Carmine . . .

The building he resides in was once a stable. Ada says there are still horses inside it. She says if you peer in through the skylight in the roof of the man's head you can see them sauntering around, a mare giving birth to a foal and the placenta as black as night. You would expect to find stars in a placenta that black, she says.

— The horses are excited. They smell of coffee and fall asleep on pillows that also smell of coffee.

Ada is lying on the couch, resting between novels. And he is also on the couch. Every time the clocktower rings, Ada says:

— It is for you.

But he is a man approaching love and replies:

— Let it ring.

And, this way, they continue into the silence beyond the ringing. Night presses its ear to the skylight and hears the thrashing of wild horses inside the old stables.

Later he pours boiling water into a teapot which has a skylight in the lid. The leaves can be observed through the skylight in the delicacy of their movements.

Ada dreams that the artist is painting a naked woman with a thick black paintbrush and the white forms of the woman can be traced to the gaps between the heavy strokes. The ink is black and oily as though it has just dripped from beneath a parked car.

And in an office block across town a drum machine and a smoke machine are rehearsing while the other two members of the band are wandering the streets affixing Pale Geranium Lake posters to other posters which already cling to the walls and available space.

— When are you going to draw me naked? she asks upon waking.

— When are you going to write a novel about me lying here naked? he replies.

— Instead of just what's in your head.

— Instead of what's just outside your head.

— I've been waiting days, she says, laughing.

— Well, write a novel then.

They laugh together in the spaces between each other's laughter. Making one continuous laughter. In this manner they continue to fill the long hours which are somehow full anyway.

— Isn't it strange how an hour is full even if you do nothing in it, she says. Hours always have enough to do.

— Karminrosa, he replies, selecting one pencil from the box.

He cannot believe his good luck. Every day is like this for the artist in the park. But today more so. His painted sticks can approximate this sky. Through the window. Just west of the fountain. She is lying there on the edge of a pencil. Ada lying there. The skylight is flung open and the sun beams downwards while the moon shines back up from below.

— The table is richly set, Ada says. A candle holder the shape of an angel. Vanishing wax.

Hours fall away, either side of his drawing of her.

Where once was the roughness of fabric, he now finds smoothness. He wonders what the sky is up to. The spaces between trees.

Across town, a smoke machine is switched off for the weekend.

OWEN MARSHALL

Convalescence In the Old City

One's real life is often the life one does not lead.
— Oscar Wilde

Only those who have experienced life there can know the feeling of
the place; for such a city travels badly by words. An insect is active
in the night there, between the paving stones of the old part of the
city, and at first light sometimes I would see small mucus domes upon
the cobbles. They made a brief defiance like fish eyes, then died
beneath the bike wheels, the boots of passers by, the sun. And in that
city there was a faint scent of the past — desperation and unrequited
injuries — which mingled with the steam from the sewer covers, the
smell of new baked saasi bread and sprays of blue, upland lilies carried
to the sanctuary, and the sleeping breath of crowded people.

At dawn and dusk there is an awkward turning: pretence fails, and
sensed in the brief hiatus as one state gives way to another is sadness
for things seen as they are. I prefer to be alone at both these times,
or if in company to avoid the eyes of others. In the old city the death
of a day or a night was a vulnerable time; one rhythm lost, another
not quite begun. A time when symptoms of illness reappeared and
achievements seemed most trivial.

I was there for a month only, a little less, restricted by convalescence to a very limited patrol; the hotel, its view and acquaintances, the
labiniska and the narrow streets surrounding. So I can't claim any
general knowledge of the country, just the experience of a short time
in the old city.

Mine was a small hotel, and the only other regular guest who was
around much during the day was a Polish engineer. I didn't see his
name written, but my guess is Debicki, Moritz Debicki. He came
from Kalisz. I have never been to Poland; never known Polish people
except for this one acquaintance. My expectation, based on films and
books, was that Poles were histrionic and libidinous, full of poetic
melancholy and the hopeless courage of lost causes. Yet Debicki was
very practical and brisk. He had come south as an engineer to work

in the heavy industry of the new city, and because it was the time of union agitation he had little to do and was on half pay until work could begin again. He found a way of turning circumstance to his advantage. He obliged with plumbing and mechanical work at the labiniska, and for the family tannery a few blocks from the hotel. The smell of the tannery remained with him after this work. Of course he was paid under the table by both concerns, to supplement his half pay, and was pleased with his resourcefulness.

I wasn't well enough to go far from the hotel, and Moritz Debicki came in to talk to me in my room many days, or sat with me a while on the ramp by the old stables which held the shade. He was a foreigner too, but more familiar with the place than I, for he had lived there for almost two years and could speak the language. He had a wish to be helpful to me — alone in the old city. Also Moritz liked to use his English, which was surprisingly good. He didn't like to waste opportunities, and if I was quiet too long from fatigue, or thought, he would prompt me to conversation again by starting up himself. 'The next day I am going to do work in the machineries of the tannery,' or 'Men and women in this country: both of them are not modern in thinking. They live in the history of their country altogether.'

I was glad of Moritz Debicki. I appreciated his practical nature, his interest in me a stranger convalescing in the hotel, and his courtesy in regard to nationality. As a Pole perhaps he considered pride in country to be everywhere a significant thing. Often when he came to visit me he would offer some knowledge of New Zealand as a greeting: a gift of his research somewhere in a city which cannot have groaned with information of Aotearoa. I hadn't the resources or freedom to repay in kind, except to praise Chopin, and the charge of the Polish cavalry against the German tanks. Moritz told me with pleasure for both our countries that New Zealand's export trade to Poland was greater than to Spain, Sweden, Austria or Yugoslavia.

Midday was a sour sweat in summer; hot, still, and the fumes of the industries in the new city drifted into the irregular streets on the hill. The men left their sidewalk chairs along the wall of the labiniska I could see from my room. They took their tall tankards inside, away from the heat and the pollution of the new industries they despised; inside, where windows were closed.

Late in the afternoon however a fresh world was begun. By four the heat was such that it defeated itself, thus the cooler air came flowing down from the hills and the mountains behind them, and the poisons of the new industries no longer reached the old part of the city. Moritz said that the local name for the cool air meant snow breath, and when it came the decorous men brought their tankards out from the labiniska and took their seats again; women moved about the narrowing streets; the hotel cook who had a lazy eye talked loudly to his staff of one.

Moritz Debicki was fond of schnapps; I never developed the taste for it. He would bring the bottle when he came to see me, and two small glasses with very thick bottoms. He might preface his visit by saying that he knew Taupo to be the largest lake in New Zealand, or that our kiwi was an oddity of nature which I should explain to him. There was a sense of unreality concerning my country when I heard it described in formal tit-bits by a Polish engineer in a hotel room above the sloping streets in the old city. As I might in ignorance have talked of prayer wheels in Tibet, or the red fields of Tuscany. Outside my window was a plant box. The grey dirt had shrunk from the wooden sides in the heat, and there were no flowers. Moritz would stand at the open window in the evening and rest his schnapps bottle in the window box. He could see the men on their chairs along the wall, and he scorned them for their lack of ambition. Moritz was resolved to be a fully qualified mechanical engineer within a year, and then return, he said, to Poland and marry a virgin of good family. There were some very good virgins and families in Kalisz, he assured me, which was after all a city of some 85,000 people.

When it was becoming dark and the snow breath had saved the old city again, sometimes the men along the wall of the labiniska would begin to sing. Songs not at all boisterous, but polite and reflective. As night came on a son or daughter would be sent by the women and stand respectfully at a distance to remind a singer of his family. And the father would leave his seat along the wall, leave his quiet, repetitious singing, and go home with the child sent for him.

In the old city it seemed to me that the electricity was different from electricity in other places, although the pragmatist will tell you that it can't be so: the light lacked penetration and was very yellow. Moritz told me that it was because the city supply was overloaded and all the apparatus second rate. I recall the singing as night came, the weak, yellow light of windows and corner lamps, and the stink of the new city moved away by the cool air of the mountains. But I don't pretend to know more than these appearances of the place, for I was there a little less than a month, and restricted mainly to the hotel and the immediate streets by not being well. I have often disparaged those who pronounce upon a place with authority after some superficial experience of it, and who have no understanding of the life and sustaining prejudices of people there, so I won't name the country or city. Yet I was there; saw the things which I describe, as you might see them yourself if you cared to. Yet nothing is ever quite the same, even in such an old city, and the earth within the window box may not crack in just that pattern again, and Moritz Debicki is unlikely to be still in that hotel where I saw him arrested for theft.

Moritz would stand at the window, or sit on the other iron bed in my room, and talk to me in his effective English. His face was lively and he would tend his moustache with the thumb and forefinger of his left hand. His interest in people was sociological rather than personal, it seemed to me: he talked of groups and classes, not individuals, to a degree that was unusual. The striking factory workers were a fascination to him, their habits and intentions, but only as a body; he had no friends among them. He knew the characteristics of the traditional minorities of the old city's population, and explained to me the utterly different lives of married and unmarried women. Yet when I praised the expressive eyes of the maid at the labiniska, he said he hadn't noticed, but that almost certainly she would be Croatian.

Our acquaintance remained a slightly formal one: talks in my room, or less often on the ramp of the stables, an occasional walk in the evenings along the streets of the old city, or a visit to the labiniska where we seemed to inhibit the regulars so that they didn't sing. Moritz and I maintained a certain reserve — on my part because I liked him but was wary of rapid intimacy which might prove a mistake. I still needed a good deal of quiet and rest. And also it was so obviously a temporary coincidence. A Polish engineer from Kalisz working in the new industries before returning to a virgin of good family, and a Kiwi teacher taking an unintended convalescence on his European tour.

Almost always I ate at the hotel, and not just to keep expenses down. Eating places were few in the old city; the locals ate at home, and it was not a tourist city to any special extent. The spread of the industries in the new city and the priorities of the government discouraged anything frivolous or deliberately appealing. The hotel food was all I needed, or felt like. The large meal was late in the evening, when the snow's breath had come, for even in summer we usually had a heavy soup. I have seen the cook adding the bowl of blood late in its cooking — displaying the addition with pride. 'It is known an excellent goodness,' Moritz told me.

On my last Tuesday I finished my soup as the two policemen arrived in the dining room. There were seven guests including myself. The police were looking for Moritz Debicki, but he was working late at one of his under the table jobs. Both men were noticeably handsome, dark, set off well by their green and black uniforms. The police in that city all seemed possible leading men; perhaps they were chosen for appearance rather than stature or skills; perhaps it was just the effect of the uniform. The senior man remained in the dining room to smoke, while the other policeman went out and waited in the foyer. Nothing was said between them; either it was planned beforehand, or their customary procedure. The hotel guests did not linger after the meal, and I was the last to go to my room. The policeman in the foyer smiled at me as I went up the stairs. It seemed disloyal to Moritz not to make some effort to warn him, and I stood by my window as if I would have the opportunity to signal to him on the cobbled street. I had little conviction though; for all I knew it could be a matter of some technicality. I learnt practically nothing of the language in my time there.

Moritz Debicki didn't pass my window, and he was arrested in the foyer as he returned to the hotel. I heard the first, quick words, then the louder protestations of Moritz. To go down was all that I could do; my uncomprehending presence was the only support that I could offer him. One policeman gripped Moritz firmly by the jacket as they argued. Their three voices echoed in the hotel foyer, but no one else came out; the hotel was quiet everywhere except the foyer.

'Is this necessary?' I said. It sounded absurd even as I said it, for who was I to stand in the entrance of a hotel in the old city and question in English the actions of authority? The policemen regarded me, but didn't reply.

'I am so arrested for robbery of the tannery', said Moritz. The police began to urge him from the hotel foyer into the street. The grip on his jacket pocket was maintained, but there was no sign of handcuffs or guns. Moritz called to me over his shoulder at the doorway. 'In your country would not occur this bungle of justice,' and as I had been addressed the senior policeman paused to nod at me.

I was ashamed for Moritz: his casual clothes shabby in contrast with the smart green and black of the police. The shabbiness was accentuated by his humiliation. I was ashamed for myself too — for my inability to be of any influence for his benefit in the situation, for my witness of his humiliation. They walked closely together across the uneven cobbles and past the labiniska wall where the singers sat quietly. I could see no car in the twilight. Moritz was still held by the pocket. One of his shoulders was lower than the other because of that grip, and his shoes were worn at the heels.

In that way was my acquaintance at the hotel in the old city taken away, and I went myself two days later. The police wouldn't let me see Moritz Debicki before I left the old city and its country. I never discovered if Moritz was really a thief, and if I would feel either of us changed because of it. I have only facts; those things that happen and then break off, as facts do, without the moral or symmetry of a story. Perhaps the justice he received was indeed a bungle; perhaps he was a thief.

Good fortune to Moritz Debicki. I hope he continues to enjoy his schnapps, that he finishes his training, that he returns to Polish Kalisz to marry a virgin of good family. Yet all I'm sure of are the facts of the place and the experience. You may see such things yourself if you go there. Often when not well, I sat at the window and watched dawn in the old city — that turning, honest time. At dawn the triangle of our lives is glimpsed; three equal, sloping sides of time and change and death. I saw on the cobble stones the mucus bubbles made by insects in the night, and watched steep houses come up against the sky.

KERI HULME

Unnamed Islands in
the Unknown Sea

[The Contents:

damned dear. In the last crazy hours before you died, I saw sights
through your eyes, sealions tombstoning, albatrosses with weary
hearts, eggs with pink yolks. Now I am myself alone again, I must
balance what I saw with what I know surrounds me. This reality
before the next.

1: the overhang. It juts like the prow of any ship but is massive. It
   broods over me. One day it will fall but I do not fear that. It has
   anciently hung here — remember the bones? Moa you said, and I
   believe that. They were old old bones, so old the rats hadn't
   bothered them.
2: the pile of seaweed at the left end. I have rewoven it, more tightly.
   It makes a ragged screen.
3: your sleeping bag. I washed it, beat it against the rock until all your
   sweated pain & foulness fled. It is nearly dry. I have rolled it, so it
   serves me as a backrest. I am undecided whether to sleep in it
   tonight. I think I might.
4: the rocky floor. It slopes towards the sea. Did it never strike you
   as odd? The roof rears heavenward and all our floor tries to slip
   away from us, downwards, outwards, away.
5: the fire — o yes. I haven't let it go out. Even if I go swimming, I
   want it there to look back to. I feed it dried kelp butts, and twigs
   from the mikkimik and detritus from the moon, feathers and
   sundried bladders and a piece of polystyrene float.
6: twelve mussels in their shells. They are placed in an arc by my feet.
   They make small popping and hissing sounds, as though they had
   minute mouths that cared to suck air. Kissing sounds. They are tea.

Then there is me clad in my despair & wet clothes; my raw feet; your weatherbeaten seabattered notebook. My notebook. My pen. I hope to God it doesn't run out.

(As you were ultimately your last clear analytic words, so I shall be these pages. And maybe they will be found by someone who doesn't understand, who doesn't read English even, or just can't be bothered reading such stained and faded script, and so burns them. As I burned those poor brown remnants of moa, which had maybe stored all the song of its living in those bones. Did moas sing?)

I have eaten the mussels. Thin meat, mussels. Even the peacrabs don't add much more than crunch. And I used to love them, mussels succulent on a scrubbed shining navy shell, topped with garlic butter or richly robed in melted cheese —

Better to remember Day 2, my feet already butchered by those bloody rocks, and me despairing because you couldn't keep the mussels or limpets down and that was all I could gather. And suddenly the waves flung a fish on the beach. It flopped weakly, one flank deeply gashed — a couta you said. I managed to hit it on the head — indeed hit with a savagery I didn't know inhabited me.

Cooking mussels and limpets had been easy — arrange them carefully in the embers and let them toast. But that red cod? Easy, you said. You sounded very tired, and you were huddled over. That seaweed, that bullkelp? Get some thickish fronds off it and split them and stick the cod inside. Never mind the guts.

You kept down the soft flesh. But it wasn't enough. Maybe it worsened matters.

I can't remember the order of days after Day 2. It could be as long as nine days I've been here.

Sometimes during the nights — ten? Eight? — sometimes during the nights we saw lights far out at sea. Distant ships perhaps, though some grew at a strangely fast rate and others stayed abnormally steady, beacons through the night, winking out at dawn. *We* saw lights? The only time you showed awareness of any of them was that night the waves danced, alive with phosphorescence. Porotitiwai, you whispered, porotitiwai, and I never thought to ask you what that means.

Do you know I have always been scared of the sea? Don't laugh. It is remorseless. There is no humanity in it.

You would have laughed at that.

I am cold and smoked and damp and so alone that I feel all the rest of the world has deliberately gone home, leaving me in the dark. I miss your laughter. O God I miss the way your arms felt either side of me as you paddled. A jaunt you said. Only thirty *k* to that island, and look at the sea. Flat as a pancake. I can get us there and back between dawn and dusk, hell I've paddled Cook Strait! And to my demur you said Think! No one's set foot on that island for bloody years! Now that's a story! And then added, your eyes full of a wicked glinting glee, That's if you came to get a story and not just see me.

I said very primly that I Am A Journalist Albeit Freelance, and a story was what I came for, and writing about scruffy field assistants cutting transects won't sell *anywhere*, so lead on MacDuff. McLeay actually, you said. From the whisky actually.

This is pointless. The rats'll eat it.

Who's going to come looking for a freelance peripatetic journo? I don't want to say what bottle I have sent out on the waves —

I used to love reading about islands as a child. Being shipwrecked on one would be heaven. You'd use the materials from your wrecked ship, and feast on the island's provender and finally when it was getting a little boring, you'd light an enormous bonfire which would hail a passing cruise ship and you'd sail happily home a better and a richer man.

God knows when I heard the plane I tried. I grabbed anything I thought would burn and a piece of smouldering kelp and rushed out on the halfmoon of gravel that is the only beach. And the drizzle made everything sodden. The fire was only smoke and a few sullen flickers of flame. Desperate — o how *weak* that reads! *desperate!* I would have burnt my hair had it been longer, I would have fed my clothes to those flames if they hadn't been wetter than the driftwood! I raced back under the overhang and grabbed my sleeping bag and folded it round the smoulder. I prayed. My feet ached so much from the running I cried. The plane droned away and as it got further and further towards the horizon the sleeping bag suddenly flared into a glorious bonfire. Nobody saw it. Just me.

It has been silent since then, if anywhere near the sea is silent. There were silences before. You would say something, mainly a coherent few sentences —

'Do you know they shake penguins out of their skins before they eat them? Catch them underwater and surface with them and shake 'em so viciously quick that the bird flies out of its skin. Then the leopard seal dines.'

Up until these few days ago I had never *heard* of a leopard seal.

I wanted to ask more but you had closed your eyes and there was another silence that lasted all night.

The days are silent too, mainly. At least, the first few — three? Four? — days. Your belly blackens. The haematoma spreads up to your collar-bones. You bleed to death inside but it all takes silent time. At least, mainly silent.

You start to curl up, going from sitting-up huddle, to lying-down hunch. And as you curl slowly into your beginning shape, you want me to see some other island. You talk against the unremitting pain.

It was a harsh place, this island you loved. A bleak volcanic terrain, sere and disordered. Some subantarctic place where the waters teemed with whitepointers and the winds never ceased.

There was mist around our island, closing the world down to just our size.

It was either cliff or swamp, you said, but we had hardwood-plant tracks and so could walk through the headhigh tussock. We could walk past the peat bogs. But if you went off the planks you got quickly lost in the draco . . . and you'd come to a cairn where there was maybe a body underneath, as though the cairn called you. Or arrive at a still inland tarn and there, deep in the water, was an unrusting trypot. We'd been there, people had been there, lots of people, but the land felt *unlived on* and somehow, it wanted people living on it, people as well as the elephant seals and the sealions and the skuas and the albatross.

This Godforsaken rock, *this* island is lived on. It doesn't want us. It already has rats and shags and the mikkimik. The rats live on the shags and each other I think. Presumably the shags live off the sea. They aren't nesting at the moment. The adult birds shuffle but they shuffle faster than I can limp. And the guano burns my feet horribly.

You said weakly, 'The wind is in my ears.'

It is so still outside. The mist hides even the sea.

There is always the wind you say, and nearly always the rain or the snow. Ninety-knot winds . . . I used to worry about the birds. And how did the cattle stand it? That small shotabout fearful herd — did they crouch into the gullies, die finally in the peaty bogs?

It was then your breathing changed.

Between gasps you say, 'Sometimes there is an unnatural quiet, a threatening calm, as the wind holds still for an hour, deciding its next quarter.'

O God he can't have spoken like that. It got hard. The blood on his lungs. I can do nothing, could do nothing. Collect limpets and mussels and stew the juice out of them and have it ready in the thermos flask so when he is ready he can sup soup. The mist pools on the rocks. We have water. The mist makes it hard to breathe. My own lungs are husking.

But your lungs are heaving in and out harnh harnh every hard intake, the sound pitching higher and higher until you are screaming —

I stay outside for the screaming —

remember thinking, But I screamed too. I screamed, What was it? What *was* it? We lay in a tangle a crush in the froth on shore. You had just laughed and pulled the right side of the paddle down hard. 'Landing!' you yelled. And then the sea lurched. Something sleek and bulky and sinuous, a grey fast violent hulk punched into the kayak punched past me into you fled past us into the onshore surf. I screamed What *was* it? until you had caught your breath. You grunted, 'Leopard seal. Wanted to get out to sea. We were in the way.' You grinned. Your last grin. 'We probably scared it to hell.'

None of the kayak has washed ashore.

I can do nothing now. I fold myself beside you and hold your hand. You say, the screaming finished, the breathing nearly finished, you say in that tired hoarse whisper,

'At new moons there are bigger currents than normal. Huge shoals of fish are swept close inshore. The sharks feed hard. Sometimes they will get in amongst a group of Hooker sealions that are also feeding hard. And then you will see the sealions tombstone — bodies rigid in the water, heads sticking straight out, while the white pointers circle and threaten and crazily decide whether to take one or to take all. They can't take all. Islands don't work like that.'

And somehow I am behind your eyes and I see the cliffs that arrow out of the grey seas to terminate in mean blade edges. I see the sheep, feral Drysdales gone surefooted like goats, gaze fearlessly down on climbing humans. I see the albatross effortfully trudge over a ridge down to the hollow where its chick roosts safely out of the wind. I see it feed the chick. I see a skua pluck a pink-yolked penguin's egg and then hungrily cruise on. I see it take the albatross's chick, a limp-necked vulnerable downy sac. I see the albatross halfway down the ridge, watch; then turn and stagger back up to the top of the ridge and launch into the wind.

And then suddenly the shags outside wave their snaky necks and shoot stinking excrement onto the rocks.

And there is no one behind your eyes.

But you did say, watching the sad lumbering albatross, you did say, because I heard you there behind your eyes.

'Don't be afraid. We are all islands but the sea connects us, everyone. Swim.'

And I had enough heart and mind left to laugh at a swimming island as you died.

I gave you to the sea. I rolled you down the sloping floor onto a quartermoon of gravel and let the sea take you. The waves toyed with your beautiful black hair, the waves toyed with your scarred strong hands. Then they too rolled you over and swam you out of sight.

I have given my message to the sea, my bottle, my message.

It is unbearable.]

[*The Notebook from the Unnamed Island off Breaksea Sound:*

It is a standard field notebook, issue item 1065, 18 cm × 13 cm, black elastic closure band, forty-six double pages lined each side, and divided by a midpage column, with red, waterstained, covers. The standard issue pen is missing from the side holder. The last ten pages, and the first two pages, have been torn out.

The notebook was found inside a plastic sandwich container (Tupperware, item CT 106), which had been wrapped in a light down sleeping bag ('Camper,' manufactured by Arthur Ellis, Dunedin). The sleeping bag, which had been extensively damaged by rats, was found tucked in the far corner on the overhang described in 'Contents'.

There was no other sign of human intervention or habitation on the island.]

[*Conclusion:*

Many people have speculated on the identity of the writer of this notebook since its recovery by two crew members from the fishing boat 'Motu' (Dunedin registration 147 DN). The unnamed 'you' may be Jacob Morehu, a field assistant employed by the DSIR on Resolution Island during the recent blue penguin (*Eudyptula minor*) counts. Two possible indicators for this identification are:

Morehu was employed during the '84 season on Campbell Island (by the DSIR), and

Morehu disappeared shortly before the now-infamous Skinned Body corpse was discovered at Goose Cove. (Morehu is not implicated. He was an ardent kayak enthusiast, and his kayak vanished at the same time. The area round Breaksea Island is marked 'reputed dangerous' on all charts, and this pertains to the unnamed small island beyond.)

However, it is much more probable the notebook is an obscure joke perpetrated by a person or persons unknown. The indicators for this Conclusion, which is that of the Department, are:

a] *nobody else* was reported missing from the *entire South Island* at the time Morehu went missing;

b] the 'Skinned Body' was almost certainly murder, and is thought to have been committed by the eccentric gunship shooter, Mike Corely, who fell into the notorious giant eel tarn in Fiordland National Park two days before the body was discovered;

c] nobody has explained satisfactorily to me why two sleeping bags should be taken on what is described as a *day-trip* in a kayak. A plastic container of sandwiches, yes, but two light sleeping bags suitable only for indoor use?]

EDITH CAMPION

Overstayers

That time of year thou mayst in me behold
When yellow leaves, or none, or few, do hang
Upon the boughs which shake against the cold —

Harry Talbut paused, looked up from the sonnet and lost himself in the blue sky. Clear strong blue giving an extra edge to the heads of trees. Nearer to him the shadow of the house crept across the lawn and began to climb that scruffy bit of bracken he kept meaning to cut back. In the distance he could hear a persistent hum that might have been a small plane but was probably a lawn-mower. Looking down he was caught by the fixed stare of his cat Sheba. Her eyes blazed love and she threw herself against his legs, twisting, turning and purring.

'It's too early, cupboard love.' His hand reached down, touching under her chin, tickling her cheek. She thrust her head into his palm and held it there. Both man and cat experienced a small ecstasy, a moment of love. 'All right. A little something for you and a cup of tea for me.'

He laid the book aside and pushed himself up from the chair. God, so many things change. Years ago he would have stood up without thinking, without having to re-assemble his bones. His body faltered but his mind . . . maybe it was not quite as sharp but at the very centre strong seeds remained — the boy, the adult male . . . the memory of love, of passion . . . his first child, his and Jessie's . . . good years, hard years but good.

A demanding meow recalled him to the present. He meowed back, drawing out the sound. Man and animal talked together this way.

In the kitchen he put on the kettle and cut some meat from a small joint and offered it to his Queen of Sheba. She looked up at him, questioning. 'Go on, it's yours.' She winked, he bent and ran his hand along her back. She settled down to eat.

Harry straightened and with both hands massaged each side of his spine. You can't really imagine it — it sneaks up. Suddenly you're saying, 'He died young, only sixty-seven.' At twenty-seven anyone over sixty had seemed past it, with no future, no reason to continue.

The kettle whistled and he poured the boiling water over the tea-bag and as he waited for it to darken he watched the young woman next door unpeg a bunting of nappies. He removed the scalding bag and waved his fingers against its heat. The young woman saw his frenzied movement and, looking a little puzzled, waved back. She had tried not to get involved with the old codger — God knows her elderly mum was bad enough — worse than kids, the old, they just sucked you dry.

He returned to the living room with his tea. Outside the shadow of the house was usurping the whole garden but the treetops still flaunted themselves in late sun.

Harry sipped his tea. It had been a great summer, a long summer. At the same time he hadn't enjoyed it. Oh, he had liked the warmth, he'd taken the odd swim but when he'd come out of the sea he had found the eyes of the young people who watched him colder than the water. They looked as if they found his ageing body distasteful and he had been compelled to wrap his bathing towel tightly against him.

Another thing he had noticed in town, as he did his shopping, was a greater impatience in shop assistants. He had the feeling of being a marked man. Watched — watched in anger. He was jostled at doorways and in queues. On buses they let him stand, looking at him with the cold eyes of china dolls.

He avoided town as much as possible, insisting to himself that he was inventing the whole thing, but there was no denying the voice of the thuggish young man who had muttered as Harry passed, 'Why don't you drop dead, you old fuck,' His friend had added, 'Yah, you're fucking up our space.'

Harry had continued down the street but his breathing had been drawn in, as if he ran and his legs felt unsteady. Looking around he had seen few people of his age in the streets. He glanced at his watch, only 4.30. At the bus stop, as he waited, he felt that sense of danger and dread he remembered from his army days before an assault. He leant against a post for support and found himself praying for his bus to arrive before . . . before what? He hadn't really known but he was sure that the territory belonged to the enemy. Here it was. Here it was, but the wrong bus shuddered to a standstill. Harry's sigh had been more like a sob. Two youths had sauntered towards him, their eyes fixed on his face. At that moment his bus drew up and he clambered thankfully on board, fell into a seat where he had sat trembling and panting. He wiped the moisture from his face and felt a trickle of sweat form and slide down his spine.

He had thrust his front door open and found Sheba waiting, 'Hello, my beauty,' and he had leant for a moment against the door, recovering; then had bent down and lifted the cat and held her against his breast.

She had purred and his heart steadied. He stayed holding her, trying to renew something of himself that he had lost that afternoon.

In the evening, looking at television news, he felt a frisson as he saw angry soldiers pursuing their enemies, their faces distorted by fear, by rage. They reminded him of the youths in town. There were some bystanders with cold faces who watched with awful detachment, having seen it all before.

Harry put his hands on his thighs, thrust himself up and walked slowly to the telephone. He dialled and waited. He heard the receiver lift but no voice spoke. 'Hello,' he said. 'Are you there, Mavis? It's Harry.'

'Oh Harry! Thank heavens. I thought it was one of them.'

'What do you mean?'

'I keep getting calls — nasty they are. Saying things . . . horrible things.'

'Such as?'

'Well, things like you're just the size and age for a nice snug coffin . . . and, get fucked, you old . . . I'd rather not say the word.'

'Don't. I get the idea. Are the voices uneducated?'

'No! Some are, the more basic messages are.'

'What about in town?'

'I don't go by myself. I try to do what shopping I must with a group of friends.' She sighed. 'I feel a bit weak against their anger.'

'Perhaps it's only a passing mood.'

'Why did you phone, Harry?'

'Just to say hello — see how you were. Would you like to see a movie or go to a concert?'

She paused. 'Harry, I couldn't face it but thank you — come and have a meal on Thursday, six o'clock.'

'Thanks. I'd like that.' He put the phone back in its cradle and looked down at Sheba, 'So it's not just me, my darling.'

He returned to his living room, switched off the TV and sat by the fire that slumbered in the grate. Sheba gauged the distance, landed lightly in his lap and folded herself into the available space. Harry continued to shift the dominant chess pieces in his mind. Was it hate?

Was it a particular sector? Certainly it was aimed at his age group and older. What did they want? His hand, cushioned by fur, moved along the black cat's spine. His fingers played with her cheeks. She pretended to bite but her purr denied aggression. He smiled and his hand rested across her shoulder. The night was still, the room warm. Harry was lulled by the cat's soft purr.

There was a crack and a shattering of glass. Harry started and Sheba leapt to the floor, digging her claws into his thighs for purchase.

Harry stood. He found himself seeking a weapon. He registered the departure of a car, probably the culprits. He picked up the poker and walked unsteadily to the front of the house. One of the glass panels at the side of the front door was smashed. The coloured glass lay in schizoid kaleidoscopic patterns. Harry shook his head. 'Oh God, God,' he muttered sadly. 'So much hate, too much hate.' And he went to comfort Sheba who had retired under the couch.

Later he phoned the police, giving his name and location. They said they would be in touch but that similar acts of violence were happening in almost every area of the city.

Next day he should have gone to collect his pension but, still feeling shaken, he put it off. Besides, his friend Mavis and others he knew were going to be on television at the opening of a new senior citizens' complex.

At one o'clock he switched on the set, letting the images break over him. Here it was. He moved the cat so that she lay along his chest, her nose just beneath his chin.

It was a large and beautiful area built for the ageing population — a hall for films, for bingo, for bridge and a courtyard protected from the wind with small trees and a waterfall of many levels. A well-planned building, mainly sacrificing steps for ramps — easier for the wheelchair brigade.

The cameras carried him outside where, in the autumn sun, people waited for the Governor-General's arrival. Harry could see that the pigeons were already looking over the ledges for future roosting and nests. He examined the group again. Was that Mavis in a pretty wide-brimmed hat, circled in daisies? His eyes were caught by a different gathering. The words that came to his mind were rabble, gangs. They wore the sort of outrageous clothes and hairstyles that Harry, in imagination, would have costumed the hordes of Attila the Hun. But what frightened him more was the cold hardness in the young eyes and faces. He was apprehensive. He feared for Mavis. He feared for them all. He feared for himself.

Thank God! There was the Governor-General. Harry relaxed. It was going to be all right. Words floated to him, 'These our seniors who have fought for a way of life, lived out their years in this country — it is most fitting that this building stands as a monument to their past and a comfort to them in the future. A place of amusement where they may meet and enjoy the afternoon of their lives.' Harry supposed afternoon was better than twilight — more hopeful.

Suddenly the Governor raised his arm and ducked. Eggs, thought Harry. They're chucking rotten eggs. The official party was withdrawing. Harry froze. The area was full of young men and women, some with sticks, some with rifles. He saw Mavis beaten to the ground, her pretty hat rolled from her head and was trampled underfoot. The voice-over had lost its way, 'Oh God! Oh no! Oh those poor people.' Harry saw one old woman try to drag herself up. A girl, her face stretched in anger, struck her savagely across the head. He saw a trickle of blood seep from the wound and then the set went dead.

Harry sat very still, taking small shallow breaths. It had started. He had felt it. He had smelt it. It had been in his bloodstream.

Carefully he set the cat down, walked to the kitchen and turned on his transistor. It was not news time but news was surging from the set.

Those collecting their pensions had been set upon. There had been many, many deaths. Similar scenes had been enacted throughout the country. 'Why, why,' asked the announcer, 'should you wish this carnage?'

There was a hesitation. 'They had their bit, didn't they? There's most of 'em rattling about in bloody mansions and we 'aven't often go' one room — they got two houses offen — we pay tax for 'em to blow on nuffin — they just live too fuckin' long.'

'But you've got parents. You can't wish this as their end.'

'It's goin' to be their end — death's death.'

'But don't you feel anything for them?'

'They give me a life like a shunting yard. A fucked-up world. What do you want me to feel? What I feel and what they feel is probably mutual.'

Harry turned the transistor off and fumbled into making tea. His kids were out of the country. He'd lost many friends in that first day of anger. Town was no longer safe. The tea was soothing. His mind travelled many roads for solutions. He put the cup down. 'Jim,' he said, 'there's Jim.'

Jim had settled off the beaten track. He liked the bush and lived in a hut he had transformed to a home. It could be reached only by foot, swing-bridge and some ten minutes' walk through scrub and bush.

Fifty-five miles. Did he have enough petrol? Fatal to stop at a garage. He looked at his watch, 4.15. Probably the early morning would be safest. He'd load the car — essentials. He would most likely never return. He was shaken by this new unexpected future. At least he was healthy enough, given his age.

He got out his pack and one large suitcase. Sheba wandered about making anxious plaintive sounds. 'You're coming. Don't fuss. You're coming with me.' He'd have to keep her in. He'd already patched the broken panel near the front door.

He found a sack and filled it with all the tinned food in the house. A makeshift first-aid kit, a sleeping-bag and blankets, he owned one pair of tramping boots, to these he added two heavy pairs of shoes, an oilskin, thick sweaters and heavy socks. Already he was tired. Night had closed down the sun. He must keep his lights off. He poured a drink and steadied himself with a quick gulp. Torch batteries, transistor . . . too much to remember.

He placed Sheba with her meal in a room, closed the door and began to lug clothes, case and other possessions to the car. There was not much order to his packing. He obeyed a sense of pressure and just got it done.

He returned to the house sweating and decided on a shower — one way or another it might be his last! It was good to stand under the warm water. He remembered Mavis and the hat with daisies and his mouth twisted, he held his hands to his eyes and tried to turn his thoughts off. Dried and dressed he added some towels to the car.

He cooked eggs — rather too many eggs with too much butter — and went to join his cat.

He turned on the TV but only black and white lines stuttered across the screen. He tried the transistor where a falsely calm voice was punctuated by the sort of music reserved for the death of monarchs: 'Everyone is to stay off the streets. There is no need for panic.' Why should you panic? muttered Harry, you're probably under forty and safe. He switched off.

He'd leave about 1 a.m. Better avoid motorways where possible. He settled down and tried to sleep but his head ached and his heart jumped about unevenly. Sheba settled beside him. Running his hand along her soft fur and relaxed body when the involuntary spasm of his body woke him and he found himself listening. Nothing there. It was near enough to one o'clock. He collected the cat basket and put Sheba in. She wasn't mad about this as it usually meant a visit to the vet.

After placing the cat in the car Harry returned to the dark house and stood in the living room. He tenderly touched the wooden mantelpiece. This house had been his shell for so many years. The kids had grown up in it. It held memories of Jessie and their lives together. He stood very still as if he listened for the dying pulse of his home. As if he said goodbye. Then he walked out into the passage to the fuse box and switched the house off.

He left the front door open. What did it matter? In the car Sheba's complaints were sharp and continuous. His fingers stroked her through the wire panel and she quietened only to take up her ˜complaints anew when he started the car. Using only sidelights he edged onto the road and turning right drove slowly to the back road out of town. There were very few lights on in the houses he passed. At the roundabout he saw two shadowy figures and found himself shaking. One stepped out to halt him. His fear egged him to drive on — knock whoever it was out of the way and go like hell — but it was against his nature so he switched on the lights which showed him a police uniform. Christ! Are they for or against us? The middle-aged cop flashed his torch at Harry. 'Where are you off?'

'I'm making for a mate at the back of beyond.'

'The motorway's clear so use it, it will be faster. We don't know what the young buggers will get up to next — they're sort of resting on their laurels. Good luck to you,' Sheba gave a doleful wail, 'and to your cat.' He stepped back and waved Harry on.

The motorway without traffic had a nightmare quality as if he were propelled through an endless tunnel. He began to think ahead to the different turn-offs he must negotiate — would he recognise them? Everything looked strange. He was travelling the main arteries, soon he would be sucked into the foothills but at least there he could use his full lights. So few houses. He felt as lonely as those sailors daring the world's edge.

He'd passed the turn-off. He reversed and turned onto the metal road heading for the ranges. As he cornered he believed the foothills cradled him, protected him. There was a straight where the road crossed the river on a narrow wooden bridge. He halted the car on the other side. Sheba wailed the woes of the traveller having no belief in journey's end. 'Almost there, almost there.' His mind captured Mavis. Again he saw her falling, falling and her hat circled in daisies, tumbling, tumbling. He thought of the meal which they were to have had together — never to be cooked, never to be eaten. He drew a shuddering sigh and rested his head on the steering-wheel. The edge of his world. There really was an edge to his world.

He started the car again. The lights gave a gold slash through the dark. The corners were sharp. Harry folded himself further and further away from the city.

Large moths threw themselves at the lights, their eyes iridescent. At last he came to the gate across the road — a no-exit road, its meaning was strong in his mind. The catch took some manipulating and he had to lift the gate across grass and low bracken. He drove through and made firm the latch. Even with the headlights the road was indistinct, better wait until dawn. Having come so far he was in no mind to take the not inconsiderable fall to the riverbed below. He wanted to live, to let the tail-end of his life wag.

In the car he took Sheba from the box and held her against his chest. She was disgruntled to find herself still confined but after one wild anxious glare at the outside, settled and produced a grudging purr. Harry's head rolled forward and the cat slid to his lap. His breathing deepened and from time to time he groaned and his hands clenched.

The day broke, the birds woke. Harry rubbed his eyes and shifted his stiff legs, shrugged his shoulders and was about to climb into the morning when he remembered Sheba. 'Not much longer.' He put her again in the box and got out of the car to a mixed bag of a day. A bit of cloud, a bit of wind, not too cold. It felt good. He could hear the talk of the river turning itself over, gossiping its way between the banks.

A half-mile of rough road would get him to the swing-bridge. It pleased him to think of seeing Jim. He needed to talk to someone, to lay those nightmare ghosts — take some of the power to haunt away from them.

Sheba objected strenuously to the lurching bumps of the road. Her arm reached through the wire and, if she could, she would have punished him with hooked claws for these indignities.

There it was. Flimsy and insubstantial, somehow to be crossed. He'd take Sheba first. He did not doubt Jim's welcome, the friendship was long and had endured many, many years.

Harry walked to the bank and looked down to the river catching the first pale morning sun. On the other side he heard the heavy-bodied flight of a native pigeon. He took one step forward, the bridge trembled, Sheba moved in her box. Harry grasped the wire and edged onto the narrow planks. In the middle the rhythm of his walk set the bridge dancing. He dared not look at the swift movement of water below.

He made it. He smiled as he recognised Jim's path — not far. Difficult to carry a creature determined to lurch about. He could smell the smoke from a fire. As he not nearer the steady 'Ugh! Ugh! Ugh!' of Jim's old huntaway warned his master of infiltration. Harry ducked under a low branch.

'What took you so long? The tea's ready — you all right?'

Harry put the cat box down and reached out his hand. Jim's hand was hard and warm. Harry found himself leaning against his old friend, almost in tears.

'Ya. I heard it all. Sounded bad enough, must have been bloody being there.'

'Oh Christ! It was unreal. But people are dead. Friends are dead and there's all that anger and hate unburied.'

'What's the screaming banshee you've brought along?'

'Do you hate cats?'

'Anything on four legs does me. It's the two-legged bastards you can't trust.'

'What about the dog?'

'Greg? He'll do what I say.' He rested his hand on the dark brown head. Greg looked up at him — God. God was touching his head. Now the hand circled the muzzle, silvered by age. 'Shut the cat in the house — give her time to get her bearings while I help you cart your stuff in.'

Two hours later assorted sacks, bundles and cases lay around the outside of the house.

Jim gave a trumpet blast on his nose, looking at Harry above the brilliant red of the handkerchief, said, 'We're going to have to get rid of the car,' dabbing at his nose, 'or hide it. What do you want?'

'Hide it. Can't tell the future.'

'Want an educated guess?'

Harry did not answer but looked at Jim who, in spite of his sixty-nine years, had all the powers of middle life — no fat, a hard face except that the eyes spoke of dreams as well as the ability to act with judgment. He had been very very handsome in his youth.

'Do you want to take a picture of me? Or have a go at that uneducated guess?'

'Oh, I suppose it could simmer down.'

'Harrry, you have a touching belief in mankind. We'll hide your car and then I'll detach the bridge, just in case shooting geriatrics becomes the in sport . . . don't worry, I can always re-rig it when, as you suggest, things simmer down.'

They drove the car deeper into the bush and, although Jim was for shoving it down the steep drop to the river, together they attached bracken and fern until nothing was visible.

'Look, Harry, there's a bit of a hollow ahead. We need this to disappear — just another shove.'

They looked at their handiwork.

'Better in the river but it'll do. A small action on behalf of optimism — your optimism, not mine. Lunch and then you look as if you could do with a sleep.'

They crossed the creaking rickety bridge for the last time. One, two, three, four. The bridge was flung upon the far bank. There it dangled and the dust rose as it hung bouncing upon the cliff.

'That's quite a streamer for our departure. Does it worry you?'

'Hell, no.' But Harry felt a small thread of regret at having lost the easy way out. What was he thinking! There was no such thing. No easy way. Even the anonymous 'they' were not going to fix it.

'What about your cat? Let her out? Can't see her swimming home.'

'I'll get her.' Sheba was asleep on Jim's bed. Harry sat beside her and she rolled a sleepy eye at him.

They had bacon and eggs for lunch.

'Food will have its problems. There are fish in the river, deer and the odd pig and goat and . . . I have developed a garden — not Eden but it will do us.'

Harry wiped his hand across the stickiness of egg and saw Sheba stalking carefully out the door. Greg's coat bristled and he moved forward on stiff legs.

'Get away out of that!' shouted Jim. The dog sat with awful dignity and turned his head away from the offensive black thing.

Harry stood, walked to the cat and patted her. He then began to look through his bundles and found the transistor.

'The reception's not great.'

'Just wanted to see,' and he turned the volume. There was a crackle and he twisted the knob until he found a voice — 'true love, true love' mooned a unisex voice. The time pips sounded. 'This is 2YA. Here is the news.' The two men listened, their mouths slightly open as if they were drinking the words. 'The Jews are making huge advances in their war against Egypt. The rebels in South Africa are being held on the outskirts of Johannesburg. Mercenary armies are being paid huge salaries to fight for the Government there. A New Zealand yacht is lying third in the Shaunessy round-the-world race. In Kentucky a New Zealand-bred, Night Flight, has won the All Comers Derby by six lengths.' There was a pause, the announcer cleared his throat. 'All citizens are to clear the streets at 3 p.m. and remain in their houses while the army completes Operation Mop-up.'

Jim grunted. 'That's your friends being mopped up, tucked underground.'

'I will repeat that message.' The two men looked into each other's eyes as they listened. 'All citizens are to clear the streets at 3 p.m. and remain in their houses while the army completes Operation Mop-up.' Harry clicked off the radio.

'They don't so much as give it elbow room — as if it never happened. As if it were some scattered debris that could be easily tidied away — forgotten.'

Harry and Jim sat on the bench and leaned against the wall of the house. A small fantail frisked around them asking sharp inquisitive questions. Greg, the dog, padded over to Jim, looked up at him solemnly, nudged his leg with his nose and sat at his feet watching him roll a cigarette.

In the distance the river turned itself round and over, bubbling and slapping its way to the sea.

Winter ate into their wood supplies and each time Jim tossed more logs on the fire he'd mutter 'at least there's plenty more where that came from', but he worried about kerosene for the lamps and soon the flour was going to give out. He'd smoked the last of his tobacco four weeks ago and for three of those four weeks he'd been edgy and irritable. Finally he forced himself out on a hunting expedition until he felt himself able to live with the deprivation. He even believed that Harry was in some way to blame, so he went bush and waited for time to take the edge off his craving.

The fire warmed the room and enlivened the walls with flickering shadows. The dog looked moodily into the heart of the flames and then threw himself on his side. Sheba jumped from Harry's knees and curled up close to Greg's shoulder, the dog gave a despairing groan but did not move.

'We've just about broken the back of winter — the only bad bit for me was the tobacco.'

'Ya. You were ready to cut my throat in the night — was as if you thought it was my fault.'

'Na, na! Well, maybe for a while but it passed.'

They had listened to the transistor from time to time but the only reference to what might be happening was that the ominous 'Operation Mop-up' was again in progress.

'I wonder if this is a worldwide movement against us overstayers?'

Jim thought, bit a piece of rough skin from around his nail. 'Could be like the Jews in Germany in that Second World War — they never gave much news, people died in a conspiracy of silence. Don't suppose we'll ever be missed.'

'Mmm. "A time to every purpose under heaven. A time to be born and a time to die."'

'We seem to be getting the bum's rush. I've found these last years good. I've been healthy, I've troubled no one and pleased myself — I guess it's the beginning of hanging on and finally letting go.'

'Yes. Yes . . . I want a full day. I don't want to be struck down at 3 p.m. I want the late afternoon and the intensity of the light before sunset. I want that. I want my whole day.'

'Tea?' Jim went outside to the water-tank The water lazily filled the billy. In the distance a morepork called, strangely disembodied, and was answered by the female. Jim turned off the tap, stepped from the small verandah and looked up at the clear sky. '". . . brave o'erhanging firmament . . . majestical roof fretted with golden fire!" That old bugger knew it all.' He breathed in the cold clear air and continued to outstare the stars.

'I'll get more wood.' Harry joined him.

'You're right, Harry, you're right. We want a full day and we'll fight for it — well, what I mean is we'll try and go when we're ready, not when they push us.'

The days lengthened and the odd kowhai tree gave notice of spring.

'I fancy pork.' Jim's statement brought a rush of saliva to Harry's mouth. 'Where?'

'We'll have to cross that ridge behind and the creek in the gully and then we'll hit a bit of scrub country and that spot's a probable. May need to spend the night out so over-feed your cat — I mean more than usual.'

Next morning they were ready before sun-up, walking through the blue-brown light. Indefatigable spiders had hung up their wares which clung to the men as they brushed past and silenced Greg's excited 'Ugh! Ugh! Ugh!' when sticky threads caught his nose and forced him to exchange sneezes for barks.

'Is he any good as a pig dog?'

'Noaw, only gets in the way. Would get himself killed. The cat would be more use.'

The bush began to steam as the sun hit the tops of trees and slid in small shafts to earth. Native birds questioned the morning with hesitant calls. The men kept an even pace in their ascent, stooping under low trees, clambering over fallen trunks, their breath hitting the air as smoke.

'We'll break at the top.'

'Give you time for a fag?'

'Bastard!'

On the ridge they could see across the land to the ocean. The sun was heaved well above the ranges, making itself profligate over farm-land and giving the first shimmer to the moody grey of the distant sea.

'I didn't think I'd like it.'

Jim turned his head. 'What?'

'Back of beyond, where you live.'

'It's always been right for me, better than the rat race, but I think even rats have more ethics than those thugs pulling down the blinds.'

'Mmm.'

The two men sat following separate roads of thought, their eyes assembling the birth of a new day. The dog looked back in the direction of home and, grunting, collapsed upon the bracken but kept his eyes steadfastly upon Jim.

'Let's move it.'

The descent was hard on ageing muscles. It was very steep and Harry found he was grasping tree tunks to halt his downward pace. Half-way he would have given his unstable eye-tooth for a break but felt like the boy who didn't want to let the class know that he couldn't keep up.

'How is it?' asked Jim.

'Harder than climbing.'

'We're nearly there. We'll boil up by the stream and rest.'

'What about the smoke?'

'It'll get lost in morning mists.' He looked around at Harry. 'You're doing just great.'

Harry was warmed and encouraged by this praise.

In the valley they collected small wood and set up a fire, taking water from the boisterous creek. 'Much further?' asked Harry.

'Nope. We follow the creek for some two miles and that should be it. We'll come out to more open country with a regrowth of bracken.'

Harry took his mug, encircling it with his hands, and watched the antics of the water — leaves and twigs flung about, borne under and then carried to small placid shadows. 'It's so busy . . .'

'Mmm?'

'The water.'

'Oh.'

Harry finished his tea and lay looking up at high white cloud, etched in branches. His eyes drooped. Jim gave him a good fifteen minutes before he doused the fire. The hissing sound woke Harry. He stretched and regained his feet awkwardly. 'Remember when we stood up without thinking? Without thrashing around like a cast ewe?'

Jim smiled, 'Speak for yourself,' and headed downstream. It took over two hours because sometimes the stream broadened and altered its headlong pace, falling into gracious curves, sulking in shallow pools beside the banks.

They emerged. Emerged to the bracken and the fuller eye of the sun. Jim paused and listened, his face and eyes concentrated. Harry was about to speak when a sign from Jim silenced him. Jim grabbed Greg about the muzzle and flattened himself. Harry followed his example.

Lying there he heard voices. Young men's voices. He had a desire to stand up and shoot the buggers.

Jim raised himself carefully and indicated two people heading up the other ridge. Jim continued to watch them, still holding Greg so he couldn't bark. He lowered himself beside Harry. 'One tall thin dark joker. The other thickset and ginger. We're lucky they didn't have dogs.'

'They may have been all right.'

'Harry, you're an incurable optimist. May well be the death of both of us.'

'No pork?'

'No pork. No shooting. We'll give them some time and head back. They've got pretty hefty packs so they could be in the ranges for a while. We'll have to be careful.'

Next day the rain beat relentlessly on the corrugated roof of Jim's home. It was almost like being submerged as the guttering overflowed and the windows streamed.

Jim lay on his bed reading and Harry wrote up his notebook which Jim insisted on calling his social diary and would ask what concert they were attending next Saturday or had they accepted for the formal dinner on Thursday.

The notebook gave Harry the illusion that he had some control of time, of the days. He liked to look back at events — the deer hunt, the fishing, the time Sheba went bush and he had been sure she was dead. Through everything he was aware of a greater freedom in himself than he had ever experienced before.

'How about a game of chess?' Jim had put his book aside.

Harry paused, looking up at the roof and listening to the staccato beat of the rain. 'Yes. Who's ahead?' They were evenly matched so it was often a matter of who was wearier.

'Dunno. I'll set it up.' He pulled up the crazy, out-of-place round chess table balanced on three elephant trunks. Lots of inlay which might have been ivory but was probably white plastic. Some aunt had given it to Jim and its outrageous design had never ceased to amuse him.

Twelve moves and while Harry waited for Jim to counter his attack he began to think of the killings. He watched Jim's hand hover above the pieces, thoughtfully he said, 'I suppose they have no reason to believe in a future for themselves.'

Jim looked up. 'Who?'

'The young thugs. They've no belief in growing old. For them Armageddon is just around the corner — where their world ends, where they topple off the edge.'

'Ya. It *is* different.' He moved his knight. 'Checkmate for the whole bloody world.'

'No going bush. No escape. Check.'

'You're putting me off. I can't plan with you exploding the world around Aunt Jane's crazy table.'

One and a quarter hours later, the game ended in a stalemate. Jim replaced the pieces in their box. 'If it clears tomorrow we'll go fishing.'

'If.' The rain continued to rattle its fingers impatiently upon the roof.

The morning was miraculous. No wind. A swept blue sky and the promise of summer in the air. The men walked jauntily out the door. Sheba stretched and strolled out as if the morning had been created especially for her. Greg cocked a leg and took a long thoughtful pee. Jim stretched his arms above his head and Harry yawned. 'Ah-ha-ha! Fishing it is. Great to be alive.'

'Where will we fish?'

'Just a step or two up the river.'

'Above the shallows?'

'Yup! That should do it — won't need lunch, have it back here.' They collected their rods, nets and waders.

'Look at that!' Jim pointed to a branch — 'Look at that beauty.'

Harry turned and saw the brilliant blue of the kingfisher as it flashed down towards the water. 'Yes . . . it's all right.'

'What?'

'The bird — the day — everything. The last bite of the apple tastes good. Teeth not so sharp . . . but the flavour is . . . memorable.'

'Ya, it's okay. Bring the plastic bucket. Display some of that optimism of yours.'

They walked up-river, sometimes wading water, sometimes tracking the bank. The sun threw down strong beams through the trees, creating patterns of haphazard light and shade.

'For God's sake, see we have some room,' said Harry. 'You louse me up when you pick small.'

'Will that do?' Jim indicated with his head.

'That's fine, great.'

They stood at some distance from each other, concentrated upon their casting. The river thrust against their legs and collected the sun on its curled surface and beneath in more constant golden shapes it caressed stones and gravel.

Harry's reel rattled. He let the fish run. 'A big one!' he shouted to Jim. 'I've got a big one.' Jim watched.

'Better than your usual tree.'

'It's a whopper.' The silver body still beneath the surface was being drawn upstream. Harry bent and lifted a very small trout from the irritated waters. He held it up for Jim to admire. Their laughter tickled each side of the river and floated up into the bush.

Greg gave warning, 'Ugh! Ugh! Ugh!' Still laughing the men turned their heads to where Greg challenged.

A rifle cracked and Jim staggered. Harry sploshed through water and caught him as he fell. 'So much . . . for your educated guesses, your blood . . . y optimism — up the river and . . .' he coughed. A second shot cut all other sounds and Harry, half laughing at Jim's 'educated guess', experienced momentary surprise and, choking on his blood, was falling. Falling, falling as Mavis had fallen.

Greg snarled and made towards the enemy, his fur bristling. Another shot but still the dog thrust his way through the water. Again the rifle spoke and the old dog keeled over. The current carried him slowly, slowly downstream.

The river continued to chatter. The bush was silent, secret. There came a sound of snapping branches. Two young men pushed into the open and paused, looking at the human island that divided the waters. One was tall and dark, his companion stocky and ginger-haired. They waded over to the bodies and stood looking down at the two men, watching the blood patterning the clear flowing water. The tall dark youth touched Jim's shoulder with his boot. 'The old bugger was laughing, they was both laughing.'

'Well, that's that, then. We'll have a good look round the camp and head out.'

They followed the track back to the shack. 'Not a bad set-up.'

The thin one entered the house. 'They got lots of stuff here, Red, and . . . Hey! Look what I found.' He stood in the doorway with Sheba in his arms. 'Want it?'

'Naw, hate cats.'

'She's nice, she's black, black's lucky.' He stroked her. She purred, her face pushed against his chin. 'She likes me. I'll take her — a sort of souvenir.'

'Suit yerself but let's move it.'

They crossed further downstream. The river was turning trout-brown in the evening light. The birds conjured up the night with final fading calls. The river chattered on and on, telling its story.

TED JENNER

In Italy Take Care Not To Miss . . .

1.

In Milan you should rub the palm of your hand along the set of railings which border the second plot (right) as you enter the Parco Sempione from the Via F. Melzi d'Eril at an oblique angle to the transverse Via Gadio situated 23 m SW; take care not to miss a single railing.

2.

Note the plentiful supply of mirrors in the bird-cages outside the pet-shop in Pisa, Via Cesare Battisti 9, and remember the two looking-glasses mounted either side of your wardrobe in Room 10, 'Hotel Orlando', Via Lavagna 14; realise that you too have been provided with the illusion of company.

3.

It is dusk in Terracina, 7.30 p.m. Convince the occupants of Via Priverno-Fossanova 57 that before a hand fluttered across the window with the folds of a curtain in its fingers you were obsessed by a circular ornament that glowed with a small but brilliant blue flame in a corner of their living-room.

4.

Calculate the average rates of ascent and descent of the unhappy Gérard de Nerval in *Les Filles de Feu* if, retracing his steps to the precipice and back — the precipice beyond the Parco della Rimembranza, Posillipo, Bay of Naples — you ascend the 750 steps of the Salita della Grotta in twelve minutes and descend them in approximately four, finding, as he did, nothing beyond the cypress trees but the brow of a calcareous rockface.

5.

c. 4 a.m. in the washroom of a hostel, the Castello Principessa Paola del Belgio, Scilla (on the Straits of Messina): you have been roused from a light sleep by a dripping tap on the central wash-hand basin, and the skylights are illuminated intermittently by the four swivelling rays of the beacon. You have a split second in every six to (a) observe a set of wet footprints encircling and even reproducing the octagonal plan of the wash-hand basin; (b) follow this entangled tracery of foot-prints, an experience which comes surprisingly close to that of reading in the verb's archaic sense: guessing, trying to make out, picking one's way along an intricate coastline.

6.
Assume that S. has also taken a seat at a table outside the bar in the Piazza Duomo, La Città Vecchia, Syracuse; you are facing her back and toying with a lemon-ice granita which reinforces the recognition — the same taut skin, tight muscles, blonde curls curving in a bow-wave around the nape of the neck. Scooping out the last of the crushed granules and watching wisps of hair quivering slightly over small, close-set ears, conclude that you will never buy another lemon-ice granita in Syracuse again.

7.
Returning to the coast exhausted c. 9.30 p.m. from a 5½ km search for an inscription near the temple of Persephone on the northern out-skirts of ancient Locri (Calabria), try the security of a half-built two-storey apartment block, many of which line State Highway 106 east of the southern boundaries of the archaeological zone. You have no cause to complain of the indecipherable if your journal is well out of reach and your Escher stairs fail to communicate with the second floor. Even so: shooting stars fall past your frameless windows; luminous coastal shipping plies a steady course past your balcony.

8.
When what had to be avoided at all costs was your Etruscan augur's sense of determinism — a stray smile, a cryptic comment overheard but never properly understood — these fleeting signatures that control your mental perspective on a day as thoroughly as the chemical action of medicine or a drug, admit that once again in Rome last night you left your clothes on the chair, your pens, pencils, journal and eraser on the small green table by the wash-hand basin, with the same unconscious regard to their dividing points or lines or planes, with the same repetition of similar parts in contrary or equally divergent direc-tions, as last Tuesday evening when you sat at another small green

table and were forced to concede that accident and order might be identical, at least in Room 17, 'Pensione Fontana', Piazza Municipio 5, Taranto.

9.

In Siena you can no longer trace the nocturnal itinerary of pavement poet Paolo Digrigoli down the Viale C. Maccari ('I embrace the soft attrition of your feet') to the Piazza Gramsci ('here I am again, about the size of an average pebble'), for Friday's heavy rain, the Polizia Stradale and the poet's rivals must have all taken their toll of aphorisms inscribed in chalk. Convinced, however, that you have not seen the last of P.D.'s work, make sure you follow one of his more recent itineraries: the Viale V. Veneto, for instance, down to the Piazza Matteoti. You will attribute your lack of success to inattention, absent-mindedness, i.e. to an attempt to compose an adequate homage ('There's no pleasure in this weaving back and forth from line to line, / This snail act, slow, slight drooling on the earth') — until you find by chance, in a script painted with the aid of a stencil, on the footpath under the fifth mimosa tree in the Viale dei Mille (in front of the stadium left-hand side), something at least twenty-four hours old: 'There's less meaning in / This tale of me and you / Than in your footsteps beating / Down the same path / As you pass me / Going the other way.'

10.

Note that the municipal authorities of Ferrara now have a detailed plan of every room in a citizen's apartment; they may even have one of his/her teeth and distinguishing features, so geometrical in late afternoon sunlight, so diaphanous, like an X-ray, is the grid upon which the shadows of this city continuously plot the habitual trajectories of its inhabitants. You have arrived on the 5.20 p.m. express from Empoli, and already the shadows in the arcade on the Piazza Trento Trieste demonstrate that every fruit-seller in a semi-circle casts a right angle; the ear-lobes of Cavour and Garibaldi lose definition in the Viale Alfonso d'Este even as their tympana become visible; the eight-year-old with a hand poised over her hoop enters a radiant trapezium in the Corso Ercole d'Este, oblivious of the figure slanting across her path at the other end of the street. Corollary: at such an hour, if someone refers only to himself, his shadow will plot a state of imminence and discontinuity. This must be why (a) you are still counting the pyramidal blocks on the western façade of the Palazzo dei Diamanti; (b) your figure is still slanting across the eight-year-old's path as she runs towards the arcade of the Palazzo Pubblico; (c) though you remain motionless, the tip of your head is beginning to climb an oblique row of pyramidal blocks, diamond shadow upon diamond shadow.

11.

A late-summer dawn in Venice, 5.48 a.m., and there is this persistent bleep coming from somewhere beyond the market gardens or the tanning factory on the Isola della Giudecca, an irregularly spaced, apparently mechanical signal you can no longer distinguish in your own memory from . . . it is on the tip of your tongue: the city, the hour, the street, the number. But, for that matter, what made you concentrate on the metal rollers of the tall waxed-paper screens beating against the gallery walls of the Ca' d'Oro in an almost imperceptible draught last night? . . . Forget it. You have an infection in your throat, you can't talk, you can't swallow, your ears are ringing with street numbers, and you really ought to join the queue outside the Farmacia Centrale, Campo Sant' Anzolo 12, where every time someone collects a prescription, his/her medication is recorded on a computer bank of rapidly increasing health profiles, so that memorable footsteps are getting frozen at last in Venice instead of being merely washed away on the next tide.

12.

Problem: Calculate the speed in metres per second of Malpensa Airport, Milan, if the Earth's rotation causes it to travel 21,600 km a day and you are standing at the bar travelling with it.

. . . one hand on the stainless steel railing, the other clutching a Cynar as you wait for BAC 437 to Gatwick, feeling the smooth metal and the viscous liquid run through the chafed creases of your index fingers like an erratum slip in an intricate text of Braille. And it's not too fanciful an analogy when your profession all this summer — as you wove back and forth in a blind passage of your own making, adapting its small-bore to the growth-rate of your segments, burrowing your way through it — was nothing less than the conversion of landmarks into signatures of yourself. But you won't accept the validity of your precise notations now that they've begun to fade in the rhetoric of another identity crisis; and though you find it remarkable, when Malpensa Airport has travelled all of 1815 km in the time it has taken you to write this much of your last paragraph, that you can never be content with the compulsive, near-sighted individuality to which the very perfection of your adjustment to life has condemned you, you only have to push yourself back against the bar till it makes a deep impression on your T-shirt, and you'll soon find the reason; you only have to feel the earth turn beneath your feet till the stainless steel railing is rubbing against your right palm, and you'll soon find the reason.

MAURICE GEE

Joker and Wife

My mother watched me for signs of spirituality, and found one or two indications. She herself was open to things, she said, but was a late bloomer. She wanted an easier passage for me, no beating on doors already open — and she raised plump fists to show how she had suffered. I tried to say the words she wanted to hear, and can't be sure I didn't mean them. I manufactured a kind of sincerity. A precondition was that she face me the right way, which she did with relentless tenderness. Then I cried for squashed tea-tree jacks and spring lambs off to the works. So short a life. Such gentle trusting eyes. 'Such tender little chops,' my father said, but his remarks only pointed up her fineness and I liked the sad smiles she gave him then.

My sympathies travelled with ease along the chain of being. I grew damp-eyed at flowers wilting in a cut-glass vase. A cloud fading in the sky — 'like the soul of someone dying,' she said — made me drop my jaw, made me breathless. We were a little mad, my mother and I, engaged in a form of *folie à deux*.

It was not a dangerous state, for growing up in my family, in our town, I had come to know very well that conflict and ambiguity were the rule, and 'oneness' a room that could not be lived in. Alone with Mum, I believed myself special; but other voices sounded, shouts and yells. I stepped outside and there behaved in a proper way. I was inconspicuous and noisy. I stubbed my toes and wore scabs on my knees. I hugged the girders on the railway bridge while a train rumbled over, and skinned an eel and baked him on a sheet of tin over a fire. Subtleties were in my scope. The goody-good girls sat with pink ears while I defiled them. 'Open the window, monitor,' the teacher said; and haughty, pure of face, I opened it and let my fart escape.

In another room I was Dad's. He taught me how to keep accounts, do the books, balance up, not go broke. His speed at adding up and multiplying filled me with a kind of love.

'Seventeen twenty-fours?' I spring on him; but the blankness in his eye lasts only a second. 'Four hundred and eight.' 'Right! Right! One thousand six hundred and fifty-one divided by thirteen?' 'Hey, I'm not an adding machine. One hundred and twenty-seven.' 'You're a genius, Dad. You're better than Albert Einstein.' 'Who's this Einstein feller, then? I bet he'd soon go broke in my shop.'

'Must you always reduce things to money? There are other things,' Mum says.

Dad grins. He loves getting her on his own ground. He looks hungry, greedy, cruel, when he manages it. 'Money bought the clothes on your back. And the food in your belly.' *Stomach* is the word we use in our house, but Dad coarsens himself in his arguments with her. 'I got you a washing machine. And a fridge so the blowies can't bomb the meat. And now you want a lounge suite to park your bottom on. Well, that's all money, Ivy. That all comes from me selling spuds and cheese. You can't sell "higher things" by the slice. There's no demand for fillet of soul this week.'

Mum had no answer. Her mind was like a jellyfish, soft, transparent, moving with the pressure of tides. 'I won't argue with you. I won't descend to your level.' And by some act of will, she seemed to float; behaving exactly as he'd expected. He watched with a grin and wet his lips. It often seemed to me he meant to eat her.

I stood in a doorway between two rooms. I was drawn to him by his quickness and cruelty, his language, so full of spikes and grins; and to her by pity. I felt that my neutrality kept a balance, kept our family from going broke.

Yet I was moving to him all though my boyhood. It was no simple fight between the spirit and the flesh. To use one of my mother's metaphors, we had all come 'out of God's mixing bowl' and had our share of conflicting desires. A higher station was her goal, and she wanted it not only in spiritual mansions but in our street. She was also a greedy woman. She spoke of her 'sweet tooth' as though she were not responsible for it, as though it were an affliction and must be treated with scones and jam and another helping of sago pudding.

'Oh dear, what am I going to do about this old sweet tooth of mine?'

'Get my pliers, Noel,' Dad says, and Mum replies with a scream as she spoons out more pudding, 'You stay in your chair. Your father's got a funny sense of humour. No one wants any more of this? Mmm. Delicious.'

Dad tells us about the old Dalmation up the valley, who pulled out his teeth with pliers when the dentist told him what the bill would be. 'He had them in a tobacco tin, rattling in his pocket. He had a grin like the meatworks.' But Mum cannot be put off. Eating pudding, she is deaf and blind. A trickle of milk runs from her mouth. She licks it with a sago-slimed tongue, and scrapes her plate as though it wears a skin she must take off. She sits back in her chair and sighs and smiles; and hears Dad now, lets his words replay in her mind, and says, 'That's hardly a topic for the table.' I think of the story of the pot that wouldn't stop cooking and think what a great Mother's Day present it would make, and see our town of Beavis awash in porridge and the cars throwing up bow-waves as they speed through it. I think of porridge squishing between my toes as I walk to school. Mum gives a lady-burp behind her hand. 'Pardon. What a tyrant the body is. But now at least I can face my night.' She means her Krishnamurti evening.

Nor was Dad any more of a piece. Mum described him fondly as 'a man's man', 'a lady killer'. He had a black libidinous eye, and I wonder which back doors he managed to slide through. I went on deliveries with him and heard a lot of cheek at doors and sensed meanings passing over my head. I saw hand slide on hand as the carton of groceries was transferred.

'Funny woman.'

'How do you mean?' With my father I keep on expecting the world to open up.

'She told me once Hell was here on Earth and we were the sinners damned by God.' He grins and starts the van. 'She's got a screw loose. Another time she told me she was a little bird in an empty house with everyone gone. She was fluttering at the window, trying to get out. What do you think of that?'

I think there's hardly time for her to say it at the door.

'She drinks too much Dally plonk' — and I see him drinking with her at a table. Groceries in a carton sit on a chair and a room opens beyond, with brass knobs shining on a double bed. That's as far as I'll let myself go.

'She's a queer old world.'

'Yes,' I say.

I don't accept my mother's view that he can't feel what we feel. He would if he wanted to, I'm sure of that, but he thinks 'being open to things' is a game she's playing. 'It's how she fills her time instead of darning my socks.' Soon I want to hear the things *he* knows. He never tells me. Yacking is for women, that's his opinion.

On Saturdays in the season he takes me on the train to Kingsland station and we walk down the hill to Eden Park and watch Auckland v. Canterbury or Auckland v. Hawke's Bay.

'Go, go, go,' he yells. 'Beautiful. Beautiful.' On the train home he says into the air, 'A lovely try,' making me blush, but I see other men smiling and nodding their heads, and understand he's speaking for them all, and I move closer to him on the seat. He's pleased not just because our team has won. It's the beauty of the cut-through that moves him, and the pass from centre to wing, and the run for the corner. The sun goes down as we walk home and the moon is in the sky. The dust road runs under swollen branches, night-black pines. He makes me stop and listen. The trees are sighing. There's a creaking sound high up as limb rubs on limb. He taps my arm. 'The creek.' It makes a muted hiss, a slide of water. Dad offers no comparisons. He uses no more words. When we get home he tells Mum, 'A chap was carted off with a broken leg.'

'That stupid game.'

'We won. We wiped the floor with them.'

'I hope you realise Noel there's more to life than football.'

I know that very well, and I lie in bed thinking of the water and the trees, and the darkness and the moon; and I understand something difficult, that brings me no ease: Mum and Dad know the same things, but know them differently.

It's unfortunate that just as Mum discovered Krishnamurti I was reading the *Arabian Nights*. I mean it was unfortunate for her. A bit of luck for me. I was set for other journeys than questings of the soul. Krishnamurti was a name I liked but I saw him riding on a magic carpet, opening caves, finding treasure. When Mum became ecstatic about his beauty, and the spirit shining in his face, I took another step away from her. Beauty of that sort was unmanly. I was frightened that she'd look for it in me. So I practised tough expressions, used tough words, I cut my sympathies back to what my friends at school might accept — and that wasn't much — and learned a kind of boredom with my mother. She blamed Dad, but he wasn't pleased to see me playing the lout. He took me aside and told me it was my job to keep her happy.

'Mine?'

'I've got the shop to think about. I'm the guy that keeps food in our bellies.'

'I've got school.'

'Well, Noel, pretend it's extra homework. Women get funny in their minds. They think life's passed them by. Let her talk about this Krishnamurky. Look as if you're floating on a cloud. That shouldn't be too hard for a clever bloke like you.'

It was too hard, and was made even harder by his winks of encouragement. And sometimes he'd get irritable and undo my work. Down went his paper and a little plosive sound came from his lips. 'Now Ivy, you can't say that. It doesn't follow.'

'He is. A saint. You can see it in his face.'

'Saints are Christians, aren't they? This guy's a Theo something. And if you're going to put him in the sum you've got to take in this lady here.' He hunted thorugh a pile of magazines. 'Countess Elisabeth Bathory. She used to have her bath in human blood. And torture peasant girls to death for fun. How's that? I'll let you have your Krishnamurk, okay? But unless you look at this gal you're only playing games.'

'What I'm saying is, his teaching lifts us above all that. Evil. And appetites. And despair.'

'Appetites, Ivy? He hasn't seen you going at the pudding.'

My mother wept. She had eyes of such rich brown the pupil and the iris ran together. They gave her large eloquent expressions — of love, of soulfulness, of despair. She melted into tears and seemed to carry huge weights of grief. I was torn inside, and hated Dad. His little licorice eyes grew round with mock incomprehension. But he came and patted her and stroked her arm, and he sent me off to make a cup of tea. When I came back they were standing by her chair. Her head was on his shoulder and she seemed to be sleeping. They rocked the way a horse rocks, and he was humming a tune in her ear. Vacantly he turned his eyes on me. 'You go off to bed now, son. Forget the tea, I'll make it.' His hand stroked her bottom. I watched him squeeze a bit of her like putty.

'Ow,' she whispered.

'Off you go. Leave her to me.'

I went to bed and imagined them, my mother and father, doing it. It was hideously disturbing, it made a swelling in my chest that hurt like an animal biting. It seemed they had betrayed me by suddenly being adult, and closing doors, and leaving me outside.

Krishnamurti. He was middle-aged by that time but his beauty was the sign he brought my mother. Many years later, in her little unit in a

286

sausage block on the North Shore, she kept a library eighteen inches square from which, in memory, I chart her journey before spirit gave way to bridge and croquet and a spot of gin. Forgotten names on faded covers: Gerald Heard, Lin Yutang, the Oxford Group. And others that return a currency. Aldous Huxley. She grew cacti in earthen pots and broken-handled mugs but could not find courage to taste them. Huxley came after Krishnamurti (after the war) but never replaced him in her pantheon.

When she knew she'd lost me she embraced her faith with a passion that at last came close to being intellectual. Dad could not make any mark on her certainties, he could not get them fixed properly in his mind, so his shots struck nothing. She spoke of 'the Beloved' and, familiarly, of Krishnaji, and it took him a while to discover they were not the same. In the end he grew tired of it and did not bother. He told me it would run its course. Now and then he roused himself to attack the members of her group: Mr Chalkley, whom he called 'the Colonel', Mrs Chalkley, 'the Begum', Mrs Brott, 'the draught mare', Miss Cole, 'the wilting violet', and so on. Mum smiled at that.

She went to her meetings on Tuesday nights, walking down our street and down the hill, and along beside the creek, under the pines, to the Chalkleys' turretted house (the 'Pleasure Dome') at the edge of a burgeoning arm of the town. She let herself in at the back gate and walked through the vegetable garden. What went on inside I never knew. I imagined incense smoking in a bowl, and glowing crystal lamps, and fingers hooked together round a table inlaid with crescent moons. Ghostly voices whispered in the dark. 'You silly boy,' Mum said, 'We sit and talk.' Looking at the pink cheeks and magnified eyes, I could not believe it.

She was never late getting home. The Chalkleys, she said, were early-to-bedders. Dad leered like Groucho Marx, but she only sighed, and went to sit in the front room, where I found her scribbling in a threepenny notebook. I did not like her independence, or her familiarity with people outside our family, and I missed the days when I had been the one to make her happy.

I sat up reading until she came home. Sometimes I played Chinese checkers with Dad, but I had given up testing him with mental. Our companionship had changed to a sharing of Westerns. We argued passionately. I liked Zane Grey but Jackson Gregory was his favourite. I reckoned there was no one in Jackson Gregory who could beat Buck Duane to the draw, and Dad replied there was more to life than being fast with a gun. 'You sound like Mum,' I said. 'God forbid,' he answered, looking startled.

That was the night she came in late. We were both aware of the clock creeping round to ten past ten. 'You'd better get off to bed.'

'A car at the gate.'

We heard her feet, scuff scuff on the gravel, then she burst in panting. 'Oh Bob,' she said, 'have you got two and six?'

'Did you get the taxi?'

'No, no, it's for Mr Chalkley. He drove me home. He's at the gate.'

'He's charging you? And he couldn't even see you to the door?'

'Please, Bob. He's in a temper.' Her eyes grew dark and undefined.

Dad fished in his pocket for half a crown. 'You're no different from these Christians. All love and buttered tripe in church but as soon as it comes to making a bob . . . Here, Noel, you take it. I'm not having my wife running after him.' He spun the coin at me but I dropped it and it rolled under a chair.

Mum got on her knees. 'I'll do it.'

'No you won't,' Dad said.

I beat her to the coin and went out into the dark and down the path. I wasn't keen to face Mr Chalkley in a temper, and thinking of him as the Colonel didn't help. The car was a big black Vauxhall, shining under the street lamp. I went round to the driver's window and waited while Mr Chalkley wound it down. He had snappy eyes, very pale, and a little rat-trap mouth under a moustache with gleaming bristles.

'Are you the boy? Noel?'

'Yes,' I said. 'Here's your two and six.'

He took it and put it in a coin purse with snap ears.

'Stand where I can see you.'

I stood looking adenoidal while he glared at my face. I felt he was counting to see if I had everything, eyes and nose and mouth.

'Now your profile.'

'What?'

He reached out and took my jaw and forced my head round. 'Huh,' he said.

'Can I go now?'

'There's not the faintest resemblance. The woman's out of her mind.' He put his car in gear and drove away. The night pressed in on me and I ran up the path, stinging my soles, and ran into the kitchen to find Dad holding Mum by the shoulders, both of them laughing, and she half weeping with vexation too.

'Ha, ha, ha,' cried Dad, and he rocked Mum back and forth, making her head bounce.

'Stop it, Bob. Oh stop it. Go to bed, Noel. Your father's gone crazy.'

'Noel, Noel, do you know what she did?'

'Don't you tell him. He's got a low enough opinion of me.' She looked at me with a kind of delight in what she'd done, her anger at herself just a game.

'She saw a man watching her. He was in the shadows under the pines. Ha! Ha!'

'I told you, it wasn't a man.'

'He wouldn't answer when she called out. Just stood there watching. So she went back and the Colonel had to drive her home. And . . . and . . .'

'Bob! It wasn't a man, Noel. It was a post.'

'A post! A post! I wish I could have seen the Colonel's face. He should have charged you five bob not two and six.' He hugged Mum and danced her round the kitchen. 'What a loony wife I've got.'

I went to bed and heard laughing, shrieking, and heard him chasing her; and later on, of course, the creaking bed. What a thing that is, what a cliché, the creaking bed; and the moaning, and the cries stifled with a hand or pillow. The pleasure and relief and the grimness and disgust they worked in me.

'Was it really a post?' I said in the morning.

'Yes. It was in the shade but the moon was shining on the top of it. It looked like a man with a bald head.' She giggled as she stirred the porridge. 'I thought Mr Chalkley was going to burst.'

'He doesn't think I look like Krishnamurti.'

'Did he say that?'

'He looked at my profile.'

'The cheek of him. Just between you and me, he's soft in the head. His wife's the clever one.'

'I don't, do I? Look like Krishnamurti?'

'You look like a hooligan. Wear your shoes today. And put some iodine on your toe. If you bring me the scissors I'll cut that flap of skin off.'

We thought she would stop going to her meetings after that. How could a skinflint like Mr Chalkley be spiritual? But no, off she went every Tuesday, with her notebook full of thoughts and her head scarf knotted under her chin. Dad and I played Chinese checkers by the winter fire. One night we made six-shooters by jamming wooden clothes pegs together. We put them in our belts and did fast draws. I beat him every time and he died extravagantly. He put tomato sauce in his palm and clapped it on his forehead and fell back in his chair with blood dribbling on his face. After that he said he had to go to the dunny. He put a new candle in the holder and went out with a magazine and I heard him treading up the path.

(Our lavatory was by the woodshed, hidden from the house by a willow hedge. The thing Mum wanted next, before a telephone, before new wallpaper in the bedroom, was a flush toilet. It was primitive going out at night especially in the rain, and having to carry a candle, and having the nightman running up your path! And she'd give anything not to keep a potty under the bed. Dad disagreed. People needed bringing down to earth. He claimed he was fond of the wetas in the dunny — the way they came out of the wall and looked at the candle flame. They had little black eyes like mice, he said. They were like devils waiting to skewer you on a fork. Dad always sat a long time up there, and I had heard Mum telling him he ate too much cheese.)

After he had been away ten minutes I grew scared. The wind boomed round the house and made it creak. I went to the window and looked into the night and saw the fuzzy candlelight through the hedge. It was quarter to ten. I wanted him to come and people the house, whose other rooms, behind their doors, surrounded me with threat and emptiness. I went back to my chair and listened for his footsteps on the path. But the wind moaned, the house shuddered, the fire gulped and sucked in the chimney. I opened the back door and stood on the porch. 'Dad,' I yelled, and heard pines thrashing in the park and a window banging in the Catholic school. 'Dad, are you all right?'

I began to think someone had murdered him. Then, as though I'd grown up in a rush, I thought of his heart, the pills he took. His visits to the doctor, and knew he'd had a heart attack up there. People often died in the lavatory, he'd told me that. I sped up the path, running lightly, making myself non-existent in the dark. I stood, not breathing, in the chasm between the woodshed and the hedge. 'Dad, are you in there?' I was hollowed out with fright, and I pushed the door back with a dab of my fingers.

The little room was empty. The candle leaned its flame away from me. The wooden lid was on the hole, with Dad's magazine tucked in the handle. I glimpsed a weta, glossy-shelled, as I backed away. The door swung in the wind and closed with a thud. Willow leaves stroked my cheek and I shrieked and jumped away. Then I peered towards the bean-frames in the garden. 'Dad.' He would pounce on me. I grinned with terror. Then I gave it up. The game. His death. It was too much for me, and I pulled my arms round myself and ran for the house. I burst in and slammed the door and turned the key and ran to my chair and sat close to the stove, feeling the heat. Dad's chair, with his dent in it, was the strangest object I had ever seen.

Five minutes passed. I watched the clock so closely I saw the big hand move. It was too soon for Mum but I begged for her. And she came early. The wind fell silent, as though for an event, and a scuttling sounded on the path. I ran to the door and pulled it open. Her arms came thrusting in. Her face was blind like the moon. She tripped on the step and lurched at the stove I thought her hands would burn on the fire-box door. 'Bob. Bob. Where is he?'

'He went to the lav.'

She gave a terrified look in that direction, and pushed at the door, ten feet away. Her eyes were leaking tears, her nose was wet. She came at me and clawed my jersey.

'Someone's out there. Someone followed me.'

Then Dad came down the path, whistling *Phil the Fluter's Ball*. He walked inside and did a little jig, with candle raised like a bottle and magazine slapping time on his trouser leg. 'What? What?'

'Oh, Bob.'

She gripped his shirt and cardigan and locked herself on him. She wanted to burrow in and hide herself. He put his arms around her, motioned me to take the candle. His face was hot beside her yellow scarf and his eyes were sheeny.

'Calm down, Ivy. What happened?'

She threw back her head to see him. 'A man followed me. He kept on walking after me. Oh Bob, he's still out there.'

Dad angled his arm and closed the door, turned the key. 'Now. We've locked him out. Who was he?'

'I don't know. I don't know. I got past the pines. And then I saw someone come out of the bracken. He followed me. Every time I stopped he stopped. And when I ran he ran. He wouldn't answer me when I called out.'

'Did he do anything? Show himself?'

'No. No. He ran round the edges of the street lamps. And when I got to the gate he climbed up the bank on to the lawn. I thought he was going round the house to beat me to the door.'

'I'll take a look.'

'Well, he'll have made himself scarce.'

Dad took her to a chair and made her sit down. He knelt in front of her and took her shoes off. Then he wet a flannel and washed her face. She closed her eyes so he could wipe the lids, but tears leaked out. She took the flannel and held it to her face and bit the fingers of her other hand. Dad stroked the back of her neck. He still had sauce in his eyebrows.

'Go to bed, Noel.' He knew from my look I had worked it out and his eyes warned me to mind my own business.

'Yes,' I said. 'Goodnight.' I went to bed. The mechanics of it, the reason, all was plain. But beyond that was another thing. I glimpsed it and it terrified me; enormous and dark and undefined, and yet with glittering features that I knew. I gave a little whimper and withdrew as it came close, and ran through litanies of school and creek; swimming and eel-fishing and games of cricket.

Through the wall I heard Dad in the scullery, running water in the kettle to make tea.

When Mum died I came up to Auckland to manage her funeral. There were mourners from the old folks club and her bridge and croquet clubs, though she had given up bridge and croquet several years before. I was offended by their geriatric glee — a term I used to put them in their place — and only later remembered that cheerfulness had been Mum's specialty. Her friends hee-heed and clacked their teeth, and told some spotty jokes; made mock assignations, had a good time. They drank to Ivy, one of the best. I gave her croquet mallet to a lady who asked for it, and gave them all something to carry away. They ran about like children, picking up this and that. Nobody wanted her books. When they had gone I put them in an apple box to send to some charity.

I was fifty-four, Dad's age when he died. Now Mum was dead. That opened up the way ahead. No one stood between me and my death. (The way behind was empty too, no wife or child.) I lifted down the books, leafing through one or two before I packed them. There he was, Krishnaji, with liquid eye and swollen mouth, wearing an embroidered Indian jacket; and a good grey suit in this one, over-coat on his arm, trilby in his hand. Mrs Besant, at his side, had a face not unlike my mother's.

She had never gone back to the Chalkleys', but had not given up books or her scribbled thoughts until Dad died. Then she put them away. After shifting to the North Shore she went back to Beavis only once. It was the time of the Gibson murder and the police were searching Beavis Creek for pieces of Mrs Gibson's body. Beavis was alive again in Mum's mind and she asked me to drive her out 'for a look-see'. First we went through the commerical part and she marvelled at the supermarkets, the new town hall — 'like a parrot's cage,' she said — and the gift shops and craft shops and boutiques with names like *Fanny* and *Jilly* and *Snatch*. A fire station stood on the corner where Dad's iron and weatherboard grocery shop had been. 'Dear, dear,' Mum said.

We went out through the factories and came to the creek. A notice at the entrance of Creek Road closed it to traffic. But Creek Road was not Creek Road at all. The pines were down. The blackberry vines were scraped from the bank and rows of liquid amber stood in their place. Houses had come over the hill and engulfed the Pleasure Dome. They crowded on its lawns and in its garden. It stood there broken, seedy, like a dolls' house when the children are grown up.

Along the road, by the bend, police vans and traffic cars were parked. Men stood in groups and frogmen were busy in the creek. The spring sunshine slid on their cold black suits.

A trafficman thumbed us to clear out.

'To think I used to walk down there,' Mum said. I was thinking much the same — my days in the creek, my boyhood of swimming and eeling.

We drove up the hill.

'What makes a man do that to his wife?'

I did not know, and did not think about it. I had long ago stepped back from that sort of thing.

We came to our house. A little square room like a pill-box sat on top. The dunny and the willow hedge were gone.

'They certainly look after it.' Lawns as smooth as a putting green. Flower-beds shaped like hearts and diamonds. The front bank, where I had cut highways for my Dinky cars and trucks, was hidden under a mat of Livingstone daisies.

'Do you want to go in?'

We looked at it for a while, then I turned the car and drove away.

'We had a lot of fun there, Noel. Of course, I was always fluttering round, trying to get out. I was a quester.' She liked the word. 'And your father was a joker. He kept me down to earth.'

'He did that all right.'

'But in all our lives we never disagreed. Not one cross word.'

WITI IHIMAERA

The Greenstone Patu

I had just sneaked into work, late again as usual, when the phone rang at my desk.

— Hello? I answered.

There was a click at the other end and muffled mutterings of the caller as she tried to answer me.

— Hullo? she called. Anybody there? Aue, damn phone!

— Auntie? Auntie Hiraina? I guessed.

I heard a long sigh of relief.

— I been trying to reach you for ages, Auntie said. Ever since the plane got in at Wellington.

— What the heck are you doing down here!

— I'm waiting for you, Tama. Can you come and pick me up?

— Oh Auntie . . .

— Never mind about work. This is important. I've come down to collect our patu pounamu and take it back home to Waituhi. Our greenstone patu, Tama. It is finally being returned to us.

Her voice was on the verge of tears.

— All right, Auntie, I told her. You just sit tight. Don't you move from where you are. I'll be there as soon as I can.

I hung up. The boss, Mr Ralston, wasn't in yet so I could sneak out before he arrived.

— Can you tell the boss I'm sick today? I asked Jenny.

— I can tell him but he won't believe it, she answered sceptically. What's up, Tama?

— You wouldn't understand, I said. After all these years, our patu pounamu is coming home.

Three months before he died, my Nanny Tama had dreamed a strange dream. He seemed to be looking through water shafted with sunlight. Suddenly, at the far end of the water, the sun had glowed upon a wedge-shaped object swimming towards him. As it approached, twisting and gliding through sparkling water, he saw that it was a

294

greenstone patu. It was one and a half handspans long and was starred by a flaw near its handgrip. As it came nearer, it called out its name.

When Nanny awoke, he'd rung Dad and asked him to come to Auntie Hiraina's house. There, he told Dad about the patu.

— Rongo, you remember the pounamu?

— The one saved from the fire? Dad asked.

Nanny had shaken his head.

— No, Rongo. There was another one.

Dad had tried to remember.

— It belongs to us, Nanny told him. It is the twin to our own pounamu; both of them were shaped from the same greenstone. I can remember old Paora telling me that his own grandfather fashioned it. It belongs to the Mahana family, and I thought it had been lost many years ago. But no, it has appeared to me in a dream and called me to find it. I have been too busy with the whakapapa to look, but I will do my best. But if anything happens to me, you must find that greenstone patu. You must promise me you will do this thing.

— I promise, Dad had said.

After Nanny died, Dad had taken up the promise he'd made to the old man. On one of my trips home to Waituhi, he had told me about the patu pounamu.

— Son, you never knew about our family's greenstone, ay. Well, I never knew about it either, because it was lost even before I was born. A long time ago, Paora's father took a haka party to a hui at Rotorua. He also took the patu with him to use in the ceremonial welcome there. Well, he fell sick on the way and had to stay at Whakatane while the rest of the haka party carried on to Rotorua. He gave the patu to the haka leader to use at the hui. After the hui was over and the party had returned to Whakatane, they found that Paora's father was still very sick. Too sick to ask for the patu to be given back to him. The whole group came on back to Waituhi. There was sickness here also. A flu epidemic. Paora's father died. So did the haka leader who'd been given the patu pounamu. All these years since, we thought that the patu was buried with one of those two: Paora's father or the haka leader. However, your Nanny Tama saw it swimming towards him in a dream. He was convinced it was still above the earth. Son, I think he was right. If he was, then we must try to find that patu. It belongs to us. It belongs to the Mahana family. We have lost so much and we must try to regain everything that we can. For the future, son. For the future generation . . .

Dad and I never spoke again about the patu pounamu. At the time, the winter was proving to be a bad one for our people. In many villages throughout the land the crops were beaten down by the weight of rain and the meeting houses were invaded by chill winds. During that time, encircled by cold and spiked with constant hail, many of the old people died.

Nanny Tama had been taken at winter's beginning. Near its end, Dad was taken too. That was a long time ago now, and I was still in Wellington.

But before he died, Dad had given the quest for the greenstone patu to Auntie Hiraina to complete.

— If ever I should die you must keep on looking for the patu, he'd told her. Promise me, Hiraina.

— Don't you worry, Rongo, she'd answered. If I have to I will find it . . .

The automatic door at the terminal building of Wellington Airport swung open as I rushed in. The terminal was very crowded but I saw her straight away.

Auntie Hiraina. In her black dress and floral scarf, a kit in her hands. Standing there in the middle of the floor, in everyone's way, oblivious to the fact that people had to surge round her to get in or out of the building.

— Tama, she sighed in relief.

We clasped each other and she kissed both my cheeks before hugging me closely.

— Still holding up the traffic, I said to her.

— Course! she answered. You told me to stay where I was until you arrived, didn't you? And anyway I was scared you mightn't find me, so I been standing right here watching that door. But now that you've arrived, let's get out of here.

— You got any bags?

— Only me, she winked. I'm only here for the day, Tama. I just came to grab that patu pounamu and then I'm on my way home. Tonight. The sooner the better. I've never liked this cold place.

She looked round and shivered. Then her face softened.

— It's really good to see you, Tama. I was praying all the way on the plane that you would be here.

We embraced again. Then I led her out to the car park.

— How's Mum? I asked. How's everyone?

— Waiting for you to come home, Auntie answered quickly.

I closed my eyes. I remembered again how bad that winter had been. So bad, that it had seemed to me and many of my friends in Wellington that we'd been left stranded by the deaths of our kaumatua and kuia. That winter had made us suddenly aware of the loss to our Maoritanga and of our own disabilities as Maori. The hearth fires were fading and needed to be stoked to flame again.

— Oh Auntie, I whispered.

Some of my friends had left the city to return to their villages and the culture submerged beneath the thick European patina of the world to learn all they could about their heritage from those old people remaining. Yet I was still here in Wellington.

Auntie Hiraina saw my despair. She pressed my shoulders, comforting me.

— We understand, boy, she whispered. We know the time isn't right yet for you to come home to us. We understand.

I shrugged my shoulders and tried to smile. I started the car.

— Where to from here? I asked her.

She gave me an address in Porirua.

— Do they know you're coming for the patu pounamu? I asked. She nodded and compressed her lips.

— They rang me up last night. They said I could come and get it, so I hopped on the first plane down here before they could change their minds. That letter my solicitor sent must have made them scared. I didn't want to do it this way but they made me, Tama. For too long our patu pounamu has been away from us . . .

After Dad died, Auntie Hiraina had not known where to look or even where to start looking for the patu pounamu. All she had to work with was Nanny Tama's dream about the patu and what Dad had told her, and their absolute belief that the Mahana family greenstone still existed.

Well, if they had believed this, then she would too.

One night, she prayed for help in her search for the greenstone patu.

There had been a rushing sound of a river. She had seen the patu pounamu twisting and turning a glowing path through sunlit water. She heard it calling out its name.

And a question had formed in her mind: If the greenstone patu was not buried with old Paora's father or with the haka leader he had given it to, where would it have gone? The answer came to her: With the widow of the haka leader. The widow. Seek her.

Auntie Hiraina had gone to my cousin, Anaru Whatu and asked him to look up the widow's name in Nanny Tama's whakapapa books. She discovered the widow had not belonged to Te Whanau a Kai. Straight after her husband's death, the widow had gone back to her own people and taken her children with her.

With Anaru's help, Auntie Hiraina found where the widow came from. Then she and her husband had gone to the woman's village. By then she would have been dead many years. But perhaps someone in that village knew about the patu.

The trip to the widow's village had taken a day and half the night. The next morning, Auntie Hiraina had gone from house to house asking about the widow.

And she had found the woman's grandson.

— Yes, I know your patu pounamu, he had said. I remember it very clearly.

— We're looking for it, Auntie had told him.

The grandson had stared at her. He had been an old man, in his seventies.

— But wasn't it returned to you? he'd asked.

— No, Auntie had told him.

The old man had cried out loudly, an animal cry of pain.

His grandmother had not known she had the patu pounamu when she left Waituhi. When she got back to her own people and found it, she was horrified. It had been her wish that the patu be returned to the people it belonged to. It was given to a member of her village who was going to be passing through Waituhi on his way north to return to us. For some reason or another, that man had not stopped at our village.

— I will find out his name, the grandson vowed. And I will let you know where you might find him.

Auntie Hiraina and Uncle had returned to Waituhi.

Two months later, they received a telephone call from the grandson.

— The man who has the patu pounamu moved to Auckland over twenty years ago. Eleven years ago, he was killed in an accident. Of his children, there is no trace. But I believe he had two sons. One of them may have your patu.

Then the old man had broken down and wept.

— I do not even know if your patu still exists, he cried. But if it does, it will guide you, its rightful heirs, to where it lies . . .

Auntie Hiraina had taken the long bus journey to Auckland. She returned the next day.

— The family who have our patu, if they have it, have moved. Nobody knows where they've gone to.

She'd locked herself into her bedroom for two days and two nights. She had not let anyone in to see her.

Then she'd opened her door. Her eyes were red and her face was strained with lack of sleep.

— I must go back to Auckland, she'd said.

She returned to Auckland and stayed with one of our whanaungas, Syd. During her first week there, the village did not hear from her. The second week passed and still no word. Then Syd rang Waituhi from Auckland:

— God must be with us, he had said. Hiraina and I have found where the greenstone patu is. It is in Wellington.

By the purest chance, Syd and Hiraina had gone out one night to a meeting at Mangere. There, Syd had met a woman whose name seemed familiar.

— Hey! You must be a relation of the man who pinched our patu pounamu! he had said to the woman.

Syd never did have any tact or brains.

Naturally, the woman had gotten angry with him and told him that although her family did indeed have a greenstone patu it had always been in the family — and hadn't been stolen either.

Auntie Hiraina had calmed the woman down.

— Does your patu have a flaw shaped like a star on its handgrip? she'd asked.

The woman had looked at her oddly and nodded her head.

With glistening eyes, Auntie had placed a telephone call to the grandson of the widow in that village so far from ours. She had then passed the phone to the woman.

At the end of that telephone conversation, the woman replaced the receiver and had not wanted to look into Auntie Hiraina's face.

— I will ring my niece in Wellington, the woman had said. She lives at Porirua and she has your patu pounamu. She inherited it from her father.

Auntie Hiraina had returned to Waituhi. The next weekend she had travelled by train to Wellington. On that occasion, I had not been there to help Auntie Hiraina. She had taken a taxi out to Porirua.

The niece had kicked her out of the house.

— I don't care what anybody says, she'd yelled. My auntie or some old man I've never heard of before, what do they know? This patu pounamu was given to me. It belongs to me. Nobody else is getting it.

Auntie Hiraina had caught the train back home. She was really wild now. She'd written to the grandson of the widow and asked him for a letter saying the patu pounamu belonged to the village. She'd asked him to give her a drawing of the patu. Then she'd written to the woman she'd met in Auckland, asking her to send a letter verifying that this was the same greenstone patu her niece in Wellington possessed.

With this material in hand, she went to see a solicitor.

— You shouldn't do it, her husband had told her.

— You think I can stop now? she had answered. When my own father heard the greenstone calling to him? When Rongo made me promise that I find it if he died? When it has even appeared to me and called to me? No.

— Forget about it, Hiraina, Uncle had continued. Such things don't mean anything these days.

— Forget about it? Auntie had yelled. Never. And how can you say it doesn't mean anything. The world hasn't changed that much that we forget about ourselves, has it? Even if it has, then perhaps we need our patu pounamu more than we think. To fight back with, to use as a weapon. To remind us who we are.

The solicitor had sent the letter. A few nights later, Auntie Hiraina received a telephone call to come and collect the family patu pounamu from Wellington.

We stopped outside the third house in a small street. Before going inside, Auntie wanted to say a prayer. When it was finished, she smiled.

— I feel better now, she told me.

We walked together up the path. I knocked on the door and a man opened it. I told him who we were and why we had come.

— You'd better come in then, he said. The wife is just visiting a neighbour. I'll give her a ring to say you're here.

He showed us to the sitting room and then rang his wife. He came back and sat with us.

— I'm really sorry this has happened, he said. I thought you Maoris were supposed to have love for each other. Well you've certainly upset my wife.

— We have no quarrel with you, Auntie answered him. All we want is what is rightfully ours.

— But all this business happened so long ago, the husband continued. As far as my wife is concerned, she inherited the greenstone from her father. Can't you understand how she feels?

Auntie Hiraina smiled sadly.

— It was not his right to give, she whispered. The patu pounamu does not belong to any one person.

— Well, the man answered. You seem to have very long memories. All I can say is that the sooner you forget about the past the better.

There was a click as the back door opened and closed. A young woman walked into the sitting room.

— You certainly didn't waste any time getting here, she said.

— I'm as sorry about this as you are, Auntie Hiraina told her.

— I'll bet, the woman answered.

She took off her coat and lit a cigarette. Her eyes glistened with tears.

— Well, she continued, you've wasted your time coming down here. I've changed my mind about giving you the greenstone.

— You tell me this? she asked. After all the evidence that was sent to you?

— What sort of evidence is that! the woman cried. My father gave me that greenstone and it belongs to me. And I've talked with my lawyer and he says you haven't got a claim to it at all. Anyway it isn't here any more so you may as well leave.

— Dear . . . her husband whispered.

— And if you ever come back then I'll call the police, the woman continued. So get out of my house. Now.

Auntie looked at me hopelessly. She got up and went to comfort the woman.

— Get out, the woman sobbed.

We walked together to the door, Auntie Hiraina and I. Then suddenly she turned and her face was filled with agony.

— I cannot let you do this to yourself, she cried. The greenstone of our family is here and you know yourself it does not belong to you. But if you must really be convinced, then let the patu pounamu choose between us.

She shoved her way back into the sitting room.

— Get out, the woman yelled. Get out. Get out. Get out!

Then it happened.

The sun glowed upon a wedge-shaped object swimming towards

us. Swiftly it approached, twisting and gliding through water shafted with sunlight. As it came, it cried out its name. Its calls grew louder, ringing in our ear.

Suddenly they were accompanied by sharp cracking sounds snapping loudly through the room. The sounds came from a cabinet panelled with glass like silver mirrors. As we watched, the panels began to buckle and snap and splinter into sharp broken shards. Imprisoned behind the glass was the patu pounamu.

The woman screamed.

Auntie Hiraina, with a cry of desperate longing, clenched her fist and punched through the breaking glass.

— Aue, she cried.

The patu pounamu was like a living thing, pulsating and bucking in her hand. The sheen of its polished surface glowed with a terrible fire.

Auntie Hiraina fell to her knees and cradled it to her tightly. Her tears fell upon it, cleansing it as she wept . . .

The bandage wasn't a very good one, but it would have to do. After all, I wasn't a doctor. The cuts weren't deep anyway. But the way Auntie Hiraina was groaning, boy!

— Well, did you have to do that? I growled at her. Did you have to put your fist through that cabinet?

We were at my flat and I was trying my best to fix up her injured hand. There wasn't much time: I had to get her to the airport within half an hour.

— But I had to grab it, Auntie answered. Because otherwise something might have happened.

— Like what! I snapped.

— Never mind, she sighed. You wouldn't understand even if I told you.

We had stayed with the young woman and her husband for over an hour. We had talked and after a while the woman had formally asked us to accept the greenstone patu of our family.

— It belongs to your people, she had said. You must take it back to your people.

— Then we'd returned to the flat.

— And now, Auntie, I said. I better get you to your plane, ay.

— The quicker the better, she answered.

We drove to Wellington Airport. I checked her in. Then we sat in

silence, waiting for her flight departure to be announced. Auntie
Hiraina held my hands.

— Boy, I sure feel tired, she sighed.

— You'll soon be home, I answered.

— You will not come home with me?

I answered her with my silence.

— When will you come then, Tama?

— When the time is right, Auntie.

She gave a wan smile.

— Then don't let us wait too long, she said. This place is no good
for you. The heart cannot survive here. It loses its warmth and forgets
to stir the blood. Blowed if I know why everyone's in such a hurry
to get down here. Nothing down here except the dollar.

She rubbed her fingers together in a contemptuous gesture. Suddenly, her flight was called. I saw her to her plane.

— You got the patu pounamu safe? I asked.

— Too right! she answered, patting her kit.

— What will you do with it when you get home?

Auntie Hiraina thought for a moment.

— You know, although this belongs to the Mahana family, I will
offer it to all of Waituhi. After all, we are all family really. I think
your grandfather, your Nanny Tama, would approve this. He didn't
really need to collect the whakapapa of the whole village, you know.
But he did it because he wanted us all to be a village family again.

Then Auntie hugged me tightly.

— Give my love to Mum, I told her.

— Yes, she nodded. And come home soon, boy. Never mind about
trying to change the world down here. Come back and help us build
up our own world back home. That's where you're needed, boy.

— You have the greenstone to help you do that, Auntie.

— Ae, she answered. But you forget why your Nanny and your
father wanted it returned to us. For the future, Tama. For the future
generation . . .

Then she wrenched away from me.

In my mind's eye I saw how it would be when she arrived back
home. The family would be waiting for her. The people would be
waiting for her. And as she held up the greenstone patu, their call to
her would ring the air with pride.

The patu would be placed with Nanny Tama's whakapapa books
and with its twin, the village greenstone that I had always loved as a
child. One an emblem of peace, the other a symbol of battle. Both

would be needed to help in the building of the future of our people.
How long would it be before I myself returned to them?

The plane soared through the sunlit sky. It seemed like a green-stone patu swimming its way back to a forgotten world beyond these hills.

Shanties

I sit in my caravan in the El Dorado caravan park and I think I am a very lucky woman. I think of those shanties we saw on the roadside.

I am very fond of my caravan. The man I bought it from painted it himself. He was a professional house painter of the old school, no spraying. The brush marks don't show or anything but it looks, well, it would have been better sprayed. It is the shape of a Walt Disney cloud, rounded at both ends. But blue. Inside it is punk pink. Very compact if a bit tatsy, but caravans often are, they seem to bring out the kitsch. The vendor showed me his product most meticulously. He pulled out the drawers. He unrolled the awning. We squatted together, heads close as children with jokes while we inspected the underpinnings. I kicked the tyres. He was selling it because he'd bought it as spare room for his daughter who didn't come. She was in Brisbane and she wrote to say she was coming, but . . . His voice trailed away. I didn't pursue it. I couldn't do anything and I didn't want to start thinking negative thoughts about my elliptical pie in the sky. I could see he was glad to get rid of it, though.

The caravan park is well run by the caretaker, Mr Kelson. Most of the residents are long-term. We're long-term, they say. Nothing fly-by-night with us, though that remains unsaid. Some are so long-term they have pretend fences which define their territory. Mr Laski's is a one-foot high white picket. One has a path to the door bordered with matching river stones painted white. Many of the homes have names emblazoned on their sleek sides. Rio Bella Vista has a glimpse of the river. Roll Your Own next door to me will never cruise again because Mrs Millrod is a widow and Cyril did the driving. Mrs Millrod is the victim of some crippling disease. She is very small and has to turn her head sideways to smile up at me. For some reason this makes even her 'Good morning, Julie' seem wise, knowing. She is uncomplaining and cheerful in her little-girl dresses and doesn't ask questions. I am thinking of painting Run Away on my mobile home but would they get it? Or El Deserto? Better just to say my husband . . . Yes, well, what? My husband and I . . . Some sort of caravan park Queen's

Message, for God's sake. The thing is, it's not only the things that happen, it's the explanations required. The new persona which must be created, the screen relit behind which I dance.

The hotel suite was vast. Mike tipped the man who delivered the luggage and turned to her, stroking a hand over his seal-coat hair. She was bouncing on the enormous double-bed in her petticoat, her shoes abandoned in the middle of the room, their heels angled. — Bit of a scream, she called. — What? he said. — The whole thing. Us. Here. Everything. He lay down on the other side of the king size, a yard across the furrows of the quilted bedspread. She stopped bouncing and snatched her narrow feet to sit cross-legged, calves flat on the bed, supple and trim as a worked-out Jane Fonda. — I mean *look* at it! She stared at the muted pastels of the overstuffed chairs, the decorator prints on the walls of the opulent anonymous room. — It's so huge . . . We could hold a levée, why not? Her hand covered her mouth in a caricature of stifled laugher. She laughed at her jokes, her faux pas, at bloody life itself. He dropped his shoulders and breathed out.

— Julie.

— Yes?

Phrases slid into his mind. — I've slaved for it. — For God's sake, woman. — Why don't you . . . Why can't you . . .

Were abandoned. — Nothing.

Her head lifted, scenting the frustration behind his silence.

— The firm's paying, he said.

— I didn't mean *that*, she said. The corners of her mouth twitched. The attempt to suppress her laughter, to humour him as though he were a fractious child, infuriated him further. He rolled over to the edge of the vast bed. He should go through the draft of his speech. See Brett. He loosened his tie. Yawned. The air-conditioning wasn't perfect. — Don't forget the laundry, he muttered. — No. She was reading the house magazine of the hotel chain. — Listen to this. The Hotel Ponçeroo is situated in central downtown Washington with easy access to . . . Can it be central and downtown at the same time? He closed his eyes. — Yes, he said. — Yes, it can, he told the darkness.

He jolted upright at her shriek, his heart lurching. She stood at the window, her feet half buried in the carpet, a two-metre bath sheet wrapped around her body. Her hair was wet, her mouth hung open with delight, not terror. She was pointing out of the window. — Look at that! He dragged himself off the bed and shambled over. She had pulled back one of the curtains on which peonies, birds of paradise and Chinese temples melded in corals and greens. It revealed a concrete service area lined with garbage cans. A rangy cat stalked its beat, planting each pad with care. Mike stared down, cluching the window-sill. — What's wrong with it? he said. — No, no. She pointed again. — *That*! A neon sign on the roof of the building opposite flashed red white red white across the bleak scene. 'Eddie's Condoms! Eddie's Condoms! Eddie's Condoms!' — Isn't that *mar*vellous! she cried. He stared at the sign, his eyelids heavy as safety curtains, hating her. — It's just so . . . Oh I can't explain. Like that weight-lifter who 'rips his glutes'. So *mar*vellous! she said.

I have been lucky also in finding a job. This is a country town and it has problems and the worst is lack of employment. People stand around. There is an air of . . . decay is too strong a word. Even the multicoloured plastic streamers above the used car lots seem listless. The place used to bustle and throb with energy like a farm generator I knew. Mr Barber made his own electricity, which seemed a God-like activity. A generator crouched at the back of his garage waiting to stutter into creation.

I have a job in the local canning factory. I sit with the other women at the ever-coming conveyor-belt as the peas roll by and we remove shreds of leaves, tendrils, all the waste scraps of a pea crop. All day our hands move rhythmically in sweeping arcs, our fingers are nimble and selective, our heads are turbaned in green. We spy for purity. We judge. We are efficient and sharp-eyed. Nothing extraneous escapes us. Once I found a feather in a can of chicken soup but that was in another country.

I am not reticent with the other women. Fouled-up relationships flow by like the peas, but nobody picks at them. There is a lot of laughter as we sit on the splay-legged plastic chairs in the canteen. We had to help Em up the day she christened the conveyor belt the steel eel.

The aircraft slipped down onto the runway. He glanced across at her and nodded. A good landing. His smile was that of a fellow conspirator, eye contact, closed lips. She smiled back then began stowing her mess of clutter in a string kit, of all things. As the plane braked to a stop a team of uniformed workmen ran onto the tarmac to align the steps. They ran bent double as though intent on avoiding detection. Three young women sheathed in green lily gowns held ropes of flower garlands. A band struck up an oompah of welcome as Brett appeared to check the cabin luggage. His upper lip twitched beneath the ragged sandy moustache. — And the little one. Right then? He beamed at them, his face proud. The door opened and the heat blasted in. Mike bent his head, then straightened quickly to run down the aircraft steps, hand outstretched to clasp the hand of the senior member of the group waiting to greet him. Julie followed, her linen suit a crumpled disaster, the orange string kit bumping her knee at every step. — I think the aircraft's got a flat tyre, she told the welcoming committee.

Unlike Washington, the air-conditioning was faultless. Brett was making notes, the ballpoint in his left hand pecking at a small pad. — Oh yes, he said. — One more thing. The helicopter. Doors on or off? They want to know which you prefer. — Oh. Off I think. Mike glanced across at Julie, who was upended over a suitcase on the floor. — Definitely, she said. She straightened up from her head down bottom up scrabbling and looked distractedly around the suite.

— What is it now? said Mike.

— My blue belt.

He looked at the easy-care non-iron hanging around her like a sack. Her lack of vanity used to fascinate him. He dismissed the thought quickly. — It doesn't need a belt, he lied.

— It does, but what the hell. The jungle won't care.

— We're not going to the jungle. I told you we're . . .

— Brett said I think we should go into the jungle and I said speak for yourself and you said . . .

— That was yesteday. We went. You didn't.

— I know I didn't. She stood on one foot as though practising balance. — No jungle?

— We go *over* the jungle, said Brett, ever-helpful.

— Ah. She raked a hand through her hair. — It's just the snakes.

— The snakes aren't going to bounce up at you.

— Not to a helicopter. No. She sounded genuinely amused. Probably was, he thought sourly.

— No doors, eh? That's great. So what is it today?

— Why don't you read the flaming programme?

— Because I've lost the flaming programme. She smiled. — One of our programmes is missing. Shot down with the belt.

His shoulders sagged. — Today we visit a hydro-electric project. We drive to the airport. We fly for two hours to an outlying island . . .

She looked puzzled. — No doors?

— God in heaven! The two hours is in a fixed-wing aircraft. The helicopter is just the last half-hour. He snatched the programme from his open briefcase and flapped it at her, stabbing an accusing finger at the print. — See!

— Yes, she said.

The drive to the airport seemed endless. The driver manoeuvred through the chaos of city traffic onto a motorway which led through an industrial hinterland of grey. The grass verge beneath the hoardings was lined with squatters' shanties built from straw mats, cardboard, an occasional length of corrugated iron. Nobody was visible. They must be at work. But where were the children? She turned to ask Mike, as if he would know. His eyes were closed.

— Mike?

— Nnnn?

— Nothing.

The car sped on.

She tried to work out the advertisements, most of them obvious. Delighted women gazed with rapture at cakes of soap. Children stretched eager arms to toys forever beyond their reach. A giant Pink Panther gesticulated with writing neon limbs above a garage. Factories became fewer.

They left the motorway and drove through a suburb. Tropical trees soared above them, their branches touching across the road. Weathered stone walls covered in cascading pink and orange flowered creepers hid the houses beyond. Women with straw brooms whisked the unblemished footpaths. The driver glanced at her in the rear-vision mirror and smiled his gap-toothed smile.

Most of the party slept in the fixed-wing aircraft. Mouths hung open, an occasional snorting snore woke its sleeper. Technical magazines slipped to the floor. Mike's rough pad was open on his knees as he stared at the jungle, searching for words. Julie slept beside him, her head heavy on his shoulder. Eventually Brett moved forward, touching the back of each seat. — Ten minutes, he said.

The reception at the tiny airport was a miniature of their arrival in the country two days before. Heat struck the tarmac and was reflected back. Officials greeted them, wives were introduced. Everyone smiled: nervous smiles, hopeless smiles, smiles of jaw-cracking intensity. Different slender young women place garlands around the same bent necks. A large corsage of white and pink orchids was pinned to the front of Julie's sack-like garment by the smallest garland lady. Photographs were taken. They moved across the shimmering runway to the helicopter which squatted nearby. — Outside or in?

Mike asked her. — Outside. The pragmatism of helicopters: up, along, down. No messing about.

The young pilot checked their safety belts, smiling and gentle. The smile snapped off, his face was blank and tough as he climbed into his seat and started the engine. They lifted rapidly. Julie stared down at the viridian landscape. People below pointed and waved, paddy fields became patches, farmers working on the terraced hillsides became toys, then disappeared. The wind rushed by, tugging and ripping at her corsage as she leant out. After a few minutes the whole thing broke loose and hurtled downwards. Her laughter tossed after it. — I've lost it! she shouted at Mike. — What? — Never mind!

She thought of the falling flowers. Imagined them drifting down, spiralling gently till they brushed the ground at the feet of a farmer, his wife, a spellbound child. Undamaged, a gift of no value, but perfect. A sign. In reality, of course, they would hurtle downwards, self-destructing, crashing to a pulp. The wire could damage even. Mike leant over to her. — *What've* you lost, he yelled.

What're you doing at Christmas, Julie? Em asks on the way back from the canteen. What I'm doing at Christmas is holing up, burrowing deep as a mutton bird into El Deserto, so I have to think quickly.

— Uh, I say for time. — Come to us, she says. I want to tell her how it happened but there is no time and anyway I can't remember. I want to tell her I can't remember.

I remember leaving, I can see the shape of the broken bit on the bottom step as I lugged my suitcase, but I can't remember a lot of it. We had a major row, I remember that. We didn't often have them. We were more subtle. After ten years we knew how to slip the knife in. Expert anatomists, we operated with wrist-turning speed, our triumph the shock on the face of the loved one, the lover who didn't know he/she had been stabbed till the pain. We used the tools of the intimate: old sour jokes, resurrected pomposities, small meannesses. You can't hone those weapons on strangers.

I can't remember how it started, even. It was the Sunday after we got back from that place. I can see the colours. Dark blue sweatshirt, old white shorts. Something about fruit juice cartons and how you can never get into the things. I can see the orange oblong in his hand as he shouts at me. See myself crouched behind the table, clutching the life-support Formica. Hear the noise ricocheting around the Living Decor Kitchen as I duck his blistering rage and slam it back.

Mr Kelson, the caretaker, is employed by the absentee owner. I admire Mr Kelson because he is so tidy. He is neat and trim, his work shorts knife-pleated. Rubbish is anathema to him. If it is small enough he stabs it with a spike and then scrapes the spike clean against the side of a small cart he made himself. It is almost a child's trolley but not quite. He trims the edges of the grass alongside the concrete paths with a wheel like a giant pastry-cutter on a long handle, then stows the shavings in his cart. Again it looks almost fun but not quite. Mr Kelson shakes me by the hand and wishes me a Merry Christmas. His hand is hard and bony, cool to the touch. He wears a cap with Hawaii Hotcha printed on it in red, a gift from his son who has made it (life-style-wise) in the States. Mr Kelson shoves it back on his head, the yellow duck's bill peak aims at the blazing sky. He looks at me thoughtfully. — I hope it all goes off all right for you, he says. — Christmas and that.

Christmas is over now so I am relaxed, lying prone on my pink bed reading an article about where people go to buy the best of things they wish to buy in Auckland, when Mike comes up my step. I fall upright. — How'd you know I was here? I hiss. We stare at each other, two cornered animals.

    — Oh God, he says.

    — Christmas is over, I say.

He looks blank. — Christmas?

I have been wary over Christmas.

    — All that food, he says, still staring.

My mind skitters, skids, runs down. I hear my voice. — Where did you go?

    — Sandra's.

I believe him. Sandra the sister, the wife and mother, presiding calm and munificent over mountains of hot food, her hands busy with portions, her eyes begging seconds from the torpid husband, her tense skinny children.

My knees start to shake. I flop onto my bed. Mike sits on the divan. Our knees almost touch. His slip-on shoes are new, shiny and black as jackboots. A blowfly buzzes, flinging itself at the tiny window. I open the window and flop it out.

    — Get out, I say to Mike.

There is a knock on the door. We stop shouting. Mike looks at me. My house. I open the door. Mr Kelson stands outside. Beside him, no higher than his chest, is Mrs Millrod, her sideways face worried, her hands clasped tight against her flowered front.

— Everything okay then, Julie? says Mr Kelson.

— Fine. Fine, I say. — This is my husband Mike. Mrs Millrod my neighbour. Mr Kelson the caretaker.

Mike is already on his feet. He shakes Mr Kelson's cool hand. He steps down onto the beaten grass to greet Mrs Millrod. Her joy beams up at him. Mrs Millrod. Mrs Millrod.

Conversation is relaxed. Mike admires the condition of El Dorado. Mr Kelson says it's not easy with the casuals. Mike says he can understand that. Mrs Millrod smiles. They leave soon, after more handshakes, more smiles. Their departure is muted, tactful.

I have to say something . . . — Do you remember the shanties by the motorway in that awful place?

The pupils of his eyes have contracted in the sun.

— I didn't mean it, he says. — I didn't mean it.

The hand on my shoulder weighs a kilo.

— Julie, he says.

I am tired beyond words. I am drowning in a deep river of sleep. I almost yawn. The effort of swallowing the thing exhausts me further.

— Forget it, I say. — Forget it.

VINCENT O'SULLIVAN

Exposures

T (time) is a shutter setting used for long exposures.

It was the heat, and the wind, that had driven him away from the town as a young man. His earliest memories, which he disliked, were the sound of naked feet slapping across lino and bare boards in the hours when he lay in bed with the light out, and on the other side of his closed door, his parents walked between room and room, so it had seemed to him, for most of the night. Between the small sitting room and the verandah, from the back porch through to their bedroom where the netting on the windows made it seem that the paddocks he looked out on were always under a kind of fog. In his own room there was a white net across his bed, a huge bandage that encased him in heat and impatience he could do nothing about. He dreamed sometimes that he could not breathe, because he was already buried. When he thought of home or of childhood it always came to that: the stifling he could do nothing to fight off, the paddocks hazed by wire and net, his parents slapping on the tacky warmth of the lino, which was green and orange squares. Those things, and of course the wind.

It would shake the house for days. When he watched his father with the black doors of the Ludo set unfolded on the kitchen table, revealing the bright pattern of the board, and his hands making a box in which he shook the dice before he threw it, the boy thought of their house in the hands of the wind. Once his mother had stood on the verandah and tried to scream over the wind's insistence. He did not even hear his father's hand fall against her several times, but saw it in that strange silence which is there, always, in the centre of its blowing. It makes a cage where nothing is heard but the bars one looks through at the bending, tumbling world. He would think as a ten year old that one day he would leave forever this place where the heat and the wind allowed him to think of so little else. He would light out for somewhere. His dad said that. 'Light out' for other places once these rotten times were over. A place where things were as still,

313

as quiet, as the ice-tray he would touch until his fingers hurt.

He married a woman who said to him that as a girl she had looked from the train window when she travelled once a year to her grandmother's at Christmas, and saw the hills behind where he lived, where the rocks she said were kind of milky and slipped in wavering heat, and once she had seen in a paddock a fallen iron water-tank bowling over and over, so quickly that it almost kept level with the train. In the calm suburb at home, in the garden where the leaves were crusty with frost some years by Easter, she would think of those things, the milky moving rocks and the huge rim of corrugated iron hurtling out there on the yellow earth. His wife said they remained in her mind as a place that must be free.

Anyone who has taken a time exposure looking towards a window inside a church may have been disappointed with the result because the window may appear on the print as a white space surrounded by a halo. This is halation.

It was extraordinary the number of places they had been to together. Neither of them was interested in cameras, so there were no evenings later on when they looked at the frozen images, the congealed days or nights that were supposed to be held by those quick and everlasting shots. Unless you were an expert it was really so much chance in any case. The light was predetermined, the emphasis depended not on you but on a fistful of Japanese machinery that you then pretended showed you life as it had been lived. But it was as close to *that*, they would say, as those rows of specimens in the lab. 'This is a fox's liver' — and you peered at a cloudy thing like a large bean floating in its liquid frame. And from that, were you meant to envisage the red nervy dash across a living hillside or the eyes quick with intelligence, crouched beside a rock? The past might be the past, but that was no reason to treat it like a corpse. No reason to use a camera to help lay it out.

So no scenes then of Radetz castle under snow, no Loch Fyne with its long slate-coloured reaches, to make them think all that was *then*, and we are trying to look at it now, its liver in a jar, its life frozen in this little coloured cube. 'No,' she used to say, 'if life goes on then it goes on organically, doesn't it? I am yesterday's dinner and today's sunburn and the warm stones at Epidavros against my sweating backside in August 1974, I don't need X-rays to prove any of that.' She said it wryly, and only when they were alone. They knew to say it beyond themselves would sound a false note. So they would joke when asked what photos they had to show. They would say they were hopeless with anything mechanical. Or they had tried a camera last trip and every shot was a disaster. They admitted to no one that they were too happy together to tempt time into giving up images that could never possibly match the real thing.

The best type of lens is the Anastigmat kind corrected for most aberrations such as astigmatism, colour refraction, curvature distortion, flare, and uneven illumination.

So when she died, after an illness that was more drawn out than most of us would hope for, Thomas and his daughter would talk about Lucy a great deal. He encouraged the girl to think she must never be silent with her grief, or spare anything for his sake. So when Rebecca said, 'Was she always as pretty as when she was sick?', Thomas would say, 'She seemed like that to me every day, love.' He did not try to say it has nothing really to do with how pretty someone is, because he knew that would sound insincere to a child. And naturally life went on. He took a job in another city, so they would not be surrounded by old friends to make Rebecca always aware of what she had lost. The girl was bright and popular, as Lucy had been. She made new friends quickly, and learned to ride the same year as they shifted towns. Sometimes she would ask her father such things as how old her mother had been when they first met? 'Was her hair long in those days or was it short?' At the end Lucy's head had been covered by a scarf. Rebecca remembered her nearly always like that, although since she was an infant she had watched her mother in front of the dressing table almost every day, the long strong brushstrokes that made her hair shiny as wire. 'Let *me* do it,' Rebecca used to say, and as her mother handed over the tortoise-shell brush, she was told, 'You need the strongest wrists in the world to do it properly.'

Thomas said, 'There was one summer in Greece when we were students when she cut it short.' But after a time the questions were fewer. Her friends would say to others that Rebecca lived with just her father, her mother had died two years ago. There was no melodrama, ever. She put on rather a lot of weight when she was twelve or thirteen, and her complexion turned raw. When she was alone in her room she put slivers of potato on her face, and tried to lie very still before she slept, with the white slices across her eyes. She would go for days without speaking more than a few words. That's adolescence for you, Thomas would think. He was patient and kind and in her schoolbooks he saw that she was writing Lucia as her second name.

Light bends when passing through a prism of glass. Thus a triangular prism changes the direction of a beam of light by bending it twice.

When he and Lucy talked about places they had visited together, the best part was what utterly different things they remembered. Take Guatemala, for instance. They had spent several days walking above and around exquisite blue lakes, where the *Indianos* passed in embroidered tunics, their perfect bodies that made you feel clumsy, as though for generations your forebears had been forgetting how to walk. It was sharing a cigarette with one of the men that he remembered most vividly. The man had pointed to the packet in Thomas's shirt pocket, and there was only one left. They sat side by side as they smoked, passing the cigarette between them. The man's teeth were red from chewing that narcotic leaf which was supposed to dull one's sense of time. His mouth looked as though it constantly bled. But Lucy remembered the designs on pottery, the symbolism of the colours that went into the weaving, and how many levels there were to that temple where they climbed until they were high above the jungle, an endless grey froth in the light between darkness and real dawn. She would draw designs and patterns to remind him. And he told her the names that for the moment escaped her — San Antonio de las Aguas, where they bought a piece of cloth, orange and green and blue, that still hung above his desk. There was a kitten in that same hotel, she said, that spent half the day on its hind legs, playing with the spiky flowers in a black vase on the lobby table. Thomas would say, But of course there was! Lucy smiled as they talked. Chichicastenango, remember? Two ugly mongrels unable to separate after they copulated, while a bemused crowd looked on and a police-man booted the dog's agitated arse, and behind them the cathedral facade, webbed and fissured by earthquake. And there was an American wasn't there, telling them mescalin had opened the skies for him, man, you would not believe it . . . Thomas's fingers had met around his wife's diminished arm and she smiled at him, alert and eager. And the Chinese restaurant, she said, with the two dead fish floating in the tank like grey soggy chips?

The wider the angle of the lens the greater will be the depth of field and vice versa.

Rebecca sat during the video clips and sorted the pictures she cut from the magazines. They all looked much the same to her father. The young men with their crotches exaggerated as though stuffed with wads of newspaper, the long-haired women whose breasts thrust upwards, their legs suggestively wide, while the microphones were raised in their hands like weapons, lollipops, organs. He wondered how much of it Rebecca was aware of. Sometimes there were scenes from Elvis films and he could scarcely credit how blatant they had been, and that was thirty years ago. The whole message was sex, to get into it, to become obsessed. And now there were half naked girls who broke up cars with enormous hammers while bands erected their guitars as though to impale the world. He loathed the whole commercial hype of the stuff yet he quite saw its vitality. If that was life, if that was fire, wasn't it better to know? Knowledge is always better than ignorance. He and Lucy believed that.

Thomas sometimes said to his daughter, 'You can't say you like the *look* of them, love?' He glanced up from his paper at an English group in black singlets, their arms pale as radishes, their heads shaved and oiled. He said it so that Rebecca would know it was a joke, a closeness between them, certainly not a reprimand.

She did not look up from her treasures. 'Don't worry about it,' she advised him.

Rebecca did well at school. For a fourteen year old she was painstaking and accurate. She enjoyed projects where she was left to herself to organise material and carry through an argument. She was capable of working as she sat in front of television, her legs crossed in her tight pale jeans. Her hair was dark, so unlike Lucy's which was straw-coloured. But she already was the same height as her mother had been. 'I'm working on images,' she said when her father asked her what she was getting ready.

When the aperture of a camera is opened light activates chemicals on a specially prepared plate so that images are left. These images vary according to how much light has been allowed to enter, and what kind of lens is placed in the aperture itself. There are drawings which accompany this information. They are very accurate, copied from an encyclopedia and done with finely controlled lines in red and black. The text is enclosed in neat boxes at the side or beneath the diagrams. *The word photo-*

graphy means writing or drawing with light. A camera picture is a picture drawn with rays of light. There were diagrams too of the human eye, of how images were received from the retina and stored by the optic nerve. There was one sentence Thomas read several times, and disliked. There was also a list of phrases that applied to photography, a brief glossary for the uninformed. *Lens shade*, one was told, *is an attachment that keeps light from striking the lens directly and making glare spots appear in the picture.*

There was a joke in the project that made people smile. A dozen photographs of different kinds were taped to the large display sheet. There was a reflecting lake among snow-covered mountains, and a white Greek village that from the distance looked like piled sugar cubes, and the famous Hiroshima photograph of a human shadow on a wall. Each exposure was technically excellent, and there were details to explain such things as timing, the type of film used, and the make of camera. And among these careful images there was a snapshot of a wedding. Heaven knows, Thomas thought, where the child had dredged it up from. It was he and Lucy on the steps of St Luke's, their faces large and blurred a few feet from the camera. There is perhaps a grin on his own face, as he turns to his wife who is holding back her veil with one hand. He had forgotten how windy it had been that morning. Rebecca must have found the thing between the pages of some book, for they would never have meant to keep it. The top edge of the print in fact cut right across both of them, and the heads were at an angle that made them tilt towards one side. Someone's elbow must have been jogged at the instant the shutter clicked. Or someone simply didn't know what to do. Thomas found it unpleasant to see himself so long ago, and not to know who on earth it might have been who moved in so close, distorting them forever. *Chopped Off Head. Make sure all of the subject appears in the viewfinder at the exact moment that you snap the picture. Otherwise you will remember things like this.*

'Couldn't you find a better one than that?' Thomas asked her.

'It was perfect for what I wanted,' Rebecca said.

Her work was so much better than anyone else's in her class. He looked again, more closely, at himself and his bride, two blurred ovals that had become a joke. He mustn't mind that. The faces were too blurred for anyone else to know. Two decapitated eggs.

On the train Rebecca seldom bothered to look out from the window. Her father said to her in the late afternoon, 'Your mother loved this part of the country. More than anywhere else.'

The girl allowed her gaze to drift across the flat country to the rise of rock outcrops, and then the shallow cliffs of the hills. She said nothing, while her father waited for her to speak. Then he told her, 'The first time I ever flew over here I couldn't get over what the hills were like from above. Like a great scoop of clinkers in a shovel. That's what I thought of. This dead ancient tumble of crumbling rock. Nothing like what it looks like from here.' He meant the ochre bleeding streaks across the bluffs. At noon they would have quivered in the glare.

Rebecca waited until her father finished speaking, closing her magazine but holding her place with one finger between the pages. The thought of a week in this place with her grandfather bored her out of her skull. She had told one of her friends that in 1946 a man had hanged himself from a post in the one rotten little street. He dressed up in his army uniform and put his medals on to do it. That was the first and last excitement the place had ever known. Tomorrow her grandfather would point out the post yet again, as if he were showing her the Eiffel Tower. She would hear from every neighbour how she had grown and Bertram the mongol from next door would grin at her until she wanted to throw up. They even let him come inside and sit at the table, snorting on his hot tea before every mouthful. Her father would take her onto the verandah and say, 'You can always bike to the river if you're bored, you know.' As if a pool in a creek were some really big deal. And of course she couldn't touch the telephone to phone her friends in town. You'd think it was gold to put a call through.

Thomas watched his daughter's head sway above her magazine. He saw how her hair was surprisingly light in such brightness, now that the sun lay almost level with the land. For a moment he saw himself as an old man sitting in his father's kitchen. His hands on the table in front of him were speckled and dry, and he wore a cardigan with old-fashioned wooden buttons. A middle-aged woman moved briskly about the room, placing food on the table and calling through the bead curtain that it was time for the party to begin. There was the sound of children interested only in food, and someone had tapped his paper hat into place. They were all told to look up, and the flash of an instamatic. There, said middle-aged Rebecca, kissing him peremptorily on the cheek.

'Can't we pull this thing down?' the girl asked him.

The sunset blazed into the carriage, forcing her to shade her eyes. 'The blind?' she repeated, frowning against the light that seemed to pour at them from some great torn reservoir behind the hills.

'Of course, if you want to,' Thomas told her.

'I want to all right,' Rebecca said. The blind closed on them like a door.

The retina is inferior to the camera because of death.

STEPHANIE JOHNSON

The Glass Whittler

She changed cities. She had actually changed countries but the people around her looked the same, only more aggressive in their speech and gestures. It was to be expeced. The city she changed to was bigger, the country harder, invaded a century earlier by more desperate men.

She slept in a room without windows and sweated at night. When she woke the sheets were damp. She would touch the man and he would be wet too, the nearest part of his body slippery. It felt like she imagined a baby's head to feel, the slime still on it. It frightened her.

She spent the days reading maps and walking. The two activities rarely had any relation to each other. The city was immense. There were strange patches of green inhabited by ancient species of animal — ibis, marsupial — and in the fountains gleaming macho men immortalised in stone. She noticed the places in the green patches where the green didn't grow properly. It was a disappointment to her — the dry earth, the sense of failure, of not being quite strong enough to survive in the opaline gassy air. She would walk quickly through these parts of the park, watching how they attracted an element. One day there was an old man, rolling in his pyjama pants, grasping at the fly, his threadbare jacket showing evidence of other daybeds. He reminded her of her night sweats. It was conceivable to end up like that. It could happen while you weren't looking.

At night the man was kind. He pretended he was responsible for the night sweats. It was an unspoken agreement between them. In the dark room the sheets never dried properly, and the flowers she put on the mantelpiece lasted forever. The scented bottle he dabbed on his face left fragrant shoals in the chilled air, a reassuring smell. If she shut the door on to the landing at any time of the day the white flowers glowed in the dark, and she could breathe in the smell of him.

When they went to bed the man would sometimes make love to her, absentmindedly. Then he would sleep, drugged with his pleasure, and she would lie alert beside him. Sometimes she would begin the slow slide to sleep, but would be jolted awake by myriads of people stacked like larvae in their cells, wrapped in white sheets like shrouds — cocoons of life that would metamorphose in the morning to the people she saw walking purposefully through the streets. At night their breathing and anxious dreams pervaded the windowless walls of the room. Sleep, when it came, was a damp door shutting them out.

In the morning the man would polish his cameras, heave his equipment into his car, and go to work. She didn't know where he went, or what he did, except that when he came home he was tired of light and welcomed the dark room. The photographs he brought back were of women — endless strips of tiny women holding bottles of shampoo, or canisters of lavatory cleaner. He would tell her stories of the women who did the make-up, the women who posed for the pictures, the go-getter people from the advertising agencies, and the sums of money involved. She shrank from them, never remembering the details. They worked a kind of violence in her.

The man interpreted her lack of interest in his work as arrogance. Sometimes he shouted at her to go back to where she came from — the tiny islands shaped like a question mark at the bottom of the world where people retained a kind of dignity, and mostly held their souls inside them at night. She considered returning, but she carried an obligation from the place of the question mark. The obligation was to see the rest of the world, or at least this ancient red continent, and report home.

Every day she looked in the paper for a job, but nobody needed a glass whittler. Nobody even knew what a glass whittler was. In the park she would roll up the newspaper and stuff it in a wastepaper basket. She would only do this after the park keepers had been around, so that it would still be there as a blanket for one of the old men. As she sat on the park benches she would feel them around her, the voices of their dead companions who didn't know they were dead, mingling sadly with the live ones. Then she would return to the dark room and sleep, the city's sleepers up and about, their wandering souls firmly involved in operating steering wheels and gear sticks, or lifting cups of coffee and cigarettes to their active mouths, or counting money with their sunburnt fingers.

One night the man returned angry and late. He showed her a photograph of a woman with warm eyes in a rumpled bed on the other side of the continent. He said she was interested in his work and that she wasn't afraid of harsh light or the huge inland expanses where the green didn't grow properly. She looked at this photograph of a woman who had a knowledge of the man shining from her eyes — and hungered for a piece of glass to whittle.

There was a kitchen downstairs which they shared with three men and a woman. After the man left, out into the night and slamming the door after him, she peeled back the moist sheets and went there.

A single wine glass stood on the bench, among the bread crumbs and dirty cups. She held it to the light bulb and saw the colours refract on the rim. In the bowl of the glass a cockroach waved its legs. She smashed the glass in the sink and gathered up the glistening fragments. The cockroach righted itself and fled beneath a saucer.

Upstairs she moulded the glass with her hands. The candles she'd lit about the dark room waved their golden heads in the breeze from her working arms making the glass glitter and blaze. Trickles of blood ran down her arms to the sheets of the bed, where she crouched intent on her craft. Her fingers twisted and kneaded the glass, her blood working as mortar, thick and scarlet.

Finally the globe hung from the ceiling, a mass of flickering emerald, indigo and vermilion, a perfect replica of a perfect world.

Below it she lay drained on the bed, splinters of glass cold in her cooling flesh. That night she slept alone, giving neither pleasure to the man nor comfort to the souls of the city.

Of course we have all visited the glass works where the men shovel the glinting shards into the flames and blow the resulting morass into objects of beauty and practicality. But I have told you this story because she was the only glass whittler the world has ever known, and in this aestival city she created her world of gentle light, without a knife.

BRUCE STEWART

Patu Wairua

I'm Rangi Wairua and and I'm speaking up so everyone will know the truth about our son Patu Wairua. He's our number eight son, the last one. Papa and I have eleven altogether. Well, you wouldn't get a closer family than ours. Moneywise we haven't got all that much but with a bit of overtime we get by.

And I've always worked hard and taken a pride in my job, I get on really good with my boss at the Porirua City Council. Papa and I have been pretty content with the way things are.

But not that Patu of ours. Perhaps we shouldn't have named him after a tapu mere that belongs to my great-grandfather. My older brother Timi said the old man is still alive — he is a tohunga and lives way back in the mountains. Whatever it is, that boy of ours was a handful right from the start.

He wasn't born with his disability, he got it trying to buck the system when he was only five years old. I'll never forget when he came running home from school — he'd only been there less than a week — well he came running home from school and said, 'Daddy, I'm going to climb to the tip-most top of that big totara at school.'

'It's too high for you. Anyway, it's out of bounds.'

It went right out of my head. It wasn't until my wife Papa rang up for me at work.

'Rangi, come to the hospital. Come quickly. Our Patu had a bad accident, he fell out of a totara. He's very sick.'

When I arrived, Papa was crying. Patu's teacher, Mr Keen, was there. 'I'm sorry, Rangi, but before we knew he'd climbed the tree . . . he wouldn't come down . . . he was right on the top rocking back and forth shouting "Look at me, look at me." I had to go up and get him, his rocking made me nervous. I started shouting at him, but he kept on singing so I shook the tree a little and he fell — it was an accident, Rangi. It was an accident.'

Patu spent four months in hospital. When he came home his face was a bit twisted. He was cross-eyed and his speech was slurred.

He went back to school, they put him in a special class. I was wild.

I went to see the headmaster. He said his staff were professional teachers and they knew what was best for Patu. I felt like a dumb Maori, apologised for taking up his time.

Papa said, 'Rangi, our boy says his school is trying to kill him. Our older kids say it's embarrassing at morning assembly because Patu sings flat and out of time and you can hear him above all the other kids. They say he pretends to be porangi. He grunts and makes awful howling noises and everyone laughs at him. It seems like they're laughing at us when they laugh at him, the kids say. What are we going to do, Rangi?'

'We'll get him some more books, Papa. Our boy loves his Maori books.'

Patu didn't start college until he was sixteen. Again, right from the start it was trouble. It all came to a head when the woodwork teacher asked the class to draw a hammer. Patu wouldn't, he said he couldn't see the sense in drawing a hammer. The teacher said that in drawing a hammer they would learn design which incorporates the best use of materials and some important engineering aspects.

Patu left the class, rushed home, picked up his precious hammer, the one he'd bought from his paper run money. And then back to school he flew — slammed it down on the teacher's desk.

'That's my hammer, it's a twenty-ounce plumb, with a fibreglass handle, and it's the best because I asked some carpenters.'

Well, the teacher did his scone and Patu did his porangi act. The class was in fits. The teacher marched him off to the headmaster where Patu did his porangi act again. The headmaster's letter said, 'in view of Patu's extremely disruptive nature' he could no longer have him at his school.

But the crunch came when I got laid off. Yes, laid off — I thought I was right in my job for keeps. My boss wasn't happy about me having to go but he said the Council was getting broke and they had to cut down. Things weren't easy, what with eleven kids and me being laid off. Also three of the older kids had left school and couldn't get jobs. And now Patu was expelled and he was a handful to have at home.

I thought it would be easy to get a job, I had a good name and good references for my work. Well, I tried everywhere, it was useless. Men were being laid off all over the place and my redundancy money was running out. There was only one thing left to do, the dole. How I hated queuing up to register as unemployed, and all the dumb questions, but in the end they gave it to me. But the money was nowhere near enough. We cut our meat down to twice a week, we couldn't afford to buy any fancy things like coffee or cheese. But even with cutting down there wasn't enough.

I told my kids either some of the older ones would have to try and get on the dole too or we'd all have to go out and steal so we could live. They all agreed to go to register as unemployed and try and get on the dole. All except Patu.

Well, the Labour Department wouldn't put them on. In the end Papa and I dressed all the kids in their best clothes and the whole tribe of us went into the office of the Department. They still said no. Now I haven't been one to get too pushy. I've always been a bit shy, but this time I was desperate.

'By you saying NO, you are turning me and my family into criminals because we're going to start stealing soon. And I don't really want to start stealing, so we're going to stay in this office and if we have to we'll even get the newspaper people and tell them. All we got left is our bodies — we'll park them here all day — all week if we have to.'

Well they got sick of us in the end so they agreed to let the eldest, Ama, have the dole. We were pleased, but even with her money we still found it very hard going.

But Patu made it harder. He made it harder because he couldn't stand the other kids just sitting around. He went out every day to see builders. He even did some labouring for free, the builder said he couldn't take him on, he didn't have enough work. He said Patu was an exceptional lad . . . maybe if things got better. One day he hitched into Wellington; it was late when he got home. Papa said she thought she heard him crying that night.

We've always been a close family, Papa and I believe in closeness. Even the big kids still lean on us, it's a good feeling. Some nights Papa gets all the mattresses down in the sitting room. And we all hop into our big bed to keep warm (it's too expensive to turn on the heater) and watch our old TV. The babies drop off, and then it's just the big ones. Papa said it's lovely being so cosy and close, she likes to turn off the lights so all you can see is the TV. It's warm, even without the heater. When the kids sang along with the commercials, Patu sang flat and all the kids told him to shut up.

We like *Koha* and the Maori programmes best. Papa told the kids what it was like then, how everyone used to work hard getting firewood and watercress and getting kaimoana. I told them about hunting wild pigs and catching eels. All the kids like to hear our stories. All the kids that is, except Patu. 'Why don't we do it now?'

'Because we haven't got a car.'

'That's no excuse. We could walk.'

Patu wouldn't stay in our big bed. He always went into the kitchen and read his books, or sometimes he did his drawings. He liked reading best though, especially Maori books. He seemed to know them backwards.

Once all the young ones were off to school there was nothing to do. So Papa and I would tell the older ones the stories we'd been told. Well it was hard remembering them all — I had to ring up my brother, Timi, to jog my memory — he learnt all our old stories from our grandfather. One day we were sitting in the sun and I was telling them a story about my favourite ancestor, Te Rangi Haeata, and the great running battles he had with the Pakeha. I knew it wasn't the first time I'd told them this story, but they always liked it and they always asked me questions. So you can imagine how I felt when Patu said, 'That story is bankrupt.'

'What . . . what did you say, Patu?' Papa asked.

'We are always talking about him, but he's dead.'

Before I could reply he was up and off and we couldn't find him anywhere.

About four o'clock that same afternoon, a big truck backed up to our front lawn. It dumped a load of car cases. I was taken by surprise. Before I could get out to tell the driver off, he'd gone. Patu and his best friend were standing there looking very pleased with themselves.

'You see all this? It cost nothing. They were going to take it to the tip,' said Patu.

'And that's where it all belongs,' I said.

'We can get lots more, too.'

'What are you going to do with all this rubbish?'

'We're going to build a marae out the back.'

And before I could answer they'd got an end each of a heavy shutter and started bustling past me on the way to our little back yard. Well, what could I say? At least he looked happy, and that was something.

It wasn't long before there was our eldest four, Patu's best friend John and two of our neighbours' kids, Sam and Jim. They were straightening out nails, cutting up car cases and nailing them all together again, and before it got dark they'd built a little rough shed. That night they were all crowded around our kitchen table with big pieces of paper, drawing plans. I hung around watching and listening.

'Where's the chook house going?'

'Over here in Sam's backyard because it's the sunniest.'

'No, we need the sunny place for a garden.'

'Okay, well where else can it go?'

'Over here by Jim's place.'

'Why there?'

'Because it's the second sunniest place.'

'Look, we're getting it all back to front. We should decide where the meeting house is going first, and then work the other things around it.'

'We haven't got enough room for all those things.'

'We'll make room.'

'How?'

'We'll pull down the fences.'

Perhaps that's when I should have stepped in, because all the houses were state houses and all the land was state land, so were the fences. But I didn't think it would even come to anything, the kids looked so happy. So I didn't say anything.

Well, how wrong I was. The next day there were about fifteen kids — four of them were pulling down the fences, three of them were digging up the front lawn, another three were building a chook house, and five of them had started on the meeting house. I almost stopped them then again, but I talked to my neighbour and he said they weren't doing any harm, 'Look at their faces.' And I knew he was right. Though I was a bit worried when two more trucks of car cases landed on what used to be our front lawn. At first the neighbours were watching through their windows, and then they came outside, leant against the walls of their houses, hands in pockets, just watching. After a while they were right in there telling their kids how to use a saw properly — or a hammer. And so was I, because I felt too guilty sitting on my bum watching.

You should have seen the kids' faces when my brother Timi brought thirty chooks home! No trouble to feed them, the kids went collecting scraps from the neighbours. In two days they were laying eggs. Patu had eighteen eggs in a big bowl, he was running around showing everybody. No one was allowed to eat them. All the young ones were jumping up and down and laughing and touching the eggs.

'Anyone think you silly buggers had never seen an egg before,' I said.

But I felt good, I'd never felt so good for a long, long time.

The kids hit the news. Thre was a big photo on the front page of our main evening paper, and it showed everyone working on the meeting house. Boy, were they excited. They cut it out and pasted it on a stiff bit of cardboard and hung it up in the sitting room. The day after the newspaper photo, a television news crew came out — they showed the garden, the chook house and someone collecting the eggs. They got some shots of everyone working on the meeting house. And when we saw it on the news that night the kids were laughing and accusing each other of being in all the 'shots'. They'd picked up this word from the cameramen.

The next day there was someone from a radio station wanting to do an interview. And just as well they were there because I saw two official-looking men jump out of their cars and come running over.

'I'm from the Porirua City Council. Building Inspectors' Department,' said one.

'And I'm from the Housing Corporation,' said the other.

'I'm afraid all this will have to come down,' said one.

'Yes, we've brought some men up from the yard to remove it all,' said the other.

'But these kids haven't done anything wrong really. And they can't get jobs at all. At least it gives them something to do,' I said.

'Yes, I can see all that, but rules are rules,' said one.

'Yes, and if we let one do it, well we've got to let the other,' said the other.

And they waved the men over to our buildings. They had crowbars and chainsaws and big hammers.

They'd hardly stepped onto the place when all our kids came rushing out armed with their rough taiaha they'd just cut from green manuka. Guess who was leading them, yes our Patu. This time I had to step in.

'Taihoa, taihoa,' I yelled because when our Patu makes up his mind you have to yell so he can hear.

And I only just got there in time because I could see the kids meant business and already the men were starting to turn to run back to their truck. When they saw me it was okay — they were all my old workmates, and as soon as Bill, the foreman, saw me he came over. 'Look, Rangi, we don't want to touch the kids' work. But we've got our jobs to look after, and even as it is some more of us are being laid off. But at least we've got an excuse now. We can say it's too dangerous. So we're off back to the yard — okay, Rangi?'

Well they went — the official people went too — and we all started work again. The boys still kept their taiaha handy.

Later that day four carloads of police arrived — it was very scary — they were putting on their helmets and visors — getting out their shields and long batons.

Luckily for us a newspaper reporter and a team from television turned up. It was easy to see the police didn't like having them there. More and more cars kept arriving, important-looking cars. There were also the same people from the Porirua City Council, and that man who was there earlier from the Housing Corporation. I recognised people from Maori Affairs. All told, there must have been about eighty people.

Meanwhile on Patu's side, kids were coming from everywhere. There was a steady stream of them cutting through the backs of the houses and through the ranks of the police and through all the important people, all armed with their taiaha. And you should have seen their faces. They were loving it. There were about two hundred of them and their numbers were growing all the time.

And then I saw him. He was a tall, fine-looking young man. He was dressed in a finely woven korowai. He had a taiaha and a mere. I couldn't believe my eyes — but then I saw everyone staring at him — especially the kids — and I knew I wasn't cracking up. He came over.

'E Rangi, tena koe,' he said, and as we pressed noses and touched foreheads I knew he was a special person — he spoke in fluent Maori. He said he was from Te Kete Aronui, it was a marae far back in the mountains. He said he had been adopted by my great-grandfather, Tane Wairua. His name was Tama.

I wanted to ask him about my koroua, Tane. But I couldn't. The police were already moving in.

Well Papa saw there were Maori faces amongst the police and the official government people, so she started her karanga. The effect of the karanga was like magic; the police dropped back and the Maoris stepped forward. Our Papa kept going, putting on her very best karanga. She didn't know the cameras were on her. They were also trying to get a good shot of the police — who looked really uncomfortable, walking sideways so's the cameras couldn't see their faces.

We were all debating which of us should speak. In the end I asked Tama if he'd speak.

'Ae,' Tama said, and he stepped out to speak.

You could see the Maoris on the other side had no idea who he was. Boy, but when he opened up, did he slay them. You could see them asking, whispering, 'Who's he?' 'Don't know.' Nobody knew and that made it all the better. What a gun, I'd never heard anyone speak that well. And the way he moved with his taiaha. It was as if someone had come back from another age. Patu and all the other young fellas looked at him with wide eyes. You could see he was their champion straight away.

When he finished he started doing the haka, Ruaumoku. Well he couldn't have picked a better haka because the kids had learnt it at school and they'd taught us. It almost seemed as if he sensed it was the only haka we knew.

He led with such ferocity. It was almost like he was possessed. It was like he was a one-man war party. And his fire became our fire. All the kids and all their dads with voices like thunder screamed: 'WHAKARONGO KITE REO O TUMATAUENGA!' He was calling the god of war, Tumatauenga, to come in to us and possess us. It was frightening and real. The ground shook. You could see the police backing away. Patu had one eye looking down to the ground and the other up to the sky, his tongue sticking out like a teko teko.

Patu spoke next. He was so fired up it was hard to beleive he was our Patu Wairua — the boy of the special class. His speech impediment hardly seemed noticeable.

'The Maori law for occupation of land is ahi ka. If our cooking fire keeps going we have right of occupation. Our cooking fires are going right here — therefore this is our land. For too long we've stood back. For too long we've been pushed around. This time we stand. We are warriors. Some of us have made a pact with death.' The boys cheered and waved their taiha. There were more and more of them. I looked at Papa. She had tears flowing.

The police spokesman had a megaphone. He said it was their job to keep law and order, and we were breaking the law.

'But we're not happy about having a battle, especially with the young people.' Therefore he said he'd retreat to consult his superiors.

One of the young kids said it was all coming out on TV because he was in the house watching Patu speak on their set.

The Secretary of Maori Affairs, Sir Wahanui Wairua, stepped forward. He's a sort of a cousin of mine.

'We are not under Maori law. He ahi ka is Maori law. We are under Pakeha law. This land belongs to the government. Those fences you pulled down are the government's. The dole you collect comes from the government. These buildings are illegal. There are proper channels to air your grievances.'

'You make up your mind which side you're on, Uncle,' yelled Patu.

'Fancy talking to his uncle like that,' said Papa as she giggled and hid her face.

By this time there were about two hundred police. They were moving forward slowly — helmets and visors — shields — long batons.

The kids started to move forward too. There seemed to be hundreds and hundreds of them.

The police spokesman said, 'I'm afraid we must uphold the law. We don't want to fight but we must uphold the law.' Just then Sir Wahanui, my cousin, stepped in between.

'Look, this could be very nasty indeed. There is another way we could do it. It is the way of the old people. We put our best man forward. And you put yours. What is your answer?'

We retreated into a huddle. Who? Who was there amongst us who could fight? 'Me,' Patu said, stepping forward.

'No. It would have to be someone good in martial arts. The police have Jim Corbett. He is going to represent New Zealand in the Olympic Games. How about you, Tama? Can you fight for us?'

'Ae.'

Tama gave his korowai and patu to my older brother, Timi, to hold.

'Why did he give you his patu,' I whispered.

'It means he does not wish to kill him . . . do you know who Tama is . . . he's our eldest sister's son — you remember, after she died he took off to the mountains. She called him Boy!'

'That's right, he was never seen again . . . he looks like one of us. Look at that ugly nose.'

Tama stepped forward — Jim Corbett bowed. Tama didn't bow, instead he said, 'He ahai koe i whawhai mo te Pakeha?'

Jim Corbett was a Maori. He understood but answered in Pakeha. 'Times are tough — I have to eat. Plus I love the art.' Jim bowed again.

For a while they circled each other, then Jim Corbett threw two kicks, so fast it was hard to see them. Tama moved to one side. Jim missed — hit the dirt.

They circled again — Tama was doing a kind of ritualistic-looking dance — it seemed he was retreating — his taiaha moved in many different patterns as did his feet. Also, he was chanting quietly. He seemed to have his eyes closed. I got the feeling he could see better without his eyes.

Jim Corbett lashed out again with a long complicated combination of kicks and punches — they were coming from all directions — all angles. I could see he was trying to catch Tama — hoping he'd dodge a punch and walk into a kick.

But Tama danced the same dance, in between everything. He seemed to do it effortlessly — seemed to have time to spare.

'What's he doing?' I whispered to my brother who knows about Maori martial art.

'I think it's the concept of Te Kore — it's a long one — Te Kore's a nothing . . . Te Kore without anger and so on and so on.'

'Sounds complicated.'

'It is — because you have to be it, live it.'

'Be what — live what?'

'Be nothing.'

'Why?'

'Well look. Look at Jim Corbett — he's fighting nothing.'

'How can you fight nothing?'

'Can't you see what's happening?'

'Yes and no.'

'He's fighting himself.'

They'd been going for fifteen minutes — Jim Corbett was exhausted. He'd completely lost his composure. He flew at Tama with wild haymaker swings which missed. He grabbed a long baton off a cop and went in swinging — Tama wasn't there. Jim threw the baton away and charged — tried to tackle — Tama kept up his ritualistic dance. Jim Corbett never even touched Tama.

Jim Corbett with bloodshot eyes was flopping all over the place — he could no longer keep his feet — he curled up into a ball and wept.

Tama kept up his dance — he kept chanting his chants, barely audible above Jim Corbett's weeping.

'Patua,' screamed our number eight son.

All the kids started chanting, led by our son.

'PA-TUA, PA-TUA, PA-TUA, PA-TUA,' they chanted. It was almost like they were crazed with killing.

Tama stopped his dance — I had a feeling that he could've stopped Jim Corbett right from the start but he was content to let Jim beat himself. He turned, walked away.

Sir Wahanui Wairua stepped forward. 'Taihoa, taihoa, taihoa. Look, the way this is going you'll have a murder charge to answer to.'

'No, Uncle Lick-plate, it was YOU who chose the way to fight, and you know our ancestors fought to the death.'

'Listen, Patu, if you knew the ways of the old people you wouldn't talk to me like that. Now if you look behind the Riot Squad you can see the Armed Offenders. I'm keeping my word, we are withdrawing. E Rangi, talk some sense to that boy of yours.'

But I was already alongside my boy. Already I'd whispered to him to drop it. And I could see he was sad and I wanted to hug him, tell him how proud I was of him. But I knew it would have to wait until later.

They took Jim away in a police car. All the police started moving out. Then the government people. Until it was only the kids and the people from our street.

The kids crowded around Tama. Some of them were practising with their bent-looking taiaha — trying to copy what they'd seen earlier.

Tama started telling us about the old tohunga, Tane, about their secret place in the mountains. Because he spoke only Maori, I had to tell our kids what he was saying. They seemed to hang on his every word. They asked him many questions, so did I. It was real late before we lay down to sleep.

The Armed Offenders Squad moved in at 5 a.m. They were backed by ordinary police in riot gear. There seemed to be hundreds of them. They moved so fast they had us surrounded in a very short time. We knew they'd come mainly for Tama — they'd find a charge of some sort.

Behind the police we could see rubber-tyred tractors moving up to demolish our buildings. The police surrounded us all three deep. They started moving in on Tama. They were a net of helmets, shields and batons.

This time Tama attacked. He cut a hole straight through the circle by slicing at their legs with his taiaha. Five of them went down (we learned later that two of them had broken legs).

Tama was gone.

It all happened so fast. One minute they had him, the next minute he was gone. I tried not to smile but it was hard because all our crowd were smiling. So I looked away, someone started laughing and that set us all going. We just laughed and laughed and laughed. And you could see our laughing stung the police — more than being hit by a taiaha. So they moved up the tractors and started crushing our buildings.

It was all over when the reporters got there. All flattened and carted away by some big Ministry of Works trucks.

Later that day Patu and lots of the kids who'd been in on the building of our car case marae came around to see Papa and myself.

'We're all going to Te Kete Aonui to be with our koroua, Tane Wairua — and Tama. Please don't try to stop us because we'll go at any rate. We are going because there is no life for us out here. And we want to be trained by our koroua, like Tama,' said Patu.

Well, Papa started to cry. I stood up to reply to our boy.

'You are right, Patu, there is nothing for you out here. Go, go quickly. Kiss your mother and go. We will stay with the young ones who are still at school. But from Papa and me, we're proud of you. Now go.'

I wanted him to go because both Papa and I knew how the police would never leave him alone until they had him locked away.

They all filed past kissing me and then Papa. Patu was last. It was the first time I saw him crying openly. Well, when they left, the way Papa cried you would've thought they'd all died. She followed them down the road, her arms outstretched, wailing and wailing. All the neighbours poked their heads out the windows, some of the ladies came up to comfort Papa, they all knew what it was about.

It's months later now. Papa is still crying for her babies, we are both lonely for them. We haven't heard anything since they left. Papa said it's my fault. She said I should have stopped them.

'Papa, they'll be back . . . you'll see, they'll all be like that Tama.'

But it's no good. She still makes me sleep by myself.

MALCOLM FRASER

An Artistic Person, Probably Male, Inspects Lovingly A South Pacific Navel

The novel begins when a schoolboy runs down to the botttom field, he and his mates passing a football backwards and forwards.

Yes, I said novel, not navel.

Fiction and charity begin at home.

(Someone who says 'Charity begins at home' means that it *ends* at home; the trouble with rugby novels, too, is that they don't get beyond the football field and the changing shed.)

After the game the boys had a shower.

Short extract from Part 1:

Fred saw Bill coming out of the shower, singing lustily as the others were. His name was Howard, friends called him Bill, to most of the school he was known as Tub — though it didn't pay to call him that to his face. He was short, squat, muscular. His balls seemed to hang in a lopsided sort of way, and one opinion was that he had only one.

For a while Fred, our hero, works on a building site as a labourer. No, better not say Fred, that's too plain, make it Andrew. One of Andrew's workmates is a Maori. Hemi is an apprentice carpenter, does his job well, and every weekend he gets stuck into the grog. Andrew doesn't drink with him, neither does Hemi go to the parties Andrew has with his circle of flatmates and friends, who are mainly students and computer programmers. One day Hemi tells Andrew that he is going to spend the weekend up north on the marae where his family comes from, and he invites Andrew to go with him. There will be plenty of people and Andrew won't be the only Pakeha, a sports team from the city will be there too.

Extract from Part 2:

Andrew went into the tent, where guitars were playing softly, and found himself a place to sit. He was next to Maria, who had been introduced to him in the afternoon. She was Hemi's cousin.

'That guy knows how to play the guitar, eh,' Andrew said to Maria, with a nod towards one of the players, who had long hair, an earring, stars tattooed on his cheeks.

'Sonny,' Maria said. 'You wanna hear him sing, too. Choice.'

Andrew looked straight into her face and smiled.

Andrew got a job with an accountancy firm and went to night school. Hemi often worked on building sites in the city, and Andrew would sometimes meet him after work for a drink.

No, Andrew and Hemi each had their own separate drinking habits.

Hemi was married by now and had a new house in the western suburbs. Andrew sometimes saw him on a city building site and occasionally took the chance to chat to him in the lunch hour.

Maria had recently come to work in the city and Andrew took her out several times to movies, and once to a play.

From Part 3:

'Maria, we won't be seeing each other for a while. For a time. Actually, I'm going to London. Overseas. Live there. For a while. Going pretty soon, a few weeks.'

Andrew was ready for the surprise in Maria's eyes. Surprise, even shock. But he had not expected the anger. The rejection.

'Bloody great. Off in a few weeks? Nice to let me know, eh brother? Jesus.'

So what did he, Andrew, mean to her? Why was she getting so . . . Anyway, there was nothing he could do about it.

That's about a third. Or say a half. The rest is quite varied, plenty happens.

In London Andrew becomes part of a group of New Zealand expatriates, who are involved in some interesting things, music, film making. He is accepted into the group mainly because of his job, which is with a merchant bank; he is able to put the creative New Zealanders in touch with Englishmen who have money to finance their projects. Fairly soon he goes to live with Aileen, who came from New Zealand with some professional acting experience, and was doing reasonably well at getting work in London, mainly in television. Not Aileen, Rosalind. Under her influence he gets used to smoking marijuana. He is happy with her, but wonders whether she needs him, whether he needs her, what the partnership means to both of them. He leaves London and Rosalind, to go to a job with a British engineering firm in Sydney. There he meets a New Zealand girl, Victoria, who is a secretary in another firm, they get married and have two children, a girl and a boy. Delete Victoria, substitute Anne. Anna.

Some years later they return to New Zealand — a transfer within the firm, which has expanded its already extensive international activities. Anna is now working for the firm also, and has a responsible . . .

The tying-up part comes along. Construction project. Taking of land. Maori owners.

There's an aesthetic shape to all this. It's a lot more than just a yarn.

One of the spokespeople for the Maori residents. No, *the* spokesperson. Proud and eloquent Maori woman. It is Maria. (Husband, children.)

Enemies? Bitter feelings?

Or do time and experience work changes?

Meetings, hearings before a tribunal. That sort of drama.

Then a tangi. Andrew has his eyes opened to something new. Another dimension.

Somehow Andrew and Maria, in spite of . . . .

Fiction is really the means by which the sexual aspects of human experience. By which the sex act is made the subject of aesthetic contemplation by readers. It can be put still more simply. A novelist makes a story, pleasing to the reader, out of men and women's . . .

To grapple with social and political themes, that lifts the narrative above the level of . . . but really it still comes down to . . .

A poet and sculptor, both smitten at heart, lay in bed stimulating a sensitive part; an explosive connection left them both this reflection — *Sure, the pleasure's intense: all the same, is it Art?*

ANNE KENNEDY

The World

1. (How big)
2. (A composition supposed)
3. (A tree)
4.
5. (What it is about)
6. (A creed)
7. (A vase)
8. (America)
9. (A flight)
10. (A book a monk)
11. (Alight)
12.
13. (A verse)
14. (A word her ear)
15. (A vase)
16. (Awash with tea)
17. (Asleep asigh)
18. (Assumed into Heaven)
19. (Deciduous trees)
20. (Descent into Hell)
21.
22. (How small)

1. (How big)

it is her greatest desire to move to the world. She will move to the world as soon as she can. The world perhaps was where she was born, and where the days of her early childhood were passed so long ago that she can hardly be sure of anything anymore. She remembers the world as she remembers dreams she has composed or as she knows anything — the most outrageous things, Reincarnation, Assumption into Heaven, Visitation, how the universe whirls about — the way she knows these things for a split second before the knowing of nothing.

2. (A composition supposed)

She supposes she was there, in the world when the world was the learning of colours, all of them grey, a street of colours muddled together. She learnt to say, Green Grass, Blue Sky, Red Roofs, although the world she knew was a flowering of cars, apartment buildings, pavements, a solitary leafless tree, a muff for her small hands, an afternoon piano, a recital of Wednesdays cooling a concert hall. She rode a streetcar along this avenue, admiring everything, knowing it as if she had put it there herself.

3. (A tree)

A lightness she remembers (the lightness of books or a liking of them) wandering among weeds. The Cow Says Blue, The Dog Says Roof, The Sheep Says Gra-ass — this as she traversed a zigzag stitch on a sewing machine smile to a silk school with a cross (-stitch) on a hill on linen, its houses, clotheslines stuck fast with their autumn blouses, trees which never lost their leaves either. She is leaving these leaves as soon as she can and she is moving to the world. Everything happens there — birth, etcetera (hers hasn't been heard of since, she is not sure where it is but it is not

4

here) she has noticed that nothing anymore in this place has meaning. Meaning has ceased. She is leaving red roofs, their therapeutic properties, leaving everything apart from *She Can Not Leave* — at least she thinks this may be so, that she will not be able to do so, sometimes, on occasions of knowing everything. In the world is everything that means anything at all. The world is everything it means, which is not such a difficult thing when compared to the part of the globe she has had the misfortune to find herself. In the world, consider the way a building was built, the way people walk

5. (What it is about)

about the streets, the way light falls, a breakage, a calamity, and also the light falling of snow. The alighting of a bookshop on a certain corner, no other, a bakery on the corner after that and a cafe on the one after that, as if she had put them there in her childhood, when she was there. She did not put the zigzag in place, where it is, it was there already, but the bookshop, the cafe, a grey street, a solitary tree, a Wednesday — she would have put them just this way, as they are, and they are, that way. Everything is the way she would have put it herself

6. (A creed)

and that is why she must move to the world. She is moving to the world as soon as possible. Hoping its end has not come in her absence. What would she do, if she had missed it? Where would she go? There is nowhere to go from nowhere at all. Even the briefest of her beliefs (she believes in the end of the world) would be shattered, if there was no world. To make sense of her various lives — in this world, the next and the one after that — she must move there. She must move to the world to find her lost birth. She has studied its vessels

7. (A vase)

as she would those of a Chinese dynasty — not much to go on, apart from *She Has Inherited Her Memory In Her Genes*. Aged five she was surprised to discover they did not live in England but in a country of the South Seas. She said to her brother (one of them): 'What about the Queen? The Queen of England is our Queen.' A map of the British Isles on the wall at school; at home an atlas fell open there quite of its own accord. 'Where do we live, on this little shape?' 'Nowhere,' said her brother. They live nowhere. Their white skin has disappeared under this white light, a coverlet thrown over the Pacific. (As a child crouched under a quilt she told her mother

8. (America)

she had a pain in her stomach: 'It's like God — it's there but you can't see it.') An article clipped from their faith on a Wednesday says, *He Believes Though He Has Not Yet Seen*. Their religion is one people are fighting about on the other side of the globe. (She says 'the globe' rather than 'the world' because the world as she sees it is not this planet in its entirety — it is only the part where she is not at this moment.) In the Twenties one of her uncles on her father's side went to New York, he and his wife and their two little girls. 'They have moved to America,' it was said, but she says *They Moved To The World*.

9. (A flight)

On their arrival in the foyer of a hotel of the world they had grave misgivings about the greyness of everything. Everything was grey, apart from a solitary tree outside on the street which was a dull silver. So uncle, familiar with green beer once a year, blue Madonnas, also red, said to the bellhop: 'Book us in to another hotel.' This accomplished, uncle said: 'Call us taxis.' This was done and soon three taxis pulled up at the door. The family and their prodigious luggage climbed into the first and into the second and into the one after that and the taxis, one after another, made U-turns (the whirling of objects

10. (A book a monk)

in the universe) to the new hotel. The new hotel was across the street. If she presses her nose up against glass she can see the bellhop waving goodbye. 'Goodbye!' (The world!) His silhouette is illuminated from behind by Heaven. Heaven and Earth she knows when she sees them, from the descriptions she has read in books. A child among weeds reads a lot. Her imagination is furnished with tasselled curtains and carpets far more sumptuous than the book-like quality of her life here (in the South Island is a place called Erewhon). If she were asked which she preferred she would say she would much rather her life were a book than be like one.

11. (Alight)

(Which it is) Disraeli said: 'If I want to read a book, I write one.' At the dinner table the conversation is an orchestration conducted from the other side of the globe — the world news, *The News Of The World*. Everyone speaks at once about it, apart from *She Is A Child Who Listens Attentively*. She listens with great concentration to a saying of Disraeli and also to what Mao said. 'Thou shalt swat flies.' And they have rid China of flies, says her mother admiringly. What is the time? It is 3 a.m. Greenwich Mean Time, says her brother (another of them), or is it the ticking of the Bay of Pigs? They have circumnavigated the globe. Mickey Savage was Irish as Paddy's pigs, says her father, Kennedy

12.

has been assassinated. She assumes from the seriousness of this announcement that it is something concerning here — a bullet travelled the curve of the earth and very shortly there will be an arrest in their street. When her mother tells her, in her next breath, she looks like nothing on earth at first she is alarmed. Nothing. On earth. On reflection (her interest in mirrors) she considers it the most appropriate way to appear here, and she cultivates an unworldliness. She is not of this world. They are not of this world but they receive radio waves of the news of the world washed up on the beach at Island Bay, collected in buckets at low tide. People hold shells to their ears. They are maps of the world.

13. (A verse)

Over the air she and her brother (another of them) hear: 'But one day you shall play in my garden, which is Paradise.' In the same breath a priest tells them their religion is not of this world. 'I am not of this world,' he quotes the famous. She believes with her strong faith that certain things cannot be seen, and the world is one of them. See, even the Catholic church says that in this part of the globe there is an unworldliness! ('I am not of this world.') A particular man with whom she has formed an object — they are as stalactites, their tears never falling, but collected before they touch the ground — she has asked him to go with her, to the world.

14. (A word in her ear)

He has replied, his lips the wings of a dove: 'Where is the world? Where in the world is it?' His belief is there is no such thing as the thing she has imagined. She listens with half an ear, the half she keeps for these parts. 'Perhaps in the world, drips will fall,' he says. (Explorers believed in a southern continent before it was known to the known world, but she has discovered, after all, their belief was groundless.) It is snowing. Her brothers (all but one) have gone before her, to the world, and her mother sighs, where in the world have they gone? They have left everything they know and soon her younger daughter will leave everything she knows also.

15. (A vase)

A teapot bought at a garage sale. A seashell map of the Chatham Islands. A sewing box cross-stitched by a great-aunt — she took holy orders and spent her days contemplating how many angels could dance on the head of a pin. A piano imported from Japan. An angel fallen from a tombstone. She is leaving these objects. 'How will you survive, with nothing to your name?' asks her mother.
She replies that in the world the world will be an object. Already it is her
heaviest

possession. Ironically an unworldliness necessary to survive in the world she has learnt here, from a priest who recommends not of this world, from her mother who rather than lamenting the breakage of something, a vase, says: 'Never mind, you can't take it with you.' She is taking nothing, when she leaves for the world.

16. (Awash with tea)

He was once a visitor to the world, and while he was there, the particular man, a particular telephone rang bearing news that a baby, his son, was to be born seven months hence — the man the object, the baby the subject of this annunciation. Immediately following it, catching a late-night boat to Calais, the man began a worldwind tour, seeing everything there was to be seen, to be seen in the world. Also he brought books to see him (*they* would see *him*)

17. (Asleep, asigh)

through the years to come confined to a small room in the Southern Hemisphere with a small thing sleeping off its birth (he has now seen everything in the world but he has not yet read every book). More and more she is absent from the part of the globe where she has had the misfortune to find herself. Lost is found. An ear has gone, an eye, also a leg. She no longer looks at red roofs or at anything blue or green, or walks about, having no interest in these book-like things. When he asks her to consider what is contained in a grain of sand, the particular man — ('The West Coast Beaches. You can't beat them. There is nothing like them in the world!') — it is to her a found speech, lost.

18. (Assumed into Heaven)

Her mother (her sighs), she has lost the four little worlds of her five sons, and watches the retreat of another, her daughter. ('What in the world!') When she was younger, her mother — walking on pavements no older than she — was taught to recite: 'I'm a New Zealander, born and bred!' while really a child of the world once removed from its wars. When her daughter says: 'I am not of the world' she assumes she means she is not of *this* world. Her own unworldliness extends to accepting the breaking of vases, the departure of children, as Heaven-sent. 'At least the trees here never lose their leaves.'

19. (Deciduous trees)

The longer she leaves leaving the harder leaving becomes and the more she resembles evergreen trees, their tresses. Her greatest fear, a dreaded phobia of creation myths — whether they exist, the way they suspend (an aria) for a fraction of a second, all departures — although her eye, her ear, her leg, have gone. Seeing them off she stood like a stilt, reciting the creed of the renunciation of everything she has ever known — 'World without world, the living and the

20. (Descent into hell)

dead, the redemption of the globe.' She renounces everything she knows apart from the things known in her bones and of these she wonders, how did they get there — and where in the world are her brothers at this moment? Two in New York, one is halfway up a mountain in Switzerland, another dead. They all catch subways beneath streets so colourful that if they care to look up they could see themselves in them. The buildings grow, the snow falls. She has moved there too, to the fall of snow. Arriving at the book she once read she says: 'My real life.' There is no need to imagine anything,

21.

to imagine anymore. It is all there already. It is already where she put it. Once she invented the conception a child makes, alighting in the landscape of her own imaginings. Her great-grandparents did the same, leaving the old world for the new, their lives for a watercolour of the South Seas. The best idea she ever had, to move to the world, was born in the colony. From then on everything, every person she happened to fall very deeply in love with, was a moment, the myth of *She Is Leaving These Parts*.

22. (How small)

The reading of a book bought in the world — he is sitting in a small room on the side of the globe that faces the ocean, furnished with the transitory flair of a piano put out to sea. Their imaginations have no other vessels. He has his books. She is one. They have marked her body with a tassel, where they are up to, a woman of *The World Has Appeared Within Her Bindings* of this desire.

RUSSELL HALEY

Lions, Attention Please!

There is a watercolour and oil sketch on paper which was painted by
Paul Klee in 1923. Four swiftly drawn lions recline in the lower half
of the work which also depicts circus folk. The paws of these felines
are indicated by small, horizontal figure-of-eight designs.

Klee, apparently, died from sclerodermia which is a chronic
progressive disease characterised by diffuse or local thickening or
hardening of the skin. Towards his end Paul Klee must have felt that
he was turning into an armadillo.

When I think of Klee, his death, and those lions, I am reminded
of mother's favourite story. Once, when she and father were young
and courting, they went to the annual feast on Woodhouse Moor in
Leeds. A feast, of course, wasn't a gargantuan meal. It was a fair with
sideshows and rides. There was a Hall of Mirrors, a Ghost Train,
many gambling stalls, and a small menagerie.

Father was determined to show it was possible to hypnotise any
animal and he chose the lions' cage to demonstrate his ability. He
engaged the gaze of a large male. I imagine that he uttered his favourite
word when talking to cats.

'Parawash, parachashishwash,' he would have said. The end of his
word rhymes with ash — tree or burned logs.

This nonsense endearment, which we heard often during our childhood, might have indicated even then that father was destined to
become an amateur linguist. Towards the end of his life, which had
mostly been spent as a furniture salesman, father could speak snatches
of Russian, German, Polish, Arabic, French and Yiddish.

But lions, attention please! Father stands before the bars of your
cage and he is going to implant a post-hypnotic suggestion in one of
your minds. You, the big male with the patched and leathery hide.

I would dearly love now sitting twelve thousand miles and sixty
years away from this conflict of wills, to know what he said to you.
Mother didn't report father's words. He might have spoken entirely
in invented *Felidae*.

We are allowed, of course, to imagine anything. Why else would we disturb this small story which has been curled up, warm and comfortable in its shell, for six decades. Mother always believed in 'embroidery' — lies were never untruths; they were inevitably 'pure inventions.'

'When you wake up,' he might have said, 'you will fly through time and space and visit our child who is yet to be born. Give him a message from me. Tell him it's time for him to get out of *his* cage.'

What on earth could he have meant by that? Am I trapped in the past just as Klee, when he died, was imprisoned in his own armoured skin?

Casual clothes were rarely worn for special events sixty years ago — not even for an outdoor jaunt to Woodhouse Feast. So father was wearing a navy-blue pinstriped suit complete with waistcoat. Mother, in spite of warm bank holiday weather, had put on a cloth coat with a fur-trimmed collar. Yes, and she'd worn her new cloche hat. Father's head was also decently covered. He sported a bowler which he used to retain even when paddling in the sea with his trousers rolled up.

The lion was shoddy in his khaki hide but he listened. He gazed attentively. Then, exhausted by not having blinked for several minutes, he cocked his hind leg and pissed all over my father through the bars of the cage.

When father was dying the weather in his mind changed. Instead of calm but overcast days and sultry nights, a dense bank of clouds appeared on his horizon and it gave birth to thunderheads and cyclones.

I climbed one of our city's volcanic cones yesterday evening and in the west there was just such a darkness. Here, that indigo band is often seen out over the Tasman Sea. That is where the sun dies nightly and those dark masses devour anything which passs through them. Canoes, our own star, funeral boats.

There must be a correct medical term for father's condition but my elder brother wrote to me and told me that Dad had begun to suffer from brainstorms.

He emerged from one particularly violent episode with something like a soft quasi-mirror lodged inside his mind. If his shirt sleeve was inside-out he was presented with a hopeless puzzle. Which way was this a-dimensional garment supposed to go? What was the real surface of this Möbius loop and tangle? Useless to point out the label. The reflective-thing in his head made no sense of the words uɐ𝖵 ꞁɘ𝗌ᴜɘH.

And that tussle to dress in the morning happened, as often as not, at 3 a.m. Because he now saw clocks in a kind of reverse image and believed, as he tried to dress in the false dawn, that it was 9 p.m. and somehow he had overslept and there was only one hour to go before the pubs closed.

Yes. He kept on drinking and smoking (two of his habits I cannot relinquish) even after a further tornado which almost finished him. He walked out of hospital where he was expected to die and was found, hours later, in a bar. Sometimes, late at night, I have tasted the bitter-sweet flavour of the beer he must have drunk on that escapade.

The wind changed today and Auckland is suffering from an early autumn deluge. The stormwater drains cannot handle the floods in our riparian street and the guava tree in the back yard, already loaded with ripening fruit, will soon shatter down its heavy branches. It is clay here, where we live, clay just a few inches below the surface. The earth cracks and yawns in summer and is heavy and sullen in winter.

This atmospheric dankness made me impatient with my hair which was too long, cresting over the collar of my shirt. I decided to trim back this mane in the bathroom but standing before the mirror, holding another looking-glass behind my head, I could not make the scissors move correctly. My eyes told me 'this way' but the nerves and tendons of my fingers were confused and would not obey. I snipped the air or I plunged the blades down to my scalp and shore off clumps of greying hair.

Then I paid attention to my face in the bathroom mirror. There was no sense of shock in seeing father's features regarding me without blinking. We have grown so much to look like each other. Yet I realised, with my throat swollen and aching, that I am older than he was when he tried to hypnotise the lion at Woodhouse Feast. How odd it is to be more elderly than your father when you are still being transformed into him.

For years I have been slowly changing. I am hardly myself any-more. This is his voice, his taste for beer, whisky and cigarettes. His thumbnails, his cough, are mine. I am my father and my father's death.

There are times when I too wake at 3 a.m. and cannot understand where I am, or *when* I am. An oddly muddled clarity invades me. Last night I awoke with a revolutionary philosophical proposition on my tongue. This axiom would utterly change the world. I spoke aloud.

'Every living thing in the universe either has, or has not, attempted to hypnotise a lion!'

There are particular animals whose gaze is hard to confront because what we see reflected back is a trapped and haunted image of ourselves. Everyone knows that wise but speechless appeal in the eyes of most primates. They tell us that they know something; just below the reflective surface of their corneas they are intimate with us. Certain animals are family. 'I know what it is to know,' they appear to be saying, 'but I have only just begun to move towards speech.'

Nor is this 'look' confined to the primates. Larger dogs wth eyes of human colour have it although I must exclude those breeds such as the Weimaraner with their ice-green or flame-yellow ghost irises. Horses may be touched with this inarticulate knowledge — I have not studied them closely enough to be certain. But pigs blink their long lashes and suggest that they are *aware*.

So in the bathroom mirror I saw my eyes, my father's, and knew that a lemur, an ape, a Dobermann pinscher, perhaps one of the larger felines, was looking out at me and struggling on the edge of language. We are all connected in speechlessness.

What were we trying to say, each to each other, in this genealogical zoo?

I think that *death* is drifting to the root of the tongue through the heavy clay of our understanding, stirring the fine stranded muscles of the vocal chords in monkey, dog, time-travelling lion and man. My young old man. Myself.

Father and mother suffered and grieved for their eldest son as I have for all three of them. When my elder brother set out on his Matchless motor-cycle and never completed his journey he could not have known that father and mother would never be the same people again. We all waited for him and he didn't arrive. After that . . . *absence* . . . a black wind blew through their flesh and I was old enough to sense its edge but sufficiently young to feel it deflected around me. Except when I tried to huddle against them. Then the spaces throughout their bodies concentrated the blast into dark spears. I too was pierced whenever I tried to hold them.

When father and mother mourned for their son, they were both younger than I am now. And I have lived twice as long as Don who will always remain my elder brother. I am hopelessly enmeshed in the tangles caused by this mirrortime; this continuous glassy tape with a single twist. I'm blown through and stab those nearest to me. Those I love.

Deaths as close as those *touch* us. We live *with* death from that moment on yet we know we can never adequately speak of it. Our tongues swell towards speech in our narrow throats and our eyes turn feral with the paradox of making language, knowledge of nothing, happen.

Lions, attention please! You, old one, will serve. And because I know you well there is little chance that I'll be pissed on. Besides, I'm looking at you in my mirror.

There! We gaze at each other. You need a haircut, old man, but I would not dare to touch your mane with scissors.

I'd like you to tell father something from me. Say it to mother too and Don. He'll hold still in the air for eternity.

Tell them a dream I had only last night.

We were all at a circus on an empty moor. Men roared on motor-cycles around the Wall of Death. There were sideshows and rides and gambling games where you rolled a penny down a wooden chute and if it fell precisely within the boundaries of a numbered square you were given coppers to the value of that numeral. The surface on which the coins spun and danced was glazed with layer upon layer of paint in which minor irregularities were magnified.

You were all emptying your small change, without winning, down those little ramps but I began to climb the bamboo tower which promised the biggest thrill at the feast.

Attached to the top of the tower were paper ropes and you had to fling yourself down on the end of these fragile chains. Some payment was extracted for this experience but it eludes me. It's there. But so far around the corner of my mind when I turn to see it, it glides away from me. It will come back, unexpectedly.

At the summit I was so frightened that I began to laugh. Imagine that — terror changing into laughter which was so intense it hurt. Tell them, if you can find the language, that I'm laughing now. Here on the end of my paper rope.

This time you do blink. Then you turn away, lashing your tail.

MICHAEL HARLOW

Interior Decorating

The postcard, a photoprint, is in sepia tones and yellowing with age. You can see, looking beyond, that there is a splendid view of the Duomo and Campanile; as you might expect, there is also a middle-distance view of the Baptistry.

However, it is the figure standing in the foreground, in front of the South Door, who appears so remarkable: a young woman with her arms raised in front of her. You might suppose she has just walked into the picture, and is turning to speak to someone, gesturing with her arms.

What is so extraordinary is that there is a flock of birds, their wings beating the air for a nesting place in the uppermost part of her body, entirely obscuring her face.

Looking at the snapshot and remembering my friend's words, I realise that for some time now his girlfriend has been falling out of the world into herself.

That is what he writes from the city of light and dark: that some-times we fall into ourselves so completely that we can hear only the sounds of other people thinking.

Or is it the other way around?

Of course, he means the girl, Marianina.

There is a strangeness in her; he is convinced — quite against the wish of his will — that *she is trying to climb into heaven on her own, which is not good for her.*

But what can he do?

Can you imagine, he asks, not hearing a sane sound, or what you think is one, for years uttered by anyone but yourself?

She is yielding to certain signs so easily that what was once remark-able is becoming the stuff of commonplace — like glancing daily at a weathercock turning in the air, or the delicate print of trees against the sky.

Signs?

Pictures, really.

And the words he hears himself saying.

The only measure, he claims, is to *hear* what you *see* before you've actually seen it. Then of course the seeing is a distinct possibility.

Don't you agree?

As you can see, my friend is a talker; he is also something of a philosopher.

Worried?

Of course he is worried.

Well, would you not be fearful when he makes it clear that his girl-friend is obsessed with *interior decorating*?

She keeps decorating the flat right there in the middle of the city, in what she says are *post-holocaust-images*.

I know . . . that her mother was once a smalltown movie star, and her father was in vaudeville, and there was an uncle in arts and crafts. But — it cannot be altogether that.

You see, there are certain darkening details.

What was once to us a comfort is no longer. When you look out, when you look in, there are those domestic signs that were and ought to be so consoling: women ironing frocks and gowns in lighted windows open to the river breezes; some small gentlemen leaning into their mirrors, carefully waxing their moustaches for a fine evening on the town; and at almost any hour you can hear automobiles turning corners on the way to dinner, or racing to a weekend in the country.

But — now, it is very different.

She stays home all day every day late into the night talking about the *fatality in her mind*. Pasting up one after the other those terrible pictures in all the rooms of the flat — even on the doorframes, the mirror borders, yesterday the ceilings, the day before the bare spaces on the floors, carpets and rugs rolled into the corners.

Until, if you can imagine it, all the spaces in the flat have been bandaged against what she insists has been a *year of terrors, and where do you suppose God has got to in such a hurry*?

And would you deny that?

There are so many of them that at first it is quite bewildering. You have to look carefully from room to room, and suddenly you realise that they are actual photographs torn from magazines, newspapers, and books.

Well, a riot of images: there are pictures of bodies with open wounds, bright gashes, bodies mangled and stripped of recognition, without limbs without heads even, bodies sometimes liquefied to a pulpy mass.

There is even the after-image of a running child pressed into the pavement.

A fossil-fact?

Soon, you begin to imagine, don't you, that there may be no bodies at all — rather, a whirlwind of torn pages, and printed light.

On one page she has scrawled in greasy red crayon: *Did you think the light could print all my desires, did you? Even if Light itself is the Healer's true God?*

To which of course I have no reply.

And it is true that I have brought her flowers freshly cut, and stuffed animals for her collection, from the stalls by the river, once even a singing bird happy in its cage.

And more.

I pleaded with her, told funny stories, then asked her for a weekend in the country. Could she? Perhaps on a windy day we could pitch the child's kite into the air. One way, wouldn't it be, to feel the wind shiver in the palms of your hands?

Or, how about an afternoon of intimate photographs, sprawling in the countryside?

But, you see, she refused straight away — and says, have I realised, after all, that *the gates to the future are being closed, if you think about it.*

What's more, she is convinced that on her daughter's wedding night *when a pillow falls it will break her ribs if not her heart.*

A delicate matter, and no occasion for dancing, is it?

All the while she is bandaging the flat against some shadow in her heart.

After a while, I began to inspect the flat each day to see where she had got to; I suppose even out of anxious curiosity — to be of some small use, after all.

It was then I discovered the glue: small, hard ice-gobbets of congealed glue, scattered everywhere — as if some fantastic snow-beast had invaded the flat, dropping one confection after another of glueturds.

I think then that I began to understand more than what I was seeing. There is a furious energy in what she is doing; and it all seems so very clear to her.

Only lately, she insists on telling me her dreams; a rare privilege and I listen attentively to her.

How admirably, she begins by picking over one fragment and then another; sorting through beginnings and endings, elaborating on middle passages, altogether a fascinating puzzle of parts.

She tells them well — sometimes even with snatches of song, filling the gaps with anecdotes to prolong my attention, or provoke my admiration.

I think I have begun to catch the look of what she is saying: *What do you do when you have just finished putting your head into heaven?*

Only yesterday, she began the day by inspecting the heels of a new pair of shoes I had bought from a shop on the way home the night before. You could smell, even through the shoebox lid, the new, uncreased leather.

Stiffening — she held them out at arm's length, the soles turned upward; points of light bouncing off the finely polished leather.

And then she showed me what I had never seen before: the imprint of the lot number, 666. Of course it may have been the signature of a shopworker.

Suddenly — I was afraid that she might fall violently to the floor. She rolled her eyes back into her head, grinding her teeth, I could hear her gasping for air, repeating over and over, *just what you might expect, just what you might expect, after all, just what you might expect . . .*

And then, as if responding to a signal for dreamtime, she fell into a deep sleep; she slept soundly for some time at the table, her head cradled in her arms.

Finally, this morning she declared that after all she was determined *. . . to carry out a raid against the unspeakable, even if there is no turning back, and amen.*

She spoke quite clearly, even calmly, almost I thought even cheerfully — reading from a torn patch of paper held in the open palm of her hand.

You will understand how much I was relieved.

There is simply no room left in the flat that hasn't been bandaged in newsprint.

Then she asked, would I care to step to the window?

I would.

I could hear it at once — humming out there on the streets. It seemed constant and everywhere in the air, and not unpleasant. She held my arm lightly at the elbow guiding my sight. Looking out as I did just above the great dome, I could see: a large, smoke-coloured ball.

Imagine my surprise when I began to notice how the globe was turning on its axis, growing larger and larger as it continued falling slowly into the city.

At that moment, despite the darkening of the sky as the sun began to slide away, I saw . . . for the very first time on the face of the turning globe, the milky contours of all the continents of the earth.

And I saw, but only for a fleeting instant, I saw the figure of Marianina above the smoke-coloured globe.

She was levitating in a shock of blue light.

MARILYN DUCKWORTH

Explosions on the Sun

Someone has safety-pinned a plastic bag inside the bars of Gillian's bottom gate.

A white shawl. Very clean. Crocheted by very clean hands. It flows out of the plastic bag very soft against her sun browned wrists. She swings it onto her shoulders and dances to the mirror, stroking it. Then thinks to discover where it has come from. A note in the bag explains it has been crocheted for her by a friend of her grandmother who wants her to come to lunch. She doesn't want her grandmother's friends. She has her own. And yet she has danced in front of the mirror and enjoyed the shawl. Madame Truffaut has put out her crochet hook and neatly hooked Gillian into her life. Last time they met she had felt the old woman was shocked by her novitiate's dress. But apparently she has forgiven Gillian her vows to the church. Now that she has renounced them.

She lives, like a witch, at the top of a white palace, at the end of the last corridor. A fat little witch in polyester. She is Belgian.

They eat sponge fingers. They fit Madame's mouth perfectly. She feeds them in greedily, as if she only eats when she has company. Gillian's French limits the conversation. They discuss the weather. She tells Gillian there have been explosions on the sun. This is the explanation for the afternoons of cloud, the phlegm at the back of the sky.

'Explosions,' she repeats. She makes a fat tunnel of her mouth to sound the 'o'. She is very serious. Gillian shudders. She wonders if the world is going to end and how soon. '*They* are responsible, of course.'

Later she realises that what the woman talks of are sunspots, familiar abnormal phenomena after all. But still hears Madame Truffaut's 'explosions' in her head. She looks up at the sky and wonders if a piece of it could fall down and crush her. And who are 'they'? It was much easier when God could be blamed for natural disasters. But Gillian has decided, after much unhappiness, not to believe in God.

She locks the top gate and is inside the cottage taking off her shoes,

when she has a strange feeling. There is someone or something outside, watching her. She hasn't locked the lower gate. She sometimes
forgets. Tonight it seems important that she should lock it. She runs
down quickly and silently in her bare feet. The tunnel of steps is
always cool, but tonight it seems cooler than usual. Round the second
bend she halts. Her keys rattle as she lowers them behind her. There
is a face looking in at the gate and she doesn't want the face to see the
keys. Did he hear them? Does he suspect the gate is unlocked?

The face is a man's — ruddy, with curling dark hair and a flash of
white teeth. Not a tourist. He looks like a satyr — not young — his
cheeks sag. But his eyebrows point upwards. He smiles at Gillian.
When she doesn't respond he turns and goes away.

She sits on the steps and waits until she has stopped trembling. The
steps are very cold. Then she runs down the last of them and locks
the gate. You have to lean on it to get the key to turn. If anyone was
waiting there they would have had the gate open while she was
struggling with the key. She hates keys. But they're necessary.

That man. She has seen him twice now, she is sure.

She thinks he might be one of them.

She wakes in the still dark and waits for the noise of a train. Here
comes one now. She can count the carriages from the sound swaying
in and out against her window. When it has gone she gets up to go
to the bathroom. The door is closed and won't give immediately. She
turns the handle a second time and pushes. Rattles the knob. The door
seems to be bolted from the inside. It must have slammed in the wind,
forcing the bolt out of place. What wind? Not a breath of air. Then
she thinks she hears whispering behind the door. She puts her eye to
the crack but can't see anything. Not even a light. This is absurd. She
will have to go outside and pee under the pittosporum bush. Who
could be in her bathroom at this time of night? Even for the South
of France this is strange. She knocks on the door.

'Is there anyone there?'

The whispering stops.

She goes outside and squats under the pittosporum bush, holding
her nightie high under her breasts.

As she moves back into the light of the kitchen she catches sight
of the spider. It hasn't had to walk very far to get here from its web
in the bedroom window. The cottage is only two and a half small
rooms. She gets the feeling the spider knows something about the

bathroom door. Supposing she trod on it now, would these odd things stop happening? She raises her foot threateningly and her lower leg begins to shake. She has never killed a spider in her life. Mosquitoes, ants, even flies — but not a spider. She puts her hand over the trembling nerve in her knee and lowers her foot to the floor. The spider plays dead.

She decides to try the bathroom door again.

It opens. There is a faint flowery smell in the air. Her grandmother must have come back to have a bath. The whispering would have been her reading Anthony Powell aloud to herself above the steam. Do books have ghosts?

If it wasn't her grandmother, then who was it?

The black-bearded tramp is sitting on a seat overlooking the port. His hair glistens with sweat, his red face is dusty. He is carefully rolling a cigarette from old butts of tobacco. Why does he always wear his coat? Is there nothing underneath? It is more important, of course, for a tramp to be modest than a failed nun on holiday from Scotland. She is walking past him with her Codec plastic bags full of cheese and fish and olives. She must have looked guilty for he invites her again to stop and talk about God. Can he know more about God than Gillian? The tramp is the imaginary badman of little girls. Bluebeard. The real badman is of course disguised — sometimes as the husband they mean to marry. The preacher tramp is kindly and slow. He isn't one of *them*. Nevertheless she is glad she didn't find him in her bathroom last night. It would be like meeting a gorilla.

She assembles lettuce, fish, eggs, olives — on her kitchen bench — and begins hungrily to make herself a Niçoise salad. Chopping, whipping and tossing, with her back to the sun. The kitchen is arranged that way. What would it be like to have no sun? If it were totally obscured by Madame Truffaut's explosions, or by something else? She shudders to think of a sunless world. A world without light. Or heat. The eskimo life has never appealed to her. She has poor circulation.

Before she goes to bed she drinks a bottle of good white wine. Blanc de blanc. Twelve percent. Tonight nothing will disturb her.

It's a fallacy that wine helps you to sleep. It might make you snore and twitch your eyelids, but it keeps the brain awake. Racing in overdrive. She can feel the heat of her body in the mattress and keeps moving to escape it.

At four o'clock she goes to the bathroom. She wishes she didn't have to go. She couldn't bear to find the door locked again. After all, it's her bathroom. Grandmother left it to her in the will. So why does she lock her away from the toilet?

Tonight she takes the few steps across the living room, past the kitchen alcove — and hears the lavatory flush. She freezes. A man has come out of the bathroom. Jeans and grubby white shirt. He sees her and sidles with his back to the wall, smiling and waving his hands as if he is trying to wipe her away. These windscreen wiper movements seem to say — 'Don't touch me. I'm harmless.'

She watches him go, perfectly calm now.

This is very odd, to find a man in her bathroom in the small hours of the morning. She tells herself how odd it is, because in fact it doesn't feel all that odd. It's as if she had put him there herself. But this isn't a dream. She pinches herself, as they used to in books she read as a child. It feels like a real pinch. But what sort of test is that?

She has forgotten to notice if he went down the steps or up into the bushes. The fence is quite high at the back.

She decides to stay awake, sitting at the table, facing the window, and watch the sun come up. If she is here in the morning, that will prove this really happened. Won't it?

Morning, and she is still here sitting at the table. She feels a bit dizzy, from lack of sleep she decides. She has been reading her grandmother's P. G. Wodehouse books. She hasn't removed any of her things. She is living here as if she were her grandmother, using her crockery, her linen, her books, her view from the window. She moved here for the view. The blue green mountains, the old ochre bell tower, the boats. It's like living in an eyrie. This reminds her of the dove that flew down across the back of her hand earlier. Was it a real bird? Yes, because she has its feather on the windowsill beside her Bible. The odd thing is that she has felt again that same sensation on the back of her hand, as if invisible wings were brushing it. She feels it now, flexing her fingers and watching the movement. There is something there, poised and feathery. She wishes it would fly away. She can hear the doves cooing in the garden above, monotonously, on and on. She feels an emptiness in her chest which is like the emptiness in her mailbox. On bad days people post stones into that emptiness.

She walks to the olive grove past empty houses. Peeling stucco. Wall boards instead of glass behind the barred windows. She peers into the darkness of one but it is so black anyone could be in that room.

Still climbing and walking, she finds deep blackberry bramble steps, going down under shadowy witchy trees. It is like being breathed into the lung of the earth. She hears voices, catches flashes of coloured clothing between branches — but there is no one there. She follows a winding *sentier* between high stone walls. She can't see and has no idea where she is going. She is a white rat in someone's experiment. Who is leading her where? She starts to turn a corner and in the passage ahead of her hears deep heavy breathing. Some large-flanked animal is padding towards her. She turns around quickly and finds another path. It is downward. There is smoke blowing across the narrow passage. Some gardener burning rubbish. As she reaches the centre of the smoke she takes a breath, chokes and sits down.

She is helped to her feet immediately. Two men support her, one on each side. The taller one on her left is the young man who had been in her bathroom. When she sees him her knees give way and he trips against her, righting himself with a curse. His hand under her elbow presses her onwards. The older man is the ruddy-faced satyr who was at her gate. They aren't merely helping her up, they are taking her somewhere.

'What are you doing?' She panics. 'Let me go.' And shakes her elbow free.

'I think you were looking for us?'

'What were you doing in my bathroom?' she demands.

The young man starts to laugh and the older man joins him. 'We want to share something with you.'

'It's down here.'

They are back on the witchy steps leading down between scented blackberry bushes. There is a great hole burnt out of the bank. The edges are charred and smoking.

'No!' She pulls back, afraid of the confined entrance. But as they draw closer it becomes larger — large enough for the three of them. Beyond she sees a long glowing passage, redlit, and at the end of it hears sounds of revelry, music and laughter.

'You don't have to come in now,' the young man says. 'Do you want to come back some other time?'

'Some other time — yes,' she says. There is a sweetish smell of smoke that is making her sick. 'I know the way.'

'Oh yes.' They laugh together. 'You know the way. You'll find us again.' And they release her. They haven't been holding her with any kind of pressure.

She runs all the way home. On the grass verge an old couple have set up a card table. They are playing euchre, wearing cocked hats made out of French newspapers. 'Peter Sellers is dead. Goodbye Mr Sellers,' a cocked hat calls out to her as she passes by. The Joker is dead.

Her strength is gone. She has difficulty climbing the thirty-eight steps.

After the humid warmth of the day the evening is blissfully cooler. She lies on her garden seat, looking upwards. A bursting green loquat falls out of the loquat tree into her lap. A healthy fruit. This isn't possible. She sits up and examines it, stroking the slightly rough skin. She looks up into the creeper-covered tree. Evil-looking fruit, black with disease, peers down at her. The ground is littered with these, and with heavy brown leaves like bits of leather. She pierces the unripe fruit with her thumbnail and it is full of sticky seeds.

They gaze up at her like eyes. Has she killed something living? She digs them into the earth. While she is doing this she notices another dove's feather, very small and pale, lying by the seat. She leaves it there because her hands are dirty.

She dreams of drowned souls. She is leaning on the rail of a ship and sees them in the water. They look like spirals under the waves. Like ammonites. She wakes and her grandmother's bed confronts her. The sculpted footboard is as high as the head. It is wood, not iron, but the curves and pointed chiselled knobs at the corners are like something in a cemetery. Why hasn't she noticed before how like a tomb it is? Of course she has this notion upside down. The bed is not like a tomb, the tombs have been made to resemble beds. Nevertheless she can't sleep in it tonight. She climbs out and arranges the mattress on the floor.

She is sitting up on her mattress, wakeful, spray can poised like a gun. She can't see the mosquitoes but can hear them dive bombing in the air, invisibly. At last she grows tired of looking for them in the lamp light — she has decided to leave this on — and shoots at random, away from her nose. The smell creeps back like a fart.

She has decided what to do today. She is going to lift the lid of Grandmother's piano and see if she can remember any of her old tunes. There are music books in the piano stool with pages missing and jumbled. She will sort them into some kind of order and try them out on the yellow keys. She had forgotten the piano. Grandmother had a table cloth draped over it and clutter parked on both levels. She wants to make a noise.

She makes a noise. This is all it is. Certainly not music. She laughs out loud at herself. She has put her hands down on the keys. They fall automatically into place over the first notes of her 'recital piece'. 'Jesu, Joy of Man's Desiring'. The fingers flutter, hesitate, stumble and go on. It can't simply be that the piano is out of tune. It is her fingers which have forgotten a remembered sequence which has somehow been jolted askew. How can this have happened? Are there other memories which are distorted like this? Playing over and over in her head, a sharp instead of a flat, a compressed interval? Well, she will have to go back to the beginning. Her first piece. 'Buy a broom. Buy a broom. Buy a broom to sweep your room.'

Some of the lower notes don't sound. She presses them and they thunk tunelessly. She sneaks up on them in a scale, fingering lightly. Still they don't respond. The silences hang like missing rungs in a ladder. She thinks she hears someone laughing outside and bursts onto the verandah, preparing to find one of *them*. Nothing. But someone is making fun of her. She peers up into the sun glare, looking for neighbours in the gardens above. Would laughter carry that far?

Later she thinks she hears somebody whistling at her gate. She is on her way down with her shopping bag, walking very carefully. Whatever or whoever whistled has passed on by the time she has descended the last seventeen steps.

In the grass growing alongside the *raccourci* a small grey snake is sunning itself. As she draws back it shoots off into a hole in the wall. The movement turns over some mechanism in her chest, so that she has to gasp for breath. She runs to get away from the spot and by the time she arrives at the Porte de France she is doubting that she saw the snake. She would prefer to think it was a trick of the light. She slows down and breathes deeply.

She has read all her grandmother's books, so decides to visit the English library.

This is housed in a church. How long since she has been in a church? Not long. Three weeks. A lifetime ago. The smell doesn't change.

In the library they are talking very loudly. The library is a social occasion and British voices are raised. Amusing anecdotes, an argument about a book order. An English gentleman gestures with a date stamp. A woman drops a cascade of books. Gillian goes behind a shelf in the small room and blocks her ears. She can't think of the name of an author. All the names have fled out of her head. In ten minutes the library will close. She reaches out for a book. Any book. Her ticket out of this place.

She finds she is walking to the olive park. She has to sit down for a moment on the old tramp's seat, opposite the port. The big olive tree in the corner has crumbled at the base, leaving a deep slotted cavity with decaying edges. Inside she can see litter, drink cans, paper. The tree doesn't seem to mind. Its lacy leaves spread a hazy shadow. She is glad the tramp isn't here. She doesn't want to talk about God. When she is rested she moves on up the *raccourci*, between ochre walls. Blue convolvulus is blooming on a bank above. Something prompts her to turn and look back at the sea. A figure is standing on the sea wall against the sun. From here it looks like him. The young man in jeans. How could she possibly tell? There is something in the angle of his chin. Like a wolf baying at the moon. If he had a beard it would point almost horizontal.

She feels very tired and sits down for a moment on a shallow step. Her skirt trails in the dust. She might as well go down as up.

By the time she reaches the Porte de France she can't see him. Some French people are arguing about a car collision, banging each other's vehicles with fists and shouting. The woman shouts loudest. Gillian goes down the steps to the Café Jardin and orders *thé citron*. The umbrella shade is cool. She stretches her legs under the table and sighs with relief. The second slice of lemon will do for her fish tonight. She wraps it in a paper serviette. Then she remembers she has an invitation to dine out tonight. She looks up past the laundry, the locksmith, to the post office clock. It is quarter to three, nearly the end of siesta. On a low wall behind the supermarket the checkout girls are lounging in overalls and green aprons. She hears their laughter. A knot of impatient shoppers clusters at the glass doors of the shop front, wheeling empty trolleys. The girls drift reluctantly towards the back entrance. Their bags of change wait to be collected and tipped into the tills. When Gillian goes home she will have to look for a job. A job like this?

Her dinner invitation has come from a retired Canadian couple who live along the Boulevarde — friends of her grandmother. She has to walk past the entrance to the olive park to reach their apartment block.

They sit on a balcony overlooking a blue swimming pool, sipping white wine and crème de cassis. From time to time the surface of the pool erupts with an evening bather. She looks beyond a tall canary palm at the glittering port and the blurred sea. Jazz rhythm rises from the park.

When it is time to go she declines her host's offer of a lift. She leaves the marble-floored foyer, walks down the wide path and sees a figure waiting where the Boulevarde begins. The young man. Perhaps she expected him to be there? Is this why she preferred to walk? Does she want to get to know the young man?

They are directly opposite the deep blackberry bramble steps where he had shown her the passage in the bank. She expects him to lead her down there again. Instead he beckons and leads her on along the Boulevarde to a roadblock. 'Chantier interdit.' Beyond the roadblock the way is dusty and uneven. The hillside has eroded and tumbled down. She hangs back.

'It's all right. It's safe to walk. I'm taking you to the old cemetery.'

'Why?'

'The view's superb. I thought you'd like to see it.'

There's a full moon so that the sky is milky. Dark cypresses circle the graveyard, black on the moony sky. Inside the gate the graves are shadowy iron cots, like Grandmother's bed, with no space for a ghost to put his feet. Other graves are enclosed dog kennels hewn in stone. She looks for eyes, but there are no eyes looking out.

They move on up to a higher level. On the way they pass crypts with iron doors, like lifts to the Inferno. One of the locks on the double doors has been breached. They swing inward to a small shadowy room. There are objects in the room — pots of flowers? She leans to look and is suddenly afraid she will be pushed from behind and the doors clang shut on her. She draws back. Now, passing other wrought iron doors, she imagines prisoners bhind the bars, rattling at them, staring out of empty eye sockets. She shudders and runs after the young man to the top level and the breathtaking view. The lights of the port, stringing along the promenade, the town below, the mountains hunched on the bright sky. The view is awe-inspiring. But she can feel death in the soles of her feet.

They look over a wall at the roofs of crypts below. It looks like a small baroque village. With lights inside, these buildings could be inhabited.

'Why did you bring me here? Yes, I know — the view. But why else?'

She is talking to herself for he has gone ahead of her, back down the steps to the lower level. She follows. She doesn't want to be alone. Round a corner he is sitting on a new double grave, like a bed. He runs his hand over the flecked and polished granite. His hand moves up to the headstone, wiping over it, feeling for an inscription. Is that what he's doing?

'There's no inscription!' she notices, following with her own hand.

He reads her thought and laughs. 'That frightens you, doesn't it? It *is* strange. Here.' He pats the granite. 'It's quite comfortable. Rest.'

She sits. She needs to sit. Her legs are weak and aching.

A moment later he has launched himself upon her, reaching for the neck of her dress, ripping, so that buttons fly like popping corn. Her heel skids on the cold granite as she tries to rise and is forced back.

She screams.

Who will hear?

All these people inscribed on headstones and not a soul to rise and help her. Not even God will hear her now, since he doesn't exist. She struggles, clawing and kicking. And then, quite suddenly he has gone. His weight lifts and his shape melts harmlessly into the shadows.

Another shape materialises, opening a new scream in her throat. The old tramp in his dusty black coat.

Is he about to show her what he wears — or doesn't wear — underneath?

No.

He holds out a hand to help her up. 'Venez.' He explains that the nasty young fellow has gone, run away. The hand she takes is surprisingly soft, like feathers, and yet she feels safe.

On the way down the hill she asks him to tell her about God.

MICHAEL GIFKINS

Not Looking for Graham Greene

Leaving Ventimiglia behind, we hustled the Renault up the valley of the Roya. The road was paved with concrete, weeds pushing through the cracks. (Ugliness and great beauty are always willing bedmates.) The town, when we reached it after half an hour, was like a vision on a postcard, the river fanning into sunlight over ancient moss-green pillows of rock. Trout, lulled by jewelled fingers, dozed. A stone clocktower announced watchfulness over the alchemist's hour between lunch and two.

I had met this woman only the night before. ('A good sort, Bianca,' Guillaume said.) The pink lurex tights and purple sweater were straight out of the American dream, circa 1960, as were the silver stilettos. And she was so big! No doubt a heart of gold beat through the red leather of her jacket — last year's Florentine *chic*.

We pulled up sharply outside a stone building no different from others that lined the cobbled square. Bianca, who was driving, leant across to free my passenger door. I smelt again the garlic beneath the Diorissimo, and through the artificially blonde ringlets, caught the ingrained patterns of acne on her cheek. What was it we were doing here? The heavy wood eroded by the centuries echoed hollowly to her knock. After what seemed a long time, the double doors were unbolted and we entered through an opening no wider than a slit.

She had a bottle of what she swore was the first wine of the season, the Italian equivalent of the *beaujolais nouveau*. Guillaume had been openly dismissive, which she rather seemed to like. I could not understand how he could be so rude, when Bianca was his guest. 'It's dreadful stuff,' he shouted. 'It looks and tastes like ink!' But he smiled as he said it. 'When you go and buy your next lot, you ought to take Diana with you too!'

The little old man still had bits of pasta in the stubble on his chin. He reminded me of my father, the way his cellar was full of tools. He pointed to the dim electric bulb and cackled, adding something that I could barely understand. 'He's saying that he's harnessed the earth's energy,' Bianca translated. She didn't seem particularly impressed.

'He'll talk all afternoon about it if we let him. He knows we've come about the wine.'

The winemaking operation turned out to occupy very little of the poorly lit space, which was like a big garage with corners disappearing into darkness. I thought there might have been tunnels in the shadows. There were a couple of plastic barrels and some bungs and lengths of hose. A box of bottles already filled and labelled we discovered hidden under sacks. It seemed that the wine was a sideline, a retail outlet that he kept going at the insistence of his sons.

'He's over eighty,' Bianca helped us, though I could almost understand. 'He says he'll live for ever, because he's plugged into the vital force.'

The shambling structure of wheels and of wood I'd refused till then to notice, because I knew it would not make sense. An old tractor seat formed a rickety perch onto which the ancient artisan now leapt. I could see pistons sunk into the dirt floor and a collection of gauges and wires. He clapped on a sort of leather cyclist's helmet studded with electrodes and began to peddle furiously. A force field formed about him and he hummed visibly at its core. Suddenly the door at the head of a stairway I had not noticed was flung open and the dingy cellar exploded into light. A woman was standing framed in the doorway. Behind her, I was sure I could hear a baby's cry.

In the square the afternoon was now so busy it was hard to remember it as it had been before. The townsfolk criss-crossed easily at this confluence of daily life. Bianca gave me two of the bottles of wine, though she'd paid for the six herself. The old man's wife (or was it his daughter?) had set an almost impossibly high price. Somewhere on that second floor (because the cellar rose two storeys) the baby continued its racket. The old man's unshaven face grinned out at us from the crack between the doors.

I had come to this place from North America to escape a boredom with myself. My passport, if it is to be believed, says that I am of an age which no one else accepts. They ask, you have a *nineteen*-year-old son? He is another reason that I left. I do not know Bianca's reasons for being here, though that is obviously not her name. The big blonde from somewhere near Los Angeles has a short and very dark Italian boyfriend. His name is Luigi, which at first I took to be a joke. You see, I call all Italian men Luigi, from the way they drive their cars. He is short, but he is very well built (not fat). Welding is his trade. Bianca has a huge iron bedstead underneath a canopy decked with stars. She sometimes says, with perfect decorum, 'After dinner we *made love.*' Luigi is too shy of her friends to say much more than good day, or when he's leaving, *ciao.* Then, embarrassed, he gets into the rusty Autobianchi that he parks at the very entrance to the drive. Perhaps he is aware that there have been others before him who are also short and dark?

I had to tear myself from my son in Toronto or else I think I would have died. Like Luigi, he is very handsome. I have a photo with me that shows him lounging with his legs across an easy chair. He is wearing slippers and doesn't think it all strange that I have left to start another life. I also have a lover, and I suspect that I have left him too. The first time I came here was in the winter of last year; it was then I met Guillaume and rented an apartment in his house. Paul (my lover) was with me and Guillaume still asks when he's coming back. 'How's that man of yours?' he asks. He seems to disapprove of what I am attempting yet I am not sure he understands either his disapproval or the attempt.

It is easy for me not to be with Paul, just as it is very pleasant to share his company. Our existence together was *civilised*, and that's a fact.

Bianca has taken a studio in Ventimiglia. It is in the high part, on the side you enter when you drive in from France. I am looking for something similar in the port area of Antibes. Bianca's studio used to be some kind of shop, there are these huge white columns and Luigi is busy welding armatures for sculptures (she thinks she'll do some sculpture). Every Thursday she works at the markets across the river, selling the Italians Italian leather clothes. Why Antibes? People will say it's because of Graham Greene.

Amy has just arrived back from Reggio di Calabria. She's travelled something like twenty-four hours by train, carrying a box of cream cakes. It was so exhausting. The train ride? (Those American girls think nothing of going straight across Europe in a day and back on their Eurail pass.) No, the relatives. They were all so pleased to see her, full of questions, but it was such an effort to understand. Would I like a cream cake? The whole family detoured via the bakery on their way to see her off.

Since her friend Mary left us, Amy hardly eats at all. They look just the same, those two, stocky college girls, brown all over. But Mary's gone on to London where there may be a job in publishing and now Amy will not leave me alone. I make dinner but she will not eat. She has neither a job in publishing to go to nor a boyfriend, but then Mary is more serious. (I fear that Mary's seriousness may finally eat her up.) Amy gobbles the mail that has been waiting. She washes out her clothes. She tries to make an international call. Her brother phoned while she was in Calabria, offering her a partnership in insurance. Should she take it up?

She is homesick. I ask her if her parents speak Italian in the home. Amy loves her father, who lately wears a colostomy bag.

People take to me wherever I go. Like Olaf and Gerde. You catch the bus up to St Agnès before lunch — it goes only the once each day. Higher and higher it climbs, past the fruit trees and the olive groves until finally you look down on the viaduct itself and the cars streaming along the autoroute into Italy. And then higher still, until it seems you may be lost somewhere among the clouds. The sea stretches beyond you to North Africa. On a clear day you might see Corsica, though it will only be an illusion, a refraction of the light.

St Agnès is the highest littoral village on the whole of the Mediterranean Sea. The bus rounds an outcrop as the driver changes down to first. Concrete bunkers with slit eyes announce the end of the Maginot Line. Then the village emerges from the mists of an even further distant time, turned in upon itself and away from the yellow-haired invaders whose longboats plundered eight, nine centuries before.

I sit with my Scandinavian friends and take ice-cold schnapps as clouds stalk the dripping streets. We are on their terrace, higher again than the village's orange-tiled roofs. Afternoon sunlight turns to spun gold in the mist. Later, in a superb display of will, Olaf will take himself in hand and guide me up the goat track to the ancient castle's keep. He says I can go higher, though there is a sign warning of the drop.

Afterwards he swallows more of his medication. The little white pills, he explains in an English made more halting by its progress, obscure the symptoms but do not arrest the disease. The motor system is degenerating. And every morning Gerde, who is still beautiful, does her 10-B-X. They show pictures of their early marriage. There they are! Holidaying with Olaf's parents just before the war. They stroll on the Promenade des Anglais. Olaf's father has just imported Swedish calisthenics and is fiercely renovating the residents of Nice. Olaf lends an arm to an equally proud new wife.

All four of them are wonderful, like film stars.

He shows me his insurance card as a magician performs a trick. I note that it allows for repatriation of his body. There is a call from

Stockholm, from their unmarried daughter, Berthe. For years now, she has been unable to hold down a job. She is not married, has never had a man. Today, she has not got up from bed.

Over afternoon tea I sit with Olaf and help him draft a letter. The house is alive with computer links, fax, all the paraphernalia of instant access, but this is a formal letter and so custom must be observed. Olaf is a world expert on the effects of weightlessness on the brain. He has proved that long exposure induces symptoms similar to Parkinson's. The letter is to his boss at NASA. He is formally withdrawing from the international space research programme for reasons of his health.

I make suggestions for improvements which he never seems to like. My coffee is cold. I can see that Gerde is anxious, would like to shield her guest. Olaf loses track of what I am saying and smiles foolishly at his thoughts. I understand the full extent of his deterioration but by then my brain is cottage cheese.

Chernobyl! One of the seven wonders of the world! The word is ringing in my ears as Bianca and I wait for the Matisse Museum to open. We have driven all this way and to find that it's a Wednesday and of course the hours are changed. Up round the Arctic Circle the Lapp hunters are throwing reindeer into pits. What else is Santa bringing them for Xmas?

And then we are fighting the Japanese to get inside from nuclear rain.

Matisse is of course one of the reasons that I'm here, but quite frankly it is disappointing, if not to say banal. Umbrellas must be left outside to avoid contamination of the carpet — try explaining that in French to an ever-eager Japanese! Photography is not permitted, but there's an elderly *kamikaze* who hasn't come all this way to be told that! Quite deliberately he is unable to understand, his three cameras clicking in rotation. Will there be an international incident? The attendant is fierce enough with children, but is that sufficient preparation for *la guerre*?

The drawings are certainly a study in economy of line, bodies fluent with a minimum of fuss. But where's the colour? A few second-string paintings are hanging on the walls, but if you really want to see Matisse, I'd say go to Paris.

This morning as I walked my *baguette* back from the baker I saw the elderly tramp pushing his supermarket trolley down the road that leads up to the station. Our relationship is on the most correct of footings. ' 'Jour Madame,' he grumbles, not quite looking me in the eye, 'avez-vous des sous?' I have a ten-franc piece already waiting. He touches his forelock in recognition of the legitimacy of this exchange and humbly I murmur, 'Pas du tout.' His hands are supremely filthy and perspiration forms rivulets in the dirt. His waistcoat (for he wears a three-piece suit with sandals) glistens with a year's supply of grease.

'The gendarmes take him in at Xmas,' Bianca volunteers (she does not find my friend particularly charming), 'and wash him and give him clothes. You knew he was a professor of mathematics?' His wife died suddenly and he was heartbroken, leaving their mansion for a life out on the streets.

'But what if it suited him anyway?' I enquire, recognising in the power of wrists and ankles something quite unmathematical. Has she noticed the soft brown of his eyes?

Over coffee we discuss such things on the avenue with the name of the city's mayor. This oily man is having an affair with a woman Bianca and I both know. I try to explain about my relationship with Paul, the parties, the dressing up, how *suitable* it all felt. Bianca is not very forthcoming about her own past, though I have heard there is a marriage to a Greek. Were there any children? I don't dare ask. For days now at a time she has been disappearing into Ventimiglia, to consecrate with Luigi the chapel they have built to love. She is vague in her responses and it seems I hurt her when I ask about her art.

We are sitting in the eighth largest city in France and men are moving in on us like flies. A Corsican bandit has died in a shoot-out with the police. In a square not a hundred metres distant a woman was raped yesterday by four men as she left a clinic where she was receiving counselling for AIDS. (In the papers they call it SIDA.) Her attackers cannot have known this, and passers-by ignore the pleas for help.

Although the Chagall Museum is no less accessible, we have it almost to ourselves. I confess to Bianca that when it came to it, I was unable to have sex with a black man that I liked. But the Chagalls are miraculous, a testament to the sustaining power of myth. Before I left to come here Paul asked me whether I would have another child. I told him it was a lot to go through, and I'd have to be very sure. 'Of what?' he asked me. I spoke then about the pain and I could see he thought I meant of childbirth. But I was referring to this present sundering of part of me from myself.

In the port of Antibes I am looking for something where I can take an upper floor. This will be my bedroom and my living area and my studio all in one. Perhaps an open space above a warehouse, or a ship's chandlers? If there is a single person who understands this perfectly, it is sure to be Félix. I will sit in his almost-empty restaurant (the tourists all gone home) and order, first the *soupe aux poissons* with its pumpkin colour and its tiny floating *croûtes* — and he will defer with a sad, timeless smile to my declining of a second bowl — and then possibly the sole, whose flesh he will remove from the supporting backbone in just seven practised gestures as I watch.

Tonight on my return to Guillaume's I inspect my clothing for any show of blood. At the market in Villefranche I bought a tiny silver ear. And then in a café washroom I pushed my fingers deep inside myself. Nothing.

I move my bed beside the window and leave the shutters open, listening to the sounds the earth makes as it opens to the rain.

My son was born in Cambridge, which I took to be the very centre of the world. His father and I tried our hardest, but it was never more than just charades. As parents we could hide a growing lack of passion, too young to recognise a true desperation of the soul. And then on our first trip to continental Europe, Paris seized me by the heart . . .

Because this was *his* break from the academy the boy's father wished to press on further and so nightfall found us in Sancerre. There, on the hilltop that breeds wines of flint and ice was a hotel whose existence seemed studiously to ignore the child. We slept, the three of us, in a massive feather bed with bolsters and woke to snow-flakes spinning in the light. My son slurped on croissant dredged in lukewarm *café au lait*. His father read Henry James (you may have seen the post-doctoral study that allows him present fame). We walked later to the castle, through the village filled with mush. It was mid-afternoon, but already almost dark; the two of them looked set to enter a North-West Passage of their own. At the castle gate we rang a massive gong of bronze and the door opened on a maddened crone whose goat-husband shat pebbles and fixed the child with a knowing yellow eye. That night his father drank *pastis* in the village with brain-damaged ex-*maquis* . . .

This morning I declined Bianca's invitation to visit St Paul de Vence, preferring my own company and the challenge of my art. I really have done very little by way of drawings and such paintings as there are exist only as ideas. The exhibition in Toronto will be the last in this act of severance. After that, the audience will know no bounds.

You are quite right to wonder about my relationship with Guillaume. To be frank, I use him, though the process works both ways. I sometimes feel he is hastening me to a conclusion of his own devising, though what this might be I am as yet too ignorant to know.

Bianca says we should all have dinner, while the nights remain this warm. There will be flares in the garden as we sit beside the ornamental pond. Carp older than this present cycle will swim within the flames. Our souls will seek purification in the benediction of the wine.

A letter today from Paul, soon to be on a flying trip to London. He is 'wondering about my health'. I dash off a note that tells him happy nothings, so that he knows there is no interest for him here. Writing to my son takes longer, on a carefully chosen card: it depicts a stranger not unlike himself, on his shoulder resting a parrot in reds and greens and gold. *Dear . . . . ,* I begin, it is a struggle to explain, *Antibes is a town like no other town before. First, there is the market, but I know you will say that there are markets throughout France. Then the port itself, where you can experience in such profusion the fruits of wealth that you never again need concern yourself about its seductive powers. You will, I am sure, especially appreciate . . .* (a description of seagoing palaces follows and of the habits of the rich).

You will have heard of course of the Picasso Museum set on the sea wall that runs behind the town. Here, there is a peculiar kind of magic that I am hard put to explain. It has something to do with the bronze figures gazing steadily out to sea, and the drawings, which display a facility that announces genius with their every line, but most especially the ceramics, plates and bowls still holding to the earth that gives us sustenance and the colours that light our lives . . .

Last week I lunched with Graham Greene who you will be pleased to know wears high-heeled Florsheim boots just like your own and prefers to read The Spectator *with his meal. Chez Félix there is always that fish that bespeaks magnificence, known unashamedly as* dorade . . .

It is hopeless, of course, but something demands that I make the attempt. How otherwise can I prepare him for this seed that cries its presence by its refusal to let me flower?

I phone Gerde up in the mountains. She sobs of their premier's recent assassination. Clouds drift over from Russia and their daughter still will not get out of bed.

At last! It is the night of the party, though we have argued about food all morning. Then there was a round-table discussion in which Guillaume refused to take my part. My suggestion was for *paella*, easy to prepare. But it was Bianca's insistence that finally won the day.

So we are to eat American. Does this seem to you rather strange? Bianca has been to her butcher, a giant of a man whose naturally harsh voice softens in her presence to the milky tones of lust. (His wife, a tiny shrew, works beside him in the shop. It is only her presence, I am sure, that prevents a godlike copulation amongst the carcases out the back.)

I suspect Bianca has bought horsemeat, for when asked she is very vague. It is a deep red, odorous equivalent of ground beef. There are also skeins of *chorito*, which as frankfurters will have to pass. Because no self-respecting French housewife would buy them, we made do with bread especially for the tourists, limp and pallid buns.

And now in Guillaume's small kitchen, the college girls fix potato salad. Did I forget to mention that quite unexpectedly Mary has returned? These sorority twins slice the warm and floury tubers. There are dog scraps on the floor and day-old milk forms a skin in the animal's bowl. Both girls sport brief and grubby tunics and jostle with endless affection.

I was going to say that Mary now seems older, but she wears the mantle of her disappointment lightly. London was not ready for such innocence, nor she prepared to accept as valid the scant returns of love. They scrabble potatoes and mayonnaise together in competitive fury. The mixture loses definition beneath their nut-brown paws.

In the garden the table is made of marble, the benches seem carved from stone. Overhead rustle the palms and fragrants from every warm country of the world. The dog chases the excitement of its own shadow. The breeze that by day carries the dust of Tunisian sandstorms now gentles candles which neither hiss nor spurt; it brings us nightsong from this sea which is at the centre of the earth.

Across the table I am talking to a retired British Airways captain. All through late summer ungainly twin-engined amphibians fill their bellies beyond the breakwater to dump their precious cargo on raging inland fires. (These droning monsters he tells me are *canadiens*.) The captain joins us in treating *les petites* as children of our own. Today is Mary's birthday and he has given her several hundred francs.

We chew our way through hot-dogs, made palatable by the wine. Guillaume presides over this abomination, amusement vying with something else. But Bianca is in her element, a creation newly hatched from myth. The colours of her clothing are of course indistinguishable from those of France.

The time has come for sacrifice and we turn to face the pool. There are eyes upon me in the darkness and Guillaume murmurs, 'Ça va, Diane?' On the silver trays the burgers contain meat now truly rank. The girls clear the ground of fragments while others fix the light.

And then they are ready! They tuck their dresses inside their pants. I am dizzy with the excitement, but with the rest of us egg them on. They are amazing, athletic as their feet thud in unison on the ground. They prance and kick together and together we all chant.

It is much more than lightheadedness, though I feel myself wired now to the ground. How can they perform for us when they have had so much to drink? Guillaume looks across and smiles to show me that he knows. Somewhere in the darkness, I hear a child cry.

Amy is balanced on Mary's shoulders and the chanting rises to a shout. I try to lift my body but find I am rooted to the spot. She launches up and backwards into a magnificent full flip. The name of their college bursts like fury from every pair of lungs.

Will she make it?

There is a moment there of doubt, then her feet strike the earth with a force that shocks us all. Like a true performer, she takes the impact in her knees.

We are all applauding, laughing, as Guillaume stands to raise his glass. Bianca turns towards me and I see her expression fill with love. There is a pulse of energy surging, healing me of myself. In the night the cry is fainter, moving far away. I feel the dark mysterious river as it starts flowing down my thigh.

ACKNOWLEDGEMENTS

For permission to reprint the stories in this collection acknowledgement is gratefully made to the publishers and copyright holders of the following:

Barbara Anderson: 'Shanties', from *I think we should go into the jungle*, Victoria University Press, 1989.

J. H. Bentley: 'Mersey Tributary', first published in *Islands*, 1985.

Edith Campion: 'Overstayers', first published in the *NZ Listener*, 1986, published with the permission of the author.

Jennifer Compton: 'An Unusual Spiritual Experience', first published in *Islands*, 1984.

Joy Cowley: 'Going to the Mountain', from *Heart Attack and other stories*, Hodder and Stoughton, 1985.

John Cranna: 'History for Berliners', from *Visitors*, Heinemann Reed, 1989, reprinted with the permission of the author and the publishers.

Marilyn Duckworth: 'Explosions on the Sun', from *Explosions on the Sun*, Hodder and Stoughton, 1989.

Yvonne du Fresne: 'Farvel', from *Farvel and other stories*, Victoria University Press with Price Milburn, 1980.

Chris Else: 'The Sphinx', published with the permission of the author.

Roderick Finlayson: 'Flowers and Fruit', from *In Georgina's Shady Garden*, Griffin Press, 1988, reprinted by permission of the author and the publishers.

Janet Frame: 'You Are Now Entering the Human Heart' from *You Are Now Entering the Human Heart*, Victoria University Press, 1983, reprinted with the permission of Curtis Brown (Aust.) Ltd, Sydney.

Malcolm Fraser: 'An Artistic Person, Probably Male, Inspects Lovingly a South Pacific Navel', first published in *Rambling Jack*, 1987.

Maurice Gee: 'Joker and Wife', from *Collected Stories*, Penguin Books, 1986.

Michael Gifkins: 'Not Looking for Graham Greene', published with the permission of the author.

Patricia Grace: 'The Pictures', from *The Dream Sleepers*, Longman Paul, 1980.

Russell Haley: 'Lions, Attention Please', *Antipodes New Writing*, Antipodes Press, 1987.

Michael Harlow: 'Interior Decorating', published with the permission of the author.

ACKNOWLEDGEMENTS

Craig Harrison: 'Eye Contact', first published in *Landfall*, 1986.

Michael Henderson: 'Rutherford's House', first published in *Islands*, 1985, reprinted with the permission of the author.

Keri Hulme: 'Unnamed Islands in the Unknown Sea', from *Te Kaihau*, Victoria University Press, 1986, permission of the author and Mary Bodger.

Witi Ihimaera: 'The Greenstone Patu' from *The New Net Goes Fishing*, Heinemann, 1977.

Ted Jenner: 'In Italy Take Care Not to Miss . . .', published with the permission of the author.

Stephanie Johnson: 'The Glass Whittler', from *The Glass Whittler*, New Women's Press, 1988.

Jan Kemp: 'The Golden Couch', published with the permission of the author.

Anne Kennedy: 'The World', first published in *Landfall*, 1988.

Fiona Kidman: 'Earthly Shadows', from *Unsuitable Friends*, Century Hutchinson, 1988.

Shonagh Koea: 'Oh Bunny', from *The Woman Who Never Went Home and other stories*, Penguin Books, 1987.

Hugh Lauder: 'Finland Station', first published in *Rambling Jack*, 1986. 'The Stone Collector', from *Over the White Wall*, Caxton Press, 1985.

Graeme Lay: 'The White Daimler', first published in *North and South*, 1986.

Cilla McQueen: 'Two Clues to Mrs Mooney', published with the permission of the author.

Owen Marshall: 'Convalescence in the Old City', from *The Lynx Hunter*, John McIndoe, 1987.

Philip Mincher: 'Traumerei', from *All the Wild Summer*, John McIndoe, 1985.

Michael Morrissey: 'Beethoven's Ears', published with the permission of the author.

Gregory O'Brien: 'Karminrosa', published with the permission of the author.

Vincent O'Sullivan: 'Exposures', first published in *Westerly*, 1988.

Fiona Farrell Poole: 'Footnote', first published in the *NZ Listener*, 1987.

Sue Reidy: 'Alexandra and the Lion', from *Modettes and other stories*, Penguin Books, 1988.

Bruce Stewart: 'Patu Wairau', from *Tama and other stories*, Penguin Books, 1989.

Margaret Sutherland: 'A Letter from the Dead', published with the permission of the author.

Apirana Taylor: 'Hera', from *He Rau Aroha*, Penguin Books, 1986.

ACKNOWLEDGEMENTS

Ngahuia Te Awekotuku: 'Makawe', published with the permission of the author.

Jean Watson: 'Ali Leaves For Delhi', first published in *Landfall*, 1986.

Ian Wedde: 'Circe and the Animal Trainer', from *The Shirt Factory and other stories*, Victoria University Press, 1981.

Albert Wendt: 'Daughter of the Mango Season', first published in *Landfall*, 1984 and subsequently in *Birth and Death of the Miracle Man*, Viking, London, 1986.

NOTES ON CONTRIBUTORS

BARBARA ANDERSON was born in Hawke's Bay in 1926. She completed a science degree at the University of Otago and, thirty years later, an arts degree at Victoria University of Wellington. She has worked as a science teacher and laboratory technician. Barbara Anderson's first collection of short stories, *I think we should go into the jungle*, was published by Victoria University Press in 1989.

J. H. BENTLEY was born in what he describes as 'a magic year, 1936, 44 squared'. He came to New Zealand in 1951 from Manchester, England. He has worked as a teacher, a postman, plastics machine operator and in forestry since attending Canterbury University College. J. H. Bentley won the *Landfall* Short Fiction Award in 1984. He is co-author with Malcolm Fraser of *A Grand New Zealand Limerick Tour*.

EDITH CAMPION was born in Wellington in 1923 and was privately educated after absconding from Nga Tawa at the age of thirteen. She studied at the Old Vic Theatre School from 1950 to 1952; and co-founded the New Zealand Players with Richard Campion. As well as a collection of stories, Edith Campion has published a novella, 'The Chain' in *Tandem* with Frank Sargeson's last work, 'En Route' in 1979. At present Edith Campion is working on another collection of stories and a novel, *Pianola*. She has 'three splendid children, Anna, Jane and Michael'.

JENNIFER COMPTON was born in Wellington in 1949. She won the Katherine Mansfield Memorial award for a short story in 1977 and has also gained recognition in Australia with plays for stage and radio. She was a joint winner of the 1974 Newcastle Playwriting Competition and received the AWGIE award for a radio play in 1976. Jennifer Compton lives in the country near Sydney, with her husband, the actor Matthew O'Sullivan, their two children, 'three ponies, a goat, a cat and a magpie'.

JOY COWLEY was born in Levin in 1936, and now lives in a remote area of the Marlborough Sounds. She writes for adults and children.

JOHN CRANNA was born in 1954 and grew up in the Waikato. He spent some years in London, and now lives in Auckland. He has won prizes in national and international short story awards, including the American Express and *Stand* competitions. His first collection of stories, *Visitors*, was published in 1989 by Heinemann Reed. John Cranna was awarded the 1989 New Zealand Literary Fund Writing Bursary.

YVONNE DU FRESNE was brought up in the Manawatu and has now retired to Makara Beach after a full-time teaching career. Her stories have appeared in most local journals and in a number of anthologies in New Zealand, Australia, USA, Japan and Europe. As well as two collections of stories, Yvonne du Fresne has had three radio plays performed and has published two novels, *The Book of Ester*, 1982, and *Frédérique*, 1987. A composite collection of stories, *The Bear from the North*, was published in 1989 by The Women's Press, Britain.

MARILYN DUCKWORTH was born in Auckland in 1935 and now lives in Wellington. Her eighth novel, *Pulling Faces*, was published in 1987. Her fifth, *Disorderly Conduct*, won a New Zealand Book Award in 1984. She has held the Katherine Mansfield Fellowship in Menton, a Writer's Fulbright, in America, and holds the New Zealand-Australia exchange fellowship for 1989.

CHRIS ELSE was born in Yorkshire, and came to New Zealand at the age of 13. As well as fiction he has written drama for radio and television. Chris Else currently works as a computer consultant in Wellington and runs Total Fiction Services, an organisation which provides support and advice to writers of fiction.

RODERICK FINLAYSON was born in Devonport, Auckland, in 1904. He was brought up in the old suburb of Ponsonby, spent much of his early life in Maori and farming districts, and since 1936 has lived with his wife and six children in Weymouth.

JANET FRAME was born in 1924 in Dunedin and grew up in Oamaru. She attended Dunedin Teachers' Training College and Otago University before teaching for a brief period. She now lives in Horowhenua. Janet Frame has written eight novels, the latest of which is *The Carpathians* (1988). She has also published her acclaimed three-volume autobiography — *To the Is-Land*, *An Angel at My Table*, and *The Envoy from Mirror City* — as well as short stories and poetry.

MALCOLM FRASER has published short fiction over the last twenty years, as well as being the author of a book of puzzles (under the name 'Wilkins') and co-author (with J. H. Bentley) of a collection of original limericks.

MAURICE GEE lives in Nelson but is currently Writing Fellow at the Victoria University of Wellington. Among adults he is best known for the *Plumb* trilogy and among children for *Under the Mountain* and the *O* trilogy. He also writes television scripts.

MICHAEL GIFKINS was born in 1945 and lives in Auckland. He is a publishing consultant who is also well known as a columnist, editor and critic, with a weekly books column in the *Listener*. In 1983 he was the Writer in Residence at the University of Auckland and was Katherine Mansfield Fellow in Menton in 1985. Michael Gifkins has published three collections of short stories.

PATRICIA GRACE was born in Wellington in 1937. She is of Ngati Raukawa, Ngati Toa and Te Ati Awa descent and is affiliated to Ngati Porou by marriage. She has taught in primary and secondary schools in the King Country, Northland and Porirua. She is married with seven children and now lives in Plimmerton. As well as short stories Patricia Grace has published two novels, *Mutuwhenua, The Moon Sleeps* (1978) and *Potiki* (1986), and two children's books, *The Kuia and the Spider* (1982) and *Watercress Tuna and the Children of Champion Street* (1984).

MICHAEL HARLOW, writer, editor, and lecturer, has published five books of poems, most recently *Vlaminck's Tie* (AUP/OUP). *Take a Risk, Trust Your Langugage, Make a Poem* won the PEN award for the First Best Book of Prose in 1986. He held the Katherine Mansfield Memorial Fellowship in 1986. A book of poems, *No Problem, But Not Easy*, is forthcoming, and at present he is writing a book of short prose texts. Michael Harlow is also the editor of the *Caxton New Poetry* series.

CRAIG HARRISON was born in Leeds, Yorkshire, in 1942. After gaining an MA from Leeds University he came to work in the English Department at Massey University in 1966, where he teaches art history and film studies. Craig Harrison has published four novels, *Broken October, Ground Level* (also a play and TV series), *The Quiet Earth* (filmed in 1985) and *Days of Starlight* (1988).

MICHAEL HENDERSON is the author of a novel, *The Log of a Superfluous Son*, and a number of short stories, several of which have been anthologised. One of his stories won a Fels Award in the United States, where he was a Teaching/Writing Fellow at the Iowa Writers' Workshop.

KERI HULME was born in 1947, 'a Fish and Fire Pig — a Maori (Kai Tahu) and a Pakeha'. She lives at Okarito on the West Coast. Keri Hulme has also written poetry, fiction, and her novel *the bone people* (1984) won the New Zealand Book Award, the Pegasus Prize for Maori literature and the 1985 Booker Prize. Other works include *Lost Possessions* and *Homeplaces*, a collaboration with photographer Robin Morrison.

WITI IHIMAERA is of Maori descent. He is currently Counsellor (Public Affairs) at the New Zealand embassy, Washington, DC. Witi Ihimaera began his writing career with *Pounamu, Pounamu* and has subsequently written seven books. His novel *The Matriarch* won the Goodman Fielder Wattie Book Award in 1986.

TED JENNER was born in 1946 in Dunedin. He combines writing (essays, poetry, short fiction, translations) with relief teaching in Auckland secondary schools. Ted Jenner has recently returned to New Zealand after working on a full-length study of the Greek poet Ibykos in London and revisiting sacred sites in Turkey and southern Europe.

STEPHANIE JOHNSON was born in 1961 in Auckland and attended Canterbury University from 1979 to 1981. She completed the Drama Diploma at Auckland University. Stephanie Johnson won the 1985 Bruce Mason Award with her play *Accidental Phantasies*. She now lives in Australia with her boyfriend and young son, Stan. Stephanie Johnson's first collection of stories, *The Glass Whittler*, was published in 1988. She has also published a book of poetry, *The Bleeding Ballerina* (1986).

JAN KEMP was born in 1949 in Hamilton and is an Auckland University graduate. She has lived mostly outside New Zealand since 1974, in Fiji, Vanuatu, Canada, Malaysia, Papua New Guinea, Hong Kong and Singapore, where she presently teaches English at the National University. Jan Kemp writes poems, short stories, and the odd critical article, and is working on a novel.

ANNE KENNEDY was born in Wellington in 1959. She now lives in Auckland. Anne Kennedy has written short fiction, and for television and films. A novella, *100 Traditional Smiles*, was published by Victoria University Press in 1988.

FIONA KIDMAN was born in 1940 and spent her early years in rural Northland and later Rotorua. She and her husband now live in Wellington, overlooking the sea. Her eleven books include novels, poetry, non-fiction and short stories. She has held the Scholarship in Letters twice, and in 1988 was the Writing Fellow at Victoria University. Other awards include the New Zealand Book Award (fiction) for 1988, and the Mobil/*New Zealand Outlook* Short Story Award in 1987.

SHONAGH KOEA was the winner of the Air New Zealand Short Story Competition in 1981 and is represented in most recent anthologies of New Zealand fiction. She was awarded the 1989 Additional Writing Bursary by the Queen Elizabeth II Arts Council. Shonagh Koea is interested in reading and writing and lives quietly in New Plymouth.

HUGH LAUDER was born in Germany in 1948 of Australian parents. He was educated in England and has lived in New Zealand for ten years. Hugh Lauder is a lecturer at the University of Canterbury and has been an editor of *Landfall* since 1984.

GRAEME LAY was born in Foxton in 1944, and grew up in Taranaki. He graduated from Victoria University in 1967, and taught in Wellington before travelling to Europe. After living in England and Germany for three years he and his wife Gillian returned to Auckland where he began writing fiction in 1973. His first novel, *The Mentor*, was published in 1978 and a second, *The Fools on the Hill*, was published in 1988. Graeme Lay also edited *Metro Fiction*, 1987. He lives with his wife and three children in Devonport, Auckland.

CILLA McQUEEN was born in 1949. She has published four books of poetry: *Homing In* (1982), *Anti Gravity* (1984), *Wild Sweets* (1986), *Benzina* (1988). Her work extends into recording, visual art, choreography and performance. Awards include the New Zealand Book Award (1983), Fulbright Visiting Writer's Fellowship (1985), Robert Burns Fellowship, Otago University (1985, 1986), Inaugural Australia-New Zealand Writers' Exchange Fellowship (1987).

OWEN MARSHALL, who describes himself as 'a South Islander by choice', is a teacher by profession, and lives in Timaru where he is deputy-principal at Craighead Diocesan Girls' School. As a part-time writer he specialises in the short story and has had four collections published. Awards include the *Evening Standard* Short Story Competition, The American Express Short Story Award, and the PEN Lilian Ada Smith Award for Fiction in 1986 and 1988. In 1981 he held the Literary Fellowship at the University of Canterbury, and in 1988 the New Zealand Scholarship in Letters.

PHILIP MINCHER has published irregularly since 1952, writing 'very rapidly or not at all'. A large number of his stories have been broadcast by Radio New Zealand, for whom he has also written several plays. He has published one volume of poetry, *Heroes and Clerks* (1959).

MICHAEL MORRISSEY was born in Auckland has lived most of his life there. He has published eight books of poetry and three books of short fiction. Both his stories and his poems have won numerous awards. 'Stalin's Sickle' was made into a television film directed by Costa Botes. In 1985 he was the first New Zealand writer to be a participant in the International Writing Program at the University of Iowa. He has also edited *The New Fiction*, an anthology of postmodern New Zealand short fiction. Currently he is working on a novel.

GREGORY O'BRIEN was born in Matamata in 1961, and has been writing and painting full-time since 1984. His first collection of poems, *Location of the Least Person*, was published by AUP in 1987. AUP also published *Diesel Mystic*, a novel, in 1989. Gregory O'Brien was the Sargeson Fellow in 1988, during which time he wrote 'Karminrosa'.

VINCENT O'SULLIVAN was born in 1937. As well as writing short stories he has published numerous books of poetry and *Miracle: A Romance* (1976). Vincent O'Sullivan is also a playright, critic and editor.

FIONA FARRELL POOLE was born in Oamaru in 1947. She studied English at Otago University and drama at Toronto University. Fiona Farrell Poole now lives in Palmerston North with her family, where she teaches part-time and writes poetry, stories, and plays.

SUE REIDY has worked full time as a graphic designer and illustrator since graduation from Wellington Polytechnic School of Design in 1976. She won the BNZ Katherine Mansfield Short Story Award in 1985. Her first collection of stories, *Modettes*, was published by Penguin in 1988.

BRUCE STEWART thinks he was born somewhere in the Waikato in around 1936. He is of Te Arawa and Tainui descent ('although a Pakeha hopped in there somewhere'). He has been a bushman, deer culler, driver, farm worker, singer, builder, jailbird and paper boy. Bruce Stewart has eleven children. As well as short stories, Bruce Stewart has written plays for both radio and television. He is a past president of the Maori Artists and Writers Society. He set up the first-ever work trust, and founded Tapu Te Ranga Marae in Island Bay, Wellington.

MARGARET SUTHERLAND has written three novels, a short story collection and a children's book. Since moving to Australia she has remarried and she works at the Migrant Health Unit in Newcastle, NSW. Margaret Sutherland has recently completed a second short story collection.

APIRANA TAYLOR was born in Wellington in 1955. He is of Ngati Porou, Te Whanau a Apanui, Taranaki, Nga Puhi and Ngati Pakeha descent. After a year at university he 'opted out' in order to write and since then has worked at a wide range of jobs including factory work, scrub-cutting, fishing, carpentry, journalism, acting, and working with theatre groups. Apirana Taylor has married for the second time and has two children.

NGAHUIA TE AWEKOTUKU was born in Ohinemutu, Rotorua, and was raised there. She currently teaches Maori and Pacific art at Auckland University, and is a museum consultant and freelance writer.

JEAN WATSON was born in 1933 and was brought up on a farm near Mangapai and travelled in New Zealand and Australia. During the 1970s she studied comparative religions at Victoria University and since 1980 has made several trips to India. Jean Watson has one son and now lives in Wellington. As well as writing short stories she has published five novels, the latest of which is *Address to a King* (1986). Jean Watson was the 1988 Auckland University Literary Fellow.

IAN WEDDE was born in 1946 in Blenheim and began to write at high school. He has published ten books of poetry, including a *Selected Poems*. Ian Wedde was a co-translator of Mahmoud Darwish's poetry and has also published three novels. He is co-editor of the *Penguin Book of New Zealand Verse* and the *Penguin Book of Contemporary New Zealand Poetry*.

ALBERT WENDT is from Samoa and the Aiga Sa-Tuaopepe. He taught at the University of the South Pacific, as Professor of Pacific Literature, for many years. At present he is Professor of New Zealand Literature at the University of Auckland. Albert Wendt has published novels, stories, and poems worldwide, and his work has been translated into many foreign languages. He is married to Jenny and they have three children.

SELECT BIBLIOGRAPHY

Only collections of short stories have been listed. New Zealand is the place of publication unless otherwise stated.

Barbara Anderson
I think we should go into the jungle, Victoria University Press, 1989

Edith Campion
A Place to Pass Through and other stories, Reed, 1977

Joy Cowley
Heart Attack and other stories, Hodder & Stoughton, 1985

John Cranna
Visitors, Heinemann Reed, 1989

Marilyn Duckworth
Explosions on the Sun, Hodder & Stoughton, 1989

Chris Else
Dreams of Pythagoras, Voice Press, 1981

Roderick Finlayson
Brown Man's Burden, Griffin Press 1938
Sweet Beulah Land, Griffin Press, 1942
Brown Man's Burden & Later Stories, Auckland University Press, 1973
Other Lovers, John McIndoe, 1976
In Georgina's Shady Garden, Griffin Press, 1988

Janet Frame
The Lagoon, Caxton Press, 1951; as *The Lagoon and other stories*, Caxton Press, 1961
Snowman Snowman; Fables & Fantasies, Braziller, New York, 1963
The Reservoir: Stories and Sketches, Braziller, New York, 1963
The Reservior and other stories, Pegasus Press and W.H. Allen, London, 1966
You Are Now Entering the Human Heart, Victoria University Press, 1983

Yvonne du Fresne
Farvel and other stories, Victoria University Press/Price Milburn, 1980
The Growing of Astrid Westergaard, Longman Paul, 1985
The Bear From the North: Tales from a New Zealand Childhood (Composite selection from the two above) Women's Press, London 1989

Michael Gifkins

After the Revolution and other stories, Longman Paul, 1982
Summer is the Côte d'Azur, Penguin, 1987
The Amphibians, Penguin, 1989

Patrica Grace

Waiariki, Longman Paul, 1975
The Dream Sleepers, Penguin, 1980
Electric City and other stories, Penguin, 1987

Maurice Gee

A Glorious Morning Comrade, Auckland University Press/Oxford University Press, 1975
Collected Stories, Penguin, 1986

Russell Haley
The Sauna Bath Mysteries, The Mandrake Root, 1978
Real Illusions, Victoria University Press & New Directions, New York, 1984
The Transfer Station, Nagare Press, 1989

Keri Hulme
Te Kaihau: The Windeater, Victoria University Press, 1986

Witi Ihimaera
Pounamu, Pounamu, Heinemann, 1972
The New Net Goes Fishing, Heinemann, 1977

Stephanie Johnson
The Glass Whittler, New Women's Press, 1988

Fiona Kidman
Mrs Dixon and Friend, Heinemann, 1982
Unsuitable Friends, Century Hutchinson, 1988

Shonagh Koea
The Women Who Never Went Home, Penguin, 1987

Graeme Lay
Dear Mr Cairney: Stories, Mallinson Rendel, 1985

Owen Marshall
Supper Waltz Wilson and other New Zealand stories, Pegasus, 1979
The Master of Big Jingles and other stories, McIndoe, 1982
The Day Hemingway Died and other stories, McIndoe, 1984
The Lynx Hunter, McIndoe, 1987

SELECT BIBLIOGRAPHY

Philip Mincher

The Ride Home, Longman Paul, 1977
All the Wild Summer, McIndoe, 1985

Michael Morrissey

The Fat Lady and The Astronomer, Sword Press, 1981

Vincent O'Sullivan

The Boy, The Bridge, The River, McIndoe/Reed, 1978
Dandy Edison for Lunch, McIndoe, 1981
Survivals and other stories, Allen & Unwin/Port Nicholson Press, 1985
The Snow in Spain, Allen & Unwin/Port Nicholson Press, 1989

Fiona Farrell Poole

The Rock Garden, Auckland University Press, 1989

Sue Reidy

Modettes and other stories, Penguin, 1988

Bruce Stewart

Tama and other stories, Penguin, 1989

Margaret Sutherland

Getting Through and other stories, Heinemann, London, 1977; as *Dark Places, Deep Regions, and other stories,* Stemmer House, Owings Mills, Maryland, 1980

Apirana Taylor

He Rau Aroha, Penguin, 1986

Ian Wedde

The Shirt Factory and other stories, Victoria University Press/Price Milburn, 1981

Albert Wendt

Flying-Fox in a Freedom Tree, Longman Paul, 1974
The Birth and Death of a Miracle Man, Viking, London, 1986